PRAISE FOR THE ...

Moonshell Beach

"Ms. Ross writes a story that wraps around your heart and ensnares you. . . . She is a master storyteller." —*Fresh Fiction*

"Ross gradually builds up the sexual tension between her characters with convincing tact in a comfortingly idyllic milieu where nearly everyone else is in love. . . . [She] satisfyingly fleshes out their mating dance with secondary characters familiar from her earlier books and tantalizing glimpses of stories to be told in future installments." —*Publishers Weekly*

"This is a lovely addition to the Shelter Bay series. Ross builds a charming town filled with good, solid people . . . making Shelter Bay a place that readers will really want to visit." —*RT Book Reviews*

"I immediately dug into *Moonshell Beach* and read it cover to cover in two days. I just couldn't put it down. . . . Shelter Bay is the kind of town I'd love to live in myself." —Love Romances & More

On Lavender Lane

"Cooking, romance, and a warm, inviting setting work their delectable magic in this tender charmer that introduces new characters (and some serious issues) and reprises previous series players." —*Library Journal*

"[A] tear-jerking tale of a commitment-shy professional cook learning to love a former Navy SEAL in idyllic rural Oregon . . . [a] savory romance." —*Publishers Weekly*

"The Shelter Bay novels have been lauded, and this one is a worthy entry in the series. The characters, especially the recurring ones, are so likable that the reader can't help getting caught up in the story . . . engrossing with just enough humor to keep the readers on their toes. I await each new story with anticipation." —*Fresh Fiction*

"Shelter Bay is a town that envelops readers in warmth. This latest entry in the series features a lovely romance that rolls in with the inevitability of the tide. Warning: It is also a foodie book that will leave you hungry—and hungry for the next book, too!" —*Romantic Times*

continued . . .

One Summer

"Ms. Ross knows how to tell a story that pulls her readers in and takes them on an emotional journey as they turn the pages. If you're looking for a fulfilling story that you can't help but fall in love with, then this along with her other novel in the series, *The Homecoming*, are two books you shouldn't pass up!"
—Night Owl Reviews

The Homecoming

"Quintessential Ross, with a terrific romance [and] mystery. Not to be missed." —The Romance Readers Connection

"Ross has again hit a homer . . . an outstanding job."
—Fallen Angel Reviews

"One of the best books I've read this summer. . . . Ms. Ross penned such emotion into her story line and created characters that you easily fall in love with." —Night Owl Reviews

PRAISE FOR OTHER NOVELS BY JOANN ROSS

Breakpoint

"An action-packed thriller that never decelerates until the finish . . . one of the better high-octane sagas on the market today." —*Midwest Book Review*

Crossfire

"The plot is riveting, the characters sizzle, and the ending will blow you away. Trust me, you do not want to miss *Crossfire*. But keep in mind once you pick it up, it's impossible to put down." —Fresh Fiction

"[A] can't-put-down-forget-the-housework-cereal-for-dinner book. The chemistry between Quinn and Cait screams off the page and practically singes your fingers." —Romance Junkies

Freefall

"A page-turning mix of danger, suspense, and passion."
—*New York Times* bestselling author Iris Johansen

"An incredible story!" —Fresh Fiction

Also by JoAnn Ross

Shelter Bay Novels
Moonshell Beach

On Lavender Lane

One Summer

The Homecoming

High Risk Novels
Freefall

Crossfire

Shattered

Breakpoint

SEA GLASS WINTER

A SHELTER BAY NOVEL

JoAnn Ross

DISCARD

A SIGNET BOOK

SIGNET
Published by New American Library, a division of
Penguin Group (USA) Inc., 375 Hudson Street,
New York, New York 10014, USA
Penguin Group (Canada), 90 Eglinton Avenue East, Suite 700, Toronto,
Ontario M4P 2Y3, Canada (a division of Pearson Penguin Canada Inc.)
Penguin Books Ltd., 80 Strand, London WC2R 0RL, England
Penguin Ireland, 25 St. Stephen's Green, Dublin 2,
Ireland (a division of Penguin Books Ltd.)
Penguin Group (Australia), 250 Camberwell Road, Camberwell, Victoria 3124,
Australia (a division of Pearson Australia Group Pty. Ltd.)
Penguin Books India Pvt. Ltd., 11 Community Centre, Panchsheel Park,
New Delhi - 110 017, India
Penguin Group (NZ), 67 Apollo Drive, Rosedale, Auckland 0632,
New Zealand (a division of Pearson New Zealand Ltd.)
Penguin Books (South Africa) (Pty.) Ltd., 24 Sturdee Avenue,
Rosebank, Johannesburg 2196, South Africa

Penguin Books Ltd., Registered Offices:
80 Strand, London WC2R 0RL, England

First published by Signet, an imprint of New American Library,
a division of Penguin Group (USA) Inc.

First Printing, January 2013
10 9 8 7 6 5 4 3 2 1

 REGISTERED TRADEMARK — MARCA REGISTRADA

Printed in the United States of America

PUBLISHER'S NOTE
This is a work of fiction. Names, characters, places, and incidents either are the
product of the author's imagination or are used fictitiously, and any resemblance
to actual persons, living or dead, business establishments, events, or locales is
entirely coincidental.

 The publisher does not have any control over and does not assume any responsibility for author or third-party Web sites or their content.

If you purchased this book without a cover you should be aware that this book
is stolen property. It was reported as "unsold and destroyed" to the publisher
and neither the author nor the publisher has received any payment for this
"stripped book."

The recipe contained in this book is to be followed exactly as written. The publisher is not responsible for your specific health or allergy needs that may require
medical supervision. The publisher is not responsible for any adverse reactions
to the recipe contained in this book.

Again, to all the men and women of the military, and their families, for their service and sacrifice.

To Maureen Hallet. When I used Google Earth to buy a lot for our new home three thousand miles away, I had no idea I'd end up living next door to such a great friend and neighbor.

And, as always, to Jay, my very own hero.

ACKNOWLEDGMENTS

With huge thanks to my fantastic publishing team at NAL—

Publisher Kara Welsh, for her unwavering support over so many years; editor extraordinaire Kerry Donovan, for her ability to see the forest for the trees and being, hands down, the best brainstorming editor ever; NAL editorial director Claire Zion, who literally changed my life when she pulled my manuscript out of her slush pile thirty-one years ago; and last, but certainly not least, Mimi Bark, who, with watercolor artist Paul Janovsky, has wrapped my Shelter Bay stories in such beautiful covers.

War is hell!

William Tecumseh Sherman

I've got a theory that if you give one hundred percent all of the time, somehow things will work out in the end.

Larry Bird

1

Tech sergeant Dillon Slater's business was bombs. And in Afghanistan's Helmand Province, Dillon's business was booming.

The landscape he was driving his Buffalo armored mine-disposal vehicle through could have come right from the pages of the Old Testament. Years of baking beneath the hot Afghan sun had turned the mud of the compounds as hard as concrete. Unlike some of the royal palaces he'd seen while deployed in Iraq, these dwellings boasted no gaudy exterior decoration. Uniformly putty colored, they were purely functional.

Children waved as the twenty-six-ton vehicle bounced over what felt more like a goat trail than a real road crossing the bleak, moonscape surface.

In earlier deployments, he'd been lucky if his EOD batphone rang a dozen times a week. But the enemy was nothing if not adaptive, and since the country had turned into the Wild West, they'd figured out that it was a lot easier to blow up coalition forces from a distance than to take them on in a shoot-out-at-the-O.K.-Corral-style gunfight situation.

In the past week alone, 212 IEDs had been discovered and detonated. Doing the math—and he had—that worked out to more than 11,000 a year. What had once been a cottage industry—guys making bombs in their mud homes—had turned into an industrial complex capable of knocking out one IED every fifteen minutes, thanks to global jihadists sharing technologies and procedures.

"Crazy," he muttered as he pulled into the area where a Ranger unit was standing around waiting for him.

He'd been called to this same spot yesterday to remove a crude pressure-plate device next to a basketball court he'd helped build. Together with other unit volunteers, he'd cleared the space and poured the surface, using Quikrete donated by some Navy SEALs. One thing Dillon had learned early on was that SEALs could get their hands on just about anything. Another thing he'd learned was to never ask them *where* they'd gotten it.

What really chapped his hide was that whatever cretin had planted that IED had been willing to take out the children who played on the court every day—often with troops. The pickup games were more than just a way to burn off energy—they served as yet another attempt to win hearts and minds. Which personally Dillon wasn't so sure was working, since more people kept trying to kill him every day. But hey, military war policy and nation building were way above his pay grade.

Unlike the previous day, when the square had been filled with civilian onlookers, today the place was mostly deserted.

Which was not good. One of the first things Dillon had learned in training was to look for the absence of normal and the presence of abnormal. Both of which they definitely had here.

Did everyone but them know what was going on? Had the kids who were usually playing roundball on this court been warned to stay away?

The hair on the back of his neck stood up as combat intuition, borne from years of experience, kicked in.

"We're being set up," Jason West, one of his team members, said from the backseat as they pulled up next to a Hummer with Arabic writing painted on the side.

On Dillon's first tour here he'd learned that the script translated to "Not EOD" (Explosive Ordnance Disposal). Having the guys on your side wanting to make sure no one mistook *them* for bomb guys was an indication of how popular Dillon and his team tended to be with the local population.

"Could be," he agreed, drawling out his words in his native west Texas twang as he considered that unpleasant prospect. "Then again, we could have some hotshot showing off to his pals by playing with us."

He jumped down from the Buffalo and went over and talked to the Rangers, the ones who had called in the possible explosive, and they reported that none of the few civilians they'd been able to question had seen anyone plant an IED.

Surprise, surprise.

One of the cool things about the Buffalo was its thirty-foot mechanical arm with both a claw and a camera attached. Returning to the vehicle, he extended the arm to get a better look at the device, which was only partially buried right behind the basket pole.

"Bingo," he said as the camera eye caught the familiar pink wire an eagle-eyed Ranger, who'd come here for a pickup game, had spotted. "This has cell phone guy's fingerprints all over it."

In the beginning, the IEDs Dillon had dealt with had been simple pressure plates. Drive over it, step on it, two pieces of metal connected, and *boom*.

They'd been crude. Hell, if he'd been into bomb making when he was a kid, he could've put one together in ten minutes for a fourth-grade science fair project. But they didn't need to be fancy and high-tech to kill.

The problem was that they also killed indiscriminately, meaning they were just as likely to take out civilians as they were American or NATO forces. Which hadn't exactly made their makers all that popular.

Then the insurgents had upped their skill set, adding command-wire remote controls to the mix. Bury one in the middle of the road, and if the patrol you'd planned to hit changed routes, you simply turned it off and avoided the collateral damage of blowing up some poppy farmer's donkey. Or wife. Or child.

Then, just as easily, it could be switched on again when the timing proved right.

In the beginning, garage door openers had been popular. More and more, though, Dillon had been running into cell phones all tied up with pretty pink wires, which tended to make his team edgier—and even, from time to time, paranoid. Was that guy over there talking on his phone really speaking to his wife, telling her what time he'd be home for dinner? Or was he about to hit *talk* and blow more Americans sky-high?

"We could wait for another robot to be brought in," said West, who'd been riding shotgun.

Their own robot, Larry, named for robot Larry Fine

in *Revenge of the Nerds*, had been injured when it rolled off a ledge two days earlier, and they were still waiting either to get him back or receive a replacement.

"If it's a setup, the longer we stay here, the more we become sitting ducks," said Chance Longstreet, who was in the back, pointing out what they all already knew. "The bastards have already gotten rid of Larry. Why let them take out some more of us?"

Although they'd all been pissed to have Larry out of commission, Longstreet, who operated the robot from a military-grade laptop, took the loss personally.

"Good point," Dillon said.

Maybe it wasn't a bomb at all. Maybe just some buried wires designed to pull the team into sniper range. Or worse yet, a kill box. The Buffalo might be armor clad, but if mortars started raining down on them from the roofs of those buildings, they'd all be toast.

Although their mission tended toward knitting them into a tight, cohesive unit, aimed for consensus, as team leader it was Dillon's call.

He had a month left downrange, and then he was going to leave the military and return to the States, where he'd signed up with the Troops to Teachers program and already had a job as a high school physics teacher and basketball coach waiting for him in Oregon.

Which should've been the good news. And it was. But there was always a flip side, and the flip side of *this* situation was that while EOD was already one of the most dangerous jobs in the military, the last thirty days were the riskiest, when fatigue, anticipation, and distraction dulled instincts.

As everyone was all too aware, in war, if you stuck around long enough, good luck ran out. Dillon was determined to be one of the ones who left this hellhole lucky.

"I'm going in."

The Taliban were not shy about their belief that time was on their side. "You may have the watches," the popular expression went, "but we have the time."

Today, Dillon vowed, he was going to employ that same patience to keep from focusing on that separation countdown clock ticking away in his head.

West sealed him into the eighty-pound Kevlar-clad bomb suit, which looked sort of like a hazmat outfit but made Dillon feel like the Michelin Man. It also increased the intense desert heat to a temperature that felt like the surface of the sun. Not helping was the additional ninety pounds of equipment he was carrying.

Finally, lowering the face shield on the bulbous helmet, he began plodding forward. Although the suit had a radio receiver, he turned it off to avoid sending out stray radio waves that could set off the IED.

Which meant that he was walking toward a bomb that he knew nothing about, without any communication with his team, an easy target trussed up in a bomb suit that definitely hadn't been designed for sprinting out of danger if things went south.

It was deathly quiet. The only sounds Dillon could hear as he took the long walk he hoped to hell wouldn't be his last were the pounding of his heart, his steady breathing, and the whir of the fan inside the helmet.

With the temperature at 102 degrees, the fan was fairly useless, and salty sweat began dripping into his eyes, making him think he should've just opted for the lighter-weight body armor and helmet. Hell, if the thing did blow, he'd go right up with it, no matter what he was wearing.

Once he'd put that thought aside, since he'd already made his decision, options began running through Dillon's mind. The explosive could be set on a timer, which meant it could explode at any moment.

Thirty feet to go.

Or it could be electronically controlled by one of the dozen pairs of eyes he could feel watching him from those buildings surrounding the deserted square, which was more likely, given that familiar pink wire.

Twenty.

Dillon dropped to his stomach, took out his telescoping trip-wire feeler, and began crawling toward the target, altering his direction because if the bomb maker was watching and saw him take a straight line, next time there'd be a pressure bomb waiting for him.

This was where luck really came in. One zig where he should've zagged, and Shelter Bay High School would be looking for a new coach.

Dillon considered another option—maybe the wire was merely a decoy, drawing him closer to a buried pressure plate, just waiting for his body to set it off.

In his business, Murphy's Law ruled.

At ten feet out, he'd definitely reached the point of no return.

His mind shifted into a familiar zone. He made it the rest of the way, took out a paintbrush from his kit, and began removing dirt and sand from what was, as he'd suspected, yet another cell phone bomb. It sometimes amazed Dillon that in this remote part of the world, where electricity and indoor plumbing were considered luxuries, every damn bad guy out there seemed to have a smartphone.

Feeling as if he were moving in super–slow motion, he began digging away at the blasting cap, trying to lift it out without causing it to blow.

Just as the wire gave way, the world exploded.

From inside the blazing fireball, Dillon heard a bell ringing. Blindly groping out, his hand found the phone, picked it up, and put it to his ear.

"Yeah?" His voice was as shaky as the rest of his body, which was buzzing with adrenaline. Afghanistan faded away and he found himself in his bedroom.

"You okay, Coach?" the male voice on the other end of the line asked.

"Yeah," Dillon repeated as he dragged himself out of the familiar nightmare. There were various versions, but all had him checking his body upon awakening, just to make sure every part was still where it belonged. "Sure."

"Did I wake you up?"

"Hell no," Dillon lied, reaching out to grab his watch, with its lit-up dial, from the bed table. It was mid-November and still dark at six in the morning. "What's up?"

"I wanted to remind you that you're having breakfast down at the Grateful Bread with the boosters this morning."

"I'll be there." If only for the sweet potato hash. The company, which Dillon understood was well intentioned, he could definitely do without.

"Thought I'd better warn you—you'll be fielding a lot of questions about the SoCal phenom."

Now that his heart had settled down to something resembling a normal rhythm, Dillon decided to try getting out of bed. Ooh-rah, both his legs were not only still attached, but they also proved capable of holding him up. Just barely.

"And what SoCal phenom would that be?"

"Templeton. A kid from Beverly Hills who was the highest-scoring freshman in the history of California State hoops last year.

"Good for him. Sounds like the Beverly Hills High JV coach is going to have a dynamite season. And you're telling me this why?"

"Because he just transferred into Shelter Bay. He's our golden ticket to the state championship, Coach."

Dillon rubbed his hand down his face, then dragged his body toward the kitchen, desperately in need of coffee for this conversation. Ken Curtis was a nice sixty-something guy who owned Harbor Hardware and had headed up Shelter Bay High School's booster club for the past three decades.

"Shelter Bay High School hasn't had a winning season for twelve years," Dillon felt obliged to point out.

"That's why we hired you. . . . Just a minute." Dillon heard a woman's voice in the distance. "Marcy wanted me to remind you that you've also got a meeting with the cheer moms right after school tomorrow afternoon. They've got a new routine they want to debut at the opening game."

Dealing with the cheer moms, dance squad, bag-lunch cadets, parent committee, and myriad other groups intertwined with the basketball team was a part of his job description that hadn't been covered in his Troops to Teacher training.

As he poured water into the Mr. Coffee, Dillon, who'd always been an optimist, reminded himself that unlike in his last gig, none of those Shelter Bay residents seemed inclined to kill him.

At least not yet.

2

Although Claire Templeton's career as a jewelry designer tended to have her working seven days a week, especially as the deadline for a new season's launch approached, she'd always enjoyed Mondays.

Monday represented the start of a new week filled with possibilities. This Monday, however, sucked.

She'd been fighting a culinary battle for the last thirty minutes and was losing. Badly. After she'd stuffed the first two batches of pancakes down the garbage disposal, the third, charred black on the bottom, had set off the smoke detector, which was blaring loud enough to wake the dead in nearby Sea View Cemetery.

She'd turned off the gas burner and was carrying a wooden chair around a stack of moving boxes when her teenage son, Matt, appeared in the doorway.

He was wearing a pair of baggy surfer jam shorts, a rumpled black Last Dinosaurs band T-shirt that had fit him a mere three months before but now ended an inch above his waist, and a petulant expression.

So what else was new?

With his heavily lidded brown eyes, tousled, too-long

dark hair hanging over a forehead tanned by the Southern California sun, and full lips, he could've stepped off
the pages of an Abercrombie & Fitch catalog.

During this past difficult year, he'd gone from golden-
boy jock to wannabe bad-boy delinquent. Which was
why Claire had left the only home she'd ever known and
moved here to the small coastal town of Shelter Bay. She
hoped that here he wouldn't face as much daily temptation as Los Angeles had offered.

"My alarm didn't go off," he muttered, cutting her off
before she could point out that he didn't want to be late
his first day in a new school.

Which she hadn't been going to say.

Okay, admittedly she'd been thinking that, but to
avoid another argument about personal responsibility
today of all days, she held her tongue as he took the
chair from her hands and moved it out of the way.

Physically taking after the father he'd never known,
he'd topped her five foot five inches by the time he was
twelve. Now, although he still wasn't old enough to drive,
he'd hit six-three, and if his oversized hands and feet
were any indication, he still had a lot of growing to do.

"You could've just knocked on the bedroom door."
His beautiful lips curled in a sneer. "Setting off the
smoke detector is definitely overkill."

He reached up, took off the white plastic casing, and
turned off the siren. Blessed silence. The only sound was
the low roar of white-capped waves outside the cottage's
kitchen window. When she'd first made the decision to
leave Los Angeles for this coastal town, Claire had had
visions of the two of them taking long walks on the
beach, healing after the rough year they'd both suffered

through, catching up at the end of the day, growing close again. As they'd been for so many years.

"I didn't set the alarm off on purpose." Was that a tinge of defensiveness in her tone? Dammit, yes, it was. "I was making your grandmother's chocolate chip pancakes." Or at least *trying* to.

Claire opened a window to air out some of the smoke, which in turn let in damp sea air tinged with salt and fir from the trees surrounding the cottage on three sides. "For luck."

Her mother, with whom she and Matt had lived since she'd first brought him home from the hospital, had always made chocolate chip pancakes for special occasions. Staring down at the gooey mess stuck to the bottom of the pan, she realized that like so many things Jackie Templeton had made look effortless, cooking her breakfast specialty was more difficult than it looked.

"That's okay," he said. Those were the first halfway positive words she'd heard from him since they'd left California. He took a box of Cheerios down from the cupboard. "It's not as if I'm going to need luck."

"You're not going out for the team?"

"I might play." Shoulders that looked too broad for his still lanky body shrugged in that blasé, uncaring way only a teenager could pull off. "Though I can't see much point in playing for a Podunk program that hasn't pulled off a winning season in nearly the entire time I've been alive."

"Which is why they'll be lucky to have you."

Giving up on the pancakes, she ran the water into the sink and turned on the disposal, sending the rest of the batter, along with this latest charred effort, down the drain.

His only response was a grunt as he poured the milk into the bowl and sat at the table, which was set in front of the window that overlooked the ocean.

The cottage itself was much smaller than the house from which they'd moved, but the sea view—which included the skeleton of a shipwreck—was definitely worth the inflated price she'd paid for it. Of course, seeming determined not to like anything about his new home, when they'd first shown up a day ahead of the moving van, Matt had complained that it was too far from town.

She reluctantly gave him points about their isolation. Considering how much it rained here on the coast, perhaps she should have looked for a place in town. A town he'd immediately dubbed "Hicksville by the Sea" as they drove past the welcome sign.

Claire strongly doubted that there was anything about Shelter Bay that could make him happy. *"Give the boy time,"* she could almost hear her mother saying. *"Kids are resilient. He'll settle in."*

Claire could only hope that was true. Because after the year she'd been through, she was rapidly approaching the end of a very tattered rope.

He continued to sulk as he ate his cereal, then surprised her by putting his bowl and spoon in the dishwasher. Taking that as a positive sign, Claire didn't mention his leaving the milk and sugar on the table.

"At least you arrived in time to make the team," she said, attempting to put a positive spin on the conversation.

Tryouts for the basketball team were being held today. After driving through the night on the last leg of their journey from L.A. to Shelter Bay, she'd managed to arrive Saturday afternoon.

"Like making the team would be a problem." His tone was thick with the derision that had become all too familiar of late. "I already got a call from some guy who heads up the boosters. He said everyone in town's excited about me becoming a Dolphin. Which is a lame name. The Normans conquered England. Dolphins do stupid tricks for fish at Sea World."

His Beverly Hills team had been the Normans, and Claire knew how proud he'd been to wear the black shirt with the orange-and-white *N* shield.

"I suspect the Miami Dolphins players might disagree with that description," she said mildly as she put the milk in the ancient refrigerator, which would need to be replaced. "And dolphins just happen to be among the most intelligent mammals on the planet. . . . Why didn't you tell me you'd gotten a call?"

They'd agreed when high school coaches started trying to recruit him back in middle school that he'd never talk to anyone about basketball prospects unless she was present for the discussion.

"You were at the grocery store. Then I forgot about it."

Not wanting to call him a liar, she wiped off the counter with a sponge. "Well, in the future, try to remember, okay?"

He shot her a dark look, then stalked from the kitchen. A moment later Claire heard the bedroom door slam behind him.

Feeling as if she were walking on eggshells, she followed. But didn't go in.

"It's supposed to rain," she said through the closed door.

"It's rained all weekend," he retorted. "And after seeing all the moss growing on the trees, if I worried about getting wet, I'd never go to school."

From the way he'd been acting, he'd probably prefer dropping out. It was something that had worried her since the day he'd been caught with marijuana in his locker. She supposed the only problem with that idea in his mind was that, if he did leave school, he'd be stuck in the house all day with her.

Right now, apparently, riding his bike in the rain two miles across the bridge into town was preferable to that prospect.

"And having my mom drive me like some lame second grader would be majorly humiliating."

"There's always the school bus." When the agent had first shown her the cottage, one of the pluses had been that the bus stopped at the corner, less than half a block away.

"Kill me now," she heard him mutter. "I'm riding my bike."

He was fifteen years old, on his way to becoming a man. So why did she feel the same way she had when, at six, he'd assured her he could cross the street by himself?

Rain began to pound like bullets on the cedar roof as the forecasted storm chose that moment to arrive. "I realize this may come as a disappointment," she said, deciding that on this she was standing firm, "but I'm still your mother. And unless you want to take the bus, since I have to go into town anyway, I'm driving you."

The bedroom door swung open. He was holding his school clothes in an untidy wad under his arm. So much for that nice crisp crease she'd ironed so he could make a good first impression.

"Why don't I just throw myself off the damn cliff?" he suggested, his tone thick with scorn. "Problem solved."

With that lovely suggestion ringing in her ears, he

strode past her into the single bathroom they were forced to share and shut yet another door between them.

As she heard the shower, which needed repairing, sputter on, Claire pressed her fingers against her eyes until she saw little dots like snowflakes and assured herself, for the umpteenth time, that she'd made the right decision in moving them here to Shelter Bay.

3

From the outside, with its white siding and pots of yellow mums, the Grateful Bread restaurant fit in with the other cheerful coastal buildings lining the street that faced the town's seawall. The only giveaway that it might not be exactly your typical small-town breakfast gathering place was its name on the oval sign, which was the same color as the bright green roof.

Inside, it was an obvious homage to the sixties band, with its obligatory peace sign, multicolored dancing-bear poster, and DEAD HEAD WAY and SHAKEDOWN STREET signs on the walls.

The boosters had claimed the coveted booth in back, which had been created from a cut-in-half VW bus painted in psychedelic colors. On the hood, a rainbow arched over a field of wheat, in the middle of which was a picture of a woven basket of various breads.

Although the restaurant wasn't that large, it took Dillon nearly five minutes to get from the door to the bus booth, as seemingly everyone in the place wanted to talk about the team and this year's season. He didn't need mind-reading powers to know that nearly everyone who cared about basketball was counting on him to be a miracle coach. Because he'd kept hearing the same question over and over again since he'd first arrived in town a few months ago.

"So, Coach," the conversation would go, "what do you think of our chances this year?"

And although he'd try to couch his answer, attempting not to be a wet blanket while also not wanting to raise expectations, invariably the next question would be, "So, you think we'll make state?"

And then, since the chances of turning the program around enough to go to the state tournament was along the lines of an asteroid landing in the center of Evergreen Park, he'd be forced to fall back on every cliché known to sports: "It's a new season. We'll be starting with a clean slate."

Or, "As long as we play all eight minutes of each of the four quarters, I'm expecting the best from our players. . . .

"They're a great bunch of kids," he assured Jimmy Ray Lovell, the owner/cook, who'd called out to him from the open window of the kitchen behind the counter. "We've got ourselves a great foundation, and I'm confident about our nucleus." Given his other job as a physics teacher, Dillon sometimes couldn't resist tossing in a little science terminology.

Before driving over here, Dillon had Googled Matthew Templeton, and the kid did appear to have the props to play high-level basketball. Considering Beverly Hills High wasn't exactly a powerhouse in California hoops, Templeton had, from the articles Dillon had read, provided most of the scoring.

Which could be a problem, since there was a lot more

to a game than mere scoring. Although he knew there were a lot of sports fans, probably many right here in Shelter Bay, who thought it was all about winning, the way Dillon looked at it, there was something immensely pure about high school basketball, before all the agents, big bucks, television, and gambling problems began chipping away at the game's soul.

The kids he was looking forward to coaching were right at the age when they were beginning to make decisions about their lives. There were always temptations, always things to lead them off course. All the time he'd been growing up, there'd been divorced parents, drugs, and the discovery that a few minutes of fumbling around in the backseat of a car could earn serious consequences it was hard to foresee when you're a hormone-driven teenager.

But things seemed to have gotten darker during the time he'd been out of the country and away from any organized game.

Part of the deal with Troops to Teachers was that he'd go to a rural or problem school in need of teachers. Which was fine with him, because unlike coaches who entered the gym every day with the glitter of championship confetti in their sights, after spending so many years watching some of the worst deeds humanity could dish up, Dillon wanted to make a difference in lives.

One problem he was facing was that a team that lost a lot expected to lose. He'd seen it happen in war. If a unit started taking a lot of losses, they began to consider themselves jinxed. Or unlucky. And when that happened, they lost their edge, creating a self-fulfilling prophecy.

Which was why he also needed to impress on his players, who'd never known the heady feeling of winning, that they weren't in it alone. That if one of them started to slide, the rest stepped up, not just on the court, but in life, and gave their troubled teammate a hand up. In order to turn the Shelter Bay program around, they'd all have to be dedicated to the cause, rather than counting on any single individual with exceptional talent.

He finally reached the bus and sat down on a chair covered in a subtle moss green fabric, rather than the expected tie-dye. Before he could look around to signal the waitress, who owned the restaurant with her husband, she was at his table, pouring coffee into a thick white mug.

"So," Vanessa Lovell began, which had Dillon bracing himself for the inevitable question about the basketball team, "are you having the usual?"

"OJ, two eggs over easy, and your husband's famous sweet potato hash," he confirmed, resisting jumping up and kissing her right on those pretty pink lips for not saying a word about basketball.

"Jimmy always gets embarrassed when people call it that," she said, coloring prettily with obvious wifely pride.

"He was on Chef Maddy's new cooking show," Ken Curtis, who was sitting across from Dillon, pointed out. "Which means people all over the country watched him cook. I'd say that makes him pretty damn famous."

"And even if it wasn't famous, it'd still be the best hash I've ever eaten," Dillon said. Which was true.

Her blush deepened as she cast a quick glance over at her husband, who was busy swirling an omelet in a cast-iron pan with a skill that made it look easy. Having tried it at home after watching the show, and ending up dropping the semicooked eggs onto the floor, Dillon knew it wasn't.

Which was why, when he wanted something more than boxed cereal and toast, he ate breakfast here. After observing the owners on more than one occasion, he'd realized that if he ever met a woman who made him feel the way Vanessa Lovell obviously felt about Jimmy Ray, and Jimmy Ray about her, he might actually consider settling down.

He'd never had any desire to get married or even live with anyone while he'd been in the Army. Having one of the most dangerous jobs in the military wasn't all that conducive to long-term relationships. Dillon figured there was a reason a lot of guys he'd worked with over the years had insisted EOD was an acronym for "Everyone's divorced."

"So," Curtis began the discussion without preamble, "what are you planning to do about the phenom?"

Dillon didn't believe in stereotyping. Both sports and war had taught him that appearances could often be deceiving. But he couldn't help thinking that a player with wealth and press coverage most teenage athletes could only dream of could well upset the cohesiveness Dillon was planning to create.

"I don't know what I'm going to do about the new student, Ken," he responded. "At this point I don't even know that he intends to try out."

"Well, of course he will," one of the two women at the table said.

Colleen Dennis was currently mayor of Shelter Bay, and from what he'd witnessed, she was a dynamo who probably could have been successful as mayor of Portland, or perhaps even in the statehouse as governor, if she'd had higher political ambitions.

"If he continues the promise he's already shown, he could be one of the highest-recruited players in the country. Which means he'd have a golden ticket to any school of his choice. Why wouldn't he want to play?" she asked.

"I certainly don't want to disparage my own program," Dillon said carefully, mindful that everyone in the place had stopped eating to hear his response to the mayor's question. "But when was the last time a recruiter was in town?"

"Two years ago," Curtis said. "A guy from Cal State Northridge."

"That doesn't count," another man at the table, Jake, who owned the Crab Shack, countered. "His rental car broke down on his way up the coast to Astoria. He was checking out their center and got stuck here overnight."

The booster club was Ken Curtis' realm. Accustomed to being supreme ruler for life and obviously not happy about being questioned, he thrust out his chest, causing the red-and-black wool logger shirt to strain at the seams. "He was still here long enough for me to meet with him at the Whale Song for a discussion about our players."

"You staked out his room," Jake said, "and practically jumped on him the minute he got off the elevator. He couldn't get into his room fast enough, and you're just lucky he didn't dial 911 and have the sheriff send a deputy over to haul your ass out of the inn."

"I don't remember seeing you there," Curtis shot back, "so how would you know what happened? Not that I'm saying you're right."

"One of my line cooks was working as a room service waiter at the Whale Song back then. When Coach here moved to town, my guy told me about your trying to bribe him to take the dinner tray in yourself. You should know that there aren't any secrets in this town."

Before Ken could respond, Vanessa arrived at the table with their orders.

Dillon smiled up at her, supremely grateful to her for forcing a time-out.

"Thank you, darlin'," he said. "I know it's going to be a good day when you bring me breakfast." He glanced over at Jimmy Ray, who'd moved on from twirling the omelet to chopping something with blinding speed. "Why don't you leave that husband of yours and run away with me?"

"You are so bad, Coach Slater." She dimpled prettily, obviously pleased with the compliment. Especially since none of the other people at the table had paid her any attention as she'd set their orders in front of them, re-filled their coffee mugs, then left the table to circle the room with the coffee carafe.

"Back to the topic at hand," Dillon said, "my point was that although the tryouts are important, I've already got an idea what I'm going to be doing with the team. I'm not sure this new kid would fit into the plan."

He held up a finger when both Curtis and the mayor opened their mouths to question that statement.

"Besides, there's also the fact that he's only fifteen."

"Fifteen and a half," Tony Genarro, owner of Genarro's funeral home, looked up from his triple stack of blueberry pancakes to clarify.

"He's still a sophomore. Which means, if he does come out for the team, he belongs on JV."

"Surely you wouldn't relegate a talent like that to the

junior varsity team!" The mayor was obviously shocked by that idea.

"That's where freshmen and sophomores tend to play." Dillon shrugged and scooped up a bite of the sweet potato hash, which damned well deserved its fame. "Varsity's for upperclassmen."

"Typically," Jake agreed, suggesting that while he and Ken Curtis might not see eye to eye on everything, on this they agreed. "But I watched some of the clips on YouTube. The kid reminds me of Isiah Thomas, back in the day."

"Thomas played both sides of the ball." When your depth was as shallow as Shelter Bay's team's was, you needed players who could handle both offense and defense.

"The kid steals like he started picking pockets in his playpen," Curtis said.

"And shoots like Larry Bird," Jake added.

"Pure swish. Nothin' but net," Tony chimed in.

Since he was the new guy, bringing hope all wrapped up in a shiny ribbon to Shelter Bay, most of the previous meetings had gone Dillon's way. He'd been optimistic without getting all crazy about the team's prospects, and they'd come up with ways to get the community involved, because, as he'd pointed out, looking at last season's attendance records, it was going to be hard to motivate the players when there were only a few dozen spectators showing up to watch them play.

But now they'd seen a different, brighter future in the six-foot-three-inch-tall sophomore from Tinseltown. And it was going to take all his persuasive powers to get them back on the program.

"From what I could tell, watching his videos online, the kid never passes."

"He didn't need to," Curtis pointed out. "Because he could make all the plays by himself."

Dillon put down his fork, leaned back, and folded his arms. "You've just made my point. If you want me to turn the team around—"

"That's why the school board hired you," the mayor pointed out.

"Actually," the other woman at the table finally spoke up, "we hired you for your impressive academic credentials and your leadership qualities."

Ginger Wells was the principal of Shelter Bay High School. She was smart, enthusiastic, and, although he figured her to be in her mid-forties, still pretty damn hot. If she hadn't been his boss—and married to her college sweetheart—he would've invited her out to dinner at the Sea Mist his first week in town.

"I appreciate the confidence," Dillon said.

"I'll be honest," Her Honor said. "I don't know anything about sports. Nor do I care. But I *do* care about what's best for this town. And if this boy is even half as good as Ken keeps telling me—"

"He is," both Jake and Ken said in unison, proving yet again that they both wanted to see Matthew Templeton in a Dolphins blue-and-white varsity uniform for the first game of the season.

"We're getting ahead of ourselves," Dillon said, trying to stand up to the booster steamroller yet again. "We don't even know if the kid intends to try out."

"He told me he was," Ken said.

Alarm bells went off like the civil defense siren the town tested once a month. "When was that?"

Dillon knew Ken claimed to bleed Dolphin blue, but he sure as hell hoped that he hadn't actually called Beverly Hills and offered the kid—or his mom—something to move to Oregon. Because recruiting kids from other schools was not only wrong; it had been declared illegal by the Supreme Court after schools in Tennessee got tired of a private academy poaching their best players.

"Saturday. When they first hit town."

"Not before that?"

"Hell no! That'd be illegal."

"As long as we're all on the same page," Dillon said, relieved. Until another thought occurred to him. "I don't suppose Marcy just happened to sell the kid's mother her house." Ken's wife was one of the most successful real estate agents on the Oregon coast.

"Yeah. Those two ladies down at the Dancing Deer Two hooked them up after Ms. Templeton told them she was thinking about moving up here. She was the one who asked them if they knew a good Realtor."

Although the siren had gone silent, Dillon still felt a little niggle of suspicion. Then again, he'd admittedly gotten jaded during his EOD days.

"Where all did Marcy take her to look?"

Ken shrugged and began pushing his cottage fries around on his plate. "If you were married, Coach, you'd know that husbands and wives don't share every little detail that goes on at work every day."

"Did *your* wife happen to mention to you that her California client was the mother of a high school–age basketball player?"

"She might have said something about it." When Dillon didn't immediately respond, he moved his massive shoulders again. "Okay, Marcy said the mom asked if the school had a basketball team. She said her kid was pretty good. So, naturally, I checked him out."

"Meaning you looked him up on the Internet."

"Yeah."

"You didn't call his coach or his parents or him?"

"No to the coach, and apparently Templeton's dad's out of the picture, but I didn't talk to his mother. And, like I told you, I didn't speak to him until two days ago. Hell, what good would it do to recruit a player only to end up getting the team suspended for the season if we got caught? Doesn't make a lick of sense."

"*When* we got caught," Dillon corrected.

Ken was, Dillon determined, telling the truth. But he'd bet that once the hardware store owner had discovered the kid's admittedly impressive stats, he'd suggested his wife try to keep the house search within the Shelter Bay school district boundaries.

"Lucky coincidence, his mother choosing to buy a house in our district," he said.

"She said she wanted to move to Shelter Bay. She'd visited this area on trips before. And the cottage was just what she was looking for," Ken said a little too defensively. "It's not like Marcy held a gun to her head and made her buy it. Besides, it's a prime piece of oceanfront real estate. She got a helluva deal because it's one of the few fixer-uppers left on the coast."

There was no point in arguing. If Ken could be believed, and Dillon hoped to hell he could, the booster had stayed within legal and ethical boundaries. Besides, he figured there'd probably be far more important skirmishes to win as the season went on.

"Well," he said, scooping up another bite of hash, "if

the kid does show up for tryouts, I'll definitely take a look at him."

"His basketball skills might not be as well rounded as you'd prefer," Ginger said, "but would it help you to know that he received a scholar-athlete award his freshman year?"

"That definitely helps. What are his grades now?"

"They've slipped," the principal admitted. "But he's hovering a bit below a three-point-oh." She paused to stir cream into her coffee.

One thing Dillon had gotten real good at was listening to what people didn't say.

"That's still not bad for a student athlete." Though if the kid wanted to play college ball, NCAA regulations required a 2.3, and many universities required higher. "So what's wrong with him?"

Her tongue was literally in her cheek as Ken began paying vast attention to his cottage fries. "He had a bit of trouble," she allowed. "Which is one of the reasons his mother decided to move here."

"Tell me we're not looking at a possible Columbine thing."

"Oh, no," she said quickly.

"Hell no," Ken seconded, revealing that the two of them had already discussed it. From the looks on the other boosters' faces, Dillon suspected he was the last to know.

"A bit of marijuana was found in his locker," Ginger revealed.

"What's a bit?"

Experimentation was one thing, not that he'd allow a kid who fooled around with drugs to stay on his team.

But he could work with that. If the Templeton kid was into selling, all bets were off.

"Less than an ounce. Which is why, along with his grades, he got off with three days' suspension."

"But the police were called?"

"Yes, it's district policy. But because of his age, and California having decriminalized less than an ounce, even though it occurred at school, it was treated much like a traffic ticket."

"Which means," Ken pointed out, "that if none of us say anything, there's no reason for the press to find out about it."

Although Dillon suspected the booster was thinking more about avoiding negative publicity for the school, if that was the only thing the kid had done, he deserved the right to come into a new school with a clean slate.

"If there's no record, how do you all know about it?"

"The suspension *is* in his school record we received from Beverly Hills," Ginger stated. "Along with a letter from his mother explaining the situation. Apparently his grandmother, who helped raise him, died after a lengthy illness this past year, and once the season was over, the boy began drifting and started hanging out with the wrong crowd."

"It happens with kids," Jake said. "I was a hell-raiser myself before I went into the corps right out of high school."

"And look at you now," the mayor said. "Business owner, chamber of commerce member—"

"And damn good cook," Dillon added. Jake's Crab Shack, among the other restaurants in Shelter Bay, had kept him well fed over the past months.

"Ms. Templeton assured me that Matthew knows

what he did was wrong and that it won't happen again,"
Ginger said.

"That's the mom speaking." Dillon knew that his own
mom, whom he'd given hell for a time himself after his
dad's death in an oil-rig fire, would've always been the
first to leap to his defense. "I want to talk to him directly."

"Of course," everyone at the table agreed in unison.

Okay. If the kid was smart enough to keep up his
grades throughout a season encompassing more than
twenty games during a tough personal time, he shouldn't
have any trouble picking up a new system.

If he was willing to give up his starring role.

Which remained to be seen.

4

Matt hated everything about Oregon. He hated the winter rain that was always drizzling on the hood of the stupid Gor-Tex jacket his mother had made him buy during the move. He hated the so-called beach with its stringy green kelp and piles of driftwood logs, and he especially hated the water that was so ice-cold that if he even tried to surf, his balls would probably go up into his throat and stay there for the next fifty years.

And making things worse was having his mom drive him to school like some little kid. He still had six more months before he'd be old enough to drive without her riding shotgun. If he had a car, he'd head straight back to California. Where he belonged.

She tried to make conversation, but he wasn't in any mood to talk, especially since if she cared about what he had to say, she wouldn't have dragged him to this lame, nowhere place.

A cold gray fog surrounded the car as they sat waiting for the bridge to open up to let a fishing boat pass from the harbor on the way out to the ocean.

"I just thought of another positive thing about playing for the Dolphins that you might not have considered," she tried again.

Not wanting to talk about the stupid team that would kill his dream of getting to the pros, Matt folded his arms and looked out the passenger window, pretending interest in the blue boat barely visible through the fog.

"President Obama's brother-in-law is the Oregon State basketball coach."

"Duh." Even people who didn't care squat about basketball probably knew that.

"Which means that the team probably draws more press attention than some others."

"So? I wouldn't be playing for the Beavers." In Matt's opinion, that was an even stupider name than Dolphins. But at least it was better than OSU's rival Oregon Ducks.

"I'd guess it also draws more NBA scouts," she said, as if not hearing him.

"In case you didn't notice, Mom, I'm not old enough for college. Or the NBA draft."

"Having given birth to you, I'm well aware of your age, Matthew." There was a snarky edge to her voice he wasn't used to hearing from her. "My point, and I do have one, is that since those reporters and scouts are already here in Oregon, don't you think they might possibly be interested in taking a side trip to the coast to check out how the number one prep player from California is doing? Especially since you're bound to receive a great deal of local press?"

As much as he hated to admit it, she might have a point.

"How many high school players are there in California?" she asked.

"I don't know. A bunch just in the SoCal CIF." Matt

guessed that the Southern California Collegiate Inter-
scholastic Federation, in which he'd played, was probably the largest in the state.

"Which put you in competition with a lot of players."

He turned away from the window toward her. "Who
weren't as good as me."

"Well, that goes without saying."

Her smile made him realize how long it had been
since he'd seen her face lit up that way. It also reminded
him how pretty she was and how much younger she was
than most of his friends' mothers. Hell, she'd only been
three years older than he was now when she'd gotten
pregnant with him.

Which, having lost his own dream, made him wonder
for the first time whether she ever resented him, since if she
hadn't dropped out of school, she'd probably be really famous.

"But with all those schools scattered all over the state,
it's unlikely that individual players, even one as good as
you, can garner that much press attention," she said. "Especially with all the big college and pro teams stealing the
spotlight.

"But here"—she waved her hand toward the bridge,
which was lowering now that the boat had passed
through—"although I hate to stoop to clichés, you'll be
the proverbial big fish in a smaller pond."

"More like a damn puddle," he muttered even as he
considered that prospect.

"Well, then, you'll just have to help grow the program,
won't you?"

Because he hadn't even considered that situation
until she'd brought it up, Matt didn't answer. Deep in

thought about possibilities, he didn't notice they were driving through town until she cut the engine in the school parking lot. Instead of the sprawling, Spanish-style red-tile-roof building he'd left behind, this had a cedar roof and four two-story wings that fanned out from a center square. Fir trees dripping with rain stood where the tennis courts had been back at his old high school.

"You sure you don't want me to come in?" she asked.

"I'm fine."

"Better than fine." She reached to tousle his hair, the way she'd done when he was a little kid, then, apparently realizing he'd hate that, pulled her hand back at the last minute. "You're the best thing that's ever happened to my life, Matt."

If he was all that important, why the hell had she uprooted him and ruined his life?

"I know it doesn't seem like it now," she said, "but if I didn't truly believe this was the best thing for you, I never would've moved up here."

She was wrong. But since he wasn't going to change her mind in the next two minutes, Matt decided not to start another argument.

"Whatever. I've got to get in," he said.

"Of course. You don't want to be late on your very first day." This time her smile was a little crooked. And it could've been a trick of the light, what with the rain and all, but he thought her eyes looked a little wet. Damn. He might hate what she'd done to their life, but he so couldn't deal with making her cry.

Pulling herself together, she reached out and, thank you, God, instead of hugging him in public, she patted his leg. "Have a great day."

Suddenly, for some stupid reason that didn't make any sense, Matt felt his own eyes burning.

Not trusting his voice, he grabbed his book bag from the backseat, pulled up the hood of his new jacket, and escaped out the door before he risked making a fool of himself in front of every high school kid in Hickstown.

5

Since the beginning of this first semester of teaching, Dillon had established a routine of getting to school at least an hour before the students arrived. It gave him time to settle in, grab some coffee in the teachers' lounge, read the paper, then get his mind into teaching mode. Which still, after all his years in the military, was sometimes a challenge.

Not that he didn't enjoy his job. He loved the kids, the challenge to find ways to engage them, and he especially loved that every day was nothing like the previous one, which was good because he'd chosen EOD partly because he was easily bored. And, after having run a summer camp for the players from last year's team, he was pretty sure, if he could keep the boosters at bay, he'd enjoy coaching, too.

The one thing that was way different from his previous gig was that teenagers weren't all that inclined to take orders, which was forcing him to find unique ways to motivate them.

This morning the booster meeting had lasted longer than he'd expected, so he arrived at the same time as the kids, who were pouring off buses and out of cars, with the underclassmen climbing out of their parents' cars, while juniors and seniors, even in less-than-wealthy Shelter Bay, tended to have their own vehicles.

As he crossed the parking lot, he paused for a moment, enjoying the view of the battalion of fir trees spearing like shaggy arrows into the pewter sky. He'd grown up in the West Texas oil patch, then spent the past several years in the deserts of Iraq and the desolate landscape of Afghanistan, so the sight of the magnificent Douglas firs draped in silvery moss never ceased to amaze and awe him.

A black Lexus RX caught his attention. First, because you didn't tend to see that many luxury SUVs in the school parking lot. Even more unlikely was to see one with California plates.

Since Templeton wasn't old enough to drive, it didn't take the deductive skills that had saved Dillon's life on more than one occasion to figure out this was the kid's mom. He was debating whether to stop and chat when he noticed that her forehead was on the steering wheel.

Concerned that she might be sick, he went over and tapped on the window. When she lifted her head to look at him, he noticed what seemed to be tears swimming in her eyes and wished he'd just kept walking.

There was a buzz as she rolled down the window. "I'm sorry," she said before he could introduce himself. "I know I don't have a parking sticker, but—"

"I'm not campus police." Actually, the school didn't have a police officer assigned to it, but since she'd come from Southern California, where crime was probably a lot more common—even in Beverly Hills—he wasn't sure she'd find the lack of security good news. "I'm Dillon Slater. I teach physical science, physics, and—"

"You're the basketball coach."

"That would be me. And I think, for the record, this is where I assure you that I didn't have anything to do with that booster phone call to your son. In fact, I didn't even know about it until a couple hours ago."

"That's good to hear."

She skimmed her left fingers beneath eyes the same soft green as her necklace, as if checking for tears. With his eye for detail, Dillon noticed that her ring finger was bare, confirming what Ken had said about Matthew Templeton's father being out of their lives.

"I usually don't let him deal with boosters," she said. "I'm not suggesting that the man who called him—"

"That'd be Ken Curtis. He owns the hardware store and has been head of the boosters for pretty much forever."

"Curtis?" Her brow furrowed. "Would he happen to be married to Marcy Curtis, by any chance?"

"Got it in one."

Her eyes turned cool. "Isn't that a coincidence," she murmured, giving him the idea that she might share his earlier suspicions as to how she ended up living in the Shelter Bay school district.

He shrugged. "Shelter Bay's a small town. Some places might have six degrees of separation, but here you'd be hard pressed to find two or three."

"Well." She looked out the rain-spotted windshield as she considered that idea. "That makes sense. It's also, quite honestly, why I chose to move here. Every time I'd come to town to visit the Dancing Deer Two after sales trips to Portland and Eugene, I'd find myself relaxing . . .

"And getting back to my point, I'm not suggesting Mr. Curtis called to make an illegal or unethical offer, but unfortunately there have been some who tried."

"Not under my watch," he assured her. "*If* your son decides to try out and if he makes the team, you can trust that everything will be not just legal and above-board, but ethical."

"I appreciate that. But if you stopped to ask my opinion, I've no idea what he's going to decide. About anything."

Her sigh was soft and, he thought, a little sad. She also looked too young to be the mother of a high school sophomore.

"That's not why I stopped to talk with you," Dillon said. "I just wanted to make sure you were feeling okay. I'm still on civilian time and haven't entered into teaching/coach mode yet."

"I'm fine." Which was obviously a lie, but he wasn't going to call her on it. This time she ran her hand through her straight fall of hair, which, even with the low clouds hanging over them, appeared woven with golden sunlight. "I'm just not exactly the most popular person on the planet right now."

From the moment Ken had called, Dillon's thoughts had been focused on the Templeton kid. It belatedly occurred to him that he hadn't given any thought to the mother, other than a niggling concern about the possibility of her complaining about undue pressure being put on her son.

"Join the club. Being the guy who hands out homework and springs pop quizzes, I'm familiar with how that feels. Want to check out the gym?" he asked in a not very subtle attempt to change the subject. "Just in case your son does decide he wants to play?"

It took her a moment to consider. "I'd like that," she said.

Dillon could hear the hesitation in her tone. "But?"

"It's almost time for school to start. Don't you have a class?"

"My first hour's open," he assured her. "I was planning to spend it watching game films from last year. Which, believe me, is not the most fun part of my job."

"Having seen the team's record, I can imagine."

A little silence fell over them.

"There's something else," he guessed as he sensed a battle going on inside her.

"I've already managed to humiliate Matt by driving him here today. If he sees me walking down a hall and thinks I'm checking up on him . . ."

"You don't have to worry. As it happens, fire regulations require an exit door on the gym. We'll go in that way."

Dillon told himself that the reason he was inviting her to see the gym was not because whatever shampoo or lotion she was wearing had her smelling like a tropical vacation—although, along with the sunshine in her hair, the pleasant scent did a lot to brighten a gray coastal day—but because he wanted to delve a bit more into whatever problems her son had been going through.

The kid could shoot like Larry Bird and dunk like Michael Jordan, but if he was going to cause conflict, Dillon didn't want him on his team.

"Thank you."

The rain was no longer hammering on the roof of the

SUV, but it was definitely more than a mist. As he opened the door for her, she picked up a small umbrella from the backseat floor.

The tide of students had already flowed into the building, leaving Claire and Dillon mostly alone as they walked toward the sidewalk. A few kids, in danger of being late, raced by, calling out greetings.

"It appears you've exaggerated your unpopularity," she observed.

"That's because the season hasn't started yet. Let's see how they feel when I fail to provide them with a championship season the first year."

"Surely no one's expecting that quick a turnaround of the program."

"In a logical world you'd be right. But there's nothing logical about small-town high school athletics. From what I've been able to tell, most folks are expecting me to provide a miracle season. The kind they write books and make movies about."

"Miracles do happen. Which, I suppose, is why those movies like *Hoosiers* get made. People want to believe in them, which isn't such a bad thing. And Matt could make your miracle more likely."

"I'm not going to lie. He probably could. However— and I'm not putting your son down in any way—I'm not sure he's the savior the boosters believe he is."

They'd been walking side by side across the asphalt parking lot, which glistened like black obsidian from the rain, the scarlet umbrella keeping them a bit apart. At his words, Claire stopped and turned toward him.

"Why would you say that?" A blond brow winged up. Her eyes frosted, chilly enough to freeze Shelter Bay. "As you undoubtedly know, he was the number one freshman prep player in his state division last year. *Every* game BHHS won was due to his talent."

"That was all too clear from watching the videos I found. Maybe it's because of all my years in the Army, but I tend to look more at the team picture. When everyone has an assigned role, everyone gets to enjoy the victory."

"Even if you lose?"

"This team hasn't had a winning season for twelve years. The only way I can figure out how to put a few games in the win column is to have all the players feel responsible for the outcome. If I let any single player do it all, the others would be more likely to slack off. Which wouldn't be good for the team or your son.

"Especially since at this level, sports are every bit as much about character building as they are wins. So we'll play the games my way, and if we lose more than we win, well, parents, boosters, and hometown fans are just going to have to suck it up and deal with it."

"That's an admirable attitude," she allowed. She began walking again. "And one that could possibly get you fired."

"If you're worried about Matt having to deal with a coaching change down the road, that's not going to happen. I came here through Troops to Teachers, a program that puts vets into classrooms. When Shelter Bay's school district requested a teacher, part of the deal was that I'd put in three years."

"That sounds a bit like the military."

"Yeah, that's exactly what I thought, when I first heard of it while I was still deployed. But hey, it works for me, and the good thing for your son, if he does end up playing, is that the same way I can't quit, the school can't fire me. Unless I do something illegal, which isn't going to happen."

As they reached the sidewalk, he put a hand on the back of her coat. Not in any sexual way, Dillon assured himself, but to guide her around the back of the building to the gym door.

"If your son plays, he'll have to find a way to be a team player. That's how I want to run things, and I'm not going anywhere."

And, it appeared, neither was she.

6

The gym came as a surprise. More spacious than the arched-ceiling gym at Beverly Hills High, which went along with the Norman medieval style the architect had chosen in the late 1920s, this one boasted high windows that let in a surprising amount of light.

"It's so bright," Claire said as she stood at the edge of a wooden floor polished to a mirror sheen, looking up at one of the ceiling-hung baskets.

"Yeah, those windows really work well, even with all our rain. Plus, the ceiling's painted with a reflective paint to better diffuse the light they let in."

"I can't imagine Matt not wanting to play here."

The steel bleachers had been painted to resemble an American flag, with red-and-white stripes and a dark blue rectangle in each top corner. A blue dolphin mascot was painted in the center of the floor and blue-and-white rally banners hung on the high walls. Along with, she noted, a lone state championship banner dating back to 1978.

"You have quite a challenge cut out for you," she said.

"You called that one right. Fortunately, if there's one thing we EOD guys love, it's a challenge." His grin, which flashed a dimple at the corner of his mouth, was quick, easy, and too charming for comfort.

Rather than acknowledge the little tug, Claire focused on what he'd just said. "EOD?"

"Yeah. We're the guys who defuse IEDs and blow weapons caches and other stuff up."

"That must be extremely dangerous."

He shrugged. "War's dangerous. For the military and civilians . . . So, how's your son with this move?" he asked in a not very subtle attempt to change the subject.

"He wasn't thrilled," she admitted. "And it's going to take some adjustment. Which is another reason I hope he'll try out for the team. Playing will be something familiar. Which should help with the transition."

"Any more signs of drugs?"

Claire wasn't surprised he knew of Matt's locker episode. If she'd been the principal who'd read the note she'd sent along with his transcript, she'd have felt obligated to share the information with his teachers and coach. In a way she was a bit relieved that she wouldn't be the only adult watching for signs of trouble.

"None. I believed he learned his lesson." She dearly hoped so.

"What about his father? I know you're a single mother," he said. She listened for any judgment in his tone and found none. "But how much is he in the picture?"

"Not at all. And he never has been."

She saw a flicker of something in his eyes. Something that looked like pity. "That's tough."

Damn. It seemed to be her day for being made to feel defensive. And she wasn't enjoying it at all.

"I understand the thinking that boys need a man in the family to serve as a role model. But that really depends on the man, doesn't it?"

When she'd found herself pregnant after a one-night stand with a man who turned out to be not just a world-class liar, but also an adulterer who'd conveniently forgotten to mention his wife, she'd come to the conclusion that not having Matt's father in their lives would turn out to be a good thing.

Because no way would she have wanted a man with such a low moral character influencing her son.

He put his hands in the front pockets of his jeans and rocked back on his heels. "I suppose it does. That's one thing sports can be good for. It gives kids a guy to talk with. Even about things they might not want to share with their moms or even their dads."

"It's an admirable concept. But I don't think it's worked that way for Matt."

While she wouldn't have changed a thing about that decision she'd made sixteen years ago, there were admittedly times Claire wondered if Matt didn't need a male mentor who could help him make the right choices during this complicated, testosterone-driven time of his life. And, just as important, make him accept responsibility for his actions.

"Obviously I'm not in the locker room with him, but over the years I've gotten the distinct impression that his athletic ability has given him a free pass when it comes to behavior."

"If he's expecting a free pass here, he's going to be in for a big disappointment."

Even though she agreed with that idea in principle, his statement triggered a spark of maternal protection-

ism. And concern about this man being former military.
"You do realize we're talking about a high school basketball team? And not a boot camp?"

"Of course. But I'm also a big believer in personal
responsibility. Every guy on the floor has to rely on every other team member to show up prepared to play.
And to give everything he's got at practice so he can be
his best. Whatever his talent level."

"Matt lives and breathes basketball." She folded her
arms and lifted her chin. "He's no slacker."

"I'll buy that he loves playing the game. That showed
from the game-film clips I saw. Call me a throwback to
the dinosaur age, if anyone had actually been around to
play roundball back then, but I see my role as teaching
the kids to incorporate discipline and the ability to make
clear-minded choices they can take from this gym to
their lives beyond the court.

"My dad died when I was thirteen. I was angry at the
world and probably could've spiraled out of control, especially since my mom, who is, by the way, a second-
grade teacher, had to take on a second job to pay the
bills, but I was lucky to have a middle school coach who
stepped in to fill that gap. So the way I see it, I'm just
paying it forward."

Her annoyance receded like the ocean at low tide. "I
like that idea." Claire also hoped that Matt would decide to play for this man, although she knew that if she
tried to push him into a decision, he'd balk and do exactly the opposite, just for spite. "Were you an only
child?"

"No, I had four younger sisters."

"You were definitely outnumbered." She also suspected he might have been forced into the role of surrogate parent.

"Definitely." From the way his eyes softened, she suspected he was looking back with more fondness than pain. "Though it wasn't all that tough, since I learned a lot of stuff about girls most guys don't."

As that small dimple flashed again at the corner of his mouth when he grinned, Claire decided the last thing this man needed was any inside information.

"If you ever need someone to braid your hair, I'm your guy."

"I'll keep that in mind."

Was he actually flirting with her? And if so, was he the same way with all the players' moms? Or just the single available ones?

He was good-looking. Okay, better than that. He was hot. But having grown up in Los Angeles, Claire had spent her life surrounded by good-looking men. And, because she wasn't a nun, she'd gone out with her share who were charming, fun, and out for a good time. Throw a stick on any beach in Los Angeles County and you'd hit a dozen of them. They'd only been in it for the moment, which had been fine with her, because she hadn't been looking for a long-term relationship. Nor was she now.

Wanting to know who was going to be coaching her son, she'd looked up his background on the school's Web site. Since she'd guess his height at a little over six feet, she wasn't surprised that he'd gotten an athletic scholarship to Texas A&M as a point guard. While that position tended to be one of the shorter players on a team, point guards were leaders, calling the plays on the floor, directing their teammates where to go, and making sure everyone got the ball at the right time.

They were, unlike most men Claire had known, adept at multitasking. Not only able to weave quickly between and around larger defenders, they were also known for their ball-handling skills.

Which drew her gaze to his hands. He'd hooked his thumbs into the pockets of his jeans. While his hands were large enough to palm a basketball, those long dark fingers would have to possess finesse, wouldn't they? In order to defuse a bomb without blowing himself and his teammates up?

His whiskey brown eyes were lighter in the center, like bursts of gold. They also had a way of looking at her as if they could see more than she wanted them to.

As he continued to look down at her, she felt the walls narrowing, boxing her in—even though the gym was larger than most she'd seen as she'd attended Matt's games around Southern California.

And as those all-seeing eyes drifted down to her mouth and lingered thoughtfully, Claire felt much too alone with him.

"Well," she said, feeling a sudden need for air, "I appreciate you taking the time to fill me in on your program. And showing me the gym. It's very impressive, and I'd feel very comfortable with you as my son's coach."

"Thank you. I appreciate the vote of confidence." A light dancing in his eyes suggested he'd recognized her unbidden, and definitely unwilling, awareness.

She glanced down at her watch. "I'd better be going. I have an appointment in ten minutes."

"Doesn't take much more than that to get anywhere

in town." He put his hand on the back of her coat again, a casual touch to once again guide her to where he wanted her to go.

And wasn't that the problem with men? Always wanting a woman to go places she wasn't comfortable going?

"I can see my way out."

He cocked his head and gave her another of those looks. "Suit yourself."

She'd been expecting an argument. Had been prepared for it. Yet, grateful as she was that he wasn't going to insist on having his way, as she walked out of the gym, the heels of her boots echoing on the polished wooden floor, Claire was vaguely disappointed.

7

Matt was seething as he walked past the jocks wearing their letterman jackets and lounging against the wall of the main hall of Shelter Bay High School. They were laughing and having themselves a good old time. And why not? They were the freaking stars of the school, and even some Martian who'd just landed a spaceship on the front lawn could've recognized it.

They were immersed in their own world, so unless you were a pretty girl they could hit on or some nerd they could laugh at, you simply failed to exist.

Matt wondered whether he'd been the same way back at BHHS and reluctantly decided he had. But since he'd also been a scholar-athlete, he'd had his share of nerd acquaintances. They might not be friends, like the guys on his team, but they didn't have to worry that he'd be singling them out for public ridicule.

He forged through the sea of kids, finding the office without any trouble. Behind the counter stood a woman with wiry gray hair that stuck out from her head in a way that made it look as if she'd put her wet fingers in a light socket.

After he'd told her his name, she typed it into her computer, and the printer began kicking out his schedule, which she handed him, along with a stack of textbooks, a temporary ID card, and a map showing the campus and the interior of the school.

"This is your locker." She plucked a yellow pencil from the bird's nest of hair and drew a circle around a rectangle on the second floor. "And here's your combination." She wrote it on the paper. "Your first class is physics with Mr. Dillon."

The basketball coach. Matt was trying to decide whether having a class with the coach would be a good thing, when the woman behind the counter called over a girl who was typing away at a computer across the room.

"This is Aimee Pierson," she said. "She'll be showing you around today. Aimee, this is our new student, Matthew Templeton." She handed her a sheet of paper. "And here's his schedule."

The top of the girl's head hit Matt about midchest. Her hair was coppery red, she had a sprinkling of freckles across her nose, and brown eyes smiled at him from behind the lenses of black-framed glasses. "Hi, Matthew."

"It's Matt." Her glasses and the way she'd pulled her long hair back into a braid reminded him of the sexy librarian in a soft-porn video he'd watched one night with the guys on his team after winning the game that sent them to state. Though she definitely didn't have a rack like the girl in the video. "And thanks for the offer, but I don't need a guide."

"Every new student gets a guide the first day," the woman behind the counter informed him.

"It's part of our Shelter Bay High hospitality," Aimee

Pierson said. White teeth encased in clear braces flashed in a smile even brighter than the one in her eyes. She plucked his map from his hand. "Oh, cool. Your locker's on the same hallway as mine."

Then, before he could insist yet again that he didn't need a keeper, she was headed toward the door of the office. Thinking that he seemed to be surrounded by bossy females lately, Matt had no choice but to follow.

"Are you that basketball phenom everyone's talking about?" she asked as they walked toward a stairway at the end of the main hall.

"I guess." He shrugged, although he liked the idea that she'd heard about him. "So, does everyone really get the hospitality treatment?" he asked. Or maybe he was just getting extra attention to help convince him to join the team.

Matt had heard stories about high school senior jocks having sex with willing coeds assigned to make sure top recruits enjoyed college visits. He'd never actually met anyone who'd admit to experiencing it personally, but he doubted there was a guy out there who didn't hope it would happen to him.

She nodded emphatically, sending her earrings dancing. He recognized the small pieces of blue sea glass wrapped in silver threads as one of his mother's designs from last year's spring collection. While he'd gotten used to girls in L.A. wearing his mother's jewelry, it seemed weird to see the earrings show up here at the end of the world.

"Everyone gets a guide the first day," she said, confirming what the woman in the office had already said. "One of the things you'll find when you read your student information package is that all Shelter Bay stu-

dents are required to do community volunteer work. I
help out Saturday mornings at Dr. Parrish's free clinic
and supplement my babysitting money working in the
office for a half hour before classes start in the morning.

"The new student guide was my idea. I'm a former
Army brat, so I know how tough it can be coming to a
new school. Especially when you're having to start later
in the year."

"No offense, but I'd rather be anywhere than here."

She nodded. "I totally understand. I've lived in nine
houses in three states and two foreign countries. Every
time I'd make friends, Dad would come home with new
orders and off we'd go again."

"That must've sucked."

"It kind of did. But it wasn't like I had any choice.
When I was a little kid, I was really shy—"

"Get out."

"No, really. I had the hardest time even talking to anyone at school and spent most of my time at home in my
room either crying or reading. Then, around fifth grade,
some boys made a paper airplane out of my homework
and threw it out the bus window, so I finally figured out
that if I wanted to fit in, I'd have to just put on my big-girl
panties and throw myself into the stream of things."

She might not be all that hot. But that comment
about her panties had Matt wondering what she was
wearing beneath that baggy blue sweater and pleated
plaid skirt. Since she wasn't wearing any makeup, he figured whatever underwear she *was* wearing probably
hadn't come from Victoria's Secret.

"When Dad retired last year, he promised our move
here from Joint Base Lewis-McChord, up in Washington, was our last."

Matt was relieved she couldn't see the image that had flashed through his head of Victoria's Secret supermodel Erin Heatherton on the fashion show runway, not wearing much more than wings, high heels, and scraps of lace.

"He teaches electrical engineering at Coastal Community College."

Although he wasn't about to call her a liar, he still had a hard time imagining Aimee Pierson being lonely and crying in her room. She was probably the most talkative girl he'd ever met.

"Does everyone in school know about me moving here?" On the HD video screen in his mind, Erin had just bent down from the end of the raised runway to throw him a kiss.

"Probably. Shelter Bay's a small town. Everyone pretty much knows everything about everyone. And all the people who care about basketball talk about you as if you're the Second Coming."

"You sound as if you're not one of the people who care about basketball."

"Oh, I don't dislike it," she assured him as she stopped in front of a gray metal locker with a combination lock. "It's just that I've never had any reason to get into it."

"Maybe you'll change your mind once the team starts winning."

She paused in twisting the dial to look up at him. "So you're going to try out?"

Try out? She made it sound as if there was any question about him making the team. Which there wasn't. "I haven't made up my mind. Though with all the rain, it's not as if there's a lot of other stuff to do."

"Oh, but there is. Of course in winter the beach can

get pretty chilly, but when the sun comes out, as long as you bundle up, it's still fun."

A boy with hair the color of a carrot was taking a stack of books from his locker across the hall and called out a hello to her. She said a cheery "hi" back, and waved.

"That's Johnny Tiernan-St. James," she told Matt. "He's a junior and probably the only kid in this school who's lived in more places than I have. He's trying out for varsity, so you'll probably become friends. He's a really nice guy. For an athlete."

Color suddenly flooded into her face. "Not that I was saying *all* athletes aren't nice people, but—"

"I know what you meant." It was pretty much what he'd been thinking when forced to walk past the jocks in the main hall.

"Good, because I definitely didn't mean to insult you. . . . If we had more time"—she glanced down at her geeky relativity watch with its rotating numbers—"I'd introduce you to Johnny, but if you do try out for the team, you'll meet him this afternoon.

"And don't worry about finding things to do around here. There are lighthouse tours, and all the nearby towns have historical museums, if you're into that sort of thing. And the Oregon Coast Aquarium and Hatfield Marine Science Center are just down the coast highway in Newport. Some Oregon State University scientists working there predicted an undersea volcano five years before it even happened."

"Did it actually blow out of the water?"

"No, there was a lava flow on the seafloor. But it still would've been way cool to see."

She said it with the same awe and excitement girls

back at his old school might've reported a Robert Pattinson—the pale, skinny heartthrob from *Twilight*—sighting. "So I guess you want to be a scientist?" Matt asked.

"Actually, I want to be a family physician. Or maybe a pediatrician, because I really like kids. Which is why I'm volunteering at the clinic. But, to the despair of my mother—who was probably accessorizing her pacifier to match her onesies in her cradle—I take after my dad. I guess nerd runs in my DNA."

It sounded like she'd guessed right. But she was pretty cute for a nerd. Of course her not liking basketball was a negative.

"From your schedule, you must like math and science, too," she said.

"They're okay," he said with an indifferent shrug as he hung his jacket on a hook inside the locker. "But I mostly take them because they're easy for me. So I can concentrate more on basketball."

Matt loved being on that polished wooden floor, doing what he did best. There were lots of times, lying in the dark in bed after a game, although he'd never in a million years admit it, that he'd fantasize about his father reading about him being drafted first into the NBA for a multimillion-dollar contract and realize the mistake he'd made, tossing his own son away and never looking back.

As good as that story was to think about, he'd never figured out what he'd do if the father he'd never known actually did show up to make amends. Would he forgive him? Or would he turn his back on the guy whose only contribution had been to supply the sperm and say, "Too little, too late, dude."

"Does that mean you won't be joining the science club?" Her question broke into the thoughts he'd been having more and more often since his mother had told him that they were leaving California, and no, he didn't have a vote.

"Probably not." After he twirled the lock, they began walking down the hall again.

"That's too bad. Next week Mr. Slater's taking a cannon down to the beach and we're going to shoot it off."

"That sounds kinda cool," he admitted.

"Oh, I think it'll be a lot of fun. Also, there's great skiing at Willamette Pass, which isn't that far away. The ski club takes a big trip there every year. Maybe you'll want to join them."

"I've never been skiing."

"That makes sense, since you grew up in Los Angeles. But you're an athlete; it shouldn't be that hard to learn. They have classes and beginner slopes, so you could ease into it. The ski trip's during Christmas break and we have a really great time. And if you don't enjoy skiing, there's snowboarding on the back of the mountain. Lots of guys really like that."

Having already blown off the science club idea, although he had no intention of risking an injury that could prevent him from playing college, then pro ball, Matt said, "I'll think about it."

"Great." She smiled up at him as they passed a couple plastered together against a locker.

The girl was blond and the guy was wearing a blue Dolphins jacket. The graduation year on the right sleeve indicated that he was a senior. Matt wondered what sport he'd lettered in.

"We have two classes together," she continued, either

not seeing the hallway make-out session or choosing to ignore it. "Mechanical physics with Mr. Slater, who's really nice and, as you probably already know, the basketball coach."

"Yeah. I figured that out when I saw the schedule."

"And after lunch is Mrs. Lessman, Honors English."

Oh, yay. Although his stupid test scores and grades had landed him in the honors program, English wasn't his favorite subject because, unlike whipping through a math problem, reading took time away from the three hundred shots he made himself take every day.

And reading lists were lame, since most of the books were written by dead writers about boring olden days. Though he'd checked online while they'd still been in L.A., and Pat Conroy's *A Losing Season*, which he'd already read without being assigned to do so, turned out to be on Dorktown High's assigned list. Of course so were two Jane Austen novels, which girls always seemed to go orgasmic about.

When he'd complained about those to his grandmother, shortly before she died, she'd briskly told him that sulking was unattractive. Then she'd added that girls liked boys who were able to discuss something other than sports and cars.

So he'd tried reading *Pride and Prejudice*, and although he'd been hoping it'd at least have some sex in it, his grandmother had turned out to be right. Just carrying it around had been a chick magnet, causing even senior girls to comment on how nice it was to see a guy willing to "embrace his sensitive side."

What he didn't bother to tell them was that he'd given up at about page fifty and settled for watching the movie.

It had been slow and way too talky, but the way Keira Knightley's nightgown kept sliding off her shoulder sort of made up for the boring parts. Unfortunately, his teacher caught his ruse when he made the mistake of including the scene in his report of Elizabeth running over the bridge and Mr. Darcy running after her to declare his great and abiding love.

Who knew that hadn't been in the damn book?

She stopped in front of an open classroom door. "Here we are."

Students were bustling around inside, talking as they took their seats. All his life he'd lived in the same house. Gone to school with mostly the same kids, though some had come and gone because of things like divorce, movie flops, and TV show cancellations. But he'd stayed. Until now.

Not able to prolong the inevitable any longer, while Aimee took her seat at the front of the classroom, Matt went over to the scarred wooden desk and handed over the form the woman at the office had given to him.

"Good to have you, Matthew," said Coach Slater, who was a lot younger than his BHHS coach had been.

He was wearing jeans, a black sweater over a blue shirt, and blue Converse Chucks. He looked kind of like Ryan Reynolds, from all the comic book superhero movies. His tone was friendly but casual, as if he didn't realize the player who could save Shelter Bay High School basketball was standing in front of him.

He introduced Matt to the class. Some managed a mumbled "hi." The girls openly checked him out, while the guys were a lot less welcoming.

"You should have been given a lab notebook," Coach Dillon said.

"It's right here." Matt held up the spiral-bound note-book.

"Terrific. Take a seat anywhere."

There were three empty seats. Two were next to girls whose glossy smiles offered open invitations that were tempting. The third was at the back of the rows of seats. Having learned early in life that kids complained about him blocking their view of the blackboard, Matt chose that one, slouching down on the seat-desk combo, which, like every other one he'd had since third grade, was too small for his height.

"I don't know how it was done at your previous school," the teacher-coach said. "But here you'll only be documenting the actual lab reports on the right-hand side of the page. The left will be used for lectures or class discussion notes. Your first line should be the title I give you. Then the page will be divided into labeled sections, which should always be included, because your note-book will be part of your grade.

"As you've undoubtedly learned, physics labs always center on a question that's being investigated. That question should be written as a purpose statement in the first section, labeled *Purpose*.

"Next is data and documentation. You can use tables, graphs, diagrams, and observations. I'm not looking for an essay here, or even complete sentences. What you will want to do is show your work for each type of calcu-lation you performed and clearly label and document your findings—because they'll be evidence you'll use to draw a conclusion to the question you've listed in your purpose.

"Then you'll write your conclusion statement, which

always refers to the purpose statement. Again, I'm not looking for an essay or thesis here, although the conclusion should be long enough to answer the purpose question.

"Finally, include any comments on why data may not have proven what you expected it to, variables to the experiment, anything along those lines. . . .

"Any questions?"

Matt looked up from madly writing on the inside cover of the lab notebook. He didn't think the guy had taken a breath while rattling off all those instructions. "No, sir."

"Great. So, everyone, listen up," he called out, stopping the low buzz of conversation that Matt guessed was a lot about him. "Today's lab is on work, energy, and power, and the question is: 'What is the effect of varying the release location of a marble along an incline upon the distance which the marble drives a paper plow along a level plane?'

"You'll write an equation to describe the effect. Presuming that there is one."

He paused while everyone dutifully wrote the question into their lab books.

"Everyone will be divided into two teams, red and blue. Your purpose will be to determine the effect of the release location—which is the distance from the bottom of the plane—of the marble and determine a mathematical equation describing the relationship between the two variables."

Another too-short pause to allow for more scribbling.

"Once you've determined that, the blue team will release the marble from a given location, which you'll have to determine, that'll result in it driving your paper plow a distance of two centimeters. Red team, you'll drive yours for five centimeters.

"Want to know what reward you're playing for on this lab assignment?"

Matt had never had a class run like the *Survivor* TV show. He just hoped he wouldn't end up getting voted off the island, which would be the pits. Like the rest of his life had turned out to be.

"A pizza party," a guy in the second row suggested.

"With beer," another said.

"Sorry, pizza's out since I don't want the lunchroom ladies to feel I'm honing in on their territory. And you'll have to wait until you're twenty-one for the beer."

"How about a get-out-of-class-free card?" someone else shouted out from the middle of the room.

"Nope. But this is nearly as good . . . a get-out-of-the-next-pop-quiz card."

That definitely got everyone's attention. Including Matt's.

"So." He held up a rumpled brown paper bag. "Come draw your chips to determine your teams, and let's get started."

Slater seemed like an okay guy. Taking a typical lab class and turning it into a challenge was pretty cool. Especially since, being an athlete, Matt enjoyed competition.

But from the way the guy had gotten right down to business, hardly taking a breath as he'd rattled off the lab book instructions, Matt had the feeling that unlike in other science classes he'd had in the past, there'd be no skating in this one.

And if the guy coached basketball in the same way he

taught his class, instead of breezing in as a savior, Matt realized that he might actually be made to prove himself on the court this afternoon.

Not that he was worried.

Piece of cake, he thought as he pulled a red chip from the bag.

8

The Dancing Deer Two boutique was located on Harborview, the main street in town. Despite the drizzle, the sight of the tidy shops with their bright wind socks blowing in the sea breeze lifted Claire's spirits, as it always seemed to do. Although residents of Shelter Bay, for the most part, had a twenty-first-century view of their place on the planet, the town also seemed to be a throwback to another, easier-going time.

When people knew one another, cared about one another, and life moved a great deal more slowly.

Since it was low tourist season, traffic was nonexistent, allowing her to park right in front of the store with its cheerful green-and-white front awning. The bell on the door jingled as she entered the boutique, which smelled of potpourri and, as always, fresh baked goods.

"Oh, you're just in time." Dottie, one of the two elderly twins who owned the shop, greeted her. "Doris has just brewed a cup of the tastiest chai tea from Lavender Hill Farm. It's a black tea with touches of orange and cranberry that makes you think of Thanksgiving."

"It sounds great. But I'd rather not think about the holiday."

"I understand," Doris said, "being that this will be the first Thanksgiving without your mother."

"I'll miss her terribly," Claire said. "But I have to admit that I also miss her cooking every day. I can't even boil an egg. My poor son's been living on frozen dinners and takeout, which has me feeling like the world's worst mother."

"I'm sure he wouldn't agree," Dottie said. She patted Claire's arm with a plump hand. "And I realize that you must have so much on your plate, what with moving to a new place and enrolling your boy in school, but you should consider taking classes at Chef Maddy's new cooking school."

"Madeline Durand has a cooking school? Here?"

While Claire might not cook, she was hooked on the Food Channel. It was one of the few things she and her mother had had in common. She'd heard from the real estate woman that the chef was helping her grandmother turn the family farmhouse into a restaurant, but a school hadn't been mentioned.

"Along with her new restaurant," both women said together. Claire had noticed, during her first visit to the boutique last year, that they often spoke at the same time, without seeming to notice they did it.

"But she's Madeline Chaffee now," Dottie divulged.

"She married her high school sweetheart," Doris said. She patted her breast. "It was so romantic. Wasn't it, sister?"

"It was a lovely wedding," Dottie agreed as she handed Claire a pretty flowered cup of dark amber tea.

"On Moonshell Beach. Her husband used to be a summer boy. Now he's settled down and is working as a contractor."

"A building contractor?" Claire perked up at that.

"He remodeled Lavender Hill farmhouse for Maddy's restaurant and cooking school," Doris said. "He's also been working like a beaver on the former cannery, which is already home to some lovely shops, with more to come."

"I noticed that while I was looking for a house to buy."

Claire didn't mention having momentarily considered setting up a retail space when the real estate agent had told her about the shops. Until she remembered that would put her in direct competition with the two sisters who'd proven such good customers.

"How are you liking the cottage now that it's yours?" Dottie asked.

"I love it."

"It's on a spectacular piece of land," Doris said.

"Which is why I bought it. That and the fact that the detached garage is perfect for my glassblowing studio. But I knew at the time it would be too small, and it is. Matt and I are already bumping into each other." When he wasn't behind locked doors, avoiding her.

"Oh, Lucas would be able to solve all your problems," Dottie said. "He put up that display wall for us just last month when we decided to expand our gift shop section." The wall in question held shelves and a glass display case. "It's proven very popular."

"I'm glad it's working out for you. Especially since it gives me another outlet for my blown glass."

Claire was used to film people buying her jewelry, but receiving a note from Irish movie star Mary Joyce, asking for a custom piece after she'd bought a more commercial item in this very store, had blown her away.

"That's something I've been meaning to mention," Dottie said. "You know about our resident whales."

"They'd be hard to miss." The whale logo showed up in the windows of seemingly half the businesses in town, and during the tourist season lines of visitors waited at the seawall to board the ubiquitous whale-watching boats.

"Well, we were thinking perhaps you might want to create glass whales for the summer tourist trade," Doris said. "Not the typical touristy cheap things you can find in all the knickknack shops, but with your usual exquisite quality and attention to detail."

"We know we could sell quite a few," Dottie picked up her part of the sales pitch again.

Claire groaned inwardly. It wasn't that she didn't know how to blow glass animals. While she'd been learning the craft, she'd taken a lesson from a glassblower at Disneyland, who could turn out Sleeping Beauty's Castle, Cinderella, or a glass slipper while customers waited. And while the artist had received a great deal of joy from people's enjoyment of his work, she knew she'd be bored in a week doing such cookie-cutter items.

"That's something to consider," she said, keeping her answer as vague as possible for now. "Well, as much as I'd love to stay and visit, I just wanted to drop off this jewelry before stopping by the market for a frozen pizza."

"You know, dear," Doris said, "you might want to drop into Farraday's Fish Monger."

"Oh, I would kill fish," Claire said. "I mean, I know it's already dead. But it's way beyond my skill set." As she'd already discovered the hard way, even pancakes were beyond her culinary abilities.

"They're wonderful at giving you instructions." Dottie jumped onto the fish bandwagon. "Steamed clams are one of the easiest things in the world to cook, since they sell them already cleaned. And you could buy a nice boiled crab—"

"Or crab cakes," Doris said. "Maeve Farraday makes them all up by hand with cooked crab. All you have to do is brown them in a pan—"

"Or oven," Dottie broke in. "Easy peasy. Maeve also makes the best chowder on the coast. They also carry wonderful artisan bread from the Grateful Bread and coleslaw that would finish off a meal nicely."

Claire was doubtful. Then again, she thought about this morning's mess of a breakfast and admitted to herself that she couldn't keep feeding Matt takeout forever. He'd always seemed to enjoy his grandmother's cooking, and she was already asking enough of him with this move and adjusting to a new school.

It wasn't as if she wasn't an intelligent woman. She had, after all, made a nice career for herself with her jewelry making, and although she'd never equal the genius of Chihuly, she was beginning to build a reputation, at least on the West Coast, for her blown glass.

How hard could it be to toss some damn crab cakes in an oven?

"Okay." She polished off the tea and made her decision. "But if I end up giving my son food poisoning, I'm going to tell him the seafood was all your idea."

They shared a laugh; then she left the store and headed to Farraday's at the docks, not far from the bait shop she spotted down the way.

"The trick," she said as the wipers swished the rain from the windshield in wide arcs, "is not to get the two places mixed up."

9

Thanks to the unrelentingly perky Aimee, lunch in a new cafeteria didn't turn out to be the horror show Matt had dreaded. Although it wasn't any fun feeling like an outsider, sitting at the nerd table, forced to watch the jocks laughing across the large room. It especially sucked when one of the guys strolled in with a hot blonde wearing a fuzzy white sweater that fit as if it were spray-painted on, a pink miniskirt, and pink UGGs. Matt recognized them as the couple who'd been tangling tongues up against the locker. They were—no big surprise—greeted like royalty.

Meanwhile, as far as they were concerned, everyone at his table could have been on another planet. Or invisible.

One of the jocks threw a French fry at another, which started a short-lived food fight, which everyone, including the teacher monitoring the cafeteria, seemed not to witness. Apparently even here in Nowheresville High School, athletes possessed star power.

Which was what had Matt making up his mind. He might have landed in a really small pond, but maybe his mom was right about that making him an even bigger fish.

"How's it going?" Aimee leaned over and asked him quietly.

"Great." He told her what he knew she wanted to hear.

Which was mostly true. At least he hadn't been forced to wolf down chips and a candy bar from the vending machine in a stall of the boys' restroom.

The hot lunch was billed as seafood mac and cheese, but it smelled like an aquarium filled with dead fish. Fortunately, they also had fish sandwiches and Tater Tots. Even Aimee wasn't enough of an optimist to try the mystery mac, instead going for a turkey Cobb salad and a Fuji apple.

"I had an idea," she said.

He took a gulp of milk from the carton. "What?"

"You could always take the late bus, but I'm working on an Oregon history project about Sacagawea with Jenny Longworth. Did you know that she—Sacagawea, not Jenny—was a teenager when she went with Lewis and Clark on their expedition?"

"No, I never heard that."

"She was. They took her along as a translator, but since she was the only person who'd ever seen the landmarks, they might never have gotten to the coast without her to keep them on the right trail.

"She also helped keep them alive by teaching them about edible plants, nuts, and berries, which Americans and Europeans had never heard of. And she did all that with her newborn baby on her back."

"That's pretty impressive," he allowed.

"She was also the first woman in what would become the United States to vote."

"I may not know everything about history, but even I know the first vote was in Seneca Falls in the twentieth century."

"That's because history tends to overlook people who aren't white," she argued. "When the expedition reached the Pacific Ocean in 1805, Lewis and Clark let her vote with the men on where they'd set up camp for the winter. That was more than a hundred years before the Seneca Falls vote.

"Anyway, I was thinking, since I already live across the bridge, and Jenny's house is just a couple streets away from yours, why don't I drive you home from practice?"

He'd been about to squeeze more ketchup on his Tater Tots, but that got his attention. "You have a car?"

"Yeah. It's not new or sexy—well, actually it's my mother's old Volvo, which pretty much looks like a blue refrigerator on wheels—but it gets me where I want to go."

"I thought you were a sophomore."

"I am. But my birthday falls at the end of this month, so back when I was in preschool, my parents had to make the decision to have me be way younger than everyone in the class, or older. Since my dad was deployed at the time and my mom said she wasn't emotionally ready to be left all alone again all day, they opted for older. Which, like most things, ended up with mixed results, but the best part is that I can drive."

"That'd be cool."

He pulled out his phone and, ignoring the TURN OFF CELL PHONES and NO TEXTING signs posted all over the school, texted his mom his plans.

As nice as Aimee was, it was bad enough sitting here at Nerd Central. One thing he so didn't need was his mom showing up and blowing any juice he was bound to get from showing off his wicked ball skills during tryouts.

10

Another of the things that had attracted Claire to Shelter Bay was its abundance of Pacific Coast sea glass, which she'd first learned about from a jewelry-maker friend who lived a few miles north in Cannon Beach. According to the archives in the historical society's museum, early residents of the town took care of their garbage by simply dumping it over the cliff. It might not be ecologically popular today, but after years of being washed out to sea, then back onto the shore, all those old bottles, dishes, and even chandeliers offered an amazing array of sand-polished sea glass. Also appealing were the agates and small shells that were scattered on the beach at low tide.

The tide was out when she arrived back at the cabin shortly before noon with several items from Farraday's, along with detailed instructions on how to prepare the dishes. Although Maeve Farraday, who ran the shop while her husband and older son fished, had been friendly and helpful, not quite trusting her skills, Claire had also stocked up on frozen bag dinners from the grocery store. Just in case.

She knew she should attack the rest of the moving boxes that were taking up so much of the floor space. But the beach was like a siren's call. After a cup of creamy clam chowder, which was even better than advertised, she went down the cliff steps in the drizzling rain. She found a small glass float wrapped in a bit of netting that had gotten caught up on a driftwood log. Probably more of the flotsam she'd read was drifting into the Pacific Northwest coast from the tragic Japanese tsunami.

Carefully placing the float into the canvas bag she carried, along with two small pieces of green glass and a handful of agates, Claire climbed back up the steps.

She'd originally started blowing glass eight years ago; when she'd tired of trying to find glass beads to add to the sea glass jewelry she'd begun making at home shortly after Matt's birth, she'd decided to make her own.

As she'd branched out with her art, she began having small showings up and down the West Coast. When the owners of Art on the River, a chichi Portland gallery, heard Claire was relocating to the Pacific Northwest, they invited her to have an exhibition the week after Thanksgiving, just in time for the Christmas shopping season.

When Claire had agreed four months ago, November had seemed a very long time away. Then she'd gotten sidetracked with all the details involved in handling her mother's estate and selling and buying a house, which left her in a bit of a time crunch.

Fortunately, at least one idea had been simmering in her mind during the drive up from Los Angeles. One she thought she'd finally figured out how to execute.

Knowing that her mother's property would be easier

to sell if the old carriage house was converted to a guest-house rather than a glass studio, she'd shipped her equipment ahead of the move to Oregon, and a glassblower she'd met at a conference had volunteered to drive down from Lincoln City and set it up in the garage for her.

Unlike jewelry making, which allowed her mind to wander to problems with insurance companies, hospitals, finding a hospice nurse, and medications, not to mention Matt's growing rebellion, she'd quickly discovered that working with molten glass required absolute concentration.

During this past very sad and challenging year, it had become an escape from all the problems raining down on her.

As she entered the studio, which, in contrast to the chilly outdoors, was an arid one hundred degrees, Claire took a deep breath and cleared her mind.

This was her domain, where fire and glass came together in a seductive dance and, she hoped, would give birth to the shimmering vision glowing in her mind.

After readying her supplies and tacking the drawing she'd done of the piece she planned as the centerpiece (and so far only piece) of her show to the wall, Claire put on her safety glasses and was on the verge of taking her first gathering of glass from the crucible when her cell phone dinged with a message.

Got ride home. C U L8R.

As brief and uninformative as the text was, it lifted her spirits. If Matt had a ride, he must have already made a new friend.

Although his text didn't say, the most likely thing would be that it was a player on the team. And the fact that he said he'd see her later suggested he'd be staying for tryouts. Claire truly hoped that was the case, because playing ball would give him a purpose and focus he'd been missing over the past several months.

Feeling more optimistic than she had in a very long while, she put Enigma on the CD player, heated the tip of her blowpipe, then dipped it into the molten glass inside the furnace, gathering the glass as she might swirl honey from a jar, spooling it onto the end of the blowpipe.

She took her time, going back and forth between the furnace, where the glass lay molten and without form, and the glory hole — a smaller furnace used to reheat the glass so she could roll and shape it on the marver.

From the first, admittedly flawed, bead she'd blown, Claire had been delighted to discover that unlike the lovely solid pieces she'd been working with for years, glass was organic. It was a living, breathing thing, hungrily taking in oxygen, which was why ventilation was imperative. Along with the exhaust fans she'd had installed in the walls, she'd opened the windows a bit to let in the fresh sea air.

Glass also had moods. It could be as calm as a soft and sunny summer day or as mercurial as a teenage girl with PMS, depending on the weather and the oxides she'd added to the sand to control the hardness and create the colors. And, all too often, for some mysterious reason she'd never understand, it would refuse to cooperate.

As it was doing today.

Glassblowing not only took enormous patience and attention to detail; it could on occasion, be ego deflating.

While she was happy with the shape, she was dissatisfied with the way the thin layers of glass had flash-fused. The colors lacked the drama she'd intended.

Discarding this first attempt into the hot pot, which was basically a fireproof wastebasket next to her bench, she began heating up her blowpipe again.

"If at first you don't succeed . . ."

11

After his last class, Matt made his way through the crush of students leaving the building, and although he still wasn't happy about the move, at least, now that he'd figured out how to get his mojo back, he was feeling like it might not be the end of the world.

He had to admit that the gym was as good as some of the best he'd played in back in California. It also, for some weird reason, had a bunch of folding chairs set up all over the court.

"It was remodeled last year," Aimee, who'd come along to watch the tryouts, said when he mentioned it. "Is it true about the gym at your old school? That it's the one where the floor opens up and Jimmy Stewart and Donna Reed fall into the swimming pool beneath it?"

"Yeah. That's it."

"That is way cool."

He shrugged, even though he secretly agreed. "I guess."

Coach Slater was already there with two other guys. One was holding a clipboard.

"You don't have to wait around," he told Aimee. "You can go to the library or somewhere."

"That's okay." She glanced over at the near-empty bleachers. "I don't have anything else to do right now, and hey, maybe you can convince me to like basketball. And I can convince you to go skiing."

"Maybe." *Not.*

The other players were strolling into the gym as if they belonged. Which they did. Watching them laughing and punching each other, the way they had in the cafeteria, Matt wondered again if this outsider feeling was the way other kids in BHHS had felt when he and his team had walked down the hall.

Of course, it had been harder to impress kids at his old school. Especially when you were a freshman. And when kids' parents collected Oscars, Emmys, and Golden Globes the way his mom collected shells, beads, and sea glass, being a high school basketball player didn't put you on as high a pedestal as it did at most other schools. Especially when you played for a 3AAA division team that had a 20-11-1 record last year and had been ranked ninety-eighth in the state.

But that hadn't mattered, because he'd been the best frigging freshman in the state, with everyone saying he could only get better. Which was going to be hard to pull off now that his mother had forced him to play on a team that hadn't even managed to have a winning season in a crappy Podunk 4A division.

In California, papers from Redding to San Diego and even over to Blythe on the California/Arizona border had sent reporters to watch him. One sports blogger had even named him "Mad Matt," because whatever gym he was playing in turned into a Thunderdome.

The name had stuck, and although his mother and grandmother hadn't liked it all that much, he'd be lying if he said he didn't fantasize about some TV play-by-play announcer calling him Mad Matt in the NBA finals.

The locker room benches and lockers had been painted the same blue that was on the bleachers. Unlike the student lockers lining the hallways, these had diamond-shaped perforations in the doors to allow fresh air in.

A poster featuring Coach John Wooden's famed Pyramid of Success had been tacked to the wall. Although it hadn't been required at BHHS, Matt had memorized the fifteen points on the pyramid back when he was a little kid playing YMCA Junior Lakers ball. A piece of blank white poster board was tacked above the door.

"Okay," the coach said after they'd changed out of the clothes they'd worn to class. Although Matt still thought a dolphin was a lame mascot compared to a Norman, it felt good to be back in uniform. Even if it *was* a practice uniform with his name written on masking tape on the back and he was having to win the right to wear it.

"It's good to see a lot of familiar faces from summer camp," Slater continued.

His mother had sprung their move on him too late for Matt to attend summer camp, but he figured he was so far ahead of the other guys in skill and talent, it wouldn't matter.

There *was* the problem that they'd already formed a cohesive unit, which he'd be bound to screw up. Which wouldn't make him the most popular guy on the team, as he'd been last year, when the other players rode his coat-tails to a winning season. But there had been a few var-sity guys who hadn't been happy having a freshman on their team.

What if this team decided to haze the new kid by making sure he never got his hands on the ball? That would keep the coach from seeing that he was the player Shelter Bay had been waiting for.

"We have a new player, transferring in from Southern California. Matthew Templeton. But he likes to be called Matt, right?" he asked.

"Yes, Coach." It had come up during physics lab, which, thanks to Aimee's wicked organizational skills, his red team had won, blowing out those loser blues.

"Coach Daniels" — Coach Dillon nodded at the guy with the clipboard — "and I have been watching the films both from the past two seasons, along with those we took during summer camp, and we've already got a pretty good idea who's going to make the roster, and, probably what you're all waiting to hear, who's going to be a starter and who's coming off the bench."

Looks were exchanged; there was a low murmur of agreement.

"Here's the thing everyone needs to know. Whatever you did last year is history. I worked with a lot of SEALs while I was doing bomb-disposal work in the military, and those guys have a saying: 'The only easy day was yesterday.'

"Along with making sure every one of you can repeat Coach Wooden's fifteen building blocks to success before tip-off of our first game, we'll be adopting that as our team motto this year."

"I thought we were Dolphins, not seals," said a kid Matt recognized as being the one who'd thrown the French fry that started the food fight.

A couple of the guys laughed.

The coach did not. He merely nodded toward the

coach with the clipboard, who pulled down the poster board, where that SEAL saying had been painted in Dolphin blue paint on the wall over the door leading out to the court.

More looks were exchanged. Matt realized that some of the guys were worried. As if just maybe this new coach was going to turn out to be tougher than he looked.

"Like I said, it doesn't matter what your record was last year," Coach Dillon said.

"Good. Because it was lame," someone muttered.

"Yeah. It was. But here's the good thing . . . you've nowhere to go but up. It doesn't matter what your shooting percentage was, the number of steals or assists you made, or even your individual state ranking."

He looked straight at Matt.

The coach might be the guy in charge, but, not wild about being singled out that way, Matt squared his shoulders and stared back.

"We're starting with a clean slate. Right here. Right now." The coach opened an equipment locker and pulled out a bunch of what looked like gardening gloves. "Okay, let's get out in the gym so you can show me what you've got."

12

After putting them through a series of warm-up exercises, Dillon handed out the gardening gloves, which would challenge their ball-handling ability. Then he set them to dribbling down the court, in and out around the chairs he'd set up earlier, as if they were skiers cutting across moguls.

Every so often he'd shout for the equipment manager to run out onto the hardwood floor and move the chairs closer together, which had some of the players bumping into each other.

All but one.

"Damned if that Templeton kid can't pivot on a dime," said Jim Thompson, the JV coach, who also taught AP senior English. "I've been watching players come up through the ranks for fifteen years and I've never seen anyone like him. He's freaking unbelievable."

"He's good," Dillon agreed. "At running and dribbling. Let's see how he is at shooting."

He blew the whistle, had the kids sit down on the bleachers, then, one at a time, gave each one three minutes to shoot unguarded.

Having never coached before, Dillon had gone to a clinic for high school coaches at OSU in Corvallis before school started. Despite what he kept telling everyone in town about needing more than a single year to turn the basketball program around, his takeaway from the clinic was that ideal shot statistics would be fifty percent field goals, forty percent from three, and, because it was something kids could and should practice on their off time at home, seventy-five percent free throws.

That was the ideal.

Being a realist, and knowing these players, Dillon knew to expect a lot less.

But nothing this bad.

"It's like they've forgotten every damn thing they learned at camp this summer," he muttered.

"It's only the first practice," Jim Thompson reminded him. "Give them time to gel."

"Easy for you to say." Dillon shook his head in frustration when his power forward threw up yet another brick. "You're not the one who's going to be living on frozen microwave dinners all season because you can't show your face in any restaurant in town."

"My wife's been taking lessons from Chef Maddy," the JV coach said. "We're mostly eating at home these days so she can try out recipes." It was his turn to shake his head as a ball went sailing over the top of the backboard into the end bleachers. "But I know what you mean. . . . Maybe Templeton's got them spooked."

Dillon followed the other two coaches' gazes to the bleachers, where the new kid was sitting all alone. By choice? Or were the other boys cutting him out of the herd? Either was possible. Neither was a good omen.

"What's the combined percentage?" he asked his as-

sistant coach, who'd painted the SEAL saying over the
door yesterday afternoon.

Don Daniels consulted the calculator on his smartphone. "It's down a bit from summer. "Thirty-three percent field goals and twenty from three."

"You've got to be freaking kidding me."

It was a rhetorical question. Don Daniels taught alge-
bra and trig. He could undoubtedly do those percent-
ages in his head. He was also the baseball coach. Since
the district budget didn't allow for assistant coaches, with
the basketball season ending in February and baseball
beginning in March, Don was able to serve as an unpaid
assistant and scorekeeper for Dillon, while Dillon returned
the favor.

"I wish I were." He looked as pessimistic as Dillon
felt.

They'd gone through the returning players. Which left
them with one guy. "Templeton." Dillon took a ball from
the center coming off the floor and threw it to the Beverly Hills phenom. "Here's your chance to show us what
you've got. But before you go out on the floor, tuck your
shirt in."

"It's not a real game," the kid countered.

There were strictly enforced rules in high school basketball; playing with your shirt tucked in was one of
them.

"That doesn't matter. I don't know how they do it
in California, but here at Shelter Bay, the coach—who
would be me—expects shirts to be tucked in during
scrimmages. And, although if you do make the team, I'm
not going to spend the entire season explaining myself
to you, just this once I will, so you'll understand I always
have a reason when I tell you to do something.

"If you leave your shirt untucked during practice, it screws up your form. So. Tuck. The. Damn. Shirt. In. . . . Now."

It was obvious from his lowered brow that Templeton wasn't happy about the criticism, but without another word of argument, he did as instructed.

Dillon didn't know what type of competition Matthew Templeton had faced back in L.A., but so far he was living up to his press. It was as if the kid had wings on his rubber-soled shoes and a computer in his brain as he proceeded to shoot a dozen layups. First from the right, then the middle, then left of the court.

"Damned if he isn't ambidextrous," Jim Thompson said as the kid switched back and forth from his left to his right hand. Again and again, never missing a beat. "If you're not going to put him on varsity, I could sure use him."

"As a sophomore, he belongs on JV." Though his skill set was definitely varsity level. "Let's see some jump shots. From ten, then twelve feet out," Dillon called out.

It was the same thing. The pebbled brown ball sailed through the air, right into the hoop.

Swish.

Nothing but net.

"Twenty feet," Dillon upped the challenge.

It didn't make a difference.

Swish from the left. Center. Right. On the rare occasion the ball did hit the rim, Templeton set himself up to recover his own rebound, then *swish!*

"Unbelievable." Don hit the keypad of his phone again. "While managing to get off twelve percent more shots than the average of what we've seen from the entire group of returning varsity players, he just single-handedly pulled you back up to fifty-six percent on field goals. And forty-four on three-pointers."

Dillon could hear the buzz of conversation behind him on the bench. He glanced back. The kids who were talking did not look all that happy to have a possible savior land in their midst. Others were sitting there quietly dumbfounded, mouths half-open at the shooting exhibition taking place on the court. Only one kid, Johnny Tiernan-St. James, who'd taken Dillon's clinic at summer basketball camp, seemed to be enjoying the performance.

"No point in wasting time having him shoot free throws, which he can probably make blindfolded," Dillon decided. "Let's put him in a scrimmage and see his defensive skills."

There was no point in having a scoring machine on your team if the other team was still able to outshoot you. Which, from what he'd been able to tell, was pretty much what had happened at Beverly Hills High.

He blew the whistle, motioned Templeton off the court, then had kids line up and call off numbers. "Even numbers will play shirts. Odd, skins."

He set the assignments, putting Templeton up against Dirk Martin, a returning senior who'd proven to be the best shooter at summer camp. He was also a power player who could plow his way to the basket, drawing fouls from frustrated opponents assigned to guard him.

Not today. Although growth spurts like Templeton's usually tended to result in a lack of finesse, the sophomore managed to tip the ball away from the older, more experienced player as if he were merely flicking away a fly.

After eight blocked shots in a row, it was obvious the

senior was getting frustrated. Dropping his shoulder and using his superior bulk, he barreled forward, trying to force the ball inside.

Not only did Templeton not give an inch, but each time Martin made the move, the kid cut him off and forced him to lose control of the ball.

"He's definitely a complete player," Don said.

He'd no sooner said that when, deftly switching from defense to offense, Templeton stole a pass from Martin to Brendan Cooper, another senior. Then, as graceful as a gazelle, he switched hands on the dribble back down the court.

There was some elbowing beneath the basket, and as Martin landed with a thud on his back, Templeton went in for the layup.

Swish.

Dirk flew back up onto his sneaker-clad feet like a rocket. "That's a fucking foul," he shouted in Templeton's face.

"I just brushed your elbow, which was trying to land in my ribs." Outweighed by probably twenty pounds, Templeton still stood his ground and thrust out his chin. "If you're looking for an Academy Award nomination for best faked-foul fall by an asshole, then I'll nominate you."

"I wasn't faking." The senior's face turned the blazing scarlet of a boiled crab. "You know damn well you charged. And everyone saw you."

They were standing face-to-face, neither one looking inclined to give an inch.

Dillon had always had a low boredom threshold, one of the reasons he'd enjoyed EOD, where every mission could prove a challenge. He might not make all the fans in Shelter Bay happy by taking his team to state this first season, but at least he wasn't going to be bored.

Deciding that he should probably intervene before those fists balled at the two players' sides began swinging and he ended up with a melee on his hands, he blew his whistle, then walked out onto the court, through the semicircle of kids watching the showdown.

The shirts on the even-numbered players were soaked with perspiration, clinging to their bodies. The other players' skin glistened with sweat. More sweat rolled down all their faces.

"That's enough. For what it's worth, I played high school ball in Texas for a real hard-ass of a coach. On away games we'd go to schools where anyone could tell the players ran the place. We'd bitch about how we'd have to run up and down the bleachers whenever we mouthed off or got in a fight with one of our teammates.

"I don't think there was a single player on the team who didn't spend four years believing we'd been dealt a lousy hand to land in such a tough program.

"But later on, when I was downrange, crawling on my belly across a field loaded with land mines, working to keep my focus so I didn't blow up myself and all the other guys around me while taking apart an IED, I was damn grateful for that discipline Coach Randall hammered into me. . . .

"So here's the deal. *This* team is going to be run by the grown-ups. Shelter Bay players don't trash-talk with opponents, and they don't disrespect or get in fights with teammates."

Dillon didn't raise his voice. Given the fact that very

few, if any, people had grown up in families like the Cosbys or the Waltons, it was logical to assume that some of these kids had learned to tune out yelling.

So he kept his tone quiet. Calm. But firm enough to let everyone know that he damn well meant business.

"Shelter Bay players don't—ever—argue with an official," he continued. "Try it and you'll find yourself suspended from the team so fast you'll think you've been shot into hyperspace.

"The Dolphins may not take state, like a lot of people around here keep talking about, but we *are* going to be a team people look up to. A team admired for our poise on the court and our leadership off the court. Each and every one of you is going to set an example for every student in this school. And for the younger kids, many of whom are your brothers and sisters, who come to the games and dream of someday wearing a Dolphins letterman jacket.

"There will be rules. And I don't care if you're Wilt Chamberlain reincarnated—every Dolphin player will be held accountable. And if those rules I just stated are broken, believe me, there *will* be consequences."

He waved an arm around the gym. "This isn't *your* court. It's mine." He jabbed a thumb against his chest to drive his point home. "And on this court, we play by *my* rules. And the first rule is from Coach Wooden's handbook—the star of the team is the team. *We* supersedes *me*. The Dolphins will be Coach Wooden's type of team at all times. On the court and off. Anyone who doesn't think they can get with the program is invited to leave now."

He paused. Waited. The only sounds were a few

squeaks from sneakers' toes being rubbed onto the polished wood floor. Not a single player said a word. Or moved to take Dillon up on his offer.

"Good." He nodded his satisfaction. "Now, go shower, change, and come back here and wait. We're going to have ourselves a little discussion here; then I'll talk to each of you individually in my office."

One of the players tentatively raised his hand.

"Travis," Dillon recognized the small forward.

"Are you choosing the team today?"

"That's the plan."

Everyone exchanged looks.

Dillon knew such a quick decision wasn't always the case, but he knew all but one of the players from summer camp and had seen all he needed to see. "We've got a lot of work to do before our first game," he said. "No point in wasting time making you all wait around to see who made the cut."

They'd strutted into the gym like the rock stars they were in their own male teenage minds. Having been there himself, Dillon could empathize. But the way he saw it, no one had hired him to be Mr. Rogers.

"Well," Jim said as the kids all walked out, far more silently than they'd entered. "That was interesting."

"You think I was too hard on them?" The way the air had gone out of their sails left Dillon feeling a lot like Voldemort from the *Harry Potter* DVD he had watched while stationed out in the middle of nowhere near the Pakistan border. Though he would've preferred an action flick with a lot of explosions, beggars couldn't be choosers, downrange especially.

Damn. Coaching a bunch of kids was turning out to

be a lot tougher than leading troops who'd already been through basic training, where someone else got to yell at them.

"Someone needed to be," the JV coach assured him. "Pete Houston was a good guy. Everyone in town liked him. Even Ken Curtis, who, if you cut him, probably bleeds Dolphin blue. But it was obvious to everyone that he'd burned out on coaching a long time ago and was mostly just going through the motions until he got enough years in for retirement."

"No one thought about replacing him?"

"Like I said, everyone liked him," Don said with shrug. "He'd played here himself as a kid. To be perfectly honest, I don't think anyone but Curtis ever had any real expectations for the team."

"Including the players themselves." Dillon had already figured that out for himself.

"Yeah. It wasn't that they didn't try," Jim said. "But they weren't getting what they needed to succeed. And I seriously doubt there was a guy on the court who ever worried about pissing Pete off."

"I'm not a hard-ass," Dillon said. "But I was hired to do a job. And I'm damn well going to do it to the best of my ability."

"I doubt there was a person who was in the gym earlier who doubts that," Don said.

"What are you doing about Templeton?" Jim asked.

"I met his mom before school and got a good vibe about his home situation." Dillon saw no reason to mention that he hadn't been thinking about Claire Templeton's maternal vibes the entire time. "So I'm going to take a chance and try him on varsity."

"As much as I'd love to have him on JV, I can't argue with that decision. The kid's going to have college coaches drooling all over him for the next three years."

"True. And we need to be prepared for that." He turned toward Don. "We also need to assure the other guys that each and every one of them is vital to the season's success. Because jealousy could end up tearing the team apart before we have our first game."

Which was something Dillon was determined to avoid.

Somehow.

13

They were freaking freezing him out. A couple of kids, including Johnny, had complimented him on his shooting, and the one who'd thrown the French fry at lunch, then made a joke the coach hadn't appreciated, had even asked him about how he managed to switch hands like that on the run, but then Dickhead Dirk had shot them all the evil eye, which shut them up.

Shields had immediately gone up. Leaving Matt on the outside.

There'd been a few minutes, when he'd been flying around the court, when he'd felt back in the groove. As if, just maybe, this move might work out.

Yeah. Right.

He was—no big surprise—the last guy to get called into the cluttered broom closet Coach Slater called an office. He'd done the math, and from the results, he knew there was one spot left on the varsity team. Which meant, Matt thought with a burst of the first excitement he'd felt in weeks, he was in. Not that there'd ever been a question.

After telling him to sit down in the chair on the other

side of the desk, the coach tilted back in his chair, rested his elbows on the wooden arms, folded his hands beneath his chin, and gave Matt a long, thoughtful look.

"So," he finally said, just when Matt was about to burst out of his skin, "how are you liking the Northwest so far?"

Matt shrugged. "We only got here this weekend. But it it's okay." *If you like rain and trees.*

"But quite a change for you."

No shit, Sherlock. "Yes, sir."

"You did well in lab today. I can see why you were named an athlete-scholar back at your old school."

"I lucked out with a good lab team today."

When the coach's lips quirked, Matt realized that Slater knew he was saying what *he* knew the coach wanted to hear.

"Right answer . . . I'm all about teamwork. In class and in life. I'm also not a believer in sophomores playing varsity."

Matt's heart plummeted like pelican diving for a fish in the surf at the same time his temper shot up. He'd done the research, and last season the team had twelve players. Six starters, and another six to come off the bench. Only eleven guys had come out of this office to high fives for having made varsity. Which meant that last remaining slot belonged to him.

"I'm a lot better than the other guys you picked for the team."

"You've got talent; I'll give you that. And skill that obviously comes from a lot of practice."

"Until we moved here, I'd shoot three hundred shots a day." Something he'd started doing in fifth grade and intended to start again. As soon as he got a basket up at the wreck of a house his mother had blown her inheritance on. "Every day."

"Good for you. . . . I was EOD in the army. Whenever I went out to take care of an IED, I never went in a straight line. Want to know why?"

Having no idea why this conversation had suddenly turned to something he didn't give a shit about, Matt said, "Yes, sir."

"Again, that's the right answer. I did that because the bad guys could be watching me and figure out my moves, so next time they could place an IED right where they knew I'd be. And if that had happened, I wouldn't be here right now talking with you because they'd still be picking up pieces of me downrange. . . .

"You're damn good, Templeton. But you're predictable."

"Predictable?" *No way.*

The coach shrugged. "It's natural. Everyone tends to get into a pattern when they play. Even the pros. The great ones will surprise you, and their opponents, but for the most part, all players have certain things they'll do over and over again."

"And you're saying I do?" He'd been playing since he was eight years old, half his life, and no one had ever said a frigging word about him being predictable. The coach was probably just looking for any lame excuse to keep him off varsity. Maybe most sophomores couldn't hack it. But they weren't him.

"Yes. You do." He turned the laptop on his desk so the screen faced Matt. It was a YouTube video of the final five minutes of the game against Santa Monica where he'd broken the school record of points scored in a single game.

"When you're going to your left, you cross-dribble three times. Then you keep going in the same direction. A good player, or a good coach, is going to catch that and predict your next move."

Damned if he hadn't done that. But it didn't mean he *always* moved the same way. Did he?

"So you're saying I should go right instead?"

"Yeah. Every once in a while. Especially if your defender's watched you go left enough times. He'll get comfortable thinking he's reading your play. That's when you change things up, catch him flat-footed, and slip right past him to score."

Matt hated to admit that the coach had caught such a lame mistake, but it made sense. "I'll work on that."

"That's the idea. Because if we're going to shoot for a winning season, every member on the varsity team's going to have to bring their A game."

"So I *did* make varsity?"

"You did."

All right!

"But you won't be starting."

WTF?

"Although it wasn't your fault, you missed summer camp. Which is when the rest of the guys started learning to use all the tools in our toolbox. So, as good as you are, you don't know my set plays."

"I'm a quick learner."

"Having watched you in class today, and seen you play, I've no doubt of that. But coming in from the bench will give you a chance to get your sea legs. So to speak."

"You do know I was number one freshman in California last year, right?"

"Yeah. So Mr. Curtis told me. But it was a different

team. And a different coach. Now you're on my team and, like I already said out on the court, we're doing things my way."

Matt could tell there was no point in arguing. But that didn't stop him from shooting this guy who was standing in the way of his dream a hard glare.

Then, knowing he might be risking being kicked off the team entirely, he stood up and walked out of the office before he started shouting.

The coach didn't follow.

14

Dillon had read the letter Matt Templeton's mother had written to explain his recent problems with his grandmother dying, so he was tempted to cut him some slack. Within reason. And not just because he was undoubtedly one of the most natural players to ever dribble a ball down the court. But because Dillon knew firsthand the anger, frustration, and pain he was feeling. If he hadn't been forced to try to fill the huge gap in his family left by his father's death, there was no telling what might have happened to him.

Shelter Bay's basketball team needed Matthew Templeton the player.

But, more important, Matthew Templeton the *boy* needed the team.

To Dillon's mind it was as simple as that.

He stood at the window of his office, watching as the kid climbed into the passenger seat of Aimee Pierson's ancient blue Volvo. The girl was not only as smart as a whip; she had a good, logical head on her shoulders. No way would she be foolish enough to be drawn into trouble by a kid with a juvie rap sheet who looked as if he should be modeling underwear.

Would she?

"Hell, she's a sixteen-year-old girl."

Which meant that Dillon didn't have a clue what the hell Aimee might be thinking. What she might do.

Deciding to tackle one problem at a time, he left his office, turned off the lights in the gym, walked out of the building to his Jeep, then headed out of town toward the coast.

"So I guess you made varsity?" Aimee asked Matt as he came out of Slater's office.

"Yeah. But I still haven't decided if I'm going to play."

Her eyes widened behind her glasses. "Why not? I thought that's what you wanted."

"I wanted to be a starter." He *should* be a starter, dammit! He'd watched some Dolphins game videos on YouTube. There wasn't a player on the team as good as he was on his worst day. "He's got me coming off the bench."

"Maybe he wants to ease you into the system," she suggested, walking faster to keep up with him. "Get you used to the different plays before he throws you into the deep end of the pool."

Her words brought up his mother's idea of him being the big fish in a small pond again. So much for that dumb idea.

They walked out into a cold, drizzling rain.

He so hated Oregon.

"I don't know all the rules of the game, but you didn't foul Dirk," she said.

"I know. So does he, but he's too much of a major tool to admit it. And what kind of name is Dirk, anyway?"

"Linguistically, it means a small dagger."

"Yeah. I'll bet his dagger's like minuscule," Matt muttered. "Dirk the Dickhead."

"He can be full of himself," she allowed. Which Matt figured was the major understatement of the century. "Are you in any hurry to get home?"

"Not really." Not that the old house his mother had bought would ever be home. "Why?"

"I thought maybe you'd like to drive over to the beach."

"I live at the beach."

"Technically you live on a cliff *above* the beach. But there's this neat cave in the cliff you might like. It's got all sorts of quartz and mica that makes it look like diamonds."

Matt hadn't found anything to like about this place so far. But it beat going home, where he'd be grilled about every damn minute of his damn day.

"What about your project you're working on?" he asked. "The Sacagawea report?"

"There'll still be time. I'm having dinner with Jenny. We can work on it afterward."

Matt wasn't in the mood to be with anyone right now. But he had three choices. He could call his mother to come to get him, which was no choice. Or walk two miles in the rain. Or check out some stupid cave with Science Girl Aimee, which would probably involve being subjected to a geology lecture. Which, he decided, was the least objectionable of the three.

"Sure."

She stopped next to a blue Volvo station wagon that was beginning to show some rust along the wheel wells. None of the girls at BHHS would be seen dead in a car like this. Speaking of dead, if it were black, it could probably pass as a hearse. Which fit his mood perfectly.

Matt was grateful when she didn't say anything as she drove through the town, which had all of one stoplight. Since there was hardly any traffic on the road, he wondered why they'd bothered putting one up at all.

The fishing boats were starting to come in from the sea, which had the ancient iron bridge opening up, leaving Aimee and Matt stuck on the town side.

"I hadn't thought about it before," she said as a blue boat chugged through the waves beneath them, "but the physics of basketball is pretty cool."

"Yeah?" He'd been playing ball for as long as he could remember, but he'd never thought of it as science.

"Everything around us has to do with physics," she said. He might be in a sucky mood, but he couldn't help noticing she was kind of cute when she got all serious about science stuff. "It's the most basic of all the disciplines, which is what makes it fun. What makes lightning, why the waves go in and out, how you can still hear a band when you're in the very back of a rock concert, even why you spin a basketball when you shoot. They all come down to physics."

"I spin a basketball because it affects air resistance and slows it down so I'm more likely to make a shot." The gesture had become as natural to Matt as breathing. He didn't even have to think about it.

"The ball's too heavy and moves too slowly to affect air resistance in any real way," she argued. "Once it leaves your hand, it travels in an unchanging parabolic path. What your backspin does is help the ball bounce into the net when it hits the rim."

One thing he'd learned early on was that you didn't question coaches. When he was in fifth grade, a coach had told him to stop pushing the ball and told him about air resistance and taught him to put backspin on it. Right away his shooting percentage had improved.

"Why wouldn't it be just as likely to bounce away from the net?"

"Because the velocity change is opposite to your spin direction, which causes an equal-angle rebound and velocity that tilts more toward the net, making it more likely that you'll score."

The horn on the bridge sounded as it began to lower. "I guess that makes sense."

"Of course it does." Her smile was quick, revealing that she was pleased he'd agreed. "It's physics." She resumed driving. "We have to write a term paper for Mr. Slater's class. Maybe you should write yours on the physics of basketball. Since you're a player, and he's a coach, it would show him another positive side of you besides just playing."

"You're suggesting I need to suck up to Coach Slater?"

"No. I was merely making a suggestion regarding your term paper. And I'll bet he understands the physics of basketball." Her tone had suddenly swung toward cool. As if he'd hurt her feelings.

"I appreciate the help," Matt said. "But I want to prove myself on the court."

"So how's that working for you?"

Okay. The snark was a surprise. "What happened to 'let's welcome the new kid to school'?" he asked.

"I believe I've already done that," she pointed out as they came off the bridge onto the coast side of the harbor. "It's after school. I'm off the clock."

The rain had stopped. For now. She turned off the raggedy wipers that had been screeching across the glass of the windshield, then shot him a look that wasn't in the least bit welcoming. "In fact, if you'd like, we can go back to the original plan and I can just drop you off and go straight to Jen's house."

"No." He raked a hand through his hair and wondered if all females were so damn changeable. "I'm sorry. I acted like a douche. . . . I'd like to see the cave. Really," he insisted as her expressive eyes narrowed.

It was her turn to shrug. When she turned on a narrow road before they reached his house, he figured she'd taken him up on his offer. But that didn't stop her from giving him the silent treatment.

"Tell me more about basketball physics."

"Why would you care? Given that you intend to prove yourself on the court."

"Because I still intend to earn a starting position with my skills, but it sounds like I'm also going to have to write a paper for Slater's class. Might as well be about something I know. And care about."

"That's always best," she agreed. The edge had left her voice, revealing that unlike a lot of girls, she didn't hold a grudge. "I'm writing mine on the physics of babies."

"What's the premise? That the amount of food that goes in is directly proportional to the amount of spit that comes out?"

"Ha-ha." Her tone was dry, but the smile had returned to her eyes. "I'll have you know that by two months, infants already show signs of expectations in their physical world, and by five months they understand that liquids and solids have different properties."

"No way."

"Way. There are studies proving it. They're fascinating."

"If you say so." They were driving along the coast road. The sun set early this time of year and it was already turning the choppy gray sea to a deep, dark blue. No way did he want to be down in some cave after it turned dark. "How much farther?"

"We're right here." She pulled off the road into a small gravel parking area. "And lucky us, we have a sunbreak."

She pointed up to the stuttering sun, which had managed to break through the clouds. Matt suspected that the Pacific Northwest was probably one of the few places on the planet where the word *sunbreak* even existed.

But since it beat going home and facing his mother's inquisition, he climbed out of the car and walked through the drizzling sunshower, which was another lame word, toward the beach.

15

Claire Templeton's car was parked in front of the small cottage, which had definitely known better days. The shake shingles, which he suspected had once been brown, had weathered to silver, one of the wooden steps to the front porch was split, and enough moss to grow mushrooms covered the cedar roof. Yet another adjustment the kid would've had to make. For someone who'd lived in the rarified atmosphere of Beverly Hills, this had to be a giant step down.

Then again, Dillon thought, as he stopped midway between the small house and the detached garage, where he heard some music playing, and looked out over the darkening sea view toward the skeletal remains of an old shipwreck glistening in the setting sun, maybe not.

Of course, thinking back on the way he'd stomped out and left with Aimee, scenery undoubtedly wasn't the top thing on Matt Templeton's mind.

He knocked on the wooden door on the side of the garage, but there was no answer.

He tried again.

Still nothing.

So, figuring that between the music and the noise of the fan that was blowing out the side of the building, she hadn't heard him, he turned the knob and walked in.

And was immediately hit by a heat as hot as anything he'd ever experienced in the Iraqi sandbox. Over the fan motors and the music, which was a mix of Gregorian chants, drumming, woodwinds, and some lyrics that sounded Middle Eastern, a blazing fire roared from inside a steel box.

Suspense, tension, danger, fire!

Hot damn.

Could any woman be more perfect?

At first Claire Templeton seemed unaware of him as she pulled the five-foot-long rod out of the hole, slanting it so a bit of the molten glass, which was glowing a bright orange from the intense heat, fell into a bucket of water.

As it sizzled, she turned and saw him. And visibly tensed.

"Is Matt okay?"

"He's fine," he assured her. It might not be exactly accurate, but it seemed to release some tension from her shoulders even as she began twirling the rod again. "I just came to talk to you about his place on the team."

"So he did try out?" She moved over to a flat surface, where she began rolling the oblong ball of glass.

"He did." He raised his voice to be heard over the fan and the music, which was swelling again into something that sounded as if the monks had gone hip-hop. "And to save you from having to ask, he made varsity."

"That's such good news," she said with a relieved smile. "And I really do want to hear all about it, but this is my third try at this today, and—"

"Go ahead. Unless having an audience distracts you."

"I've given demonstrations before. And taught a few classes." She was back to the glory hole, reheating the glass. "So I'm fine. But I'd appreciate you staying by the door so I don't have to worry about dropping molten glass on you. And if you wouldn't talk right now, that'd be helpful."

"No problem." He leaned against the door and folded his arms as she added more color to the glass.

She was wearing jeans, a long-sleeve L.A. Lakers T-shirt, and sneakers. Her hair had been pulled into a high ponytail through the back of a baseball cap, and her face, free of makeup, glistened from perspiration, which made sense because from her comment about a third try to pull off whatever she was trying to make, she'd been working in this hellish oven for a very long time.

When she put her lips to the end of the rod, blowing as casually as she might into a straw, the glob on the end of the rod expanded.

It was as if he'd turned invisible as she slipped back into what he recognized as a zone. Watching her carefully, which was certainly no hardship with the way those snug jeans hugged her ass, Dillon suspected that part of the reason her movements appeared so natural was that she was working from muscle memory. Something he was all too familiar with himself.

One of the reasons the Army's basic training was so brutal was to make sure that when in a battle situation, troops didn't have to stop and think to aim and shoot at the bad guys shooting at them. Their bodies took over and responded as trained.

Whatever she was working on kept getting larger, and as she turned it, the shape began to form.

It was when, after opening the center, she held what

appeared to be a tall vase or bowl upside down and began twirling it, creating a wavy top, that he realized what
the emerald core at the center of the sunset bright colors
was.

"A green flash," he said, forgetting he'd agreed to stay
quiet.

She glanced over at him. "Very good. That's exactly
it."

The highly elusive pulse of dazzling green, lasting
only a few seconds, occasionally appeared on the ocean's
horizon, at the very top of a setting sun, just as it was
about to sink into the water. Although he'd been living
in Shelter Bay several months, he'd been lucky enough
to see it only once. But damned if she hadn't captured it
perfectly.

"My mother, who illustrated children's books, once
did the drawings for a book of Scottish myths. One leg-
end said that a green flash will magically banish all pains
of the heart for any lucky enough to see it," she said.

"Now, there's a thought." Remembering this morning's tears, Dillon wondered what pains Claire Templeton's heart might be harboring. "Maybe you can use it as
a marketing incentive. Buy a vase; banish a heartache. . . .

"Anyway, I really like those bubbles. They look as if
they're sea foam rising up from the bottom of the sea."

"Thanks. My goal is usually to keep bubbles out of
my glass, but I decided to play with soda ash on this
one to accentuate the idea of liquidity. As you probably
know, soda ash is actually the common name for sodium
carbonate."

"Na_2CO_3," he said. Though he admittedly hadn't
given it any prior thought, he would have assumed that
jewelry making and glassblowing had more to do with

creative arts than science. He'd been way off the mark
with that one.

"Exactly. No one knows exactly when the first glass
was made, but we do know that the Egyptians were
making glass containers from soda ash as early as 3500
BC. If I place it on a piece of glass, then put a new hot
layer over it, a chemical reaction occurs that causes it to
release a gas. Which creates those bubbles."

Dillon was already attracted to Claire Templeton.
But in the past ten minutes that attraction had just
spiked.

"Not only does she play with fire and danger; the lady
knows her chemistry. I don't suppose you'd agree to
marrying me and having my children?"

"I'm sorry," she said mildly as she broke the bowl off
the rod and put it in another oven, where, he guessed, it
would cool. "But I'm afraid my schedule is all booked
up."

"Damn. I was afraid you were going to say that." He'd
have to work on getting around that ice wall she was
capable of putting up. Fortunately, EOD had taught him
patience. "But it's still a stunning piece."

When he'd seen Claire Templeton earlier today, tears
swimming in her eyes, she'd seemed almost fragile. Looking at the emotion she'd poured into this glowing piece
of hot glass, he realized she was anything but.

"Thanks. I don't usually go for such bright colors."
She pulled off the gloves and hat, then wiped the perspi-
ration from her forehead with the back of her hand.
"But it just felt right today."

"Your muse must've been feeling fiery." That idea
had him wondering what inner fires might be simmering
inside a woman capable of infusing so much emotion

into a piece of glass. And wouldn't he love to be the guy to tap them?

"I've been feeling like a volcano about to erupt for months. I suppose that bowl is the result." She rubbed the back of her neck. "Which is TMI. And I'm drenched."

"Not surprising since it's like Dante's inferno in here. How hot is that oven, anyway?"

"Twenty-four hundred degrees. Which is what it takes to turn sand into glass, glass into a liquid, then back into a solid again . . .

"What time is it?"

"About quarter to seven."

"That late?"

"I guess you lose track of time when you're working."

"When I'm in the zone," she admitted, confirming his earlier thought. "When were tryouts over?"

"Five thirty, give or take a bit."

"Matt texted me and told me he had a ride home. So I guess he's out celebrating with his teammates. I know it risks sounding like a helicopter mother to admit I'm a little worried he didn't let me know his plans—"

"He's not with the team." Which was something they were going to have to discuss. "He got a ride home with a girl."

"A girl? She must be older."

"A bit. But she's still a sophomore. She's a great kid. Honor roll, lots of extracurricular activities, and she's in science club. I'm the adviser."

"Well." She didn't look exactly thrilled at the prospect of Matt's having hooked up with a girl on the first day.

"They're both in my class," he volunteered. "They worked together on a lab project and I didn't get any of those kind of boy-girl vibes going on. She's one of the hospitality volunteers who introduce new kids their first day. She lives out here somewhere, so she's probably just giving him a tour of town on the way home."

"I suppose that makes sense." But she still looked a little distracted. From the kid's attitude when he'd been informed about coming off the bench, Dillon suspected the past year hadn't been easy on either of them.

"While I suspect you didn't drive all the way out here to tell me in person that my son made the team, I really do need a shower. Would you mind coming in while I freshen up first? I could offer you a glass of wine."

Although he was more of a beer guy, Dillon wasn't in any hurry to leave. Besides, he really did need to talk to her about the kid.

"Is that an invitation?"

She lifted her chin, looking anything but fragile as her eyes shot him a warning. "For wine. Nothing more."

"Works for me," Dillon said.

16

He was standing at the window, looking out at the darkened sea, when Claire returned to the combination kitchen / living room after what may have been her fastest shower ever. Part of her was sure he wasn't the kind of man to burst into the tiny bathroom while she was naked, but that hadn't stopped her from locking the door.

Which wasn't being paranoid. Just reasonably cautious. As any woman should be with a strange man in her house.

"It gets dark so fast this far north," she murmured as she came to stand beside him. The beam from the lighthouse on the cliff jutting out into the sea flashed on the wreck below, which, along with the veils of fog drifting in, gave it the look of a ghost ship.

"True enough. But come next summer the long days will make up for it."

He turned his head and looked down at her, a smile beginning to form on his lips.

And then it happened.

Their eyes met. And held.

As she drew in a breath, Claire's mind was wiped as clear as one of those glass facets on Shelter Bay's lighthouse.

She had no idea how long they stood there, her looking up at Dillon Slater, him looking down at her. Finally, as the rotating beam flashed across the ship yet again, she managed to break eye contact.

"You came here to talk about Matt?"

"Yeah." He dragged his hand through his hair, looking as disoriented as she felt. "I think we've got a problem."

Since this was the second time in a single day she'd felt that vivid awareness around him, Claire was beginning to figure that out for herself. She also couldn't help noticing that he'd used *we*. Something she wasn't accustomed to with any of his previous coaches. Not that Matt had ever proven a problem. Until this past year.

"Oh?"

"Let me pour you some of your own wine. Which, by the way, is very good."

"Thank you. It's from a Willamette Valley vineyard. . . . Am I going to need alcohol for this conversation?"

"It couldn't hurt."

He walked through the maze of boxes over to the counter and poured the pinot noir into one of the glasses she'd picked up, along with two cartfuls of other household necessities, at a Costco in Newport before she'd reached Shelter Bay. Her mother's extensive collection of Waterford hadn't fit into the far more casual lifestyle she'd planned. Nor had all the sets of china and sterling and formal furniture. Fortunately for them, the owner had been willing to sell the cottage furnished, and although most of the pieces would have to be replaced, at least they weren't relegated to sitting on the floor and sleeping in sleeping bags.

"That bad?" She sank down onto the tattered sofa she'd covered with a muslin slipcover for now. *Please, don't let him have already gotten kicked off the team.*

"At some places, it wouldn't be, no. But, like I told you, I really need these kids to be thinking as a unit."

Their fingers brushed when he handed her the glass.

"Matt was a total team player at BHHS." When the sudden thought of those fingers on her body caused her blood to warm, Claire took a long swallow of the ruby-hued wine and wished she'd taken a colder shower.

"He was the *star* of the team. Big difference." He sat down in the chair on the other side of the heavy plank coffee table she'd already decided to paint a distressed white to lighten it up. "He made this Dolphin team, but not as a starter. I had him coming off the bench."

"That makes sense." Relief flooded over her, washing away that unexpected and decidedly unwanted stab of sexual awareness. "After all, he doesn't know this team's plays yet. This will give him time to learn."

Claire was thinking how reasonable it sounded, when something else he'd said struck home. "You said *had*." As in past tense?

"Yeah. Your son didn't seem to agree with us about the plan."

She took another sip as her mind whirled with Matt's possible reactions. None of them at all encouraging.

"He walked out," the coach revealed. "I'm not sure he intends to come back. To the team," he clarified, not wanting her to think he'd taken off to hitchhike back to California or some other dumb kid stunt.

She stared out at the well of blackness looming outside the window. The fog was wrapping around the house, clinging to the window, making her all too aware that her son wasn't at home, where he belonged.

"Was he angry?"

"He sure as hell wasn't happy. . . . Look, I drove out here to talk to him, but it's probably just as well he isn't here right now. Hopefully he's blowing off steam, and it gives us a chance to discuss what to do."

Before she could ask if he had any thoughts about that, because she was rapidly running out of ideas, she heard a strange sound coming from the refrigerator.

"Oh, my God." Although the white fridge was on its last legs, this wasn't the rattle she'd been hearing all weekend. "My clams are crying!" It was an odd sort of sighing, sobbing sound, as if they were calling for help to escape.

He visibly perked up at that. "You have fresh clams?"

"I bought them at Farraday's this afternoon. Mrs. Farraday gave me instructions on how to steam them, but she never mentioned that I'd have to deal with the guilt of murdering them."

Despite the seriousness of their earlier topic, he laughed.

"Maybe *you* find it funny." She folded her arms across the front of her sweatshirt. "But you're not on the verge of becoming a clam assassin."

"They have no idea they're not still buried back in the mud and sand," he assured her.

"How do you know? I mean, it's not as if anyone can interview them on refrigerator death row to find out what they're thinking."

"They don't think."

"Then why are they making all that noise? They were quiet in the car."

"They have siphons they stick out of their shell when they're under the tide, which is how they breathe, eat, and expel carbon dioxide and waste. Then the water recedes, and they squirt out their extra water and close their shells. That's all that's happening now."

"You're sure?"

"I'm a science teacher," he reminded her. "I may be teaching physics at the moment, but I took a lot of biology in college."

There was another loud series of clicking noises that had her imagining opening the refrigerator door and coming face-to-face with a giant clam like in some black-and-white horror movie.

"I don't know if I can do this."

What on earth *was* she going to do? She probably couldn't just take them back down to the ocean once they'd been dug up, could she? But when she'd bought them at the fish market, it hadn't really sunk in that she was going to have to steam them alive. The idea was enough to put her off shellfish for the rest of her life.

"Well, it's probably not up there with killing a spider, but I could do it for you."

"You cook?"

"That would be an exaggeration. But Sax Douchett— he runs Bon Temps—"

"I've eaten there. The food's delicious."

"You're not going to get any argument from me. His grandmother's Come-Back sauce is flat-out addictive. . . . Anyway, I was over at his house one night this past summer and he boiled up a mess of clams and crabs. It's not that hard."

Maybe not for him. But as much as she hated the idea of being a cold-blooded shellfish murderer, throwing the poor clams out in the garbage wouldn't solve her problem, either.

"Well, then," she said, making her decision, "could I invite you to dinner? You can talk to Matt as soon as he gets home. I also have crab cakes and a sourdough rosemary garlic bread."

He grinned. "You've got yourself a clam executioner."

"Did you have to put it that way?"

"Sorry." But his eyes were laughing at her. As the strange clicking and sighing continued to come from the refrigerator, Claire realized that while he was undoubtedly right about clams not having the capability to think, they certainly did manage to shift the mood for a few brief moments.

Unfortunately, there was still a serious issue to settle.

"Would you be willing to give Matt a second chance?" Claire couldn't remember ever begging for anything in her life. Not even when the father of her unborn child had informed her that her pregnancy was her problem. But she'd be willing to beg for her son and a chance for a new start in Shelter Bay.

"Sure. As long as he apologizes and accepts that he doesn't get to call the plays. Both literally and figuratively."

"He needs this," she said. "The team. The discipline daily practice will bring to his life."

"You know that. And I know that." He polished off his wine. "Let's hope he knows it."

17

The first thing Matt noticed as Aimee let him off in front of the house was the Jeep Grand Cherokee with an SBH faculty parking sticker.

Busted. Because who else could it be but the coach, who'd probably told his mother all about his sucky attitude? As he'd walked on the beach to the cave—which, he had to admit, was pretty freaking awesome—he'd decided that by walking away from the team he'd be cutting off his nose to spite his face, as his grandmother always used to say. Now he was going to have to grovel his way back, and although he'd rather eat wet sand, he figured he didn't have much choice.

"There you are!" His mother smiled as he walked in the door, but that worry was back in her eyes. Matt's first thought was regret that he'd been the one to put it there. His second thought was that she and Coach Slater were drinking wine as if they'd been having themselves a private party.

At first he was pissed about that. Until he realized that maybe his mom had been softening the coach up.

"I was getting concerned," she said.

"I was on the beach. A friend wanted to show me this cave."

"A teammate?"

"No." He wasn't sure he even had any teammates. He risked a glance at the coach, whose expression was giving nothing away. "This girl who drove me home."

"Aimee Pierson, right?" Coach Slater said.

"Yeah. I mean, yes, Coach," Matt said.

"How did you meet her?" his mother asked.

Not in any third-degree way. It was more like she seemed happy to have something positive to talk about. And, Matt suspected, she figured he wouldn't blow her off in front of the coach. Especially if she knew what had happened, which he figured she must.

"All new kids get someone to show them around the first day. She was assigned to me."

"Isn't that nice?" Yeah, she was definitely grateful. In fact, she sounded more as if she'd just won the lottery, instead of her kid meeting a girl who drove him home.

"Yeah. I guess." He shrugged, hoping she wouldn't be dragging him into town to rent a tux for the winter formal that he had no intention of attending. "And it's not like going to the beach was a date or anything. She's into science stuff and wanted to show me some rocks in the cave."

"There's mica," the coach told Matt's mom. "And some pyrite."

"Fool's gold." As soon as he'd clarified what pyrite was, Matt realized that, being a jewelry designer, his mother probably knew that.

"Maybe you can show it to me someday," she suggested.

He shrugged, wishing they'd just get down to the reason the coach was sitting in the living room. If he was going to be kicked off the team, he'd rather just be told straight out than have to endure all this dancing around the subject.

"If I remember where it is," he said, although he knew exactly where Aimee had turned off the road.

He was thinking the problem was that hanging out on the beach with your mom would be even more humiliating than having her drive you to school, when she dropped a bombshell. "Coach Slater is staying for dinner."

"Shut up." The words were out of his mouth before he could pull them back. "I mean . . . really?"

Why? He couldn't remember the last time his mother had gone out to dinner with a guy. Let alone invited one home.

"He may be saving you from food poisoning." She answered the question he'd managed not to ask out loud. "I picked up some clams and crab cakes from the fish market, but even though the woman who owns the market gave me instructions, I was still worried. But Dillon—Coach Slater—knows how to cook them, so I invited him to stay."

That kind of made sense. After all, even his mom had to be getting tired of takeout. And it wasn't like there was a Thai or Chinese restaurant on every corner that'd deliver. But something was different.

She was different. A bit edgy. And, now that he looked at her more closely, either she was wearing some makeup on her cheeks or she was blushing. He sniffed. And she had definitely put on perfume.

Matt couldn't decide whether her going to all that

trouble for the guy who was holding his high school and college basketball future in his hands was a good or bad thing.

"Okay," he said, figuring that was a safe enough answer. "I guess I'd better get started on my homework. And my paper for your physics class," he told the coach.

Coach Slater arched a brow. "You've already picked out a topic?"

"Yeah." Matt decided he owed Aimee for this one. "The physics of basketball . . . like how, if I catch a hard pass into my chest, it's less likely to knock the wind out of me."

"And that's physics?"

Matt knew the coach knew the answer to this and was just testing him to see if *he* did. Again, thanks to Aimee, he was ready.

"Everything all around us is physics." Okay, *that* part was sucking up. "The ball coming at me has momentum. If I increase the time I decelerate the ball, by holding it against my chest, I lessen the force. Increasing T, time, causes F, force, to get smaller."

"Is that true?" his mother asked.

"Absolutely," Coach Slater said. From his narrowed-eyed gaze, he was probably trying to decide whether Matt was blowing smoke or actually knew what he was talking about. "It's the same theory that makes an airbag in a car work. The time it takes to decelerate is lengthened, which results in a lower force when the bag hits you in the face."

"I'm impressed," his mom said.

She was easy. He glanced over toward Coach Slater, who was still studying him like he might've looked at one of those bombs he was going to have to detonate. He was working on figuring him out.

"Of course," he said finally, "catching the ball into your chest also makes it less likely you'll drop the ball and turn it over."

Which was true.

"Too bad you decided against playing, where you could put all that basketball physics knowledge to a practical use."

Damn. There it was. What Matt had been afraid of the minute he'd walked in the door and had seen the coach sitting there.

"About that." He'd practiced what he was going to say when he got to school tomorrow. The groveling part and the sucking-up part. Aimee had even helped him edit his words so he wouldn't sound so full of himself. But the carefully rehearsed words had totally flown out of his mind.

And he wasn't getting a freaking bit of help from the coach, who just sat there, arms folded across his chest, looking at him. Waiting.

"I need to apologize. For walking out that way."

Another long silence. Matt could feel the sweat rolling down his back, and his palms were soaking wet. He could also feel the waves of sympathy coming from his mother and didn't dare look at her.

"I disrespected you." There. Hopefully he'd hit on what the coach wanted to hear.

"True. But you also disrespected your teammates. Which is equally important. Give me one reason why I should give you a second chance."

Because you need me? Because I can turn your program around? Because if I don't play ball I'll die?

Knowing that the first two reasons wouldn't fly, he decided to go with a version of the truth. "I need to play."

After another long pause that had Matt's gut twisting up in knots, the coach nodded his satisfaction. "That's a start."

18

Feeling as if she were walking on clouds, Phoebe Tyler basked in the pleasure of her new home. The one-bedroom apartment on the ground floor of one of Shelter Bay's Victorian houses probably could have fit into the kitchen of the McMansion she'd lived in before escaping her abusive marriage.

But the size didn't matter. What mattered was how free she felt. And how, after so many years as a virtual prisoner, she was finally safe.

She also had a job as a sous chef at the Lavender Hill restaurant and cooking school, which allowed her to move out of Haven House, the shelter she'd first lived in when she'd arrived in Shelter Bay after fleeing her abusive husband. And she had friends who'd thrown her a surprise party and filled her empty apartment with furnishings and other necessities. It had been, she'd thought, a bit like a wedding shower, but certainly more fun than the one where her deceased husband's controlling mother had held court shortly before Phoebe had made the worst mistake of her life—walking down that white satin runner and marrying Peter Fletcher.

"Bygones," she reminded herself firmly as she picked up a globe that had been a housewarming gift from Kara Conway Douchett, Shelter Bay's sheriff. Inside the clear glass, swirls of various blues and greens were reminiscent of the sea she could see in the distance from the widow's walk at the top of the house. "You survived. And you've moved on."

She skimmed her hands over the top of the chest that Flynn McGrath had surprised her with. The retired stockbroker turned artist who worked with reclaimed wood had restored an old cannery into a workshop, with space he rented out to other artists and even some bakers from Haven House.

Like so many others in town, he'd taken her under his wing, and she suspected that Lucas Chaffee, who'd done the remodeling work and was married to Phoebe's chefboss, had suggested he donate a piece to help her set up housekeeping. Having seen the prices in his furniture gallery, she'd been floored when the deliverymen had shown up at the door.

Of course she'd bought a few things for herself with her salary from the restaurant, but the generosity of seemingly everyone in town still amazed her.

"You have friends." Framed photos taken by Gabriel St. James of Kara and Sax Douchett's and Maddy Durand and Lucas's weddings shared space atop the chest with others of her previous life growing up on a ranch in Arizona—one of her at twelve, barrel racing on her beloved quarterhorse, Butterscotch. Another of her parents, celebrating their wedding anniversary in Sedona's red rock country. The love they still shared for each another after forty years shone in their eyes and their smiles. It was what she'd always dreamed of having for herself.

"There's still time."

She was young and, as the therapist who visited Haven House every week had pointed out, she had her entire life ahead of her. A life she was becoming more and more impatient to share with her child. As if sensing her feelings, the baby turned a series of somersaults as she continued to study the family photographs that Peter had never allowed in their sprawling Tudor in Colorado. He'd been an expert at manipulation and, as she'd learned, even brainwashing.

Shortly after they'd married, he'd changed the checking account to solely his name. He did give her an allowance for personal spending—treating her like a child rather than an equal partner—but since he chose her clothing and her hairstyle and slowly cut her off from her friends, she'd had nothing to spend any personal money on.

Which was how she'd been able to hide enough away to finally escape.

He'd made all their plans, often not telling her what those plans were until almost the last minute, which kept her not only unaware of what was going on, but also on edge and anxious.

He'd gradually isolated her so badly that even after he'd beat her, or, in his words, "discipline" her, she had absolutely no one left to turn to.

She'd lost more of herself every day, becoming quieter, never offering an opinion of her own, which would be ridiculed, but assuring him how smart, how clever, how *right* he always was.

Eventually, over time, she came to believe his accusations, that she was stupid, incapable of succeeding at anything she might want to try, and useless. Even in bed.

As she lived in constant fear of displeasing him, the map of her world had narrowed to the gilded prison she'd known she'd be living in until the day she died. Which, she also knew, could be any day of her husband's choosing.

And then life changed. In the bedroom where she'd first learned that a wife could, indeed, be raped, a new life had sparked.

And a strength she'd believed that he'd stolen from her forever rose, like a phoenix from the ashes, to protect her unborn child.

Which was when she'd risked her life by contacting an underground railroad of women who helped others escape danger and abuse. With the clandestine group's help, she'd ended up here in Shelter Bay, where she'd been protected and, with a great deal of help, began to recover the strong woman she'd once been before her marriage.

Since her arrival she'd made friends. Close friends who cared about her. She had work she loved, and as much as she reveled in a weekly paycheck after all those years of having to depend on her husband for money, even more special were the compliments she received from diners about the food she'd prepared.

Lately, Chef Maddy had even begun letting her train new students, many of whom were new arrivals to Haven House; others were tourists and foodies willing to pay to learn how to cook the restaurant's simple but delicious farm-to-table food.

And speaking of farm-to-table . . . when the doorbell chimed, she quickly checked her hair and makeup on the mirror hanging on the wall of the tiny foyer, then opened the door.

As always, Ethan Concannon took her breath away. When the former Marine turned organic farmer had first shown up in the kitchen of Haven House with a delivery of vegetables, he'd startled her. Having just escaped her husband, she'd found him too large and too male. Yet as soon as he'd smiled, Phoebe had been amazed to feel chords being strummed within her that she hadn't believed still existed.

She been drawn to him at the same time the idea of getting involved with any man made her jittery. But after they'd spent more time together, she came to realize that any man who could coax a seed to bloom into gorgeous vegetables that looked as if they belonged on a Renaissance painting would possess a great deal of patience.

Over the months he'd let her know how deeply he cared about her. Including taking her into his house for protection when her husband had threatened her. But understanding how badly she needed to regain her independence, he'd never pushed her into a more intimate relationship than she was ready for.

Today he was taking her to veterinarian Charity Tiernan's no-kill pet shelter. Having grown up with ranch dogs, Phoebe had decided that now that she was settling down into a stable relationship, she wanted her child to have the same opportunity to love a pet as she had. Charity had already chosen two young rescued dogs, both of which she thought would be a good fit.

"Damn, you look gorgeous," he said as he entered the living room. Before she could complain that she was nearing the size of one of Shelter Bay's whales, he gathered her into his arms, bent his head, and treated her to a slow, deep kiss that had her toes curling in her sunshine yellow rain boots.

"Flatterer," she said after they'd come up for air.

"It's not flattery. It's the truth." He nuzzled her neck. "And you smell good, too. Like spring."

"It's lotion from Lavender Hill Farm." The fresh green scent carried an undernote of white flowers that made her feel pretty and feminine. Something she hadn't felt during her marriage.

"Lotion?" He ran a broad, calloused hand down her side, from breast to hip. "Would you happen to have put it on all over?"

She felt the blush rise in her cheeks even as she lifted her arms and linked her fingers behind his neck. "I believe that's for me to know and you to find out." She allowed herself one more glorious moment of contact, then backed up. "After we check out Charity's dogs."

He shook his head in mock exasperation and skimmed a finger down the slope of her nose. "You do realize you're a tease."

"I know." Imbued with a heady sense of freedom and female power, Phoebe laughed. "Come on." She linked her fingers with his. "Play your cards right, Farmer Boy, and I may just let you play explorer later."

"Be careful. I just may take you up on that." He nodded with satisfaction at the thought.

And wasn't that exactly what she'd been angling for? The idea of finally making love with this man she'd fallen in love with caused lovely gold ribbons of anticipation to flow through her body.

The bedroom was only a few feet away. And even as

she appreciated him giving her these past months to regain her independence, Phoebe had come to the realiza-
tion that if she didn't make the first move, she and Ethan
could still be playing this waiting game while waving her
child off to college.

Which was why she already had her own plans for
tonight.

"They say anticipation is a good thing," Ethan said.

"So they do," she agreed.

Thinking about the fresh sheets she'd rinsed with lavender before spreading them on the bed, the beeswax
candles waiting on the dresser and bedside table to be
lit, Marvin Gaye's "Let's Get It On" (recommended
by Kara after Phoebe had shared her frustrations), designed to seduce, waiting in the CD player, had her heady
with anticipation.

He helped her with her parka, then, hand in hand,
they left the apartment. They'd just reached his truck
when a man approached them.

"Ms. Stephanie Fletcher?"

The fact that this stranger knew her former name
chilled her blood and caused every nerve ending in her
body to screech an alarm. "It's Phoebe Tyler." She'd le-
gally changed it after her husband's arrest.

"Either one will work."

He held out a piece of paper. "Have a good day," he
said as she took it from his hand. Then he turned and
walked away. Like every process server she'd ever seen
in the movies or on TV.

This can't be good.

"Let me read it first," Ethan said, proving that once
again they were on the same wave length.

"No." Her fingers had a death grip on the paper. "We'll read it together."

She hadn't gotten past the first two lines when Phoebe's head lightened and began to spin.

Right before everything went black.

19

The dinner went surprisingly well. Apparently wanting to get back into his coach's good graces, Matt could have been the poster boy for manners. It also helped that they spent the entire time talking basketball, with Dillon Slater giving him a crash course on the new plays he'd be expected to learn.

It was, Claire thought, as she dunked a piece of bread into the tasty white wine, butter, and garlic clam sauce, as if a lightbulb had been turned on inside Matt. The dark cloud that had been hovering over his head for weeks had lifted, and he'd visibly brightened by the time they got to the marionberry pie she'd picked up at Take the Cake bakery for dessert.

As good as it was to see her son engaged and excited about something again, she was also pleased by how well the coach was bringing Matt out of himself. There were times, when they were arguing about who was the best point guard in history, when he almost seemed like his old self.

"It's gotta be Steve Nash," Matt insisted. "He kicks ass in every category."

"Which is why he was voted league MVP twice," Dillon allowed. "I'll bet a lot of college coaches are kicking themselves for not having seen his potential when he graduated high school. Santa Clara College was the only school that offered him a scholarship."

"No way. That's just wrong." The shocked look on Matt's face told Claire he hadn't known that fact. She also saw a bit of worry move across his eyes.

"It's a tough world out there," the coach said as she topped off his coffee mug.

He had such pretty brown-and-gold eyes, Claire considered as she felt herself falling back into them yet again. And those long thick lashes were decidedly unfair to have been gifted to a man. While days would go by before she'd think to put on makeup, if she didn't at least put mascara on her blond lashes, they didn't show up.

"There are more than a million basketball players in men's and women's high school basketball programs," Dillon said.

That dragged Claire back to the conversation she'd only partly been listening to. "That many?"

"Give or take. Some years more, some a bit less. Want to guess how many get college scholarships?" he asked Matt.

"Half?"

"On average, fifty thousand."

"No—"

Claire knew that before Matt had wisely shut his mouth, he'd been about to argue that number. She also knew that the coach wouldn't have any reason to make it up.

"That's only five percent," she said.

Despite the seriousness of the bombshell he'd just

dropped on her kitchen, he smiled. "And she does math, too."

"*You* got a scholarship," Matt said, finding his voice again. Though it cracked slightly. And his complexion had paled.

"I did. Of course, I knew a trick."

"What trick?"

"I knew I wasn't big or tall enough to be all that attractive to the pros. So, right there, that diminished my odds, because college programs like having their players go pro because it adds to the number of students wanting to go there. And gets them better professors."

"Surely you're not saying professors actually decide whether they'll teach at a school by how big a success its sports program is?" Claire asked.

Foregoing a traditional college, after graduating from BHHS, Claire had enrolled in Los Angeles' Fashion Institute of Design and Merchandising. Which, needless to say, had not had any sports program.

"Not every person. And not every program, obviously. But yeah, it makes a difference, because a strong team brings in more money in ticket sales and merchandise. Which, in turn, results in more income to the college or university, which, in turn, is available for professor salaries."

"That's depressing," she said.

"It's reality."

"So what did you do?" Matt asked.

"I gave up the idea of getting any sports scholarship and went for an academic one instead."

"*You* were a scholar-athlete," Claire reminded her son.

"I think the definitive word there, Mom, is *were*."

"Surely any college admission officer would overlook your grades slipping during such a difficult personal time."

"Fortunately," Dillon said, "your slide happened the last semester of last year and the beginning of this year. You still have nearly three years to pull your GPA up."

"See?" Claire said. "You just need to work a little harder. You're so smart, Matt. If you apply yourself to your schoolwork the way you do to basketball, I know you can achieve any goal you set for yourself."

Hadn't her own mother given her the same pep talk when the home pregnancy test had shown that little plus sign her freshman year at FIDM? Having Matt had admittedly altered her path to that glittery life she'd imagined for herself—having her jewelry routinely appear on red carpet runways, and partying with the stars—but with her mother's help she'd managed to complete her BA in five years and had been able to have a career while being a stay-at-home mom. And she wouldn't trade her son for all the Oscar parties in the world.

"None of us get a free pass," the coach backed her up. "Having strong grades is a big advantage in the recruiting process. An academic scholarship doesn't count against the total allowed to the athletic department, which right away makes you attractive to coaches, because it frees up one for a player whose grades might not be that high. Plus, there's an additional advantage that a lot of programs are looking for players they might not have taken otherwise, if those players can help raise the team GPA."

"Well." What had begun as distressing news could turn out to be a good thing. Claire had been trying to get Matt focused back on his schoolwork. But he'd remained stubbornly resistant to all her appeals. Now it appeared Coach Slater had shown up at her door with the magic bullet. "That's certainly something to think about, isn't it, honey?"

"Yeah." Matt's voice was flat and more subdued than it had been earlier. She suspected that was, in large part, due to hearing those cold hard numbers.

He'd always been assured he was the best. That the basketball world was his oyster. She knew he didn't apply himself as much as he could in school because, quite frankly, he hadn't needed to. He'd been born with a gift for math and sciences—which she'd long ago decided he must have gotten from his paternal genes because everyone in her family tended to live in their creative right brains. Even Matt's father, who'd come to FIDM from New York City to guest lecture on merchandising, had been a textile designer before joining the executive ranks of some of the world's top fashion businesses. With those genes woven through his DNA, Claire had never figured out where his sports talent had come from.

Apparently Dillon picked up on Matt's decided lack of enthusiasm, because he tabled the discussion for now.

"So, anyway, getting back to our point guard rankings, as good as Nash is—and he's damn good—he's got a way to go before I'll credit him with being the best. It'd help if he had some finals experience under his belt. The obvious choice is Magic Johnson, who's definitely in the running, because not only could he shoot, he could play all positions when he was needed, which made him a total team player. But I'm still going with Isiah Thomas."

"You said everyone needs to be able to play both sides of the ball," Matt argued. Claire couldn't decide if it was a good or bad thing that he was willing to argue with his coach. On one hand, he'd gotten a bit of his spark back; on the other, would Dillon Slater see it as a lack of respect? "Thomas was a scoring guard."

"He let Joe Dumars handle more of the passing," the coach allowed. "But he could and did play both offense and defense. Where he stood out, in my opinion, is his absolute leadership. Who could forget the sixth game in the 1988 finals against the Lakers when he checked himself back in the game and hobbled through the fourth quarter on a badly sprained ankle, scoring twenty-five points?"

"I wasn't even born in 1988," Matt pointed out. "But even *I* know Detroit lost that game."

"In points, maybe. But not only does Thomas hold the record, that game he reached a level he'd never reached before by winning. He didn't give up. He stayed mentally strong and persevered. And that never-say-die, never-give-up-the-dream mentality was, hands down, what made him the best."

Claire knew Matt believed she'd snatched his dream away from him by bringing him to Shelter Bay. Now she could practically see the wheels turning in his head as he considered the coach's words.

"You think I gave up?" he asked.

"You've been through a lot, but I wouldn't have put you on the team if I didn't think you had it in you to be the kind of leader Thomas was. I'm not going to lie, Templeton. It's going to be a rough year. The other teams in the league are used to the Dolphins providing a check in their win column. And yeah, that's not going to change overnight. But we're damn well going to make them work for it. And if we do, we can win more than we lose."

"Hell with that," Matt said. "I think we're going to state."

The coach surprised Claire by laughing at that. A deep, rich sound that slipped beneath her skin and sent alarm bells jangling.

20

Kara Conway Douchett couldn't deny that she loved having her husband sitting beside her in the birthing class. While many of the other husbands were obviously uncomfortable surrounded by so many females talking about detailed physical aspects of pregnancy, Sax seemed to take it all in stride.

Also, there was the fact, she thought with wifely pride, that he was, hands down, the sexiest man in the room. None of the others, in her opinion, came close.

With Jared deployed for most of her previous pregnancy, she hadn't experienced much sexual desire over all those months. Or perhaps, she thought, since sex hadn't been available, she simply hadn't allowed herself to think about it.

Lately, perhaps because her body was being flooded with hormones, she thought about sex. A lot.

Although the exercises they were being led through were designed to encourage relaxation, the feel of her husband's strong hands moving across her shoulders, then down her spine to the small of her back, then lower still, did nothing to instill calm.

By the time they made it all the way through the series of prescribed exercises, she was ready to jump him.

"All right." The nurse-practitioner leading the class
said the fatal words. "It's time for the video."

"I'm so sorry," Kara said as she and Sax got back into
the car. After what he'd told her about his harrowing
missions in Iraq and Afghanistan, his reaction to the
birthing video came as a total surprise.

"You're laughing at me." He leaned his head against
the back of the driver's seat. His face was an unhealthy
shade of gray and his eyes were closed.

"I am not," she said, not quite truthfully.

Hearing the faint crack in her voice, he turned his
head toward her, opened his eyes a slit, and shot her a
glare. "Admit it. You're finding this funny."

"Funny?" She put a hand on her chest, as if shocked
by the accusation, even as she struggled to rein in the
laughter that was rising in her throat. "Of course not."
Okay, that was a lie. "What kind of woman would find
humor in watching a grown man swoon in public?"

"I didn't swoon," Sax replied, repeating what he'd
said at the time. "Or faint, or pass out, or any other
smart-ass euphemisms you might be thinking up. I merely
became a little light-headed."

"I stand corrected." She pressed her lips together but
knew he could spot the laughter in her eyes. She'd never
been able to get anything past this man. Not even back
when he'd been close friends with her high school sweetheart, who'd later become her first—and now late—
husband.

Then, making it worse, a laugh escaped her lips.

"It wasn't all that funny," he muttered.

"It wasn't. Not really." Her breaking into full-fledged, out-of-control laughter belied her words. "I'm sorry," she said again. Taking a deep breath, she struggled for calm. "It's the hormones," she insisted. "They swing all over the place these days.

"But if you could've seen your face!" She choked, then managed, just barely, to recover. "I honestly didn't have any idea the video was going to be so graphic."

Having given birth before, Kara had taken the video in stride, while many of the women in the room had looked horrified. Admittedly, Sax hadn't been the only husband who'd looked ill. He was, however, the only SEAL present, which undoubtedly had upped his embarrassment level.

Remembering another time, when Kara had been pregnant with Trey and wept in his arms, there was no way Sax was going to be annoyed at her musical laughter now.

But when those graphic images flashed through his mind again, Sax's stomach lurched. Willing himself not to hurl, he dragged his hands down his still-sweaty face.

"It wasn't the film," he lied. "I think it was the sliders I had for lunch. The shrimp must've been bad."

"I had them, too," she pointed out. "And I'm feeling fine. Besides, the Crab Shack always gets one hundred percent on its state health inspections. Jake doesn't serve bad seafood."

She really was enjoying this. As he viewed the sparkle in his wife's eyes and the curve of her luscious lips, Sax decided that he'd be willing to toss his cookies every day to make this woman he'd loved seemingly forever laugh.

Never one to dwell on failure, he put the humiliating incident behind him. "I think," he said, "that since this time of day between the lunch rush and dinner is always slow at Bon Temps, and Cody's capable of handling whatever business drifts in, maybe I ought to go home and crash in bed for a while."

Kara had not only been Shelter Bay High School's valedictorian; she was still one of the smartest people he'd ever known. While she might not have realized that he'd fallen head over heels in love with her their senior year of high school, she'd definitely had his number since they'd both landed back in town.

"You just want to have sex."

"I always want to have sex with you." That was the absolute truth.

"Me, too." Her teasing voice had slipped into that warm silky tone he immediately recognized.

"Guess it's the hormones," he repeated her earlier claim.

"No." She unfastened her seat belt long enough to lean across the center console and touch her lips to his. "It's you. And since Trey won't be home from school for another hour . . ."

The kiss, which was short and potent and included a hot bit of tongue teasing, cleared his head and sent the blood flowing south.

"Sweetheart," Sax said as he twisted the key in the ignition while she buckled up again, "you are playing my tune."

21

Phoebe was curled up in a ball, looking small and defenseless between the flowered sheets that had been a housewarming gift from Sedona, the pretty blond baker from Take the Cake. Her beautifully delicate face was as pale as marble and tears had left tracks down her cheeks.

After carrying her back into the apartment and putting her to bed, holding her as she'd cried herself to sleep, Ethan had remained sitting beside her for a long, silent time. And as the minutes stretched into an hour, then longer, he thought about the two very different women who'd made such a difference in his life.

He'd loved Mia, but their marriage had been one of youthful optimism. Sure, they might have had their problems, especially when he'd come home from deployment and they'd had to figure out how to settle back into being a family. Also, it couldn't have been easy for her when he'd separated from the service and tried, for a very short time, to work on his parents' farm.

Unfortunately, working with his brother, who'd resented Ethan's college degree and new environmental ideas, had been like mixing gasoline and a flamethrower.

It had been Mia, who'd grown up on a farm herself in Idaho, who'd convinced him to buy Blue Heron Farm, although she'd been killed before they'd been able to settle in. With herb gardener Sofia De Luca's help, he'd turned the farm organic and had been, if not as happy as he and Mia had planned, satisfied with both his work and his life.

Then he'd walked into the kitchen of Haven House and felt his well-ordered, comfortable world tilt on its axis.

Dammit, Phoebe had been through so much with her bastard husband. But she'd never given up. Although he'd wanted her from the first, falling in love with her had felt totally natural. And right.

Knowing she needed time, he'd mustered up all the self-discipline the Marines had drilled into him to give her however much time she needed. There'd been a moment, just a few months ago, when he'd thought they could move on. Until Fletcher had shown up in Shelter Bay and thrown a monkey wrench into Ethan's plans to move their relationship to the next level.

And now, just when he'd thought they'd be able to move on for good, despite being dead and supposedly gone forever, the bastard was back in their lives . . .

She looked so vulnerable. No one looking at her would imagine the battle she'd waged—a delicate, amazingly brave David against that murderous, larger-than-life Goliath. Ethan had vowed that whatever it took, he would not allow anyone to hurt this woman ever again.

Her hair was spread out on the pillowcase, which smelled like the lavender he knew she bought at Lavender Hill Farm. Unable to resist the lure, he stroked it, kissed it, inhaled its familiar fragrance. Her lips were unpainted and parted ever so slightly.

Phoebe Tyler was Sleeping Beauty in the flesh. And amazingly, she was his.

She sighed, not sadly, but, he thought, with pleasure, which was surprising after the hit she'd taken. He wondered if she could be dreaming of him.

Which would only be fair, since his dreams had been filled with her for months.

He'd helped her move in, had even put her pretty white iron bed together. Not wanting her to risk climbing a ladder in her condition, he'd painted the walls a soft hue the color of sea foam. He hadn't been in this bedroom since that day. Gauzy white curtains framed the windows; the sunny faces of perky daisies she'd placed in small white bud vases brightened the gray Pacific Northwest view; ivory candles stood in distressed white lanterns, waiting to be lit.

It was definitely a woman's room. A man wouldn't feel comfortable here unless invited. Which, from the way she'd flirted with him before that process server had arrived, he'd suspected had finally been about to happen.

Her eyes fluttered open. "Ethan?"

Her weeping had left her eyes red rimmed and shadowed. But the uncensored emotion in them was the most beautiful thing he'd ever seen.

"You were expecting someone else, perhaps?"

"No." Her smile as soft as her voice, she reached across the sheet, took his hand, and lifted it to her cheek. "I'm glad you're still here. Thank you for staying."

"I wouldn't leave you." Waves of emotion, like from a tropical sea, washed over him. "Ever."

Then, unable to resist, he lowered his mouth to hers.

He kept the kiss gentle, lacing it with all the tenderness swelling his heart. She sighed as she allowed herself to sink into the warmth of it.

Nibbling at her lips, Ethan tasted his way from one corner of her mouth to the other. "You taste like temptation," he murmured as he dampened her bottom lip with the tip of his tongue.

"Chef Maddy's been teaching me all about flavor profiles." She twined her arms around his neck. "But we haven't covered that one yet."

"It's sweet . . . and warm." He skimmed his tongue up her jaw. "Ripe."

She trembled as he circled her ear. "Ethan."

"God, I love to hear you say my name." He punctuated his words with slow, melting kisses. "Say it again."

His hands slipped beneath the hem of her sweater.

"Ethan," she said, her voice somewhere between a sigh and a plea.

Although it took every ounce of willpower he possessed, he kept his kisses light, his hands gentle. "Again."

Just when he thought they were finally going to forge a future together, Fletcher had, yet again, infiltrated himself into her life. Into their lives.

"About that subpoena," he said, having come up with an idea while she'd been sleeping.

"No." She framed his face in her hands and brushed her lips against his. "I don't want to talk about all that right now." Her warm, sweet lips plucked at his, encouraging a response. "I just want to make love with you, Ethan."

She drew her head back and, although her confidence had grown in leaps and bounds in the past months, in her remarkable eyes Ethan could see faint seeds of doubt. "If you want to . . ."

How the hell could she not know that making love to this woman was what he'd been thinking about ever since he'd found her in the kitchen of the shelter, her hands deep in bread dough?

He drew her back against him, gathering her close, inhaling the herbal scent of her hair, the fragrance of the silky flesh behind her ear. "Let me show you exactly how much I want to make love to you."

Take it slow. As he brushed butterfly kisses over her face, a soft, excited laugh slipped from between her lips.

"I've been waiting for this for what seems like forever," she murmured as his mouth glided along her jawline.

"That makes two of us." She was so unbearably soft. And warm. And special.

He undressed her slowly. Tenderly. She lifted her arms as he pulled the sweater over her head. Then pulled the jeans down her legs.

"Wow. I didn't even know they made bikini panties for pregnant women."

"Remember when I went to Portland overnight with Kara, Sedona, Charity, and Maddy?"

"Sure." He'd played poker with the guys and lost every hand because his mind had been fantasizing about spending the night in some luxury hotel with a view of the river and city lights, and making love to his Phoebe in an oversized marble tub.

"Kara found out about this amazing maternity boutique," she said on a light gasp of pleasure as he slipped his finger beneath the low-cut waistband. "Charity, who apparently is rich, though you'd never know it because she's so nice, insisted on practically buying out the lingerie department for me."

He could feel her light laugh beneath his fingers. "I told her I didn't have anyone to wear them for, but all of them said that didn't matter. That I should wear them for myself."

"Tell them thank you for me."

The shadows in the room deepened. When he reached to turn on the lamp, she caught hold of his hand.

"I want to see you, Phoebe." He lowered his mouth to hers again. "All of you."

"I'm fat," she protested. The complaint was little more than a whisper, but Ethan had no trouble hearing it in the hushed stillness of her bedroom.

"Not fat." His fingers dispatched the clasps of the lacy bra. Hot damn. He hadn't lost his touch. "Beautiful," he said as he scattered a trail of kisses across the slope of her breasts.

She was still tense. He could feel it. Sense it.

Ethan had waited too long for this moment not to want it to be perfect. So he was willing to forgo the lamp. But no way was he going to make love to Phoebe in the dark.

He stopped his caresses just long enough to snag the lighter lying beside the candle on the bedside table. He touched the flame to the wick, bathing her in a warm yellow glow.

Her heavy breasts were the color of porcelain, but so much warmer. Her flesh was drawn tight against her belly, outlining the child she'd run away from a dangerous marriage to protect. The child she was still having to fight to keep.

The child Ethan swore she *would* keep.

"You," he said, as he kissed a white stretch line, "take my breath away."

"You don't have to lie." Even as she protested, when he skimmed his tongue over her navel, she arched her back in pleasure.

"I'll never lie to you, sweetheart. And especially never about this." He kissed his way up to her breasts, running his tongue over a taut nipple. Her flesh was so hot, Ethan was amazed it didn't sizzle at the wet caress.

Basking in the pleasure of the fragrant damp flesh, he moved to the other nipple. "There's something really hot about a warm, ripe woman."

"Now you make me sound like a fruit from one of those trees in your orchard," she complained. But he could tell she enjoyed the idea.

"Absolutely," he agreed. "And before the night's over, Phoebe, my love, I'm going to taste every delicious bite."

There was no storm. No flare of fireworks. The earth did not move.

Instead there was flickering candlelight and the scent of melting wax. Sweet, whispered words. Tender, murmured promises.

Fingers linked, lips melded, legs entwined as Ethan finally slipped into her as easily and as perfectly as if they'd been created for each other. Which to his mind, they had.

And as the flickering candle burned low and a huge harvest moon climbed high in the sky, showering its light over the room, Ethan and Phoebe soared over it.

22

It was raining. Again. As he gulped down three packages of microwave instant oatmeal, Matt made a mental note to start checking his feet every night before bed to make sure they weren't becoming webbed. Aimee had assured him that Shelter Bay summers were awesome, but he was beginning to suspect that her bar might be set a lot lower than his.

"We have a problem," his mother said as she sat down across from him.

He wondered what her first clue had been. The problem was obvious. . . they were living in the wrong damn state.

"What?" he asked around a mouthful of oatmeal.

"That gallery in Portland, the one where I'm having my exhibition next month? The hotel room they booked only has one king bed."

"So?"

"So, because of some Christmas boat parade thing, the hotel's booked solid. I couldn't get two rooms."

"Why do you need two rooms?" He took a long swallow of milk.

"Because I don't want you having to sleep on the floor."

"Why would I do that? I'm not even going."

"Of course you are. You have that night free. I checked your schedule."

"I'd rather just stay home and watch a video." He paused, thinking about their conversation last night. "And work on my term paper for Coach Slater's class."

"But you'd be alone."

Which was the freaking point. She had no idea how much he'd been looking forward to her going away for that show. "What, you don't trust me?"

"I didn't say that."

"You said yourself I need to apply myself to get my grades up."

"I did, but—"

"So, that's what I'm going to do. You've got to admit that me working on the physics of basketball and getting started on that English reading list makes more sense than hanging around some gallery with phony artsy-fartsy types."

"Excuse me? I'm artsy-fartsy by your definition."

"No, you're not. You're my mom. And I realize you have my best interest at heart." He figured that, along with the mention of getting started on the damn list, would soften her stance. "But since I'm too old for a babysitter, you're just going to have to bite the bullet and trust me."

"Of course I do," she said, not quite convincingly, making Matt wonder how long it would be before they got beyond that stupid pot fiasco.

What nobody knew was that it hadn't even been his stash to begin with. Not that he ever would've ratted out the owner. Even if she hadn't been a girl who'd taken off her shirt and bra while they'd been studying in her bedroom while her parents had been at some movie premiere red-carpet deal.

"But what if something happens?" his mother was asking as Matt was imagining, not for the first time, what Lila Greene might have looked like with the rest of her clothes off. What really sucked was that before he'd had an opportunity to spend more time with her and find out, he'd been busted by that pot-sniffing German shepherd the campus cop had brought in, and her movie-producer parents had banned her from seeing him again.

"Like the house catching on fire," his mother said.

"You taught me how to dial 911 before I was three," he reminded her.

"Like it or not, I'm your mother. I worry."

"Well, don't. Everything'll be copacetic. Really."

He'd never been so happy to hear anything in his life as he was the beep of the horn on Aimee's janky Volvo outside the door.

Feeling as if he'd just gotten a reprieve from death row, Matt jumped up and grabbed his jacket and book bag. "See you after practice."

He managed to escape before she humiliated him by going out to meet his new "friend." Which would undoubtedly lead to her giving Aimee the third degree.

"Let's roll," he said as he threw his bag into the Volvo's backseat. "Now."

"We're not late."

"I just want to get the hell out of Dodge."

"Bad morning?" Aimee asked.

"It could've been," he said as she pulled away from

the house. Matt did not look back. "If you hadn't shown up just in time. Like Black Widow from *The Avengers*."

"Thanks. But I'd rather be Katniss from *The Hunger Games*, who's a heroine because she's wicked smart, and not because of how she looks wearing a catsuit."

Matt decided not to point out that there was nothing wrong with Scarlett Johansson poured into black latex. In fact, Black Widow claimed a major chunk in the hot-chick section of the pie chart that was his brain.

"Pull over," he said after they'd turned the corner.

"Did you forget something?" She pulled the Volvo over to the shoulder of the narrow, winding road.

"Yeah." He unfastened his seat belt, leaned across the console, and kissed her smack on the mouth.

It wasn't a long kiss. He didn't use any tongue and kept his hands in her hair instead of letting them wander into dangerous territory. But it still left her eyes as wide as an owl's when he pulled his head back.

"What was that for?"

"I owe you."

"For what?" She looked a little stunned. Which was weird. He couldn't have been the first guy to ever kiss her. She was sixteen. She had wheels that would let her go anywhere she wanted. With anyone she wanted. And the back of that station wagon offered a lot of possibilities.

"Because you saved me. From my mother, which, believe me, is no small deal. But also because your basketball physics lecture got me back on the team."

"I'm glad." She touched her mouth with her fingertips. Her nails were short and unpolished. "But a simple thanks would've been sufficient. You didn't have to kiss me."

"It was a spur-of-the-moment thing." He shrugged, wondering, as he refastened his seat belt, if she was afraid he might want to become a couple just because she'd rescued him from high school oblivion. "It didn't really mean anything."

"Don't worry, I didn't think it did." Her cheeks turned a bright pink as she put the car back into drive. "Because boys like you never kiss girls like me."

"Boys like me?" What did that mean?

"You're, like, from Hollywood."

"Technically Beverly Hills."

"Even worse. I'll bet the girls at your old school look like they belong on *Gossip Girl*." The wipers were really squealing this morning. He could hardly hear her voice, which wasn't as perky as it had been yesterday. "Which I so don't."

"I think you're cute."

"Maybe if the light's right. On a rare good day. I'm a nerd, Matt. I've been a nerd all my life."

"So?"

"So . . ." She shook her head. "I don't know. It doesn't matter. Let's just drop it, okay?"

"Fine." The temperature inside the car had dropped twenty degrees. "If it makes you feel better, like I said, it was a spur-of-the-moment impulse. It wasn't as if I was hitting on you for sex or anything like that."

"Oh, yeah." She smoothed a hand over her hair where his hands had been tangled in it. "Thanks. That totally works."

Matt didn't need to be Dr. Phil to realize she was being snarky again. Fuck. Was there anything more complicated than girls? She'd told him she was also driving

Jenny Longworth to school, and as they pulled up in front of the other girl's house, Matt decided scientists would unlock the code for cold fusion before any guy managed to figure out the mysterious workings of the female mind.

23

Claire was in the midst of tackling moving boxes when there was a knock on the door. She opened it to find a wide-shouldered man in a Gor-Tex jacket, jeans, and lumberjack boots standing on her front porch.

"Hi." Little lines fanned out from brown eyes as he smiled. "I've brought your basketball setup."

"I didn't order that." Though it was on her to-do list. Hopefully for this week. Okay, maybe next, given all the work she still had to do for her upcoming exhibition.

"Sorry. Dillon Slater sent me over with it. I guess he forgot to mention it."

"Yes. He did."

"Well, then." He held out a hand that had more than its share of nicks and scars. "I'm Lucas Chaffee."

"The contractor, right?"

"That's me. Dillon knew I had an old portable setup from before I installed a permanent one at my wife's and my place—"

"Your wife being Maddy Durand."

"Maddy Chaffee now," he corrected easily. "I see you're getting caught up on all the Shelter Bay stories."

"Dottie and Doris mentioned your marriage when I was in their shop yesterday and said I needed a contractor." And here he was. Could this be a portent that life was finally turning around?

"This is a way cool cottage, but it could use a little TLC. Not just for appearances, but for structure." He pulled a pocketknife out of the front pocket of his jeans and stuck it into one of the pillars holding up her moss-covered porch roof. "You've got dry rot."

"I read that on the inspection report." But she'd decided that even if she and Matt had to live in the Whale Song Inn while she had the cottage torn down and a new house built in its place, the land, which she'd bought at what would be seen as fire-sale prices in California, was worth it. "Which is ironic considering how wet it is here."

His answering grin was as charming as Dillon Slater's. But even if she hadn't known he was married, it wouldn't have strummed those chords the way Matt's coach's smile had. *Don't go there!* she instructed her rebellious mind, which had dreamed about the man last night. A hot, X-rated dream involving sex on the beach in the rain.

So not only was she subconsciously lusting after her child's teacher, whom she'd just met, but she was also on the verge of becoming a cliché—a sexually frustrated cougar. She'd bet her entire stash of beach glass that Dillon Slater was younger than her own thirty-three.

"The term's misleading." She was relieved when Lucas Chaffee's voice dragged her thoughts back to her rotting porch. Which wasn't the least bit sexy.

"It's actually caused by the brown rot fungus, but it does need moisture to get started. After that, it can take off and spread like, well, fungi. I'm really not here trolling for business. As I said, Dillon just wanted your son to have the basketball setup, but you'll want to get it taken care of as soon as possible."

"You come very well recommended, so yes, I'd like to discuss some options with you. But I've got a gallery showing shortly after Thanksgiving, so I'd rather not even think about doing any work until after that."

"The cottage has stood here since the thirties. I imagine it'll stand for another few weeks. What did the report say about the electrical?"

"That, fortunately, had been updated. And I had additional circuits installed in the garage for my equipment."

"Super." This time, while she still wasn't attracted to him in *that* way, his easy grin had her wondering if all the men in Shelter Bay were so sexy. She'd met Sax Douchett a few times while eating at Bon Temps, and he certainly fit in the hot category.

"I'll get started on the basketball rig. It's portable, with wheels, so Dillon figured you could set it up at the end of the driveway so your son can keep up with his practice shots. Then, once you get the house restored, you can get something more permanent."

"Coach Slater certainly seems to take a personal interest in his players."

"He's hands-on—that's for sure. But if you're worried that your son's getting special treatment because he's the Beverly Hills phenom who rode into town on a white horse to take the team to state, you needn't worry. I've watched Dillon with some of the other players whose families have been having a rough time during this recession. He's not one to play favorites."

"That's good to know. Though do people really expect Matt to solve all their problems?" And technically, he'd ridden into Shelter Bay in a black Lexus, but that wasn't the least bit pertinent to the discussion.

"Yeah. Some do. But you don't have to worry about Matt being under impossible pressure, because Dillon's been working overtime to keep expectations reasonable."

"I have the feeling high school basketball holds a higher priority here than it did in Beverly Hills."

He laughed. "Yeah. I'd say you're probably right. There's not a lot of movie premieres and charity balls to go to in Shelter Bay, so once the winter rain sets in, high school hoops are pretty much the top ticket in town."

As he went out to his truck and began taking out the backboard, rim, pole, and what appeared to be a brand-new net, Claire hoped the amiable, handsome contractor was right about Dillon Slater protecting her son from Shelter Bay's fans' expectations.

24

"Marry me," Ethan said as Phoebe lay in his arms the next morning.

She'd awoken still basking in the afterglow of their lovemaking and the feeling of sleeping in his arms. Then she'd remembered that horrid subpoena and it had felt as if an icy wave had washed over her.

"What?" Startled out of her worrisome thoughts, she looked up at him.

"You must have thought about it. I have."

"You have?" She'd hoped. But he hadn't said anything, and having loved the place they were already in, she hadn't wanted to risk their closeness by asking.

"I love you. And I'd gotten the impression you love me—"

"You know I do." She hitched up to a sitting position, and although he'd already seen and tasted every bit of her body, feeling suddenly modest, she tucked the flowered sheet beneath her arms. "More than I ever thought possible."

There'd been a time, while planning to escape her dangerous marriage alive, that she'd sworn to never,

ever, consider getting involved with any other man. Not that Ethan was just *any* man.

He sat up as well. "Then what's standing in our way?"

"I'm pregnant, for one thing."

"You wouldn't be the first pregnant bride to walk down the aisle. Hell, Kara was pregnant when she and Sax finally tied the knot this past summer. And you won't be the last." He ran callused fingers that had both soothed and aroused so wonderfully last night over her bare shoulder.

"I can't plan a wedding. I have a new job, a baby on the way, and now Peter's parents' custody grab to fight."

"There's no way they have any claim on your child."

"Their grandchild," she pointed out.

"Whom they don't deserve and shouldn't be allowed to be anywhere near because they raised a monster." He splayed his broad fingers over her sheet-covered stomach. "They're not going to take anything more away from you. I promise."

"I can't believe they're claiming I'd be a bad mother."

The complaint had accused her of illegally establishing a new identity by buying forged documents. It had gone on to accuse her of abandoning her family, adultery, and living with a man who was not her husband while still married.

The pages of legalese did not add that the only reason she'd been living in Ethan's farmhouse was because her husband—their son—had, on more than one occasion, threatened to kill her. And had even attempted to follow through on that threat. Which he would have succeeded in doing had it not been for this man sitting next to her in bed.

"They're grasping at straws. You'll get a lawyer who'll

prove that you'll be a far better and safer parent than they could ever think of being. Meanwhile, if you're bringing your baby home to a stable marriage, that's got to weigh heavily on your side."

"That's why you're proposing?"

He shook his head. "No. That's why I'm suggesting getting married now. In a perfect world, since this is a slow time for farming, I'd wait until the baby's born and you can fly again, then take you both to some tropical island where I can feed you breadfruit and make slow love to you all night long."

"When we're not feeding the baby," she said dryly, even as his suggestion sounded like, well, paradise.

"Time slows down in the islands," he said. "Even more than here in Shelter Bay. We'll have plenty of time. Meanwhile, getting married can checkmate your former in-laws, because although we both know you're going to be a dynamite mom, they won't be able to play that working-single-mother card against you. Your child would be born into a family with both a mother and a father."

It was so tempting to just let Ethan leap in to solve her problem. But she'd worked so hard to regain her independence; she didn't want to allow herself to crumble just when things got a little tough.

Okay, a lot tough.

"I want to marry you, Ethan." She took both his hands in hers and lifted them to her lips. "I've dreamed of it."

"That makes two of us. So why do I hear a *but*?"

"Because I don't want to let the Fletchers be the impetus to our getting married. That's giving them a power they don't deserve."

"That's one way of looking at it. But did you consider

that you're giving them power by letting them prevent us from having a life together?"

"I don't know." She was so torn.

"Am I at least allowed to make a suggestion?"

"Of course."

"Call Charity."

"How can a veterinarian help? Other than show any investigators who come around to check me out that I've already adopted a dog for my child?"

"Her stepdad's a hot-shot judge in Washington State. He probably knows someone back in Colorado who can make the Fletchers go away with a single phone call."

"Do you think?" Hope fluttered in her heart, which was torn between her very real fear of her former husband's powerful, wealthy parents, and her joy at being loved by Ethan Concannon.

"Absolutely." He kissed her again. "Trust me," he murmured against her mouth.

"I do," she said as his wonderfully clever lips caused her wounded heart to take wing.

25

Matt grabbed some utensils and a handful of paper napkins, then pushed his tray down the cafeteria line. Today he had a choice between spaghetti, which looked a lot like white worms drowning in a dark orange sauce, and a gray meat loaf that reminded him of one his mom had tried to make while his grandmother had been in the hospital. That had turned out as dry as Huntington Beach sand and as heavy as a brick. This didn't look any more promising.

The side dish was spinach boiled until it looked like the seaweed strung all over the beach below the cottage. And, seriously, orange Jell-O?

"What is this place?" he asked as he sat down across from Aimee. Although he was starving, he'd skipped the nuclear waste, and since the kid in front of him had snatched the last turkey club sandwich, he'd settled for an apple and milk. "A hospital or a school?"

"That's why I try to remember to check out the menu at least the night before. If there's nothing that looks like it was created by a human for human consumption, I brown-bag it." She reached into the brown bag in question. "My mom, who has the metabolism of a humming-bird, always packs enough for two people. Want a salmon salad sandwich with capers on whole wheat? Or sushi?"

"I'll take whatever you don't want, thanks."

"We'll split."

She took out a plastic container and had just divvied up the food onto one of the paper plates her mother had provided when Brendan Cooper, who'd initially compli-mented Matt on his shooting the previous day, stopped by the table.

"Hey, Templeton. What are you doing at this table?"

Matt looked across at Aimee, who appeared to be waiting for the answer. The other kids, he noticed, had taken a sudden interest in the nutrition information on their milk cartons.

"I like it here."

"Here?" Cooper looked down at the others at the table as if noticing them for the first time. "Seriously? Dude! You're a Dolphin." The way he said it had Matt half expecting a flare of trumpets from the band table across the room. "Which means you belong sitting with the rest of the dream team."

It was what Matt had wished for yesterday. It was also what he wanted at this moment. But he'd already hurt the first person who'd been nice to him. And not, he was sure, because it had been her job. But because she was a warm, caring person.

"You should go," Aimee said. "Didn't you tell me Coach Slater wants you all to bond as a team?"

"Yeah, but—"

"Go." She made a little shooing gesture. "I'll see you later in English."

Matt felt bad ditching Aimee, but it wasn't like he was

leaving her all alone. She'd probably been eating at the same table with the same kids all year.

"Look who I rescued from the geek gang," Brendan announced. "The Beverly Hills phenom himself."

Matt wondered if he'd have been so complimentary if Dirk the jerk were here. For some reason, although the thirty-minute lunch period was half over, his nemesis hadn't yet shown up to hold court over his minions.

"Hey, your mom made you sushi?" one of the kids asked, spotting the lunch Matt had brought with him.

"Aimee's mom made it. She shared it with me."

"Wow. You California guys move fast," Cooper said as Matt sat down in the space on the bench that Johnny scooted over to make for him.

"She was my assigned greeter yesterday. That's all."

"Good to hear. Because, like Coach said, we Dolphins need to keep up our image. You having a flat-chested brainiac as a girlfriend just doesn't cut it, dog. You know what I'm saying?"

Matt did. Back when he'd been rolling around on top of his homework beneath the pink-flowered canopy of way-hot Lila Greene's bed, he'd thought the same way.

"Aimee's a nice girl," he said at the same time Dick-head Dirk strolled in with the blonde, who today was wearing a pair of skintight jeans, a ribbed tank top, and a denim jacket studded with red rhinestone hearts. Today's UGGs were the color of cranberries.

Acting as if Matt were invisible, Dirk glanced down at the tray in front of Johnny. "What the hell is that stuff?"

"The sign said meat loaf."

"Well, then, you'd better eat it. Because no Dolphin ever lets his meat loaf." He basked in the expected laughter from his sycophants, then pulled the blonde against his side and grinned down at her. "Right, babe?"

She rolled her eyes and shook her head.

"You wore me out," he announced loudly. "I need nourishment." He pulled a five-dollar bill out of his wallet. "Why don't you go get me some chips and a drink?"

"That's not very a nourishing lunch," she said.

His eyes narrowed to slits. Dangerous slits. "Make it Doritos. And a Coke. And regular, not that diet stuff you drink."

Obviously pissed at his behavior, she nevertheless sashayed off.

"What do you think you're looking at?" Dirk asked Matt.

Apparently having become visible, Matt shrugged. "Just admiring the scenery," he said mildly. Along with every other guy at the table.

"Don't." With that warning lingering in the air, Dirk went to the far end of the table, swung his legs over the bench, sat down, and began talking to the French fry kid.

The buzz of conversation that had stopped when Matt had shown up at the dream team table resumed.

"So," Johnny, of the hyphenated name, said, "I hear the coach had dinner at your house last night."

"News gets around fast."

"It's a small town."

"Yeah, I've already figured that out for myself. But it wasn't like people are probably trying to spin it. He came over to tell my mom about my bad attitude. Then stayed to show my mom how to cook clams."

"Bad attitude?" Johnny took a bite of the meat loaf.

"Yeah. I let him know I didn't like coming off the

bench, which didn't go over real well. And you must have either a suicide wish or a cast-iron stomach."

"You spend enough years in foster care with people who are in it just for the money—which they don't spend on groceries for the kids living with them—you learn to eat just about anything you're lucky to get." He took a long, thirsty slurp of milk, which suggested that the meat loaf was as dry as it looked. "Guess you didn't do much Dumpster diving for dinner in Beverly Hills."

"You'd guess right. Do you have a problem with that?"

Skinny shoulders shrugged. "Some of the guys don't like the idea of a rich kid breezing in and winning a spot on the team."

"I may have lived in Beverly Hills, but I'm not rich. My grandmother got the house in a divorce. Since it was paid for, we stayed. Both she and my mom had to work. Even though Mom inherited the house and sold it to buy our place here, she's still not anywhere near rich."

"It wouldn't matter to me if you were. I hit the jackpot when I ended up here in Shelter Bay with my sister and we both finally got adopted. Which is how I got my last name. Since both my mom and dad had names they were already known by for their careers, they kept their own names, and then my sister and I got both."

"That's kind of a cool way of handling it," Matt said, thinking that the possibility of his taking on *his* father's name had been a moot point in his family.

"Yeah. Mom and Dad are both way cool. They even took us to Hawaii with them when they got married. So no way am I going to begrudge anyone else their good luck."

He picked up a forkful of greasy spinach, then put it

down again. Apparently even the former sometimes-starved foster kid had his limits. "I'm coming off the bench. But I'm not nearly as good as you. Hell, I was surprised to make varsity."

He was pushing the spinach around. "You want to come over and shoot hoops after practice? I heard you have this goal of three hundred shots a day, and since you don't have a setup at your place yet, maybe we can work out a trade. You can use the hoop my dad set up to keep sharp and maybe give me a few pointers on how to improve my game so I don't get busted down to JV."

Realizing that he had no idea if Aimee was thinking about sticking around like she did yesterday to drive him home—unlikely since he'd manage to insult her twice today—Matt glanced over at her table. And saw her looking at him. Had she been watching him this whole time? Or was it just some weird coincidence that their eyes would, like, meet across the crowded cafeteria?

She turned pink, the way she had when he'd kissed her, and forced a smile that was obviously fake. Then, giving him the indication that he'd turned invisible again, she picked up her tray and took it over to the recycle bins.

"Sounds like a plan," he said.

26

Frustrated that spending two hours in her hotshop hadn't resulted in anything she'd be willing to show, Claire had returned to the task of emptying moving boxes when there was another knock at the door.

This time four women were standing on her porch. Each carried a covered dish, which made her feel a bit as if she'd fallen down a rabbit hole and landed in the 1950s.

"Hi," the woman with gypsy hair falling in wild curls below her red knit cap said with a smile Claire had watched hundreds of times on television. "I'm Maddy Chaffee—"

"I know exactly who you are," Claire said. "I'm a huge fan of your show. Although I can't boil an egg, I cook vicariously through you."

The TV chef's laugh was even warmer in real life than on television. "Thank you. Maybe, once you get settled in, we can remedy that situation."

"Doris and Dottie suggested I attend classes at your school."

"We could definitely work something out," Maddy

assured her. She turned toward the other women. "This is Kara Conway Douchett. She's our sheriff and married to Sax Douchett, who owns Bon Temps."

"I've eaten there many times." Claire smiled at the very pregnant woman. "How clever of you to have married a man who can cook."

"I tell myself that every night," Kara agreed with a bold, friendly smile.

"And I'm Charity Tiernan," the third woman introduced herself. "I'm the town vet and I run a no-kill shelter. Just in case you happen to find yourself in the market for a dog or cat for your son."

The other women laughed.

"Watch out for her," Kara warned. "Before you know it, you'll end up adopting a pet you never knew you needed."

"Actually, since you mentioned it, I've been thinking about getting a dog." Matt had always wanted one, but her mother had been allergic to animals.

"You guys can drop by anytime. We live above the clinic. In the yellow Victorian on Harborview?"

"I've seen it. It's a lovely old house."

"Thanks. I fell in love with it on the Internet, and although it took some work, I love living there. Even better now that I've filled the rooms with a family. . . . If you want, you can just talk with your son about what type of dog you think you'd like and I'm sure we can find the perfect match for you. Unfortunately, due to the economy, we've no shortage of canine candidates."

"She's a great matchmaker," said the blond woman, who bore a striking resemblance to Malibu Barbie. "Which is how I ended up living with Butter, a rescued Persian."

"It took a while, but I wore her down," the vet said.

"I own Take the Cake," the cat owner said with a friendly smile. "I'm Sedona Sullivan."

"Oh, I was just in there yesterday and bought the best pie I've ever eaten."

"Thanks. I'm sorry I missed you. I was probably in back with my hands in dough. I keep thinking I should add pies to the sign, but then I'd have to redo the entire logo, and the former CPA in me cringes at the thought of dumping a design I already have so much invested in, so I've been procrastinating."

Belatedly realizing they were all still holding those dishes and standing on her porch, Claire said, "I'm sorry. Would you please come in?"

"We'd love to," Charity said, "if you're sure we're not interrupting anything."

"We mainly just wanted to welcome you to town," Kara said.

"And feed you," Maddy added. "We all know first-hand how stressful moving can be, so we thought you might like a few meals."

"*Like* is a major understatement," Claire said, resisting throwing her arms around all of them for a huge group hug. "If you don't mind a mess, please come in. I still have some pie left, and I do know how to make coffee and tea." Not that it was difficult to put the little cups in the machine and hit the brew button.

"Moving's always a mess," Kara said. "Fortunately, Sax and I agreed that we're never moving again. And I, for one, never turn down pie."

"But we can't stay long," Charity said as they entered the house and put their dishes on a counter cluttered with boxes. "I know you have a show in Portland soon, so you'll probably want to get back to work. And Kara's got a doctor's appointment."

"Not for another forty-five minutes," the sheriff said. "And it doesn't take more than twenty minutes to get anywhere in town." She sat at the round table. "The trick will be getting back onto my feet." She frowned down toward her black boots. "Which I can no longer see."

"When are you due?" Claire asked.

"Although I feel and probably look like one of Shelter Bay's whales, not for another three weeks."

"I remember when I was pregnant with Matt. That last month seemed to take forever."

"Doesn't it? It was the same way with Trey, my son," Kara agreed. "Of course, at the time my first husband was deployed, and I was eighteen, alone, and scared to death."

"I was eighteen, too," Claire shared as she cut the remaining pie into five pieces. "But I had my mother, who stepped in and helped a lot."

"My mother missed Trey's birth," Kara said. "Since I got pregnant in high school, then eloped, I wasn't exactly her favorite person at the time."

"I'm sorry." Claire's mother had been a rock. Only now was she beginning to realize how much she'd depended on her.

"That's okay." Kara shrugged. "She and I had a double wedding this past summer, so life moves on."

"That's nice. I lost my mom this summer. I can't count how many times a day I miss her."

"I'm so sorry." When Kara's eyes misted up, Charity reached into her purse, pulled out a Kleenex, and handed it to her. "Thanks." She dabbed at her eyes even as she managed a crooked smile. "Hormones," she complained.

"I remember those well."

"Wow," Sedona said, looking out the window at the shipwreck. "You've got a dynamite view from here."

"That was my main reason for buying the cottage," Claire said as she placed the plates of pie on the table. "I knew it was going to take a major renovation.

"Fortunately," she said to Maddy, "your husband comes highly recommended."

"He's always been good with his hands," the chef said, which drew knowing laughs from the other women.

"Maddy and Lucas were high school sweethearts," Charity volunteered.

"It was like something out of one of those old teen romance movies," Kara said. "Lucas was the rich summer boy and Maddy, who'd been orphaned, was the herb farmer's granddaughter. Everyone thought for sure they were going to get married; then Lucas made the bonehead move of breaking up with her."

"Well, technically I broke up with him. Which was what he wanted me to do," Maddy said, shaking her head. "Because I wanted to get married and he wanted me to stick to my dream of going to Europe to expand my culinary skills. . . . Fast-forward, I ran off, heartbroken, then later made the mistake of marrying the wrong man."

"I—" Claire slammed her mouth shut so hard her teeth rattled, but she knew the damage had already been done.

"You know." Maddy smiled. "Don't worry, just about everyone on the planet has seen my former husband's sex video."

"I haven't," Claire said honestly. "But I did hear about it."

"It was not a fun time. But it turned out well, because I came home to lick my wounds and figure out what I was going to do with the rest of my life. What I never expected was for Lucas to be here, too."

"He'd agreed to add an addition to her grandmother's farmhouse." Sedona continued the story, patting her heart. "And the sparks were still there."

"Maddy didn't want to admit it," Charity said.

"But it sure was fun watching him wear her down," Kara said. "One of the things you'll learn," she confided in Claire, "is that living in a small town requires us to invent our own entertainment."

"And Lucas and Maddy definitely provided a lot last spring," Charity finished up.

"I met your husband this morning," Claire told Maddy as she joined the other women at the table. "He had some great ideas."

"He always does. I was kidding about the hands thing. But he really is an excellent contractor."

"From the work he did at the Dancing Deer Two, I can see that," Claire agreed.

She took orders for three cups of coffee. Kara had come prepared with her own tea bag of an herbal blend from Lavender Hill Farm.

"Sax became the caffeine police the minute I told him I was pregnant," she said with sigh. She took a bite of the pie and moaned. "Oh, my God. That's so good! And fortunately, I'm eating for two, so calories don't count. That's my story and I'm sticking to it."

The others laughed, and for the next ten minutes Claire enjoyed the type of girl talk she couldn't remember having in, well, perhaps going all the way back to school. Her days had consisted of work and having lunch with her mother, who, as a children's book illustrator, also worked at home. She did get away on sales trips and to trade shows, but while there was a social aspect to those occasions, they were also focused on business.

"Did Matt or Dillon tell you about the basketball team crabfest?" Charity asked.

"No. Is that what it sounds like?"

"If it sounds like a fund-raiser, you're right. It's also this Friday night at Bon Temps. It's like a typical school spaghetti supper, but with a local coastal twist. The menu is boiled Dungeness crab, salads, bread, and desserts. Along with soft drinks, coffee, and tea."

Terrific. Wasn't that just what she needed? "I can't begin to handle spaghetti. Let alone crab. I probably would've given Matt food poisoning last night if Dillon Slater hadn't steamed the clams I bought at Farraday's."

Sedona arched a blond brow. "Wow, that was fast work on his part. Isn't he too cute for words?"

"Really?" Claire pretended nonchalance. "I didn't notice."

The obvious lie caused the other women to laugh.

"Seriously," she insisted as looks were exchanged. "He just came over to talk about Matt's place on the team. Then my clams began crying—"

"Oh, that's so creepy when they do that," Kara said. "I grew up eating them, but I'm still always afraid that when I open the refrigerator, there's going to be a giant clam waiting to suck me in. Just like some old black-and-white horror movie."

"I know! I felt exactly the same way."

"Great minds," Kara said. "Dottie and Dorothy told me I'd like you. And they were right." There was a trill from her purse. She dug out her phone, then sighed as she read the caller ID. "It's Sax."

"There's a surprise," Maddy said.

"I think that's a record," Sedona said. "It's been at least ten minutes since he called."

"It's because of those damn Braxton Hicks," Kara muttered. "He won't stop hovering." She hit the button, then rolled her eyes as she listened to what Claire took to be husbandly words of concern.

"No, darling. I'm fine. Really . . . Yes, of course I'll call you if I go into actual labor. But don't hold your breath, because it isn't going to be for another three weeks. . . . No, really? . . . Thanks for letting me know. Whatever would we do without that expectant father book? And yes, I know I have a doctor's appointment today, and if you don't hang up and get back to work, I'm going to be late.

"No. I won't speed. I'm the sheriff, remember? It'd be humiliating to be stopped by one of my deputies. Goodbye. I'll see you this evening. Thanks to Charity bringing up the basketball crabfest, I'm now craving Jake's butter-roasted crab, so how about you, Trey, and I going out to the Crab Shack for dinner? . . . Great . . . Love you, too."

She hung up and shook her head with exasperation. "Thanks to my beloved husband's news flash, I now know that babies have been known to come early."

"You should call Phoebe," Maddy suggested. "In case Dr. Parrish failed to inform her of that possibility."

"Speaking of Phoebe," Charity said, "has anyone spoken with her today?"

"No. She asked yesterday if she could take the day off to stay home to help the new dog she was adopting from you settle in."

"That's just it," Charity said. "She never showed up."

"What?" Sedona and Maddy said at the same time.

"That's not like her at all," Maddy said. "She's always very dependable.

"Oh, she wasn't exactly a no-show. Ethan called and said something had come up and they'd have to put off the dog adoption for few days. Which is fine, since I don't exactly have a line outside the door waiting to take the dogs home. But there was something in his voice. . . ."

She glanced over at Claire. "I'm sorry. It's rude to be talking about someone you don't even know."

"I've seen her on a couple of your shows," Claire said. "She's very good."

"She is. You'll hear the story, so we might as well fill you in."

As the women told her about the former Stephanie Fletcher, now Phoebe Tyler, Claire realized what a strong bond they'd formed. She hoped that their visiting was their way of letting her know that their circle could include one more.

"I just realized we got sidetracked and I never finished filling you in on the crabfest," Charity said. "You don't have to worry about cooking. Jake, from the Crab Shack, is a member of the boosters, so he boils and donates the crab.

"The boosters pay for the drinks, and Sax is not only supplying the space, but tossing in some popcorn shrimp with his famous Come-Back sauce as an appetizer. Also, Sedona's sweet enough to supply the cupcakes, Lavender Hill Farm kicks in the salad, and the Grateful Bread supplies the rolls and bread. All the families have to do is buy tickets, show up, and let the boys serve them dinner."

"I can handle that," Claire said, trying to imagine Matt serving her dinner. "I'm glad you let me know. It'd be just like Matt these days to spring it on me ten minutes before we were due at the school."

"Give him time," Charity said. "Gabe and I adopted two children last year. There was an adjustment period, since both Johnny and his sister, Angel, had practically grown up in foster care. But Johnny's making honor roll and he's on the team with Matt. He says your son's a phenom."

"So they say. His dream is to get to the pros, though I'd much rather have him concentrate on his schooling and get an education. Which is why I was so grateful Coach Slater gave him a wake-up call about grades and scholarships last night."

"From what I hear from Johnny, Dillon's a great teacher," Charity said. "He's smart and clever, and he really likes kids."

"Partly because he's still part kid himself," Kara suggested.

"That's what makes him fun," Charity countered. "How many other men do you know who set off cannons?"

"Not my husband, fortunately," Kara said. "Considering I like Sax having all ten fingers."

That said, she pushed herself out of the chair. "I'm afraid we have to get going, but it was lovely meeting you, and although I know you're busy, I do hope we'll be able to get together over the holidays. . . .

"Oh! That reminds me of what I wanted to ask you. I swear, my brain's in a fog these days."

"Pregnancy brain," Claire said. "I remember it well."

"The main reason we came here today, along with bringing you some meals for while you settle in, is so I could introduce myself and invite you to Thanksgiving dinner."

"Oh, that's very nice, but I wouldn't want to put you out."

"Don't be silly. We have a huge house we're just rattling around in. Sax and his brothers will be doing all the cooking. They actually enjoy it," she said with a roll of her expressive eyes.

"I've already invited some other people who don't have family here, and since this will undoubtedly be a difficult year for you, not having your mother, it might be good for your son to have some other kids around."

"Gabe and I'll be there with Johnny and Angel," Charity volunteered. "When Matt gets sick of all us old fogies, he can go shoot hoops with Johnny."

Claire had planned to get a takeout turkey dinner from the market's deli. But Charity had a point. It would be good for Matt and her to start having a social life.

"I'd love to come," she decided. "Thanks for inviting me."

"It'll be fun," Kara said simply as Maddy helped her slip back into her coat.

Claire stood in the doorway watching the SUV until it had turned onto the road and disappeared around a tight S curve. For the first time since arriving in Shelter Bay, she was actually feeling optimistic.

27

"I like her," Charity said as they drove toward the bridge to return to town.

"She is nice, isn't she?" Kara agreed.

"Though it's sort of amazing that her son is fifteen years old and she's never learned to cook," Maddy said.

"Not everyone cooks," Charity said. "My mother's gone her entire life without knowing how to feed herself. And Marcy Curtis said that Claire and her son lived with her mom, who died this past year after a lengthy bout with cancer. Maybe she'd been their family cook."

"Well, we'll still have to get her up to speed," Maddy decided. "If I have to give her private lessons in her house."

"Well, if I were you I'd wait until after Lucas replaces that ancient stove," Sedona said. "Maybe it's a good thing she doesn't cook, because she could well burn the place down. . . .

"That was clever how you worked your way into sneakily inviting her to Thanksgiving dinner," she said to Kara.

"I wasn't being sneaky. I was totally telling the truth about inviting people who don't have family."

"Ah, but I grew up Catholic," Maddy said, "where we're taught all about the sin of omission. Which you pretty much committed by not mentioning that Dillon Slater happens to be the other person you invited to dinner."

"It was also clever how you conveniently failed to mention that he asked you to invite her," Charity pointed out.

"So? And here I thought you, of all people, would approve of matchmaking," Kara shot back. "Is there anyone but Claire Templeton left in town without a dog or cat?"

"There are a few holdouts," the vet said dryly. "And I do approve. Which was why I was complimenting you on how you slipped it in."

Kara's phone, which she'd stuck in the cup holder, rang again. She glanced down at the caller ID and grinned.

"Would you take that," she asked Sedona, who was riding shotgun, "and tell Coach Slater that his date for Thanksgiving is set?"

28

Matt had stopped by his locker after lunch to get his English textbook when an amazing pair of breasts came bouncing toward him. They were attached to Dickhead's blonde.

"Hi," she said, a little breathlessly, as if she'd been working out. Or maybe—he thought back to what her boyfriend had implied earlier—having sex in Dirk the Jerk's backseat. "I'm Taylor Bennington."

"Like Bennington Ford?"

"That'd be it." Her glossy lips smiled, revealing blinding, perfect white teeth. "Daddy has another dealership in Boise. When this one came available last year, we moved here so he could get it started." She tossed her hair in a sexy way. "It sucks being the new kid in school, doesn't it?"

"Yeah. But I doubt you had any problems." He thought back to what Aimee had said about the girls at BHHS. She'd been mostly right. Except for a small minority, most of them had looked a lot like Taylor Bennington.

"Isn't that sweet of you to say?"

As a group of freshmen plowed by like a school of minnows keeping tightly together for defense in a sea of sharks, she bumped against him. It *could* have been an accident. The way her chest stayed plastered against his definitely wasn't.

"I'm going to be your cupcake girl," she said.

"Cupcake girl?" *Was that, like, a euphemism for something else?*

"The cheer squad always brings cupcakes for the players on the away games. We're each assigned players."

She treated him to another dazzling smile that could've lit up the rainy day from the California border up to the Washington State line.

"I asked for you." Eyes as blue as a sunny summer sky back home sparkled. "I hope you're not one of those health nuts who hate cupcakes."

"What's not to love about cupcakes?"

"That's exactly what I always say. Especially since the cupcakes at Take the Cake are purely orgasmic." The thought of Taylor Bennington in the hot, noisy throes of orgasm nearly took the top of Matt's head off. "What's your favorite kind?"

"Kind?"

"Cupcakes. My favorite is Better Than Sex."

"That sounds good to me." Though he had no empirical evidence—yet—he seriously doubted *any* cupcake could be better than sex.

"Great. That's what I'll get you, then. And surprise you with some other flavors. Also, the other reason I wanted to talk with you is that my parents are going to be in Oahu for some Ford dealers' convention the night after the team's season opener," she said. "So naturally, I'm having a party at my place. Please tell me you'll come."

Matt thought about his mother being away in Portland that night. He knew she'd hit the roof if she found out he was going to a party that was going to be totally lacking in adult supervision. But, hey, *she* was going to be out of town. And what she didn't know she couldn't worry about.

"Sweet," he said.

"Oh, great." She clapped her hands, then rose up on the toes of those red UGGs and kissed his cheek.

Matt was debating turning his head, just the slightest bit, and kissing her mouth when the bell rang.

"Well, I'd better get to class," she said. "Mr. Petterson is always so cranky when I'm late. It's like he's in permanent PMS. Sometimes I wonder if he must've been a girl in another life. The other day he told me I was flirting with an EMD. I mean, is that petty, or what?"

"EMD?"

"Early morning detention." She sighed heavily, which did interesting things to her breasts. "You know, like *The Breakfast Club* movie? But without the dancing and the pot."

She waggled a good-bye with her fingers, then rushed off, allowing him to finally touch his cheek where she'd left behind a glossy imprint.

It was the same type of impulsive, casual kiss Matt had given Aimee this morning. Even less of one, since only the corner of her glossy pink lips had gotten anywhere near his.

As she melded into the crowd dashing to classrooms and he sprinted off to class, Matt told himself that she'd just been being friendly to the new kid. It didn't mean anything.

Did it?

29

Although Claire had had good intentions of getting at least two pieces done when she entered the studio, concentration was proving impossible.

The trick, she knew, was to watch the glass, listen to it. Let it speak to her. Let *it* tell her what it wanted to be. Instead of trying to force the glowing, living material to gather into what *she* wanted to create.

Unfortunately, her mind kept drifting to Dillon Slater. Focus proved elusive as, instead of paying attention to the pale glass forming on the end of her pipe, she was remembering last night's hot dream. But she had no business imaging Matt's coach making love to her while the winter rain pounded on the roof.

Finally, after spending another futile two hours in the sweltering studio, Claire decided she was getting nowhere fighting the glass.

Frustrated, she looked into the fire hole, watching as all the failed attempts bled and died on the glowing red coals, melting down into a single mass. The thing to do, she decided, as she poured the water bottle she kept for hydrating—vital in such dry heat—over her head, was to expand her horizons.

Experience had taught her, going back to her early days of jewelry making, that when her muse grew stubbornly silent, nothing came from trying to force it.

She was in and out of the shower in less than five minutes. She blew her hair halfway dry, braided it, and went out to explore her new home.

Unfortunately, a quick glance out the windows revealed that while she'd been struggling to create something good enough to show in Portland, another storm had blown in from the sea, causing the rain to drum on the mossy roof and pound against the windows like a shower of stones. It was not a day for beachcombing or strolling along Shelter Bay's colorful waterfront.

As she took out the newcomer welcome packet Marcy Curtis had given her, a brochure for the aquarium in the town of Newport, just south of Shelter Bay, caught her eye. Grabbing her sketch pad, some pencils, and her Gor-Tex jacket and umbrella, she was headed out the door when her cell phone rang.

"Hey," she said, trying to hold down her anxiety over why her son might be calling. "What's up?"

He had a friend. A teammate he was shooting hoops with after school. And—hallelujah!—better yet, it just happened to be Charity's adopted son.

"Of course I'll pick you up at Johnny's house. His mother dropped by with some friends—and, get this, some already cooked meals for us—so I know exactly where it is. Just give me a call when you're ready. And, Matt, honey . . . have a great time."

Feeling as if a huge weight had been lifted off her

shoulders, Claire drove down the coast road, and ten minutes later she was immersed in the magical land of the sea. At one exhibit, the surf ebbed and flowed against docks and piers and tide pools much like the ones on the beach below the cottage. Taking out her pad, she quickly sketched the anemones and sea pens, which resembled bright pink and orange old-fashioned ostrich-feather plume pens.

Continuing on the glassed-in passage, through the dark and quiet canyons of the reef, through the sparkling waters out into the vast blue expanse of open sea, she reveled in the colors of blood stars, bat stars, brilliant sea urchins, and ghostly transparent moon jellyfish that appeared to have been created from liquid, amorphous glass.

Dazzled by the colors swimming in her head, she stopped in to a gift shop to purchase postcards and a photography book of what she'd just walked through. With her muse once again fulfilled and excited, she couldn't wait to get back home to work.

"That's a stunning necklace," the woman behind the counter said as she rang up the sale.

"Thank you." Claire had tumbled the deep aqua sea glass oval making up the pendant until it was smooth and translucent, then wrapped it in swirling silver strands that represented the power of the surf during a winter storm such as today's.

"May I ask where you bought it?"

"I made it."

Having been about to hand Claire her credit card receipt to sign, the woman paused.

"You're an artist?"

"Jewelry and blown glass."

"Isn't that interesting?" She handed over the receipt. "Do you do glass whales and paperweights and such?"

"Although I enjoy them, my own work is larger. And I think my muse must have a very low boredom threshold, because I've never been able to make the same piece twice."

"Do you sell your jewelry locally?"

"I'm at several stores in Portland, Salem, and Eugene, but since I was living in Los Angeles until last week, I never really had time to establish a market in the smaller towns. Though I have sold pieces to the Dancing Deer Two in Shelter Bay."

"I love that shop," the woman said. "And the cookies are great, too. Would you be interested in placing any items on consignment? I'm manager here, and I just know they'd sell like hotcakes. Or even better, crab cakes."

Fifteen minutes later, Claire was headed back up the coast road, with a new consignment contract in her purse and dozens of shimmering, colorful images dancing in her head.

The rain stopped just as she reached the sign welcoming her to Shelter Bay. As she passed the next sign declaring the town to be home to Navy Cross winner Sax Douchett, a double rainbow, sparkling like jewels in the light of the sun that had broken through the pewter clouds, appeared in front of her car.

Deciding to take that as a positive omen, she drove across the bridge heading toward the cottage that was beginning to feel more like home every day.

30

Phoebe should have been floating on air. She'd spent the night making love to a wonderful, sexy man. But unfortunately, in the cold light of the mid-November day, reality had returned.

"I swear, he's like a shark," she said as she paced the apartment floor the following afternoon. "Just when we think it's safe to go back into the water, there he is."

"No," Ethan said firmly. "He's not."

"Well, maybe not him. But his parents. Which is even worse, since they have the bottomless pockets."

"But you have right on your side. And the law. And"—he bent his head and brushed his lips against hers—"you have friends in high places."

She laughed at the twist on one of his favorite songs. Had it only been last week they'd been dancing to the Astoria band Sax had brought in for country night at Bon Temps? As if on the same wavelength, he gathered her into his arms, which wasn't so easy to do with the baby between them, and began twirling her around the floor, singing the lyrics to one of Garth Brooks' signature songs in her ear.

"I can't stay upset when I'm with you," she said, the worries that had begun bedeviling her again sliding away as he crooned about slipping down to the Oasis.

"That's the point." He cupped her butt—which was considerably larger than it had been when they'd met—and slowed the dance to a sexy sway. "You brought sunshine back into my life, Phoebe."

His breath fanned her hair as he nuzzled her neck. "I'd put my feelings into cold storage after losing Mia and Max. If it hadn't been for the farm, which I knew Mia would want me to make a success, I probably would've let myself spiral down into a deep black pit of self-pity.

"So I threw myself into making it the best organic farm in the state."

"The country," she said.

She felt his smile right below her ear, where his lips had been stimulating a now familiar warmth. "You're prejudiced," he said.

"True." She lifted her arms, twined them around his neck. "But it's also true that Blue Heron Farm sets the standard."

She'd once wondered if she could allow herself to fall in love with a man who'd loved another woman so deeply. Over the months she'd come to realize that it was precisely because Ethan had been the kind of man to fully give his heart that she could give her carefully guarded one to him.

He'd loved Mia. Deeply. But now she was blessed to have him love her. Just as deeply. And, although her child wasn't one of his blood, he'd assured her while they'd been waiting for Charity to arrive that he would love her son as if he were his own.

"I have an idea."

"About Peter's parents?" They'd already spoken with Charity, who had immediately promised to call her step-father for advice.

"No. About us." He brushed his lips against hers. "We're not going to let them into our lives any more than we have to. I called Charity again. She said she could meet us at the shelter this evening. So what would you say to going out to dinner? Then dog shopping."

How did he always know exactly the right thing to say—and do? Phoebe had quit believing in soul mates when she'd given up on Prince Charming. But Ethan Concannon had her rethinking the concept.

She went up on her toes and kissed him with all the love and happiness that was filling her heart.

"I'd say yes."

31

"You live above a vet clinic?" Matt asked as Johnny pulled into the driveway of the yellow house overlooking Shelter Bay. He was starting to feel like the only kid in town without a car, which really sucked.

"Yeah. But it's soundproof, so it's cool. And the living quarters are totally separated from my mom's work. You know," he said, "they're going to make you choose a volunteer job at school."

"Aimee Pierson told me. I guess she works at some doctor's clinic on Saturdays."

"Yeah. Dr. Parrish. She's our family doctor and is pretty cool. . . . Anyway, do you like animals?"

"What kind of animals?"

"Dogs and cats?"

"Sure. I've always wanted a dog, but I've never been able to have one because my grandmother was allergic."

"That's the pits," Johnny said as they got out of the Ford Escape crossover with HARBORVIEW VETERINARY CLINIC painted on the doors. "Maybe you can get one now. But meanwhile, maybe you might want to volunteer with me. Along with being a vet, my mom runs a no-kill shelter. Since she's really picky about fitting the right animal with the right family, there're always some dogs living there.

"I work Saturday mornings, cleaning the runs and feeding and bathing the animals. It sounds like scut work, but it's actually kind of neat, because they're always so happy to see you."

Matt had already been trying to figure out what he was going to do. This sounded like a good possibility. "Maybe," he said, thinking out loud, "if I found the right dog, my mom would be so happy I was doing something useful, she'd let me bring it home."

"No sweat." Johnny's grin split his freckled face. "You find a dog you want, and we'll get my mom on it. Because no one can resist her. She's like a friendly bull-dozer."

At that moment, the bulldozer in question arrived home, pulling up beside them. "Hi, boys," she called out as she jumped down from the driver's seat, then went around to open the back passenger door. "How was practice?"

"It was okay," Johnny said with a shrug as a little girl who looked about six climbed off her booster seat in back and came running toward them. Her shiny flowered raincoat was open, revealing a pink tutu and Tinker Bell T-shirt over bright green leggings. "I need to work on my shooting. Matt here is going to help me. This is Matt Templeton."

"I figured that out," she said with a warm smile that had *welcome* all over it. "You favor your mother."

"You think?" He'd sometimes wondered, as he'd shot past his mother and grandmother in height, if he might look like his dad. Not that he cared.

"It's mostly in the eyes," she decided, giving him a longer look. "They're a different color, of course, but they're very similar. And expressive."

Except for Dirk the Dickhead, everyone in Shelter Bay seemed really, really friendly. It was, in some ways, beginning to freak Matt out a little bit.

The little girl tugged on the hem of his jacket. "I'm Angel," she piped up. Her huge grin revealed a missing front tooth. "I learned to do a *sauté* in dance class today. Do you want to see?"

"Sure."

"Great!" With that she took off, doing circles of running leaps around the front yard, arms outstretched as if she was trying to fly, her pink boots making squishy sounds on the rain-soaked lawn.

"I met your mother today," the vet said.

"Yeah. She told me."

"It must be wonderful to have so much talent. If I hadn't really liked her, I'd be envious."

"You have talent with animals," Johnny jumped in loyally. "She's even better than that dog whisperer guy on TV," he told Matt.

"My son exaggerates," she said with a laugh, reaching out to ruffle his carrot red hair.

Matt would've died on the spot if his mom had done that in front of any guy he knew, but he figured since Johnny had been a foster kid, he was probably more grateful than a lot of kids might be. Kids like himself, he admitted, thinking that maybe he'd been tougher on his mom than he should've been. She had been trying to do the right thing. Even if she'd screwed up his life in the process.

"Some movie stars have bought her stuff," he said, not wanting to seem to be lacking in family loyalty.

"I know. I was at a wedding where Mary Joyce gave a close friend of mine a lovely glass piece your mother made as a gift. You must be very proud of her." She shared another of those warm smiles. "She's certainly proud of you."

"Matt thinks that maybe he might want to volunteer at the shelter," Johnny said.

"We can always use an extra hand," she said. "And it'd also be convenient for you to get to know the dogs, since your mother said she's been thinking that the two of you could use one."

"Really?" That was news to him.

"Oops." She shook her head. "Don't tell her I spilled the beans, okay?"

"No problem."

He was going to get a dog? He hoped she wasn't planning on adopting some foo-foo dog that she'd dress up like a doll. A lot of his friends' mothers had ones like that back in L.A. Some even carried them around in their designer purses like accessories. He'd die if any of the guys saw him walking some fluffy puffball.

"How would you guys like a snack before you play?" She took a pink box from the backseat of her SUV. "I picked up some cupcakes."

"From Take the Cake!" Angel said as she came leaping up to them and switched to spinning like a top. "This is my pirouette," she informed them all. "But it's hard not to get dizzy."

"Did you get chocolate peanut butter?" Johnny asked his mother, catching his sister to steady her when she began to wobble.

"Absolutely. I wouldn't dare come home without it, since it's your favorite. But I also got a mix because

Gabe likes the carrot, and although I got your text about bringing Matt home, I didn't know what he'd want.

"You take Dancing Queen into the house before she gets so dizzy she throws up that lemon custard cake she ate at the shop," she said, handing the box to Matt to carry. "I've got to run into the clinic and check on a cat I spayed this morning."

"That's so she can't have any kittens," Angel said, having to looking at Matt upside down because Johnny had thrown her over his shoulder, fireman-style. "Mama says there are too many homeless animals already. So we shouldn't be adding to the population."

"Makes sense to me," Matt said as he followed them into the kitchen.

Twenty minutes later, Angel was busy with a Disney princess coloring book while their mother began briskly getting things out of cupboards to start dinner. Which made Matt miss his grandmother. Not for the cooking, which he'd come to realize she was really good at, but just for the fact that somehow she'd been the one who'd made them a family. He knew his mom was his mom. And she was always the one who'd set down the rules about bedtimes and making sure he did his homework and stuff, but his grandmother had always seemed like the glue that had held them all together.

And now she was gone and he and his mom were getting tossed about in the same way that ship that wrecked beneath their small, ugly house must have been tossed before it crashed up onto the rocks.

But hey, they were getting a dog. He just hoped he'd be able to talk her into a real dog. Like a lab. Or a boxer.

They took turns shooting as they warmed up. Matt

dribbled the ball twice, then put up a fifteen-foot jump shot that sailed through the net.

"I'm glad we're not playing for money," Johnny said after he tried to duplicate the shot five times, missing four of those attempts, one of which sent the ball rolling into a bed of winter brown bushes. "Because I'd be in a world of hurt."

"It's okay to miss. Even the great ones do. The trick is to make sure you're still in place to make the shot when you do. . . . I'm going to try to miss, and you try to get the rebound, okay?"

"Ready."

Matt stood at the end of the sports court Johnny's father had built and drove toward the basket, throwing up a jumper that hit the rim. Before Johnny could even launch himself up to catch it, Matt had grabbed the ball in midair and stuffed it into the basket.

"He shoots! He scores!"

"That was amazing," Johnny said.

"I was lucky." Which was only partly true. The other part was all the hours he'd put in practicing controlling his own rebounds. "The trick is to never take your eye off the ball. That's where you have an advantage over the other players."

"Well, now that you're on the team, I think the Dolphins are going to have an advantage over all the other teams in the league," Johnny said.

As they practiced the rebounds from the left, right, and center, Matt felt an inner click. He was getting his groove back. And it felt really freaking good.

They were sitting on the front porch, waiting for Matt's mom to show up, when Johnny said, "I saw you with Taylor today. At your locker."

"Yeah." Matt scuffed at a worn place on the steps. "She invited me to a party."

"You know she's having sex with Dirk, right?"

"So he wants everyone to believe." Matt hadn't liked the way the douche had treated her at lunch. She deserved better.

"Oh, she is. Totally. Not that there's anything wrong with that. I'm just saying that he's already pissed about you being on the team. And being better than him. You might want to tread carefully."

"Thanks for the advice."

"No problem." Johnny was tossing the pebbled ball back and forth between his hands. "You ever have sex?" he asked casually.

"Sure." When Johnny shot him a look, Matt decided that friendships, and this looked like it might turn into one, shouldn't be based on lies. "Sort of. Not exactly. I got to second base."

"Better than striking out," Johnny said.

"You ever have sex?"

"Yeah." His tone was flat, with none of the boast Dirk had shown off when he'd showed up late for lunch.

"Was it great?"

"No. One time was with an older girl in a foster home. I was thirteen; she was seventeen. I had no clue what I was doing and felt like a total failure when she laughed at me for lasting all of thirty seconds.

"My next time was two years later. With a stay-at-home foster mom. She'd call me in sick, and we'd do it while her husband was at work. It lasted about three months before I got moved to a different place. Looking back on it, I think my social worker had suspicions about all my excused absences from school."

"Was she hot?"

"I guess." He frowned at the memory. "At least she thought so."

"Wow. That's, like, every guy's fantasy."

"It's probably better as a fantasy. Because in real life it pretty much sucked. . . . But here's the only reason I'm telling you about it. Because the one thing those times taught me is that sex should be important. Any girl who's willing to have sex with me someday is getting a flawed guy. A guy whose total sexual experience is pretty much humiliation, fear, and guilt."

"I think most guys are probably afraid. At least the first time," Matt said, wondering what the woman looked like and thinking that still didn't sound so bad.

"Probably. But if it's a first time for both of you, then you've created a memory. Maybe one you can build on. Maybe not.

"I'm not saying that everyone should do the promise ring, celibate thing. Just that the same way I suspect moms tell their daughters not to give themselves away too easily, it's probably the same for guys. But nobody talks about it that way, especially guys in sports, because playing ball is all about being macho. But the one thing my dad has taught me is that being a man is also about respect. For other people, and yourself.

"Whew." He blew out a long breath. "Sorry. I didn't mean to give you a lecture. I was mostly wanting to warn you Dirk has pretty much claimed Taylor for his own this year. You might not want to get in the middle of that."

"I appreciate the warning." But Matt couldn't deny that after the way the guy had tried to freeze him out of the team, taking his girl, even if they didn't end up having sex, could be sweet. "Thanks."

"Like I said, no problem." They bumped fists just as Matt's mom pulled up in the Lexus. Matt ran to the SUV, then paused after opening the door. "That thing you said, about the girl getting a flawed guy?"

"Yeah?"

"I think you're wrong about that."

Worrying that he'd just opened them up to a weird bromance thing, Matt climbed into the passenger seat and closed the door.

As they drove away, he looked back through the side window and saw Johnny, still sitting all alone on the porch, bouncing the basketball.

32

"So did you have a good time?" Claire asked as she headed down Harborview, back toward the bridge.

"It was okay," Matt mumbled. "His mom brought home cupcakes."

"That's nice."

"Yeah."

Could the conversation be any more strained? Claire wondered. Next they'd be talking about the weather. Which would be rain. Rain. And more rain. Wouldn't that be stimulating?

"She told me about the crabfest when she and the others dropped by today."

"Sorry. I forgot about it."

"That's okay. It sounds like fun."

"If you like crab."

Which Matt always had. But apparently he was still determined not to like anything about Shelter Bay. "She also mentioned that she runs a no-kill shelter."

"Yeah." She felt him shoot a glance her way, but when she looked toward him, he quickly turned his head and stared out the window. "I'm thinking about doing my volunteer work there."

"That'd be a great choice."

Claire didn't add that she'd feel more comfortable knowing that the vet and her husband would be keeping an eye on him. Heaven knows, having adopted two foster children, they must be accustomed to dealing with kids with issues.

"I was thinking," she said carefully, her fingers tightening on the steering wheel, "that maybe we could adopt one."

"A dog?" She could feel him looking at her again but this time kept her own gaze glued to the road.

"Yes. Unless you'd rather get a cat."

"Cats are okay, I guess. But dogs are cooler."

"I agree. I always wanted a dog," she confided truthfully. "But Mom's allergies ruled them out. I did have a goldfish for a while."

"Which isn't much like a real pet," he said.

"No. It wasn't."

Another silence settled over them as darkness began to surround the SUV. But this one felt less strained.

"What kind of dog?" he asked.

"I haven't really given it that much thought. When I was growing up, I always wanted a collie. Like Lassie."

"That'd be okay."

"If there's one at the shelter, we might want to look at it. But I do wonder if all that fur would be hard to handle with our rain."

"Maybe a short coat," he suggested. "Like a lab. Or a boxer."

"Two more possibilities," she agreed. "Of course, we'll want to look more at personalities than just focusing in on one breed. But I read on the shelter's Web site after talking to you this afternoon that Dr. Tiernan-St. James has a degree in animal behavior and she makes certain that all the dogs she has up for adoption can, with a little love and kindness, settle in well."

"So you're not thinking about getting a little dog you can dress up?"

"I'd have nothing against a small breed. Or a mixed one, which the Web site said we'll most likely end up with. But you've known me fifteen-plus years, Matthew. Have I ever seemed to be the type of person who'd put a dress on a dog?"

"No," he said. "You've always been pretty normal."

"Why, thank you." She also sent up a silent thank-you to Charity Tiernan. "I'm going to take that as a compliment."

Although he didn't answer, she could feel the tension lessening even more.

Just wait until he got home, she thought with almost giddy anticipation.

Thanks to the floodlight Lucas Chaffee had set up with the basketball pole, Matt saw the addition the moment she reached the house.

"You got me a basketball rig?" His voice reminded her of how he used to sound on Christmas morning, when he'd come wandering out in his footed pajamas, all wide-eyed at the wondrous bounty Santa had left behind.

"Coach Dillon sent it over." Wanting to leave the driveway free, since she had the feeling he'd want to try it out right away, she pulled up at the curb in front of the house. "Lucas Chaffee—he's a local contractor who'll be fixing up the house—put it up. He said when we get the house done, we can make a more permanent one."

"This is just the coolest thing!" His grin reminded her of the old Matt. The bright sun around which her entire world had revolved for so many years.

As she heated up the braised short ribs Chef Maddy had supplied for their dinner, Claire listened to the familiar bounce, bounce, bounce of the basketball on asphalt, which brought her mind back to the man responsible for Matt's happiness. While part of her selfishly wished she'd been the one to put that smile on her son's face, Claire was relieved to see him so enthusiastic about anything again.

Although she hadn't wanted to admit it, even to herself, she'd been afraid that if she couldn't find some way to break through that tough shell he'd spent the last year building, he'd get himself into even worse trouble. It was a bullet she seemed to have dodged, at least for now, because of Matt's coach.

Which brought her mind circling back, as it seemed to do so often, to Dillon Slater. . . .

Though she'd planned this move down to the last detail, the man had turned out to be one complication she hadn't counted on.

"He can only be trouble if you let him," she assured herself as she set the table.

So what if his deep voice strummed chords she'd forgotten even could be strummed? His Bambi brown eyes could stare down into hers until doomsday, sending as many enticingly sensual messages as they liked.

She was a grown woman, capable of making her own choices. And she wasn't the least bit interested.

"When did you turn into such a liar?" She slapped the paper napkins onto the placemats with enough force to create miniature tidal waves in the water glasses. "But

it'll still be okay." She placed the forks next to the napkins with more care.

Dillon Slater could become a complication only if she
allowed him to be. For now, at this particular moment in
time, with the mouthwatering aroma of braised beef
wafting from the oven, and her son's basketball bouncing on the driveway of her new, soon-to-be-renovated
beach house, life was good.

33

"I love her!" The moment Charity had brought out the golden retriever, Phoebe had lost her heart. "She's perfect!"

"Goldens are wonderful companion dogs," Charity said as she wrote up the adoption paperwork. "They're one of the few breeds who truly build a strong lifetime bond with their human family, which is why it's so rare for them to come up for adoption.

"Unfortunately, they are prone to separation anxiety, which is how Sunny ended up with me. With both her humans working long hours, she tended to get bored and think up things to do to get in trouble. But with you and Ethan sharing her, she should be in doggie heaven." Charity reached down and scratched behind the dog's ear, causing it to wiggle its fluffy gold butt in a canine happy dance.

"Since I'm a believer in full disclosure, I have to warn you that she'll shed."

"I have a Swiffer," Phoebe said. "I can handle some dog hair."

"The upside is that it's a double coat, which makes it weatherproof."

"A handy thing for this area, with all our rain," Ethan said.

"She's very patient, which will be a plus once your baby starts walking and undoubtedly jumps on her. And she's strong enough to be able to take whatever rough-housing an older child will give her. And, being two years old, she's well trained and housebroken."

"She's perfect," Phoebe repeated as she signed the adoption agreement Charity handed her. For a moment she was almost able to forget the trouble the Fletchers had brought down on her so suddenly as she imagined this beautiful, sweet dog playing with her soon-to-be-born child.

"And you two are perfect for her. And I'm glad you both came by this evening, because I received a call from my stepfather just before you arrived. He's not sure about the details, but there are rumors floating around Colorado that your former father-in-law might be under federal investigation."

"For what?" Phoebe asked in surprise.

"He doesn't know. Yet," Charity qualified. "But he's going to make a few calls to people he knows in Washington—DC, not the state—and see what else he can find out."

"So they're just rumors?" Ethan asked with a frown.

"Yes. At this point. But believe me, Benton, my stepfather, is superconnected in high-up legal circles. If the Fletchers have any skeletons in their closet, he'll unearth them."

"I don't know how to thank you." Words couldn't begin to describe the depth of Phoebe's gratitude.

"Just be happy. With your new dog, your baby, and this guy here. You've created a wonderful new life for yourself, Phoebe. None of us who care about you will let those horrid people take it away."

As Sunny thumped a thick yellow tail on the floor, as if to signify canine agreement, Phoebe thought, yet again, how of all the places that underground railroad might have taken her, she'd been beyond fortunate to end up here in Shelter Bay.

34

Claire had never been to New Orleans for Mardi Gras, but each time she visited Bon Temps, she felt as if she'd come close. The night of the crabfest was no different.

Gold, purple, and green carnival masks hung on Tabasco-hued walls, and bright beads, like the kind thrown from floats, had been hung from light fixtures.

The high school pops band was playing on the small stage. What the teenage musicians lacked in professionalism, they made up for in enthusiasm as they belted out show tunes interspersed with the Dolphins' fight song, while the cheerleaders tried to get everyone to sing along. Spirit banners painted by various school clubs hung on the bright red walls next to the masks.

Although she felt some chilliness from a few of the parents—she suspected they were concerned that Matt would take away from their sons' playing time—the boosters were more than friendly, and nearly everyone else who'd shown up to support the team made a point of stopping by her table to welcome her to town.

"I'm having a good time," she said to Charity, who was sitting next to her at the long table.

"I'm glad. It is fun, isn't it?" Charity said. "Sometimes it blows my mind that I'm actually the mother of a teenager, but fortunately, Johnny's such an easy kid." She glanced over at her adopted son pouring water into a pitcher at a nearby table. "He looks so grown up."

"I know." Claire was struck at how adult her own son, clad in slacks, a white shirt, and a black tie, looked as he moved around the room, a model of polite manners and charm as he served the crab dinner. She also watched all the young girls' eyes following him.

"They grow up so fast," she said, focusing in on one blond cheerleader, who, from the hungry look in her gaze as she'd sassily flirted with him when he passed with a tray of bright red boiled crabs, looked as if she could be trouble. "I hear I have your Johnny to thank for Matt deciding to volunteer at your shelter."

"We're happy to have him. And I'm so glad you're coming by next week. We have some wonderful dogs to choose from."

At that moment, a little girl who reminded Claire a bit of Zuzu from *It's a Wonderful Life* came spinning up to the table. She was wearing a pink tutu, striped pink and yellow leggings, a glittery pink T-shirt that read I HAVE HAPPY FEET, and sneakers that flashed as those happy feet moved up and down.

"Hi," she greeted Claire with a bright smile that was lacking a front tooth. "I'm Angel. And I'm a ballerina."

"I can see that," Claire said. "I've been watching you dance with the band. You're very good."

"Madame Zelda's the best teacher ever. Mommy says that's because she used to be a really famous ballerina in Russia. Are you Matt's mommy?"

"I am."

"He's nice."

"I like to think so."

"Oh!" She lifted both hands up to her mouth. Her short nails had been painted with a sparkly pink polish. "I almost forgot. Mommy," she said, "Daddy told me to come get you. He said it's *really* important."

"I hope it's nothing serious," Claire said to Charity.

"If it was all that serious, he wouldn't have sent Tinker Bell," Charity assured her. "I'm on the crabfest committee. It's probably something like we're in danger of running out of coleslaw or another emergency."

Just as she stood up, Dillon walked by.

"Dillon," Charity said, snagging his arm, "come sit by Claire and keep her company. She doesn't know that many people yet."

Before Claire could assure her that she was perfectly capable of introducing herself to other town residents, Charity was off, following the dancing sprite, causing a faint sound, like the one made when the angel Clarence finally earned his wings in *It's a Wonderful Life*, to chime in the back of Claire's mind.

"Why do I get the feeling I've just been set up?" she asked dryly as the coach sat down at the butcher-paper-covered table next to her.

"Beats me." He popped some shrimp from a bowl in front of him into his mouth and looked around. "The place is really packed. I'm just glad I was able to find a place to sit down. It's a little hard to crack crab standing up. . . . So how goes the glassblowing?"

"I've been blocked," she admitted. "Other than the green flash, I haven't been able to come up with anything creative that works with it." She'd begun to wonder if it was possible to actually run out of ideas.

"That's probably not surprising. I'd imagine all the changes in your life haven't exactly put your mind in a creative space."

"True. But inspiration struck when I was down at the aquarium the other day."

"Cool place." He nodded approvingly. "I took the science club there last month. They have some great programs. Maybe we could go together sometime. I have an in with the research scientists there. I could give you a behind-the-scenes tour."

"That sounds interesting, but I'm afraid I have a lot on my plate right now," she said mildly as she realized a couple at the next table over were openly eavesdropping.

"Just let me know if you change your mind. I'm glad you're here," he said, seeming to take her rejection in stride. The fact that it irked just a bit didn't make a bit of sense, since she didn't want to get even slightly involved with Dillon Slater. "I have a proposition for you."

The conversation around them came to an abrupt halt. A smile quirked at the corner of his mouth. Looking around, he spotted Kara and Maddy, who'd just come out of the kitchen.

"Would you two ladies mind saving our seats for about five minutes?" he asked. "I need to talk with Claire."

As neither woman seemed all that surprised or curious about what was going on, that niggling little chime sounded again in her mind. Louder, and a bit more insistent this time.

"Of course," Kara said. "Hey, Claire, it's good to see you."

Brief greetings were exchanged; then Dillon scooped

Claire's jacket from the back of her chair. "Let's go out on the porch," he said, "where we can have some privacy."

The chime was now an alarm bell. "Unless you're going to tell me that Matt has a problem, we don't have any reason for privacy."

"Now, see, far be it from me to argue with a lady, but that's where you're wrong."

They wove through the tables, past the bandstand, to the porch overlooking the harbor. Although a light mist was falling, the porch roof kept them dry. Claire had also discovered that the cloud cover when it rained actually kept the temperature up.

"It's the maritime climate," he said when she mentioned it after he'd asked if she was cold. "So I've been thinking about watching you blow glass the other day."

"Have you?"

"I have. And I was wondering if you'd be willing to give a demonstration to the science club. I think they'd really go for it."

She was surprised he just hadn't asked her that question back inside the restaurant. "I'd be happy to. Do you think they'd enjoy blowing a glass paperweight?"

"You'd make their day. Who wouldn't want to give someone a special thing they've made with their own two hands?"

"When would you want to do it?"

"I don't want to interfere with your exhibit work. Maybe after the first of the year?"

"I think I could fit it in before that so they'd have a Christmas gift. How about sometime the week before Christmas?"

"Great. Thanks. That's way cool."

"That's it?"

"Well, there is another thing."

Make that a siren. "What?"

The flashing green, gold, and purple neon sign overhead illuminated his face enough that she could read his intention.

"This isn't going to happen," she warned.

"Why not?"

He was close. Too close. "Because we don't know each other."

"Good point." His breath warmed her lips, and despite her protest, as she held her breath, waiting for his kiss, he surprised her by nipping at her chin. "It just so happens that I've got a few ways in mind we can remedy that. Starting right now."

"I can't." Oh, he was good, she thought as her heart speeded up. But she was no longer that naive girl who could fall for such practiced seduction.

"Can't? Or won't?"

She put a hand on his chest and was surprised to discover that despite his outwardly easy charm, his heart was beating as rapidly as hers. Which caused a little jolt and made this situation all the more tempting.

"Both. Because I've never been one for playing games, I'm not going to deny I'm tempted. But you just happen to be my son's coach. There are undoubtedly a great many parents in that restaurant who are hoping their sons win athletic scholarships. If they thought you were giving Matt more playing time because you were involved with me, it would not only hurt the team; it could hurt my son. A lot."

"I think you're overstating the problem."

"I don't believe I am." Mrs. Martin, whose son Dirk

was a senior on the team, had definitely iced her when they'd been introduced. "And it's time we went back inside."

He didn't stop her when she took a step back. Nor did he argue, but merely shrugged and said, "Your call."

But as they entered Bon Temps and Ken Curtis called him to the bandstand to give a speech about the upcoming season, Dillon bent his head and murmured next to her ear, "Just think about it, Claire."

As if she was going to be able to think of anything else.

35

As with everything else in her life lately, Claire's trip to the shelter did not go as planned. Matt had been talking about a lab or a boxer, and she'd been fine with that. Until this black-and-brown dog came up to them, sat on her haunches, and held out a paw.

"That's Jessie," Johnny said.

"What is she?" Claire asked, even as she bent down and shook the paw. At which point the dog rolled over and bared her stomach. "She looks like a miniature Doberman pinscher. But larger." She also had floppy ears and a long tail, but Claire assumed that was because they hadn't been surgically changed to the AKC standard.

"Actually, min pins aren't related to Dobermans at all," Charity explained. "*Pinscher* actually means *terrier*, and those were bred as barnyard ratters. Their breeding ancestry includes dachshunds, Italian greyhounds, and perhaps German pinschers, which is what Jessie is."

The dog, hearing her name, rolled back up onto her feet and again held out a paw. "It's her trick," Charity said. "I've no idea how she learned it, because her previous owners swear they didn't teach it to her. She's incredibly smart, but her breed also has a strong will, so she needs gentle but consistent discipline. And because she's high-energy, she'll need daily exercise."

"We can do that, can't we, Mom?" Matt was on his knees on the grass, scratching behind her velvety ear, causing the dog to groan with canine pleasure.

"I suppose so." Claire turned to Charity. "I read on your Web site that you prequalify all your dogs?"

"I definitely do. Jessie's a bit of a Velcro dog, needing to keep close by people, but that's because her life has been through so much upheaval lately. We got her when the owners found out she was pregnant, so suddenly she was not only having to become a mother at her very first heat; she was in a strange environment with people she didn't know.

"But she'd be a wonderful companion. As you can see, she's very outgoing and a very quick learner." She turned toward her son. "Show Mrs. Templeton the trick you taught her."

"Sure." He grinned. "Jessie, sit."

She sat.

"Now, stay."

She didn't move a muscle.

"This needs a bit of backstory," Charity said. "After helping in the clinic and shelter, Johnny's decided he wants to go to OSU and become a vet. And OSU's century-old rival is U of O."

"The Ducks," Matt said dismissively, suggesting he found the name even less suitable for a mascot than the Dolphins.

"So . . . Jessie," Johnny said. When he paused, her ears pricked and she seemed to go into high alert to listen.

"Would you like to be an Oregon Duck fan? Or would you rather be a dead dog?"

On cue, she dramatically fell to the ground, rolled over, and stuck all four legs in the air. And held that pose until the teenager snapped his fingers.

"Okay," Claire said with a laugh as the dog jumped up and gave Matt's face a wet swipe with her long pink tongue. "You won me over. . . . Matt, what do you think?"

"She's perfect, Mom!"

All the youthful joy she'd once been accustomed to seeing in his face was back as he hugged the dog, who, since she was in a shelter, obviously needed him as much as he needed her. Of course, in three years he'd be off to college, and she'd be stuck walking and feeding and disciplining his dog. But at least she wouldn't be left with a totally empty nest.

"There's just one more thing," Charity said. "Johnny, would you go get Toby?"

He took off running.

"As I said, Jessie's been through a lot of changes. She's young and was a bit overwhelmed to suddenly be faced with a litter of pups. Which is when Toby decided to adopt them. And, as it turns out, her."

"Toby is a dog?" Claire asked.

"Exactly. He's one of our golden paw boys, meaning he's a senior citizen. The two of them are pretty much inseparable, and I'd really prefer adopting them as a pair."

"Oh, I don't know—"

"Mom!"

"Matt, our own life isn't exactly settled right now. You have your sports, and we have to fix up the house, and—"

She felt her heart turn over as Johnny returned with

a ball of black fluff in his arms. The little dog leaped out of the teenager's arms and went running over to Jessie. Watching them exchange enthusiastic dog kisses, as if they'd been separated for years and not merely minutes, Claire knew she was toast.

"Toby spends much of his day dozing," Charity assured her. "Most of the time you won't even realize he's there."

"But Jessie will," Claire said as she watched them together. Jessie was on her feet, chasing Toby around the yard. At first Claire worried, then noticed that the younger and larger dog kept letting Toby think he was knocking her down.

"As you can see, they've formed quite a bond," Charity said.

Claire caved. "Prepare the paperwork," she told Claire. "For them both."

"Thanks, Mom!" Again Matt reminded her of the happy son he'd once been. "You totally rock!"

36

Matt hadn't had any real intention of joining the science club, and the idea of giving up a Saturday morning he could've been playing ball sucked, but the prospect of shooting off a cannon was impossible to resist.

Since the town's only real cannon was too big to move, the coach had built his own with help from the school's metal-shop teacher. It was currently sitting on the beach, its barrel pointed out to sea.

"Okay," Coach Dillon said as they gathered on the sand in front of the old shipwreck they'd be aiming at. Not that there was any chance of anyone actually hitting the ship's skeleton, but it exponentially upped the cool factor. It wasn't raining today, but the sky was still as gray as the metal cannon barrel. "Who knows where gunpowder was first invented?"

"That's easy," one kid said. "China."

"You're right. It was easy. Who knows why or how gunpowder was invented?"

"For fireworks," another guy called out.

"Nope. Who wants to try again?"

"Someone, perhaps a Taoist monk, was looking for the secret to longevity," Aimee said.

"That's exactly right. The Chinese were big on ingesting chemicals for health reasons. For the bonus question, can you give me the time frame?"

"No one's exactly sure," Aimee said without missing a beat, "but sometime in the first century AD."

"You nailed it."

Matt would've expected more enthusiasm from Aimee for being the only person on the beach besides the coach to have known that. But she'd been uncharacteristically quiet ever since they'd all gotten on the school bus to drive out here. Although he'd been sitting across the aisle from her, she'd pointedly ignored him.

While everyone else on the bus was talking and laughing and having a high old time, the silence between them had been deafening.

"Good answer," he said, trying to get a conversation going now.

"Thanks," she said tonelessly.

"I guess you knew it because you're interested in medical stuff. Since you're going to be a doctor."

Instead of answering, she merely froze him out, then walked across the wet packed sand to stand as far away from him as she could.

Well, that went well, he thought as he kicked at a piece of seaweed. His house was just above the beach, and he was seriously considering just saying the hell with this and going home when the coach zeroed in on him.

"Templeton. Can you tell us what makes gunpowder explode?"

It was a trick question. And he knew the answer.

"It doesn't," he said. "It just burns really fast."

"But it *does* explode," another kid said.

"It better," someone else called out, "because I gave up going to the arcade to come blow stuff up."

"It explodes when it's compressed," Matt said. "And when it burns, it releases gases larger in volume than the original powder. The same way steam has more volume than water."

"Or like how the steam inside the kernel of popcorn keeps expanding until it bursts the shell," Aimee said.

"Good team answer." The coach, seemingly oblivious to the tension between them, grinned.

"To cut to the chase before it starts raining again, the Chinese held the secret to gunpowder for a long time. By the 300s AD, a scientist, Ge Hong, had written down the chemicals and described the explosion, but although it was cool for fireworks, it wasn't until somewhere in the 900s that they thought to turn it into a weapon.

"They started putting small stone cannonballs inside bamboo tubes and shot them out by lighting the gunpowder at the other end. Which is the same principle as the one we'll be using today.

"And, since Templeton caught the trick to my question, I'm going to let him choose the first powder man to light this baby up."

"Powder *girl*," Matt said, looking across the top of the cannon straight at Aimee.

He could tell she wanted to refuse. Only because he'd suggested her. But maybe she couldn't resist the opportunity to be the first one to set off the blast, or perhaps she didn't want to cause a scene, because she merely shrugged her parka-clad shoulders and mumbled, "Thanks."

"Okay," the coach said. "Since it's not only dangerous

but environmentally wrong to go shooting cannonballs into the surf, we're going to be using melons. And the chemicals we'll be using are . . . ?"

"Potassium nitrate, sulfur, and carbon," everyone said in unison.

The coach assigned a kid to load the cannon; then he gave Aimee a lighter and a long stick. "Don't want to blow off your hand."

"If she does blow it off, at next month's meeting we can try using her own stem cells to grow her a new one," a kid in a blue aquarium CAMP FINSTITUTE counselor slicker suggested. Which drew a laugh from nearly everyone. Aimee—surprise, surprise—didn't crack a smile.

She took the lighter and touched it to the wadded cotton at the end of the stick. After bringing the flame up to meet the wick, she hesitated a moment to make sure it had caught, then quickly stepped back.

Ka-boom!

The resultant explosion echoed off the cliffs and water, earning loud cheers.

Even she managed a smile. Which she ruthlessly cut off the moment she caught Matt looking at her again.

As everyone lined up to take their turn, Matt grabbed her by the wrist and practically dragged her behind a towering stack of driftwood logs. He suspected the only reason she went with him at all was to avoid calling attention to them.

"What do you think you're doing?" she asked, shaking free and putting her hands on her hips.

"You didn't talk to me the entire bus ride out."

"Maybe because I have nothing to say to you." She lifted her chin. "And more to the point, I have no desire to hear anything you might have to say."

"Not even that I'm sorry?"

Her eyes narrowed. "For what?"

Another trick question. One that had him feeling as if he were on the verge of sinking into quicksand. Over his head.

"Whatever I did to piss you off."

She stared at him. Then blew out a long, frustrated breath.

"You really don't get it, do you?"

"Get what?"

"This." She reached up, pressed her palms on either side of his face, and crushed her mouth to his in a hard, grinding, teeth-clashing kiss.

Heat sizzled through him, flames flared, and when another boom rocked the ground beneath his feet, Matt couldn't tell if it had come from the cannon or from inside his head.

Then, just as suddenly as it had begun, she pulled back, furious emotions swirling in her brown eyes.

"Remember that," she said, "when you're throwing your useless self away on that basketball groupie Taylor Bennington."

Before he could find his voice, she spun around on a booted heel and went marching back to the others.

Leaving Matt confused, aching, and totally tied up in knots.

37

The sun had set, but as Dillon pulled up in front of the cottage, he saw Matt shooting hoops in the driveway beneath floodlights. It was drizzling, but although he'd grown up on sun-drenched beaches, the wet ball didn't seem to be affecting the kid's shots.

As soon as Dillon got out of the Jeep, a small black-and-brown dog that looked like a scaled-down Dobie and another that resembled a black dust mop came running up to greet him, tails wagging. Apparently the good Dr. Charity Tiernan had struck again.

"Getting your daily shots in?" he asked on what sounded, even to his ears, like the lamest conversation opener ever. He rubbed both dogs' heads, causing the larger of the two to drop to the ground, roll over, and begin wiggling in dog ecstasy so he could rub her stomach. He obliged.

"We've got our first game coming up." Matt told Dillon nothing he didn't already know all too well. It was mostly all he was able to think about these days. Well, that and Claire Templeton. She'd gotten not only into his mind, but under his skin as well. Which was what had him showing up at her door again. "Don't want to lose an opener. It's bad luck."

"You guys will make your own luck on the court," Dillon said. "But it's always a good thing to start the season in the win column."

"Why are you here?"

And wasn't that a question Dillon had been asking himself? Especially since she'd already made her feelings clear about getting involved with him.

"I need to talk to your mom."

"What did I do now?"

"Nothing." Except work his tail off both in class and on the court. "You're fine. This is just a . . . booster club thing." With the exception of bad guys who were trying to blow him up, Dillon was not accustomed to lying to anyone. Let alone a student. Which just went to show how badly the woman was messing with his head.

"Oh." Matt turned back to the ball, sending up a one hander from the far end of the driveway. *Swish.* "She's in her hotshop. In the garage." He tilted his head in that direction, bounced the ball twice, and sent it sailing into the basket with his other hand. Ken had been right about one thing: The kid from Beverly Hills was a phenom.

"Thanks."

She looked to be finishing up as Dillon entered the garage, which was not only as hot as the surface of the sun, but as bright.

"Wow," he said, looking at the shelves lining the walls. "You've been busy." They'd been empty the first time he'd been in here. Now they gleamed in the light from the overhead halogen fixtures like Aladdin's treasure cave. "Guess you got your mojo back."

"I did." She pulled off the heavy gloves and wiped her glistening forehead with the back of her hand. "I have to admit that I was starting to get seriously concerned when nothing was working, because I've never—not even when my mother was dying—been blocked before.

"Then, as I told you, in desperation, I took some time to go to the aquarium, and everything just clicked. Plus, I think having Matt settling in and getting back into the groove eased my mind enough that I was able to reconnect with my subconscious."

She did seem more relaxed than he'd seen her. And, Dillon thought, totally in her element surrounded by fire and all that brilliant colored glass. "I have you to thank for that."

"He's a good kid. He just needed time to adjust after a rough year."

"Don't we all."

A little silence settled over them. Maybe it was hopeful thinking, but Dillon wondered if she was considering asking him to stay for dinner again.

"I really like this," he said, filling in the conversational gap by turning toward a tall piece of clear glass with a remarkably lifelike coral jellyfish with light bluish green tentacles trailing down floating inside it. As she'd done with the green flash, clear bubbles rose from the bottom, giving the sense of movement.

"Except for a few commercial pieces I've done for places like the Dancing Deer Two, I've never been drawn to creating such true-to-life pieces," she said, coming to stand beside him. "Usually I've done more free-form, letting people decide for themselves what a piece might represent. But when I was walking through the aquarium tunnel, through the different life zones, I noticed what I've always, on some subconscious level, known. I'd just never really thought about it before."

"What's that?"

"On land, with the exception of some insects and other animals who've learned to camouflage themselves over the eons, plants and animals look different. But what I realized while I was walking through the passage, surrounded by all that teeming sea life, is that in the sea, they often look alike."

"I've never given it any real thought, either," he admitted. Which could well be because he'd grown up in the oil patch of West Texas, a very long way from any sea.

"Well, as you know as a physics teacher, there's a school of thought that glass is neither a liquid nor a solid. Because liquid molecules are disordered and not at all rigidly bound."

"While solids' crystals are rigidly bound little armies," Dillon said.

"Exactly. Glass molecules are disordered, but rigidly bound. Which is why, when people in ancient times looked at wavy cathedral windows being thicker at the bottom than the top, they believed that if given enough time, glass would eventually melt into a liquid onto the ground."

"Theoretically, maybe. If you were able to wait around two million years or more."

"True. Which is why it'll never be proven. As for the cathedral windows, the simple fact is that there was much less quality control at the time, and before our modern float-glass process was invented, most window glass was rolled, which resulted in a lot of the rippled glass you see in old windows of houses even now. When builders got pieces of glass that were thicker on one edge, it was only natural to put that side down."

"Makes sense. I've always liked that old wavy glass."

"You're not alone. A lot of people think it gives old homes more character. In fact, Lucas asked me if I thought I could make some windows for the house he and Mary Joyce are going to build. She thought it would remind her of the farmhouse she grew up in back in Ireland."

"Interesting idea. Are you going to do it?"

"It could be a fun challenge, and I'm considering it seriously enough to start studying up. There's still so much to be discovered about the thermodynamics of glass, but it seems to me that glass is actually a separate entity somewhere between solid and liquid.

"Anyway, that's a long story for why it seems natural to use water as a theme for glass objects."

"Especially since so many things in the sea are transparent," he said, immediately seeing her inspiration.

"Exactly. That's what I love about the jellyfish." She beamed because he understood.

Claire Templeton was an attractive woman. But when her face lit up and her eyes sparkled with enthusiasm, she was, hands down, the most compelling woman he'd ever met. He also wondered if she knew how sexy she was when she started getting excited about molecules.

Physics and fire.

Could any female be more perfect?

"You can actually see right through jellyfish," she said, "which makes them especially perfect for glasswork. It took a bit of trial and error to keep them that way, especially when I was putting on the striping. But unlike stone, or even wood, glass can create an organic, almost moving quality, which is what I was shooting for."

"You definitely pulled that off. How did you get the colors?" The dome of the jellyfish faded from turquoise to pale green.

"The light turquoise color came from adding copper oxide, and the palest green is sea glass that I found on the beach, probably originally from a 1900s Coke bottle, which I melted back down," she said.

"That's really recycling," he said, thinking that she'd taken it back to what those original glassmakers had worked with.

"Isn't it? Oh, and it might be over the top, but I decided to add a bit of phosphorous powder to a few of them, like this cobalt blue one, so it'll glow in the dark. It's not for everyone, but I called the owners of the gallery and they sounded really excited about displaying a few pieces in a dark side room lit with black light. I think it should really show well and add fun to the showing."

The jellyfish in question was floating across the inside of a huge globe, its wavy glass tentacles trailing behind like ghostly ribbons. Below was a brilliant yellow coral reef teeming with colorful fish and plants.

"You've done an amazing amount of work since the last time I was here." Since he didn't see a dinner invitation on the horizon, he decided to take matters into his own hands. "I'd say you need a reward. How about letting me buy you dinner? I owe you one after you shared your clams and crab cakes."

"Which you cooked."

"After being in this place all day, you don't need to stand over a hot stove. I was thinking of going to Bon Temps for dinner. Why don't you and Matt come with me?"

Her brows knitted as she looked up at him. "We've been over this. Even if I had time to date, which I definitely don't, you're too much of a complication."

He put his hand on his heart. "Ouch. That sound you just heard was my ego deflating."

"As if," she countered with a bit of sass he found every bit as appealing as her smile.

"Don't think of it as a date," he suggested. One of the things he'd always done best when confronted with a roadblock, on either a basketball court or a minefield, was to figure out a way around it. "You have to eat. I have to eat. And I've never met a teenager who doesn't have to eat."

When he sensed her weakening, just a bit, he charged for the shot. "When was the last time Matt had Cajun food?"

"I'm not sure he's *ever* eaten Cajun."

"Well, then, after how hard he's been working on the court and in class, don't you think he needs a reward?"

She shook her head. "That's playing dirty."

He decided against telling her that he wasn't playing. At all. "It's just dinner, Claire. Three people sharing a meal in a public place. Would it make you feel better if I promised not to kiss you over the popcorn shrimp, then ask you to go steady?"

She laughed, as he'd hoped she would. "You're impossible."

"Just hungry." And not just for Sax's crab jambalaya. "How long will it take you to get ready?"

She sighed dramatically. "Give me twenty minutes," she said. "Meanwhile, since you were thoughtful enough to send Lucas Chaffee over with that basketball setup for Matt—which I really appreciate, by the way—you might as well go shoot some hoops."

38

He might be trouble. With a capital *T*. And he was definitely a complication. But as Dillon shared with Matt what Claire suspected was a highly sanitized version of his days in EOD, she realized she was actually having a good time.

The restaurant was crowded, which wasn't surprising, given the warm atmosphere on a drizzling winter night, the fire blazing away in the tall stone fireplace, and the quality of Sax Douchett's cooking.

"I could eat this stuff all day long," Matt said when Sax came over to see how they were enjoying their dinner.

"That's why it's called Come-Back sauce," he said. "It's my *grandmère*'s secret recipe."

"If you bottled it, you'd probably make a fortune," Claire said.

"Maybe so. But then, if that happened, I'd land myself in a business that took up all my time, when I'd rather just feed people and enjoy my family."

Having heard from Dorothy or Dottie the harrowing story of how he'd ended up as the sole survivor of a SEAL mission in Afghanistan, and having seen the sign at the town line announcing Shelter Bay to be the hometown of Navy Cross recipient Sax Douchett, Claire couldn't think of anyone who deserved a calm and happy life more.

"I think that's a much better idea," she agreed. "A slower pace is partly the reason I moved here."

She felt Matt, who was seated at her left, tense.

"How are you liking Shelter Bay?" Sax asked Matt.

He shrugged. But at least the glower was gone. "It's okay," he mumbled around a mouthful of dirty rice. "I like playing ball."

"Word on the street is that you've got some wicked skills on the court. I was a baseball guy myself, and to tell the truth, when I was your age, I thought this place had to be the dullest spot on the planet."

"Obviously you haven't ever visited the oil patch in West Texas," Dillon said dryly. "At least Shelter Bay has an ocean. . . . Matt, you surf?"

Another shrug. "I did."

"Come summer you'll have to get back into it. I've been thinking of taking it up. Maybe you can give me some pointers."

Although Dillon had promised not to kiss her over dinner, Claire could've leaned across the table and kissed *him* when her son visibly perked up.

"People surf here?" He made it sound like another, far distant, alien planet.

"Sure." Dillon scooped up some crab jambalaya. "I saw a lot of surfers out last summer. There are apparently good breaks all up and down the coast. Including some for winter surfing, but those are for experts only."

"Which I am," Matt said.

"That may be. But you're also important to the team, so why don't you just save risking your neck until the season's over?"

"I guess that makes sense," Matt agreed reluctantly.

"All the folks counting on you to take the team to state probably wouldn't be real thrilled if you crashed a surfboard into the cliff before playoffs," Sax agreed.

"Not you, too!" Dillon said.

"I didn't say I was one of them," he assured Claire. "I'm just passing on what happens to be the main topic of conversation since you and Matt arrived in town.

"A town which," he said, turning back to Matt, "might seem like dullsville to you now. I didn't grow up with the bright lights of L.A. but was definitely happy to leave when I was eighteen. But a funny thing happened. After college and the military, I discovered that this place exactly fits who and where I am in my life now."

"You never know where life's going to take you," Dillon agreed. "I sure never imagined living on the Oregon coast. But after my winding road led me here, it turned out to be just where I belong."

"When I was fifteen, I was positive I'd be living in Florence, Italy," Claire said.

"No way," Matt said. "You never told me that."

"It never came up." The truth was that she'd never wanted him to believe, even for a moment, that she'd changed her life plans because of him. She had, but she'd never regretted her decision for a heartbeat.

"What were you going to do in Italy?" Dillon asked.

"I was going to study at Le Arti Orafe Jewelry School and Academy. Jewelry has been an important part of the art of Italy since the Renaissance, and Florence has always been the gem in that crown." She smiled at the memory of the young girl with the fanciful dreams.

"Then you had me," Matt said. "So you couldn't."

"Oh, no." Wasn't this the exact reason she'd never brought it up? If she hadn't been feeling so relaxed and comfortable, she never would have now. "I'd already decided, for various reasons, including financial ones, to go to school in Los Angeles, which also has an excellent design college."

"But L.A. isn't Florence."

"No. But Florence isn't L.A." She smiled and resisted, since they were in public, patting his hand. "Besides, I'm terrible at languages."

"So," Dillon said, leaping in to help her out when that hadn't taken the frown from her son's face, "we shot off the cannon this morning."

"Since you still have both your hands, I guess it went off without a hitch?"

"Sir Francis Drake would've been damn proud to have our cannon on his *Golden Hind*."

"Drake was the pirate, right?" Matt asked. "I didn't know he got all the way up here."

"Technically, according to my historian brother," Sax said, "he was a privateer, which is basically a pirate for hire, in the pay of a government. In his case, the queen of England."

After a quick glance around the room to see that everything was running smoothly and that the servers were handling the dinner crowd, he turned a chair around, straddled it, put his arms on the top of the back, and continued his story.

"My brothers and I used to play pirates all the time growing up and would pretend the cave on Moonshell Beach was where Drake hid the bounty he'd get from attacking Spanish galleons on their way back from China and Japan. And that the wreck on Castaway Cove beneath your and your mom's cottage was the skeleton of one of those galleons. Which it's not, but when you're a kid, it's fun to pretend."

"It also makes for a better story than some wannabe pirates sinking a merchant ship because they mistakenly thought it was carrying a shipment of Klondike gold bound for San Francisco, which is what actually happened," Dillon said.

"True. But there were a lot of wrecked galleons along this part of the coast. Since they were so heavy and more cumbersome, Drake used his lighter, faster ship to drive them into the cliffs; then he'd let the sailors who wanted to escape leave.

"Afterward his crew would loot the ships, which sometimes took days; then he'd blow them up. He got so effective that the Spanish started calling him 'El Draque, The Dragon,' and the king of Spain put a twenty-thousand-ducat price on his head. Which would be about ten million dollars today."

"That's dope," Matt said.

"We always thought so," Sax said. "No one's ever quite figured out where his secret port was. Some believe it was Whale Cove down at Depoe Bay. But that's open and easy to see, and a lot of galleon captains would've loved to have sunk his ship. Not just for the bounty, but to get rid of him. So most people think it was probably Tillamook Bay up north.

"Whichever, he was effective enough that Queen Elizabeth knighted him after he gave her enough to pay off her entire foreign debt."

"That's even cooler than Captain Jack Sparrow," Matt said.

As he and the two men discussed pirates, both real and fictional, Claire sat back, sipped her wine while looking out at the bridge lights reflecting on the water of the bay, and felt the chains that had wrapped around her heart this past year begin to loosen.

Her ease was short-lived.

"How come you never told me about Florence?" Matt asked as soon as they were back in the cottage and Dillon was driving away.

"I told you, it just never came up." Which wasn't a lie. But it was a hedge.

"Because you gave up your dream because of me?"

"Oh, honey." She wanted to put her arms around him, but feeling the now-familiar wall going up between them again, she allowed him his space. "Of course not. I was already going to school in L.A. when you were conceived."

He folded his arms across his chest. "If it wasn't for me, why didn't you go?"

"As I said, it was partly because of the money. Your grandmother got divorced my senior year, and although she was given the house in the settlement, California doesn't have alimony, so she had to find a new career. There simply wasn't any money for me to go study in Italy."

"Your father could've paid."

"I suppose he could have. He chose not to."

Which seemed to be the story of the men in her life. After Matt's father had refused to acknowledge his unborn child, friends at school had told her she should get a DNA test and sue for child support. But to Claire's mind, right or wrong, if she had forced him to pay, someday that money could come with strings. Which she hadn't wanted to risk.

"Why did Gram have to get a new career? She already had a job designing sets for movies and TV shows. She even had an Oscar nomination and an Emmy." Not that Claire's mother ever talked about those days, but both the *L.A. Times* and *Variety* had included them in her obituary.

"She never really discussed it." Which was absolutely true. Once Claire's father had packed up and left the house, it was as if he had died. "I suppose she wanted an entirely new start." And, given that her producer-husband had left her for his much younger assistant, Claire had always suspected the entertainment business had lost its gleam. "That way she could work at home, too. Which turned out to be a good thing for us, since she was there to take care of you while I went to school."

And perhaps, Claire considered, her mother stepping in so completely had kept her from entirely moving on with her own life. Was it possible that she'd become so comfortable with the way things were, with the three of them making up their own family unit, that she'd never been all that interested in changing the status quo?

That thought had her remembering back to when Matt was seven years old and she'd dated a television screenwriter who'd written a few episodes of *Friends*. He'd been smart, talented, and funny and had even seemed to genuinely like her son. But her mother's disapproval of the way he cut his hair, his clothes, the fact that he spent so much free time surfing, even his Canadian nationality, eventually did in the short-lived romance.

For the first time in a very long while, Claire was forced to wonder if, just perhaps, her mother, who'd always seemed so strong and independent, hadn't wanted to be left alone.

"You've always been the most important thing in my life, Matty," she said, slipping back into his childhood nickname. "And you've no idea how proud I am at how you're turning around what was a very small slip into a new life here. Especially when I know how much you must miss your old school."

He shrugged. "It's not so bad. The Dolphins may be the Bad News Bears of high school basketball, but Coach Slater is the best coach I've ever had."

"Really?" She could tell that he cared more about his players than others Matt had played for. But because he ran a closed practice, she hadn't had any idea about his actual skills.

"Yeah. He sees stuff no one else does. It's like he has superpower vision. And he always knows where everyone's going to go. Before you even go there."

"Maybe that's from his military days," she considered. "I'd guess defusing bombs requires a lot of attention to detail. And intuition."

"I guess so. Do you like him?"

And didn't that question come out of the blue? "Of course I do. He's a very nice man and he's been very good to both of us."

"No. I mean, do you *really* like him? Like that guy you went out with when I was in second grade."

Okay. That was a major surprise. Here she'd just been thinking about her failed relationship with the writer, who was now happily married, living in the San Fernando Valley with three kids.

"You remember Nash?" That had been his name. Which her mother had ridiculed, too. *"What was his mother thinking," she'd asked derisively. "Why not just name your child Chevrolet? Or Chrysler?"*

"Sure. He was nice. He took us to Lakers and Kings games. And taught me how to ice-skate. For a while I thought it'd be cool to be a hockey player."

She'd forgotten the winter of his hockey love. After she and Nash had stopped seeing each other, he'd never put on those skates again. She'd finally given them away to Goodwill when they'd moved.

"So," he pressed, "do you think you could like the coach in that way? Like a boyfriend?"

"I'm not sure people have boyfriends at thirty-three."

"Lila Greene's mother had a boyfriend. And she's older than you. And married."

"She did?" Claire waved away the question. How inappropriate was it to be gossiping about a former neighbor's sex life with your teenage son? "Never mind. I don't want to know. And as for Coach Slater, although he's a very nice man, I'm way too busy right now with the upcoming show and the renovations we have to do on this house to even think about getting involved."

"The show's going to be over soon. Maybe you can think about it then."

"Matt—"

"Just think about it, okay? And not just because it'd be cool to have him around more, but because he likes you."

"Because I'm your mother."

"Jeez." He rolled his expressive eyes toward the ceiling, which was dotted with brown roof-leak splotches. "Believe me, Mom, me being your kid has nothing to do with it. He likes you. A lot."

"I think you're misconstruing things."

"Guys know this stuff," he insisted.

This was so not a conversation she'd ever planned to have. "Speaking hypothetically," she said, treading carefully through this conversational minefield, "if you're right—"

He nodded emphatically. "I am."

"Would that bother you?"

"Hell—I mean, heck—no. You know what you said about Gram wanting to start a whole new life?"

"Of course."

"Well, maybe this is your chance. I'm not always going to be here," he reminded her unnecessarily. "I'll be going off to college in less than three years. You don't want me feeling guilty about leaving you alone, do you?"

She couldn't help laughing at that. "Of course not." Since they were actually getting along so well, she reached up and ruffled his hair, the way she used to. "How did you get so smart?"

"I guess it's in my genes, since I've got a smart mom," he said. Which may have been the first compliment she'd heard from him since he'd turned twelve. "There's something else I need to tell you. About that pot."

"Oh, honey." She shook her head. "It's okay. I totally understand. Anyone can make a mistake, and—"

"It wasn't mine."

"What?" And wasn't tonight just turning out to be

one surprise after another? "But it was found in your locker."

"Yeah. I know. But it wasn't mine. I guess, since I'm not going to BHHS anymore and we're not living in the neighborhood, I might as well tell you the truth. It was Lila's."

"Lila Greene's?" Daughter of the adulterous next-door neighbor?

"Yeah. She kept some of her stuff in my locker because it was closer to the cafeteria and more convenient for lunch."

"Did you know about it?"

"I knew she smoked sometimes," he said. "And before you ask, I never did because I didn't want to screw up my lung capacity on the court. I didn't realize she brought the stuff to school."

"And yet you never said a word." Even when it looked, for a short time, as if he might be expelled.

His shoulders lifted in that shrug she'd grown to hate. But instead of a lack of interest, this spoke of helplessness. "She told me that her father had warned her if she was busted again, he'd send her to boarding school." He held up both oversized hands, palms up. "What was I supposed to do?"

Telling herself that it was all water under the bridge, Claire didn't respond with the obvious. He should have told his mother the truth.

"It was a difficult situation," she allowed. "But let's agree that if anything like this ever comes up again, we'll talk about it. And figure out a workable solution."

"Okay. I guess that's what I should've done back then, huh?"

This time she followed her heart and wrapped her arms around him. "Bygones," she said. "This is a new start for both of us." Because she was afraid she was going to cry, she backed away and glanced up at the myrtle-wood mantel clock, another thing that had come with the house. "Now, you'd better start getting ready for bed so I don't have to turn you in to Coach Slater for breaking curfew."

As he laughed, sounding much like his old self, and left the room, Claire had to admit that Dillon Slater might represent more trouble than she was prepared to deal with, but he was also responsible for giving her son back to her.

39

After a great deal of consideration, Phoebe had come to a decision.

Since she'd discovered that cooking soothed her nerves and cleared her head, she'd been in the kitchen fixing Ethan a crab bisque when the answer suddenly came to her. It seemed so right, she was amazed that she hadn't seen it right away.

He was sitting across the apartment's combination kitchen / living room, feet up on the coffee table, reading the latest issue of *Acres* magazine. The radio was tuned to KBAY, the town's country station. Pulling the saucepan off the stove (she could always reheat it later), she crossed to stand in front of him.

"What I said?" she began. "About not being able to marry you until this problem with the Fletchers is settled?"

"You don't have to worry." He put the magazine down, took her into his arms, and began stroking her back in a way that may have been meant to soothe but had her thinking of dragging him into the bedroom and tackling him on that pretty white bed he'd put together for her. "I understand."

"That's the thing." She pulled away enough to look up at him. "I was wrong. Their custody suit came so out of the blue, I wasn't thinking straight."

"Who would have been? I sure as hell never saw that coming."

"I should have. His mother is a master manipulator. But here's the thing. . . . I was so focused on not allowing her to push me into a marriage that's everything I've always dreamed of, I didn't realize that once again I was letting Peter pull the strings.

"I swore when I left Colorado in the middle of the night to come here that would never, ever happen again."

His hands cupped her shoulders, his fingers digging a bit too deeply. "Are you saying what I think you're saying?" Hope and love and myriad emotions too complex to catalog were in his eyes and on his face.

His dear, dear face.

"I'm saying I want to marry you, Ethan. As soon as possible."

He lifted his eyes to the ceiling, which he'd painted a pretty pale sky blue for her. "Thank you, God."

Then, as Rascal Flatts' "I Won't Let Go" began playing on the radio, he began dancing her around the room, singing along with the lyrics that he'd fight her fight and stand by her and never let her go.

And unlike all those times when Peter Fletcher had caused her to weep, Phoebe's tears were born not from pain and fear, but from love. And much, much joy.

40

Sax and Kara's house was, like Claire's, set on a cliff overlooking the sea. That was the only similarity.

She knew movie stars in Beverly Hills who didn't own homes as large as this sprawling white, red-roofed house. But she knew none whose homes were as comfortable and welcoming.

"You have a stunning place," she told the couple, who greeted her and treated the pumpkin pie she'd brought from Take the Cake with the same pleasure they might have shown if she'd given them a deed to their own diamond mine.

No, she thought, as Matt immediately disappeared with Johnny Tiernan-St. James and she followed Kara—and the amazing aromas—into the kitchen, where J.T., Lucien, and Leon Douchett had pans simmering and pots boiling, with the six-burner range in full use. These people had no use for diamonds. Because they had a more valuable commodity. A family.

And another guest.

Which was not surprising, given what Kara had said about inviting others in town who didn't have family to celebrate the holiday with them. What she'd failed to mention was that one of those people just happened to be Dillon Slater.

Appearing not the least bit surprised to see her, he lifted two bottles of wine—one red, one white.

"You're just in time," he greeted her, another clue that he'd been expecting her. "Sax made me bartender before he and Cole went outside to deep-fry the turkey. So what can I get for you?"

Claire had two choices. She could be peeved at having been set up this way or she could relax and enjoy the day. And the company.

"The chardonnay would be lovely," she said. "Thanks."

"My pleasure." For a fleeting moment, as he bestowed a slow, unreasonably sexy smile on her, it was as if they were the only two people in the kitchen.

The cheerful conversation, the bubbling pots, the oil sizzling in heavy cast-iron pans, all faded away as he poured the wine and handed her the stemmed glass.

She took a sip of the chilled wine, hoping it would cool the heat the intimate look he was giving her sent flashing through her veins. It didn't.

"This is wonderful." Damn. Instead of sounding light and casual, a guest complimenting her host, her voice had come off as breathless.

"It's from a friend's winery," Sax's mother said. "Sax serves it in Bon Temps." Maureen Douchett, who had to be in her late fifties or early sixties, was stunning, harkening back to the golden days of Hollywood glamour with her glossy black hair, emerald green eyes, and red lips, which smiled a warm welcome. "He doesn't make a lot. But what he does make is very special."

Claire couldn't disagree.

"Are you sure I can't help?" she asked, feeling guilty watching all the work going on in the bustling, steamy kitchen. "I can't cook, but I could help peel potatoes or set the table—"

"The kids set the table," Kara said.

"And the men do all the cooking." Maureen smiled her satisfaction at that idea over the rim of her own wineglass.

"Well, most of the men," Dillon said. "J.T. and I, who apparently are not to be trusted, have been relegated to peeling potatoes and shrimp."

"When I was growing up, I was convinced the reason Cajuns had kids was so they'd have someone to peel their shrimp," J.T. said from behind a counter piled high with shells. "Since I was the youngest, I usually got stuck with the job."

"It's because you're so good at it, darling," the most famous woman in the room said with a smile immediately recognizable to movie fans all over the world. Claire, who was used to going to the occasional party with celebrities, was surprised to be having Thanksgiving dinner with Mary Joyce, a major A-list movie star.

"You're just trying to butter me up," he complained without heat.

"The men also do all the cleanup," said Kelli, who was married to Cole, the eldest Douchett brother.

"Which makes this about the most perfect day on the calendar," Mary said. "And yet another reason to love America. The average Irishman would probably have trouble finding so much as a pot in a kitchen in his own home."

"OMG," Matt, who'd come in with Johnny to get

some popcorn shrimp and Cajun devil peanuts, blurted out. "You're Mary Joyce."

"I am indeed," the actress said, the lilt of Ireland in her friendly tone. "And you must be Matt. The basketball player everyone's talking about."

"Um . . . yeah . . . I guess so." His cheeks flushed. "I mean, yeah, I play basketball for the Dolphins."

"My husband and I are looking forward to watching your first game in a few days."

His Adam's apple bobbed as he swallowed. "You're coming to our game?"

"We wouldn't miss it," J.T. said. "Believe it or not, Mary spent all that time in L.A. and never once got to a Lakers game. So she's never even seen basketball."

"We're not the Lakers," Johnny said. "But Coach Dillon is teaching us their triangle offense."

"Well, as I said, I'm looking forward to cheering you all on. My older brother played football during his school days back in Ireland. There was, for a short time, talk about him possibly becoming a professional, but he wanted to be a war photographer instead."

"My dad was a war photographer, too," Johnny said. "Now he just takes pictures of people."

"My brother got out of the business as well," Mary said. "He's now a farmer in Ireland."

"I really like your movies," Matt blurted out. "I've seen all of them bunches of times."

"Well, isn't that lovely." The smile she bestowed on the teenager had him turning red up to the tips of his ears. Partly, Claire suspected, because the actress was nearly naked in her Selkie films.

"My Maureen could've been a movie star," Lucien

Douchett, Sax's father, informed Claire as he deftly whisked a roux with one hand while stirring a pot of shrimp and crab gumbo with the other. "But she turned down a big Hollywood producer to marry me and stay in Shelter Bay."

"It was a very small offer," Maureen said as she went over to the stove and kissed him on his weathered cheek. The look they exchanged was so intimate, Claire almost felt as if she were intruding on a personal moment.

Having grown up a single mother who was the product of a divorce herself, she honestly had never believed that type of love existed. Sax's parents and grandparents, Adèle and Leon Douchett, were living, breathing proof that it did.

"You're a lucky woman," she told Kara as they watched Angel following Trey Douchett around like a lovesick puppy. The tiny ballerina had informed Claire that when she grew up she was going to marry this boy she'd "loved forever."

Listening to the absolute determination in the little girl's tone, although it was highly unlikely, Claire almost believed her.

"I tell myself that on a daily basis," Kara said.

"Me, too," Charity said as Angel demonstrated an arabesque, which had her wobbling a bit on one leg, to the ever-patient Trey. "When I moved here I was a runaway bride. Now I have a fabulous, talented husband and two children whom I couldn't love any more if I'd given birth to them."

"I was wondering if I could ask you a favor," Claire said, feeling suddenly uncomfortable.

"Of course," Charity said without hesitation.

"I have a showing in Portland next week and will have to stay overnight. Matt insists he's old enough to be left alone, but—"

"Of course he should stay with us," Charity said without hesitation. "Johnny would love it."

Relief swept over Claire. "Thank you."

"Don't mention it. It's no problem at all, and, as I said, Johnny really likes Matt. I suspect they share that fish-out-of-water feeling, although Johnny's fit into school much better than I thought he would."

"That's probably something he learned being moved from foster home to foster home," Kara suggested.

"Probably so. I never liked moving, but I got so I could deal with all the schools and all my mother's marriages," Charity agreed.

"You make me feel a bit guilty," Mary said. "I lived in the same house I was born in, attended the same school, then went off to university. Then came here and met J.T. My life, compared to so many others, has been very blessed."

"You lost your mother when you were just a girl," Charity pointed out. "That couldn't have been easy."

"No. But I was fortunate to have my gram and my older sister."

The bond between the women was obviously very strong. But, just as when they'd shown up at the cottage, there was nothing cliquish about them. They welcomed Claire into their group as if she'd always been part of the fabric of their lives, and if they did bring up Dillon a few more times during the conversation leading up to dinner, she understood that it was only because he was a friend as well. And they wanted him to be as happy as they all appeared to be.

*   *   *

The dining room, which was about twice the size of Claire's cottage, was packed with people. The table groaned with platters of surprisingly moist deep-fried turkey with giblet gravy and an andouille sausage and corn bread stuffing; baked ham with a sugarcane-bourbon glaze, because, as Leon informed her, no Cajun holiday dinner was complete without two meat main courses; corn *maque choux* Lucien had made by braising corn and vegetables until the corn became creamy, then adding bits of crispy bacon; shrimp and crab gumbo, again, made by Lucien, with shrimp peeled by J.T.; fried oyster patties and crab cakes; a sweet potato casserole utilizing the potatoes Dillon had been peeling when she'd arrived; green beans with bacon and onions; spicy corn bread; and dirty rice.

Conversation flowed like wine, back and forth across the table, as they shared old stories and teased one another in ways she sensed were family jokes. She also learned that the house had originally belonged to Sax's grandparents, who'd inherited it from a wealthy lumber baron's widow. When it became too much for the elderly couple to take care of, they'd moved into town to live with their children, passing the house on to their middle grandson.

After dinner, Angel danced, Lucien played a clarinet and Sax his guitar, accompanying Maureen, who entertained with her still strong voice. The house was redolent with spicy scents and flavors, laughter, and lots and lots of love.

Which had Claire thinking back on Thanksgiving with her mother, who'd thought that roasting an entire turkey for three people was a waste of time and effort. So they'd always dressed up and gone out, where stuffy waiters delivered expensive meals and wouldn't have thought of breaking into song or telling a joke.

"You look as if you're having a good time," Dillon said as they stood side by side on the porch after a sinfully rich pumpkin bread pudding, watching the sun sink into the ocean in a dazzling display of gold, ruby, and bronze.

"I am." She turned toward him and smiled. "Enough that I'm not even going to be upset that they sprung you on me."

"What makes you think you weren't sprung on me?"

She looked up at him and saw the answer in his eyes but asked anyway. "Was I?"

"No. Kara's newly married. She's in love. So it's not so surprising she wants everyone else she knows to experience the same thing."

"Love isn't contagious. It's not like the flu."

"I used to think that. Especially watching everyone I knew get divorced. But here we are in a house filled with people who definitely offer contrary evidence."

"That's not very scientific."

"Sometimes you just have to go with your gut and figure out the science later," he countered easily. "You sure are a picture today, Claire."

She'd noticed that his Texas accent and syntax came and went with his moods. Like now, it surfaced when he was relaxed and enjoying himself. Or when he was yelling at the team on the sideline. Or when he went into seduction mode, which she braced herself for now.

"I'm overdressed." Her blouse was cream silk, her slacks a black lightweight wool. Kara had told her that dress was casual, but certain that she didn't mean Claire's usual jeans and T-shirts, Claire had delved deep inside her closet and pulled out something that she knew her mother would approve of.

When Cole Douchett had opened the door wearing worn jeans and a faded WHO'S YOUR CRAWDADDY T-shirt, she realized Kara had, indeed, meant *casual*.

"Maybe just a bit, for this company," he allowed. "But I can help you out with that."

"How?" she asked, knowing that she was walking into a verbal trap.

"This is a big house. I figure we can find ourselves a little corner somewhere and I'll mess you up a bit."

As if to demonstrate, he cupped the back of her neck, beneath her hair, and brushed his mouth against hers. His lips were warm, the air cool, his kiss tender and undemanding.

"That's a start," he decided, smiling against her lips.

Then kissed her again.

A third time.

Each time, his lips lingered a bit longer. His thumb brushed a gentle pressure against her chin, inviting her lips to part.

Which she'd just done, when she heard an all too familiar voice calling her name.

"Mom?"

She jumped back, feeling as guilty as if she'd been caught stealing dollars from the church poor box.

"I'm out here, Matt," she called back.

"Johnny's got to go feed the dogs at the shelter. I told him I'd come with him."

"Fine." She was all too aware that she was still out here all alone with the man she'd sworn to stay away from, and her voice wasn't nearly as steady as she'd have liked it to have been.

"And we thought we might go to a show afterward. The Orcas is having an *X-Men* marathon."

"Just be home by eleven," she said. "You know the team curfew."

"And your coach just heard you," Dillon called out. "Wouldn't want me calling and checking up on you boys later, now, would you?"

"No, sir." Claire heard a faint disappointment in his tone. "Thanks, Mom."

"You're welcome. Have a good time."

She heard a door close. A minute later, the Escape pulled away from the house with both boys in it.

"Now he knows we were alone."

"Anyone ever tell you that you worry too much?"

"I'm a single mother of a teenage son. It comes with the territory."

"I understand that. But here's a little life lesson I picked up one dicey day in Kandahar. If it doesn't blow you up, in the great scheme of things, it isn't all that important."

Before she could respond to that, he skimmed a finger down the slope of her nose. "You'll dream of me tonight," he predicted.

"Arrogant ass," she muttered.

But about this, Claire knew he was right.

41

Dillon had decided early on that if the Dolphins couldn't beat the other teams on shooting and defense—which they couldn't, at least at the beginning of the season—he was going to make sure they could outrun them.

Which was why, over the past weeks of preseason practice, he'd been ruthless in his conditioning program, making the kids run up and down the bleachers and do laps around the gym and, as a change of pace, on the school's cinder track on those rare days when the rain didn't threaten to drown them.

Everyone complained in the beginning, but by the first game of the season, when they opened on the road, he felt confident that there wasn't a team in the league whose legs were as strong.

"We're going to wear them down," he said, walking up and down the aisle of the team bus as they headed up the coast to play the Agate Beach Pirates, who, Ken had informed Dillon, had been the Stoners back when they'd been established after World War II. Over time, as the name brought to mind something less inspiring than the rocks that scattered over the sand at low tide, the administration had decided to change mascots.

"They're going to see us come out on the floor and think we're the same team they're used to wiping their floor with. But we're going to be like sharks in a fish tank. We'll sniff out the weak ones, never let up, and wear them down. Which will lead to what?" He put his hand to his ear.

"Turnovers!" the players roared as they did every time he asked the question.

"Right. And what is the one sure thing about turnovers?"

"The team with the fewest turnovers wins!"

"And what does Coach Wooden say about finishing a game?"

Along with running the players ragged since their first practice, Dillon had been determined to teach them the history of this game they were playing. To hammer into their minds the knowledge they needed to win when all the odds were against them.

"It's not who starts a game. But who finishes!"

"And who's that going to be today?"

"The Dolphins!"

What they might lack in skills and talent, they definitely made up for in enthusiasm.

"You bet your asses," he said with a grin.

He returned to the front of the bus and sat down next to Don Daniels. "Sometimes I really freaking love this job," he told the assistant coach.

Agate Bay was a division powerhouse and it showed—from the state championship banners hanging from the rafters to the trophy case in the lobby that overflowed with only a fraction of the shiny hardware the teams had collected over the years. And then there was the packed house of very vocal fans.

Having been told by Ken that they also introduced the team players NBA-style, Dillon had the AV guys at school set up a loudspeaker in the gym so the kids would get used to it. But it wasn't the same as the real thing. As the roars rocked the roof and searchlights flashed each time a Pirate ran out onto the floor, Dillon could feel his Dolphin players' spirits deflating.

He could give them all the *X*'s and *O*'s. He could quote John Wooden, Phil Jackson, and Pat Riley until he was blue in the face. They weren't perfect. Hell, most days Dillon wasn't even sure that—with the exception of Templeton—they were any good.

"Just go out there, run their tails off, and remember the basics," he told the players, who were gathered around him on the sideline after the over-the-top, bells-and-whistles introduction meant to intimidate visiting teams. "And most of all, have fun."

In the beginning, nerves showing, they forced shots, trying for three-pointers and dunks they couldn't even make in practice.

"You're trying too hard," he told Dirk Martin after pulling him from the floor and putting his best friend, Cooper, in to replace him after he'd forced yet another shot to the rim. "Last year you might as well have been out there on your own. This year you've got Templeton. Whatever problems are between the two of you, keep them in the locker room. Don't take them out onto the floor. And use him."

At the end of the first quarter, the Dolphins were behind by only six points, which Dillon considered a miracle, right up there with the bread and fishes and water to wine. They might not be making any shots, but their legs were getting ahead of the Pirates, keeping them from making a lot of the attempts.

By halftime, they'd slipped six more, putting them twelve points behind. And when Martin threw away a ball instead of passing to Templeton, who'd been open, Dillon realized that the antagonism between the boys had returned. And, dammit, it probably would, every time they were under pressure. Which, given the team's skill level, and the toughness of the season's schedule, meant they'd be fighting each other during every damn game if he didn't do something.

Now.

"Okay," he said in the locker room, "we've got them right where we want them. Now it's time to get serious and shut that crowd up. And we're going to do that by making sure our captains get the ball as often as possible."

"Captains?" Templeton asked.

"As in two?" Martin scowled at that idea and shot Claire's kid a dark look.

"Two," Dillon confirmed. "Guys, you're looking at your new team captains."

"Jeez, Coach," the cocaptains both groaned at once. Revealing, Dillon thought optimistically, that his two best players finally had something in common. They both hated his brilliant idea.

"I don't care how you two hotshot ball hogs get along off the court," he said, "but when you're playing, you're going to not only cooperate; you're going to lead. Is that straight?"

"Yes, sir," they both mumbled. Which wasn't exactly the level of enthusiasm Dillon needed from the boys.

He lifted his hand to his ear. "I can't hear you."

"Yes, sir!" Now, *that* was better.

"Good. Now go and show them that the Dolphins may get down, but they're never out. And by the way, there's a dead spot on the floor you can use to your advantage."

"A dead spot?" Templeton asked.

"I didn't see any dead spot," Martin said.

"It's three feet from the sidelines opposite their bench. Stay away from dribbling there, and if you can get them to fast break in that direction, you should be able to steal a dribble when the ball slows down.

"Now, before we go back out there, what's our motto?"

"The only easy day was yesterday!"

"Hoorah," Dillon said.

The conditioning had paid off. Although the locker room had radiated with antagonism, his two best players did somehow manage to put their antipathy aside as they put on the Templeton and Martin show.

The first half, each had been concerned with his own scoring, but suddenly, they were passing the ball, creating opportunities for their other teammates, and defending like dual demons.

They'd also managed to do what Ken had assured Dillon *never* happened. They silenced the home crowd. The gym, infamous in high school hoops for its deafening noise, became as quiet as a church on Monday morning. During the third quarter, there was only the sound of the leather ball bouncing, the squeaking of soles on the polished wooden floor, and the labored breathing of the Pirates as they were taken by surprise and outhustled.

Then, as the Dolphin fans realized that the momentum was actually changing, something they definitely weren't used to seeing, they began to wildly cheer their team on.

With five minutes to go in the game, they'd not only made up the difference; they were two points ahead. Then Templeton, instead of taking an easy layup, decided to dunk it.

The ball clanked like a brick off the back rim, high into the air, but fortunately Martin grabbed it and scored with a layup.

Frustrated by the showboating, Dillon yanked Claire's son off the court. "What's the freaking first commandment?"

"The team always comes first."

"And the second?"

"Thou shalt not miss a dunk."

"Remember that next time. For now, put your butt on the bench. If I need you, I'll call."

The Pirates' legs were gone. The Dolphins had spent the final quarter controlling the clock, keeping the ball from their opponent, running them up and down the court, essentially putting on a basketball clinic.

"I hate to tempt fate," Don said as Templeton, now back in the game, shot, making three points, "but it's going to be really hard for them to lose now."

"I know."

Dillon was not exactly thrilled to find his team on the winning side of a blowout. His initial concern, going into the game, was that they hadn't known how to win. Now he worried that they'd foolishly, mistakenly think the rest of the season was going to go the same way, and slack off.

As yet more proof of their inexperience, when the

buzzer rang, his ebullient team went wild, jumping around at the center of the floor, throwing high fives as if they'd just won the NBA finals.

Which earned them an admittedly deserved foul for excessive celebration, but the Pirates, now totally off their usual brilliance, missed the free throws, officially ending the game.

Only then did Dillon look up into the stands to the visitors' section, where he'd known, from the moment she'd walked in, that Claire was sitting with the entire Douchett clan, along with Charity, Gabe, and Angel, who'd swapped out the ubiquitous tutu for a miniature blue-and-white Dolphins cheerleader outfit.

The woman who'd infiltrated his dreams and banished his nightmares, the single mother whose love and unyielding sense of duty to her son were the only things keeping them apart, had begun jumping up and down like a teenager, waving plastic blue-and-white pom-poms and hugging everyone around her.

Their eyes met. When she flashed him a dazzlingly brilliant smile, the first he'd been treated to, Dillon's breath clogged in his lungs and his mouth went as dry as the Iraqi sandbox.

The earth teetered on its axis, tectonic plates shifted, volcanoes erupted, and if a wave train of a tsunami had suddenly washed over the gym, he wouldn't have been the least bit surprised.

Because the well-ordered, comfortable, postwar world he'd created for himself in Shelter Bay had just exploded.

And, on the verge of exploding himself, Dillon knew that neither it nor he would ever be the same.

42

After Thanksgiving dinner at the Douchett home, Claire locked herself away in her studio and, except for attending Matt's games, spent most of her waking hours sketching and blowing the glass pieces for her exhibition.

Despite a less than encouraging beginning, since her visit to the aquarium, the previously temperamental glass had come alive, singing in a way she'd never experienced before. So much so that, after waking up to see what appeared to be a glistening of ice crystals on the steely water outside her windows, she decided, although she'd already created what she'd thought would be her final piece, to try one more.

The process was hot, laborious, and prone to failure, but she wasn't about to let that stop her.

"The only easy day was yesterday," she said, quoting the SEAL saying Dillon had the team repeat before every game.

She began by swirling the glass from the crucible onto her blowpipe. As long as she'd been working with molten glass, she found the fact that the mere wind of her breath could create such beauty almost miraculous.

Since the slightest change in breath at the crucial moment could be the difference between perfection and another piece tossed into the scrap bucket, she quickly shaped, reheated, then shaped some more.

When she was satisfied, she began rolling the piece on her marver, coaxing it into the form that would begin its final transformation as she layered on frit—bits of crushed colored glass—in swirling shades of deep smoke blue, steel blue, and opal white designed to resemble the storm-tossed, white-capped winter sea churning outside her windows.

"Good," she murmured as she twirled the glass downward, then suddenly stopped, causing the edges to ripple like the tops of waves. "But not quite finished."

A *ghiaccio* was a Venitian technique popular in the sixteenth century that she'd achieved only a few times. But as heady creativity surged through Claire's veins, intent as she was on her creation, an earthquake could have split open the floor beneath her sneaker-clad feet and she wouldn't have noticed.

This time she drew in a deep breath. Then she plunged the multihued bowl into cold water, causing a sudden, fine crackling of the surface. Thus, the definition of the word: *ice*.

Then—and this was the trickiest part—she quickly returned to her blowpipe and blew more clear glass she used to layer over the crackled ice.

As she carried the bowl to the annealer to slowly cool, she found herself wishing she had someone to share her success with.

"Sometimes," she said to herself as she closed the oven door, "total independence can suck."

43

Phoebe was sitting on the couch, knitting a square for Project Linus—a charity that made blankets for sick and needy children that Sax's grandmother had gotten nearly every woman in town involved in—when the doorbell rang. Sunny, her and Ethan's adopted golden retriever, rose from where she'd been snoozing on the rug to accompany her to the door.

When Phoebe looked through the peephole and saw who was standing on the other side of the door, her stomach clenched.

"It's Charity," she told Ethan as he came over from the kitchen area, where he'd begun preparing dinner. Although she'd assured him that she was perfectly capable, he'd insisted, when she'd arrived home from cooking for the Lavender Hill Farm restaurant lunch crowd, that she spend the rest of the day off her feet and relaxing.

"Well, you'd better let her in." Although his voice was typically calm, she could see the shared worry in his eyes.

"I bring more tidings of good news," Charity said as she entered the apartment, pausing momentarily to pat the welcoming dog's head. "And an early Christmas present—the Fletchers dropped the suit."

"What?" Phoebe turned to Ethan, who looked as surprised as she felt. "That fast? How?"

"It seems your former father-in-law has been under investigation for something to do with natural gas licenses. I didn't really follow all of it, but it appears that bribery might have been involved. Along with extortion."

"That doesn't surprise me at all," Phoebe said.

"Like father, like son," Ethan muttered.

"There's more. It appears Peter wasn't his only child."

"What?" All right, *that* came as a surprise.

"Apparently he's been spending a lot of time in Washington, DC."

"He always did. That's where the lobbyists are."

"True. Including one particular one who, it seems, he's been having an affair with for the past eight years."

"No!" Phoebe's surge of emotion caused her child to do a backflip. Sitting back down on the couch, she pressed her hands against her stomach. Revealing a strong sensitivity to emotion, Sunny placed her large, furry head in Phoebe's lap, as if to comfort her. "Are you saying he has a secret child with this woman?" Phoebe asked as she stroked the golden retriever.

"That's exactly what I'm saying. And he's been siphoning money to pay for her living expenses in a pricey Georgetown home. Plus private school for his daughter. Also some really to-die-for vacation trips to the Caribbean, Mexico, and Europe, including a birthday trip for the little girl to Disneyland Paris this past August.

"Which gets particularly sticky when you consider that Fletcher Gas and Oil went public a decade ago. So, by paying the woman consulting fees averaging in the seven figures every year for eight years to keep her quiet when she hasn't done a lick of work for the company, it appears he's been embezzling from shareholders."

"Oh, wow." For a fleeting moment Phoebe almost felt sorry for her former mother-in-law. Then she reminded herself that the woman had been trying to steal her child.

"I do feel sorry for that little girl," she murmured. "Bad enough that her father's never acknowledged her publicly. But her mother must not be the most nurturing parent, either, to use her daughter as a bargaining and blackmail chip."

"That part sucks," Charity agreed.

"Well, it certainly doesn't make the guy an ideal father in the eyes of any court," Ethan said.

"That is true. My stepfather learned this from an attorney friend who's familiar with the case. It hasn't gone public yet. But it's about to break, and I suspect, Phoebe, that your former father-in-law might find himself going to federal prison."

"Too bad it'll probably be one of those country club ones for the rich one percent," Ethan muttered.

"Unfortunately, you're probably right," Charity agreed. "But a prison's still a prison. He's going to lose his freedom, undoubtedly the chairmanship of his own company, and his reputation. Not to mention all his business and political friends, who won't want to be connected with him in any way.

"Unsurprisingly, his attorney realized that there's no way he can win a custody battle while being under threat of incarceration for several federal crimes. Especially when you already factor in his son's actions toward you and Ethan. So they had no choice but to drop the suit. Which they would have lost, but now you won't have to go through all that stress of depositions and perhaps even court appearances."

"Wow," Phoebe repeated, her head spinning. "I can't imagine how furious Peter's mother must be."

"Like the evil queen in Disney's Snow White, just before the boulder falls on her," Ethan guessed.

"That's probably a good analogy," Charity said.

"She's always enjoyed playing society queen bee," Phoebe said. "It's how she's defined herself."

"Well, that's going to be a bit difficult with the king behind bars," Charity said dryly.

Phoebe knew that this would go down as one of the most amazing days of her life. As she sat there with a woman who'd become her friend and the man she loved with every fiber of her being, and her sweet new dog, who'd fit so perfectly into her life, she looked around her lovely apartment again and thought of how far she'd come since she was that terrified, shattered runaway wife who'd arrived on the doorstep of Haven House.

"I love this apartment," she said.

"You've done a great job with it," Charity said.

"I have. Thanks to all of you who chipped in to help furnish it. And I'll definitely keep and cherish every gift. But"—she held out her hand to Ethan—"I think it's time for me to go home. To our farm."

44

Although the Art on the River gallery was packed to the rafters, Claire knew the moment Dillon entered. He stood at the edge of the main room, watching her with an unblinking male intensity that set every nerve ending in her body to jangling.

Don't look at him!

Although it took every bit of concentration she could muster to laugh at some obscure arty joke—revolving around the idea of Van Gogh being reduced to cranking out TV beer commercials to pay for reconstructive surgery on his ear—while she was being bombarded with testosterone bombs, she was all too aware of him headed her way.

But before he could reach her, a redhead specializing in steampunk wall murals stepped in front of him, deftly stopping his progress.

She was wearing a black-and-red corset adorned with black ostrich feathers, a layered black ruffled skirt that barely covered the essentials, black lace stockings attached to the corset with elastic straps, and stiletto-heeled, over-the-knee leather boots. She'd accessorized the look with a black derby and attached illusion veil, a gun belt worn low on her hips, black lace fingerless gloves, and a *lot* of ink, including a dirigible that floated across her breasts.

Claire recognized that maddeningly sexy smile he exchanged with the artist. Watched as the woman reached into her generous cleavage—made even more impressive by the uplift of the corset and that airship tattoo—and handed him a small white card. That she was offering Dillon something was obvious. Claire would bet it wasn't a mural.

"Congratulations," he said when he finally reached her. "Your show appears to be a grand success."

"It's going well."

Better than well.

She'd nearly sold out. Including the green flash piece, which she'd purposefully priced high because, if she were to be perfectly honest, once it was done, she hadn't really wanted to sell it. Unlike a piece of jewelry, the mercurial temperament of glass made it impossible to create exact duplicates of any piece. However, since she needed the money for the renovations she was planning with Lucas Chaffee's guidance, she didn't really have any choice but to put it up for sale.

"You've drawn quite an eclectic crowd."

"Portland's art community is nothing if not colorful," she agreed.

"I know I've been away from the States a lot, so I haven't exactly kept up with popular culture, but is that woman over there actually wearing a ray gun in her holster?"

"It's steampunk. According to Matt, who reads some of the books, apparently it borrows from elements of science fiction like H. G. Wells and Jules Verne and has something to do with steam power in an alternate history or a postapocalyptic period. But I'm certainly no expert, so don't quote me."

"I wouldn't even try."

"I'm sure that woman who gave you her card could explain it in much more detail."

"She probably could. But I'd much rather talk with you. . . . Can I buy you a drink?"

"It's an open bar. Drinks are free."

"Even better."

Those dimples deepened as he smiled down at her. He appeared larger than she remembered him. Almost overpowering. He was wearing black jeans, a black cashmere sweater, and a black leather bomber jacket that gave him a dangerous look.

"I'm not here to play. I'm supposed to be working."

He rocked back on his heels and glanced around the white pillars holding her sea-swept glass collection. "From all the red dots on the tags next to your pieces, I'd say you can risk taking a couple minutes for a break."

He put his hand on her back and began herding her toward the bar that had been set up next to a Christmas tree that soared to the open loft ceiling.

"I don't remember saying yes," she said.

"You didn't say no," he countered. "And I did drive all the way up here. Surely you wouldn't be so cruel as to make me go back to Shelter Bay without at least having one drink with me?"

"Which brings up a question. What *are* you doing here?"

"Well, I could make up some excuse, like I had a meeting with Shelter Bay High's Nike rep, but that'd be a lie. I came up to see you. And maybe offer some moral support, which you don't appear to need."

Not sure how to respond, she didn't say anything right away.

"Plus, there's another reason."

"And that would be?" she asked him.

"I wanted some time alone with you. Away from all the prying eyes of everyone in town."

She looked around. "This is hardly a private venue."

"True. Though it *is* anonymous since the only person in the place I know is you. But it's also why I booked a room at the hotel."

"*My* hotel?"

"I figured that would be more convenient than staying in one across town. It'll make it easier to walk you to your door after our date."

"That's more than a little chauvinistic."

"You want to walk me to my door? Although it might dent some less confident guy's male ego, I'm down with that. . . .

"What would you like to drink?"

What she would have liked was for him to get back in his Jeep and return to Shelter Bay, where he belonged. She didn't want him here in Portland, let alone staying at her hotel. He was too hot. Too male. Too damn tempting.

"I'll have a champagne cocktail, please," she said to the bartender.

"Dark beer for me," Dillon said.

Speaking of chauvinism . . .

Instead of handing her fluted glass directly to her, the bartender gave it to Dillon, who passed it on. As their fingers touched, she felt a jolt of emotion so strong it shook her, but when she risked a glance upward to see if he'd been similarly affected, his friendly expression gave nothing away.

"Nice tree," he said, though he wasn't looking at it, but at her. The tree in question was black, with black-and-white lights, white satin bows, and clear glass ornaments.

"It's supposed to represent a white-tie affair."

"Festive." His tone said otherwise. And although she could appreciate the tree as an artistic statement, she'd have to admit that when it came to Christmas, she was definitely a traditionalist.

As he continued to look at her, long and deep, Claire took a sip of the seasonal red cocktail and, as she tasted the tang of cranberry and citrusy Cointreau, willed both her mind and her body to calm. "I know I've been distracted lately, but I believe I would remember you asking me out on a date."

"Would you have said yes if I had?"

"No."

"I figured as much. Which is why I decided just to take matters into my own hands. And speaking of which, I'd really like to get my hands on you, Claire. All over."

She glanced over at the bartender, who was doing his best to hide a grin and failing.

Having watched Dillon pacing the sidelines of that basketball game, and listening to what little Matt had shared about practices, Claire realized that he might be the most determined individual she'd ever met. Which meant that as much as she didn't want to have this conversation, she wasn't going to be able to continue to ignore it.

Taking his arm, she practically dragged him a few feet

away, putting the black-and-white tuxedo tree between them and the eavesdropping bartender.

"Okay, that hands-on thing?" she said. "I know the feeling."

"Well, now." He rocked back on his heels. "That's a surprise. Oh, not that you've been thinking about it, same as I've been. But that you'd admit it."

"I'm not the kind of a woman who plays coy, Dillon. I'll admit I'm attracted."

"That's a start. . . . You've changed your scent."

"What?" The sensible, sane, *reasonable* explanation as to why an affair was impossible momentarily fled her mind.

"You usually smell like a tropical vacation. Tonight you're walking on the dangerous, just a little wild side."

"You should probably know that I'm the furthest thing from dangerous. I wouldn't want you to be disappointed."

He laughed at that. "Sweetheart, I've dealt with IEDs less dangerous than you."

"I'm also not impulsive."

"Yet you packed up and moved to Oregon."

"That's different. I was protecting my son. Who," she said firmly, "has to be my main priority."

He lifted his beer bottle. "As he should be."

She'd been sexually impetuous once in her life. That had resulted in her son, which she'd never regret. But she'd always sworn she'd never make that mistake again. Even when she was so, so tempted.

"We've been through this, Dillon. It's unethical for you to be dating the mother of one of your players."

"So you keep saying." He tipped the bottle back and

took a long swallow of the beer. "Which, I have to tell you, kind of hurts my feelings."

"Surely I'm not the first woman to turn you down."

"No. But you're the first who's questioned my integrity."

"Me?" It was her turn to take a long drink. "How on earth did I do that?"

"You're suggesting that if we went out, and things heated up, I'd actually risk another player's chances for college by giving Matt more playing time. Simply because I was sleeping with his mother."

"I didn't say that."

"Not in those words. But you're implying it."

"I honestly don't believe you'd play favorites. But that doesn't mean that others, especially parents of some of the seniors, like Mr. and Mrs. Martin, wouldn't think it."

"Anyone ever tell you that you worry too much?" He reached out and idly twined a strand of her hair around his fingers. "Have I mentioned that your hair reminds me of summer?"

"No. Possibly because you realized what a bad line it is."

"It's not a line. The first time I saw you, sitting in your car in the school parking lot, I thought how it looked as if it was streaked with sunshine. I didn't say anything at the time, because we didn't know each other yet, but I hadn't had the most promising breakfast, being hammered on by boosters about Matt, and was feeling frustrated. You've no idea how much you brightened that rainy day. . . ."

"So, have you eaten yet?"

"I've been busy." And too nervous even to think about food.

"I figured as much. What would you say to a late supper?"

When she opened her mouth to respond, he put his finger against her lips. Although she knew it was only her overly active imagination, Claire could have sworn she felt the sizzle.

"You have to eat." He smoothly, logically pressed his case. "And you probably need to unwind before going to bed."

That was definitely true. Gallery shows required an amazing amount of energy, requiring the artist to be continually "on" to potential buyers. She'd smiled so much tonight she was certain her face muscles would ache in the morning, and was so exhausted she felt on the verge of melting into a puddle right here on the black-and-white marble floor, yet at the same time, both her body and her mind were buzzing with adrenaline.

"I'm used to working alone, with just my own thoughts," she said. "Events like this not only take me out of my comfort zone; afterward I'm too exhausted to crash."

"It's the adrenaline. I always felt the same way after a mission."

He continued to toy with her hair. The gesture, while not overtly sexual, felt inordinately personal. Claire was not used to people invading her space. But there was something so compelling about Dillon Slater, she couldn't back away.

"You have to be in a zone to defuse an IED. By the time I'd reach the target, I'd pretty much be all alone in my own head, the way you looked when you were blowing that glass. I had to give it my entire focus, but at the same time, I never forgot that if I screwed up, even the slightest bit, they'd be picking pieces of me out of the sand and dirt for a very long time.

"So by the time I was done, I'd be totally drained. But at same time it felt as if a nest of hornets were buzzing around inside me."

He'd nailed it. Claire had always gravitated to the arts and men who worked in creative fields, which was why she was surprised to find herself having anything in common with a former bomb disposal expert who spent his days teaching kids physics.

"What I was going to say, before you cut me off," she said, returning to the original topic, "was that I'd like to have a late supper with you. Just as a friend, if that's the way you're willing to keep it. For now."

Claire knew she was playing with fire even more dangerous than what she worked with in her hotshop every day. But the simple truth was that she was didn't want to be alone. Not tonight.

"Terrific. You flew up here from Newport, right?"

"I did, and Lorenzo, one of the owners, picked me up at the hotel and drove me over here."

"Great. So we don't have to deal with two cars going back to the hotel. When can you escape?"

He'd no sooner asked the question when the gallery owner, wearing a gold silk duster over black slacks and a black silk shirt, came up to them.

"Congratulations, dearheart," Lorenzo Batista gushed. He framed her face in his hands while air kissing both her cheeks. "The show was an absolute tour de force."

"I knew you'd sell out," said Lorenzo's companion, who'd dressed to dazzle in a black sequin blazer, starched white tux shirt, black bow tie, black velvet slacks, and mirror-bright Christmas red patent leather shoes. "In fact, two people even got into a brief but heated bidding war over that ice sea bowl, which had it going for fifty percent over what we'd asked."

"The loser asked if you'd be willing to make another," Lorenzo said.

"But Lorenzo told him that you were no philistine who worked on demand for the masses," the second man assured her.

"That sounds awfully full of myself," she worried.

"Oh, don't worry, darling." Lorenzo waved a hand, showing off his gleaming woven gold wedding ring. He and his longtime business and life partner had gotten married in Vancouver, British Columbia, last month. "With this new inspired sea-swept series, you've catapulted yourself into serious-artist territory."

"Like Monet and his water lilies," his husband said. "Or Georgia O'Keeffe and her flowers."

"That's definitely an overstatement." While it was always lovely to have her work admired, Claire had a logical enough head on her shoulders to know that she was nowhere near those two artists.

"Not for long," Lorenzo said. "I'm very aesthetically sensitive, and it's quite clear that something's definitely set fire to your emotions since your move to our Pacific Northwest." He glanced over at Dillon, who'd remained silent during the exchange. "Or perhaps that's *someone*," he murmured.

He extended his hand. Diamonds flashed, gold

gleamed. "Welcome to Art on the River. I'm Lorenzo Batista, proprietor and admirer of our darling Claire. This is my husband and business partner, Raphael."

"Lorenzo and Raphael recently got married," Claire informed Dillon.

"Congratulations," he said easily as he shook both their hands. "I'm Dillon Slater."

"The green flash!" Raphael exclaimed. Then, when he saw Claire's puzzled look, he put both his hands over his mouth.

"Now you've done it," Lorenzo said with a long, dramatic sigh. "I believe, from Claire's expression, that Mr. Slater preferred to keep his purchase a secret while waiting for a more intimate time to tell Claire the news."

"What news?" But a suspicion was niggling.

"That I bought your flash."

"You?"

While they'd been setting up the display, each piece of the collection claiming its own pillar beneath a spotlight, Claire had waffled about whether she'd wanted to sell the piece that had been born from such a burst of inspiration. And which had opened up a long flare of inspiration that she'd never, thus far in her life, experienced. But when she'd expressed her ambivalence to Lorenzo, he'd informed her that he'd received a call at home on Thanksgiving from a patron asking to buy it.

At the time, she'd assumed it was someone who'd seen the piece in the catalog. Never in a million years would she have expected that person to be this man.

"It's a special piece. Not that they're not all amazing, but having watched you make it, I feel a special connection with the green flash."

"She actually let you into the sanctum sanctorum of

her studio?" Lorenzo's gaze went back and forth between Dillon and Claire. "That's certainly a first."

"Darling, you've been keeping secrets from us," Raphael chided with a back-and-forth swish of a finger.

"Dillon is Matt's basketball coach," Claire began to explain.

"Ah." Lorenzo nodded. "That explains the sexy, loose-hipped athlete's stride."

"You definitely turned more than one head when you walked into our little gallery tonight," Raphael told Dillon. "I thought for a moment Lorenzo was going to have the vapors. If I were a jealous man, I'd have worried."

"I suspect you don't have anything to worry about," Dillon said. "As for being there when Claire made the piece, I'd gone to her studio to discuss her son. And was privileged to see its birth."

"That's a good way of putting it," Lorenzo said. "Because creating glass is a form of artistic birth."

"The roaring glory hole's pretty damn cool, too," Dillon said.

Watching Raphael and Lorenzo's response to that now familiar grin, Claire realized those dimples transcended gender. Because both men looked as enthralled by Dillon Slater's smile as the steampunk princess had been.

"Claire and I were discussing slipping out," Dillon said. "She hasn't eaten all day and I'd like to remedy that."

"Just because I agreed to dinner doesn't mean I'm not perfectly capable of feeding myself," she insisted. As if to prove her point, she snatched a cracker topped with smoked salmon and caviar from the tray of a passing waiter and popped it into her mouth.

"Of course you are," Dillon agreed. He slipped his arm around her, his hand settling possessively on her waist. "But it's been a long day and I know you haven't gotten much sleep preparing for this show."

He smiled down at her, then looked back toward the two men, who were watching with great interest. And she noticed, spotting the dancing light in Lorenzo's dark eyes, amusement. "I hope you won't mind me stealing your artist away."

"Of course not," both Lorenzo and Raphael said at the same time, reminding Claire of Dottie and Dorothy.

Which had her wondering if that was a common habit with people who lived together for a long time. It also caused a little twinge of envy that none of her relationships had lasted more than a few weeks. Which was, admittedly, most times her own doing.

"I should stay." Claire plucked Dillon's hand away. "One of the buyers might want to ask me questions."

"I believe, between the two of us, Lorenzo and I can handle any situation that arises," Raphael said.

"We have had a great deal of practice," Lorenzo confirmed. "Don't worry, darling. So long as the food and alcohol lasts, I'm sure no one will even miss you."

"Thanks," she muttered. "You really know how to boost a girl's ego."

But her smile softened her accusation. There was no way she could be annoyed with them. Partly because they had become friends, and because she suspected that their newly married state had them wanting everyone else they knew to have a hearts-and-flowers romance of their own.

Lorenzo put his hands on both her shoulders and this time kissed her on her forehead, as if she were a child.

"Thank you for gracing our humble gallery with your beauty," he said. "Both your own and that of your stunningly evocative work."

"Not to mention paying for the Greek honeymoon cruise we've booked for after the holidays," Raphael said.

"I'm delighted to contribute. And thank you both for setting up such a dazzling event. I realize that much of tonight's success was your doing."

"Which is why we get fifty percent." Raphael's quick grin and cocky statement lightened the mood, making them all laugh.

45

"I like your friends," Dillon said as he and Claire left the gallery and began walking along the river back to the hotel a few blocks away on the opposite bank. Although he'd left his SUV in the parking garage, he'd offered to call a cab. But Claire decided she'd rather walk.

"They're wonderful people who were early supporters back when a lot of people were telling me that I ought to stick to jewelry. Which I love making, but I wanted another creative outlet, if that makes sense."

"It does, and I, for one, am glad you didn't listen."

A full moon rode across the sky, its light edging the dark, gathering clouds with silver. "You didn't have to buy that piece."

"Are you kidding? The minute I saw it I wanted it. But I didn't say anything because I didn't want you to feel obligated to give me any special deal. So I just called the gallery and had them put me on the invitation and catalog list."

"It was the most expensive piece listed."

"And well worth it. It's a hell of an investment. Not that I'd ever sell it. Every time I look at it, it's going to remind me of that day. I don't think I've ever been hit by as much of a punch as I was when I walked in and saw you looking so hot. By the way, I've been meaning to mention that you look gorgeous tonight."

"Please. It's a plain black dress."

She dragged out the simple black sheath, with a sweetheart neckline that skimmed her shoulder blades, long sleeves, and a flared skirt, whenever she needed to make a public appearance. Preferring to keep the focus on her work, and uncomfortable in the spotlight that exhibitions required, she thought of it as a blank canvas. Tonight she'd paired it with a three-strand necklace she'd created from natural pearls and garnet.

Her wool coat, which she'd just bought last week at the Dancing Deer Two, was a seasonal scarlet. Although it was much brighter than what she usually wore, the minute she'd seen it in the boutique's window, she'd wanted it.

Knowing that she'd be standing on her feet for hours, she'd worn practical black flats, which ended up giving him even more of a height advantage but made walking through the crowds who'd gathered along the river to watch the parade of Christmas ships much easier.

"Sweetheart, you are definitely a case for not gilding the lily. You look super in anything. Why detract with a lot of dazzle when you can get the attention of every guy in the room just the way you are?"

"You weren't kidding when you said you learned about women from your sisters, since that was, of course, the perfect response." She thought about the steampunk dominatrix and wondered if he was going to keep that card. Not that she cared.

Liar.

"So I guess I should take back my space gun and cancel my tattoo appointment?" she asked.

"Depends on the tattoo," he answered as they edged around a group of Japanese tourists. "And where it is."

The boats were beginning to make their way down the river, decked out in flashing Christmas lights that reflected on the water.

"Oh, now I wish Matt were here," she said as one floated by sporting the outline of a huge fish, which, from the lit-up words CO HO HO, she took to be a salmon. It was wearing a Santa hat created from twinkling red lights. "Though he'd probably pretend to hate it."

"Next year," Dillon suggested. "He'll be acclimated by then."

"I hope so. Though he is doing so much better. And I realize I have you to thank for that."

"Your son's a good kid," he said.

An elderly street saxophone player was sending Christmas carols out over the waterfront. They paused to listen to "I'll Be Home for Christmas," which had Claire thinking how home wasn't necessarily where you came from but where you chose to make it. She and Matt were already beginning to settle in. Hopefully by next Christmas they'd have set down new, transplanted roots.

Others, drawn by the music, had joined them. There was a scattering of applause as the last note lingered on the chilly air. When Dillon tossed some bills into the candy-cane-painted bucket, the musician complimented him on being with the most beautiful woman in the city.

"He's right," Dillon said as they continued on their way.

"Flatterer."

"It's not flattery if it's the truth. Can I take your agreeing to have supper with me as a sign you're reconsidering your moratorium against getting personally involved?"

"No. It merely means that I'm hungry. And, just for tonight, I'm willing to suspend judgment."

He took her hand, linked their fingers together, and gave her another of those slow perusals that warmed her blood and made her pulse race. "Tonight is a beginning."

46

"We're not going to have any alcohol, right?" Johnny asked as he and Matt drove up into the hills where Taylor Bennington lived in Shelter Bay's sole gated community. "I mean, if we break training, we get kicked off the team."

"No alcohol," Matt promised.

"Good. Because it took me a really long time to land myself in a family, and I'd hate to blow it."

"You're not like a dog," Matt said. "Your parents aren't going to get rid of you."

"Shows how much you know about real life."

"My dad never stuck around," Matt reminded him.

"Oh, yeah. I forgot about that. Sorry."

"No problem. It's not like I knew the guy or anything." It wasn't anything like what Johnny had gone through with his mother.

Most of the inside house lights were off. Matt might have thought they had the wrong address had it not been for the music throbbing from inside. Both sides of the street were lined with cars, forcing Johnny to park a few houses away.

"Quite a crowd," he said as they walked up to the door, where a sign had been taped telling them to come on in.

"Yeah. It looks like word got out," Matt said. So much for his chances of being alone with Taylor. He figured he'd be lucky to find her in this crowd.

He was wrong.

They'd no sooner entered the house when she came running up to them. Running being an exaggeration, since her dress was so short and so tight, and her heels so high, it was kind of amazing she could walk at all.

"There you are! What kept you?"

Matt figured he'd lose any cool points he'd gained from the game if he admitted he'd had to wait until his mother's scheduled call from Portland before her show. "I got busy," he said, forcing his most nonchalant shrug.

"Well, you're here now." She flashed her perkiest cheerleader smile. Although he couldn't quite tell in the darkness of the room, he thought her eyes looked a little too bright. She linked her arm with Matt's. "Let me get you something to drink."

"Coke'll be fine," Johnny said.

"Are you sure? Because we have a full bar. And I'm a really good mixologist. My dad likes a cocktail when he gets home from the dealership."

"Coke's great," Matt confirmed, backing Johnny up.

Her lips, painted a rosy red tonight, made a sexy little pout. Then she immediately brightened. "Oh, well. It's early yet. Maybe you'll change your mind."

It was already ten. And he wasn't going to change his mind. Exchanging a look with Johnny, Matt figured they were thinking the same thing. That there was no point in arguing.

Matt pulled the tab on his Coke and looked around. Most of the team seemed to be here, along with other jocks from the football and baseball teams. The girls were all pretty much clones of Taylor, which, for some really weird reason, had him thinking of Aimee, whom he suspected he wouldn't be seeing here tonight.

"Do you like video games?" she asked Johnny, her smile and eyes bright.

"Sure."

"Great. We've got a killer game room." This time it was Johnny's arm she linked with as she practically dragged him through the crowd to a really impressive room.

"Tristan," she called to a long-haired guy who looked a couple of years older than everyone else in the place, "come over here.

"This is my brother, Tristan," she said, introducing him. "He's taking a break from college while he figures out what he wants to do with his life. Tristan, this is Matt and Johnny."

"Hey, dudes." As opposed to Taylor's bright sparkle, his eyes were decidedly unfocused.

Fuck. Wasn't that all Matt needed? To get busted at a pot party?

He was trying to decide what to do when Taylor said, "Come dance with me, Matt."

Matt paused, caught between what he knew he should do and what he wanted to do.

"Go ahead," Johnny said with a careless roll of his shoulders. "I'm okay here."

Still not entirely comfortable with the situation, Matt allowed himself to be led into another room, where music pounded and strobe lights flashed.

"Nice setup," Matt said.

"Isn't it?" Although the pulsing hip-hop beat wasn't exactly designed for slow dancing, she twined her arms around him like a python and pressed her body up against his, swaying in a way designed to create flames.

"Where's Dirk?" he asked as she ran her fingers through his hair.

"I've no idea. We broke up."

"Really?"

"Really." She sighed and wiggled closer, like she was literally trying to crawl inside his skin. "Small-town boys are so immature." She took hold of his wrists and placed his hands on her butt. "Sometimes I think about moving to Hollywood," she confided.

"Really?"

Matt was beginning to wonder what was wrong with him. He had hot Taylor Bennington's very fine ass in his hands, her lush boobs were pressed against his lower chest, and she was grinding against him like he was a stripper pole, which caused his body to leap to attention.

But unlike when he'd been rolling around on Lila Greene's canopied bed, his mind was totally disengaged. He glanced around and saw another couple dancing pretty much the same way, but the guy's right hand had disappeared down the front of the girl's jeans.

"Would you like me to give you a tour of the house?"

"Um. Okay. If you want to."

"Goody." One leg was now wrapped around his calf. "I thought maybe we'd start upstairs." Her hand slipped between them to play with his belt buckle. "With the bedrooms."

There it was. The freaking golden ticket. So, why didn't he just reach out and grab it?

Sensing his hesitation, she went up on the toes of those high spindly heels and pressed her open mouth against his.

Her tongue slithered inside, seductively engaging his with a hotness that even Lila, who'd been pretty experienced, couldn't touch.

But as Matt compared her skilled expertise to Aimee's raw, unpracticed, passionate attack—knowing that he'd probably throw himself off the cliff for turning down what would undoubtedly be hot, blow-his-mind sex—he heard himself saying, "I'm sorry. But I have to leave."

"What?" She pulled back and stared up at him.

"The team's got an eleven o'clock curfew."

"Oh, that." Her smile returned. "Don't worry. Not a single player on the team has ever paid any attention to a silly old basketball curfew."

Having a good idea how she knew that and realizing that he was probably just one in a long line of Dolphins to be given a tour of this house, Matt suffered an immediate and epic ego fail before finding Johnny and telling him it was time to go.

47

Claire and Dillon were crossing the bridge when a light rain began to fall. When they reached the other side, they dashed into a small French dinner club where the jazz was cool, the house wine tasted like buttery sunshine, and the round tables were so small their knees touched beneath.

Over bowls of steamed mussels served with fragrant hunks of artisan-baked sourdough dipping bread, they talked easily about the team, which had gone on to lose two games before winning again, which Dillon hoped would be the start of a streak.

She told him about the renovations she and Lucas were working on, while he shared stories about his sisters, all of whom were happily married and raising families back home in Texas.

"I think Lorenzo was right," he said as he topped off her glass from the carafe the waiter had left in the center of the table.

"About what?"

"That this collection could well establish your name in serious art circles."

She laughed at that. "I hadn't realized you were an expert on glass art."

"I'm not. But I know what I like."

And he liked her. Although she'd claimed that her dress was nothing special, the way the neckline skimmed across her shoulders made him want to touch his lips to that smooth, fragrant flesh.

She'd worn her hair up, he supposed to appear more formal, and to show off those delicate silver earrings he knew were her own creation. He was accustomed to seeing her without makeup, but whatever she'd done to her face—darkening her eyes and brightening her lips—added an exoticism that was another layer to the California girl who'd first caught his eye.

"Plus," he added, "I was listening to all those people who probably know what they're talking about. And the buzz was definitely there."

"I am proud of the collection." Her face lit up with a smile. "I was offered a commission tonight," she revealed. "From an architect who's designing a waterfront home for some tech mogul in Seattle. The owner's putting in an indoor lap pool. It's going to have colored neon tubes beneath a glass ceiling that opens on clear nights."

"Good luck with that," Dillon said.

"I was thinking the same thing," she said with a light laugh.

"What does he want you to do?" Surely she wasn't going to waste her incredible talent making neon tubes?

"He wants me to create an underwater garden. With sea anemones and sea flowers."

Dillon immediately saw the potential. He even indulged in a quick fantasy of making love to her in a pool with a glass sea garden shimmering beneath the water. "The question will be, to people swimming in the pool, are they manmade? Or from nature?"

"Oh, you *do* get it." When her eyes got a little misty at that, Dillon figured he could live to be a hundred and never understand the female mind.

"Yeah. Right away. But I didn't mean to make you cry."

"You didn't." But she did dash away a bit of moisture below her left eye with a knuckle. "But I recently realized I haven't really had anyone to talk with about my work, at least on a personal level, since my mother died."

"I'm sorry." Damn, could he have screwed this up any worse?

"Don't be. I was just thinking how, at this precise moment, I'm as happy as I've been in a very long while."

Dillon had a few suggestions as to how they could try to make her night even more memorable, but he knew better than to push.

But that didn't mean he was going to let her get away, he thought as the singer launched into a sultry, breathy version of "Let's Fall in Love." Not yet.

"Dance with me," he said.

Claire could have said no. Perhaps she even should have. But lulled into a sense of pleasure by the mussels and the music and, yes, the company, and assuring herself that it was just dancing, that people did it all the time without it leading to anything more, she let him lead her out onto the postage-stamp-sized dance floor.

She fit perfectly in his arms. Perhaps too perfectly, she

considered as she settled against him, enjoying the fluid way his athlete's body moved her around the wooden floor.

"You smell so good." He nuzzled her neck as his fingers skimmed up and down her back. "And feel even better."

He was humming along to the song, which was all about taking chances, and not being afraid, and falling in love.

"You keep making it sound so easy," she complained as he actually sang the line about not being shy, "but our situation is complicated."

"So you keep saying." He pulled his head back far enough to look down at her. "And I get your point about the fact that we've found ourselves in a sticky—"

"It's not sticky if we avoid it entirely."

"Now, see, here's my problem with that." His fingers were doing that light, feathery seductive rhumba on her back again. "I don't want to avoid it. Because I want you."

"Has anyone ever told you that we can't all get everything we want?"

"Sure." His smiling lips brushed against her temple. "But here's the deal. That only makes me want it more. And more determined to win it."

"I'm not a prize to be won." She knocked away his hand when it began playing with her dangling earring. "And if you don't mind, I'd like to go to the hotel now."

"Your call," he said easily.

The rain had stopped, but fog rising from the river was swirling around their feet as they walked the rest of the way to the waterfront hotel, where they stood side by side as the elevator took them up to the seventeenth floor, awareness humming between them.

"By the way, how did you manage to get the room

next to mine at the last minute during the holiday season?" she asked. "I couldn't even get one on a different floor for Matt."

"Vet connections. I know a guy who knows a guy. Who knows a guy. Who pulled some strings. Hotels always keep a few rooms open they don't advertise. Plus, it wasn't last minute. I booked it the day you made the green flash. When you told me about your show."

"Why?"

"Why do you think? I've been up front from the start about my feelings, Claire. About wanting to be with you." The fingers that skimmed over her lips were calloused, and although she'd never considered herself a very sensual woman, she suddenly ached to feel them everywhere on her body. "And you've already admitted that you want that, too."

"Of course I do." Her lips parted beneath his thumb. "But we can't."

"Now, see, that's where you're wrong." That seductive Texas drawl was back as he treated her to a slow, devastating smile. "We can." That tantalizing touch traveled to the corner of her mouth. "And we will."

"My son is important to me," she insisted. "Our having an affair would not only be unethical—"

"I've been thinking about that. And you're wrong. Because lots of high school coaches have their own kids on the team. Even in college. And nobody cares. In fact, lots of times it's considered a good thing. No one's going to think I'm playing favorites, Claire. And those who do just aren't paying attention to reality."

He had her there. But she still wasn't entirely convinced. "Even so, I've already made him miserable by moving here—"

"He's starting to fit in," he interrupted her yet again.

"Which is exactly why I'm not going to put aside my responsibilities and risk hurting him for a dalliance, or an affair, or a quick roll in the sheets."

"Believe me, Claire. When I do finally have you in my bed, where you belong, there'll be nothing quick about it."

Oh, she did believe him. And wasn't that the problem? She'd never been so tempted. So torn. But she also knew she was right.

Because her pulse had gone impossibly jittery, she forced herself to look straight up into his eyes. "I'm not going to put aside my parental responsibilities to play games with you, Dillon."

"I'm not playing games, sugar. Not about wanting you."

But he did lower his hand. They stood there, face-to-face, inches apart, the energy between them as palpable as sheet lighting on the horizon before a coastal storm.

Then, finally, after what seemed an eternity, the bell dinged as they reached their floor. Dillon stepped back, letting her exit first, then walked down the carpeted hallway beside her. "But one of the things EOD taught me is patience. So, although it's going to mean a lot more cold showers, I'm willing to wait until you're ready."

She wanted to tell him that he'd be waiting a very long time. It was what she should tell him.

"Thank you for a lovely evening," she said instead as they stood outside her door.

"The pleasure was all mine. And hey, if you're serious about that no-involvement deal, at least we'll always have Portland."

As she entered her room and shut the door between them, Claire wondered if she was making a mistake. It wasn't as if anyone in Shelter Bay would know if she and Dillon Slater spent the night together.

Then again, when Matt found out his coach had come to Portland, and he would, if he asked if anything had happened, she wanted to be able to tell him the truth. She'd never lied to him. And she wasn't about to start now. But while he might like the idea of his coach and her in a relationship, she suspected there wasn't a teenager on the planet who wanted to think about his parent having sex.

She'd put her bag down on the desk and had taken off her earrings when there was a knock at the door.

Her foolish heart fluttered in her chest as she looked through the peephole and saw him standing there.

"Did you forget something?" she asked as she opened the door.

"Yes." His smile was slow. Sexy. Devastating. He cupped her cheek. When his fingers felt like sparks against her face, Claire knew she was sunk. "This."

His mouth claimed hers with a hot, hungry passion that created an instantaneous flare of heat.

He didn't coax Claire into the mists; he dragged her weak-kneed into the flames. His lips didn't tease or tantalize. They plundered.

Her body flamed, her mind emptied, as a dark, dangerous desire unlike anything she'd ever experienced surged through her veins.

And then, just as suddenly, he released her.

"One more thing," he said, his drawl amazingly tinged with good-natured humor. She dragged a hand over her upswept hair, which had begun to tumble down. "What?"

He caught her trembling hand on its second pass and brought it to his lips. "I'm leaving that door between our rooms unlocked. Just in case you happen to change your mind."

He waited until she went back into the room, flipped the lock, and put on the chain.

Only then did she hear him walk back to his adjoining room.

He was whistling.

48

It had taken a Herculean effort, but Dillon had managed, just barely, to keep from dragging Claire back into her room and doing what she'd already admitted she wanted as much as he did.

He flung himself onto the bed, his skin burning as if some Taliban torturer had put matches beneath it, and, turning on the news, he tried to concentrate on the weatherman's charts and arrows predicting—what else?—more rain.

But his mind kept going toward that door, imagining the luscious woman on the other side.

The news had segued to *Letterman* when the door opened and she was standing there. She was wearing a white satin nightshirt, and in the flickering light of the TV, he could see the pebbled hardness of her nipples. Her hair was down, tumbling over her shoulders. Her long legs and feet were bare.

"This is just for tonight," she said.

She was wrong. But as he dragged his gaze back to her face, Dillon knew this was no time to argue the point.

"Deal." He turned off the TV, then pushed aside the sheets to go to her, but she held up a hand.

"This is my decision," she said. "My move."

Again, there was no way he was going to argue with that.

Desire had claws as he forced himself to lie there on his back. Wanting. Waiting.

And then she was standing at the end of the bed, bathed in the colored lights of the city outside the tower's windows.

"I want you, Dillon." She undid the first button on the nightshirt. "I think I've wanted you since that first moment in the gym."

Another button.

"I remember it well."

"Do you?" She smiled like the seductress he suspected she just might have lurking inside her. "Sometimes I lie in bed at night and think about what might have happened if you'd just taken me. Right there and then."

Two more buttons opened, revealing breasts that gleamed like porcelain in the lights of the bridge below.

"I think one of us would've gotten a really bad floor burn," he managed as he struggled not to swallow his tongue.

"Probably." She sighed. Then with a flick of her fingers, she released the final button and shrugged the shirt off her shoulders, where it fell to the carpet in a pool of white satin.

"You want me, Dillon?"

"Only like I want to breathe."

She held her arms out to him. "Then take me."

He didn't need to be asked twice. Leaving the bed, he

dragged her against him, chest to chest, thighs to thighs, mouth to mouth, as he pulled her down onto the mattress.

He'd wanted to be gentle. Whenever he'd imagined being with Claire, he'd fantasized taking her slowly, tenderly, showing her that he understood that some things—some very special people—were worth waiting for.

But needs that had been pent up since that first day burst free, like a tsunami crashing in from the sea. He rolled over, pressing her into the mattress, and took her breast in his mouth.

When her gasp filtered through the roaring in his head, Dillon struggled to pull back.

"I'm sorry."

"Don't you dare apologize." Her fingers grabbed his hair, pulling his mouth back down. "Take me."

She was wild beneath him, every movement a demand that he take more, go faster. He left her only long enough to retrieve one of the condoms he'd optimistically brought to Portland. Then he was back, braceleting both her wrists in one hand, holding them above her head.

His free hand cupped the source of her heat, ruthlessly sending her soaring. She peaked instantly, bucking against his touch, her back arching bowstring tight.

Even as she poured over his hand, he whipped her up again. Higher. Harder. The second climax left her shuddering.

"Claire."

She murmured something incoherent and tossed her head on the pillow.

"Look at me."

Her eyes were dazed as they met his.

"You're mine." When he slipped his fingers into her, she arched up against him. *Take me.* "Say it."

"Yours." The single word was torn from her throat, a ragged thread of sound.

Digging his fingers into her hips, he lifted her, settled between her warm silk thighs, and plunged into her.

She cried out again, not in pain, but pleasure, and wrapped her long legs around his hips, holding him in a viselike grip as he drove her deeper and deeper into the mattress, and they rode out the storm together.

Feeling as if he'd been turned inside out, Dillon finally collapsed on top of her. Neither said a word for a long, long time.

There was only the rough sound of steady breathing and the distant hum of night traffic on the street below. The earthy scent of their lovemaking mingled with the fragrance of flowers emanating from her damp skin.

"Are we still alive?" he asked.

"I think so."

"Good." Afraid he was crushing her, he rolled over onto his side, taking her with him.

"Well, that was certainly worth waiting for," she murmured.

"You'll get no argument from me."

"I've never done that before."

"Come into a man's hotel room wearing only a nightshirt?"

"Well, that, too. But I've never had so many. . . . I mean, usually I'm lucky to have one. . . . Never mind."

"Don't stop now." Dillon grinned as he left the bed to dispense of the condom, then returned to draw her into his arms. "You're doing wonders for my ego."

"As if you'd need any more ego strokes," she murmured as she lifted her lips to his.

The storm behind them, for a long delicious time they indulged in the slow kisses and tender touches they hadn't taken time for earlier.

"I honestly can't believe how you can make me feel," she sighed.

"How's that?" He pressed his lips to the little heart-shaped birthmark at the base of her spine.

She exhaled a slow, rippling sigh of pleasure. "As if I'm floating about three feet above this bed."

"That's a start." He skimmed his tongue up her spine. "Let's see if we can make you fly."

As the hour grew later and the kisses grew longer, Claire discovered that Dillon Slater was definitely a man of his word.

49

Even though Claire had insisted that Dillon's and her night together in Portland was going to be a onetime thing, after they returned home to Shelter Bay, she realized it was going to be impossible to return to the way they'd been. Too much had happened between them.

Not just the sex, which had been amazing, but a bond had formed that had begun that first day when he'd shown her the gym, then driven out to the cottage to talk with her about Matt. The night he'd cooked the clams and gotten through to her son about paying more attention to his classes when she hadn't been able to.

As she'd predicted, it proved impossible to keep their relationship a secret, but to her relief, everyone seemed pleased that yet another couple had found love.

After Mary Joyce had mentioned the small Irish town of Lisdoonvarna drawing thousands to their annual matchmaking festival every year, the mayor was quoted in the *Shelter Bay Beacon* as saying that Shelter Bay should consider promoting itself as a place for visitors to find true love in order to draw in even more tourism business.

As Christmas approached, the town began to look less like the whale-watching capital of America and more like *It's a Wonderful Life*'s Bedford Falls before George Bailey's loss of faith had shown it as a dark and tragic town. Students from the elementary, middle, and high schools painted holiday scenes on local business windows, tinseled lit garlands and wreaths with huge red bows were strung across the downtown streets, and fairy lights sparkled in the branches of trees all over town.

A Douglas fir donated by a local Christmas tree farm towered over the lacy white Victorian bandstand in Evergreen Park. And to the delight of Shelter Bay's children, who got to be passengers, a small, brightly painted Santa train chugged around the park.

"You used to love going to tree lightings," Claire said, coaxing Matt when he'd balked at attending with Dillon and her. The annual Beverly Hills lighting had taken place on Rodeo Drive, all the better to encourage holiday spending.

"I used to be six years old," he retorted without heat, not bothering to look up from watching Oregon State blowing out Arizona at home. He was sprawled on a La-Z-Boy that had come with the cottage. While she planned to get it reupholstered when her remodeling was completed, for now she'd covered the duct tape on the arm with a holiday plaid wool throw she'd bought from Dorothy and Dottie's expanding home decor section. Jessie was snoring happily at his feet, while Toby was curled up in front of the fireplace.

"Lots of kids your age will be there," said Dillon, who was sitting on the couch next to Claire. "Johnny—"

"He doesn't have any choice. If Angel wants him there with her, he'll walk through fire to get there."

"I won't argue that," Dillon agreed easily. "The cheer squad's going to perform a dance."

Matt folded his arms and, for some reason Claire couldn't discern, glowered a bit at that idea. "Good for them."

"And the Madrigals are performing Christmas songs."

"Which I get enough of here." He shot his mother a look.

"I like holiday music," she said. "You used to, too. I still remember when you performed 'Rudolph' for your second-grade Christmas play. . . . He looked so cute," she told Dillon. "My mother made him a costume with a nose that actually lit up and blinked. I'm sure I have a photo of it somewhere."

Now that her show was over, she really ought to do something about all those boxes of photos that had piled up over the years. Perhaps, Claire considered, she could make Matt an album for a present. Oh, he wouldn't necessarily appreciate it all that much now. But someday, when he had children of his own, she knew those memories would be important.

"Aimee's in Madrigals," Dillon said.

Matt didn't answer, but Claire saw his shoulders tense at that announcement.

But later, over a surprisingly successful clam linguini Maddy Chaffee had taught her to make just yesterday at the restaurant's school, Matt said, with exaggerated casualness, "I guess I could go. If it means that much to you."

Claire had no idea what had happened between her son and the girl Dillon had assured her was special, but she wasn't going to pry.

"It does," she admitted. "Because it's our first year

here. And the first holiday season without your grand-mother."

"I miss her," he admitted. "A lot."

"Me, too," Claire said as Dillon took her hand be-neath the table. "A lot."

50

What Dillon had worried about was coming true. After their first exhilarating win, the little team that could stalled out on their way to state.

"We can't even buy a break," he told Don Daniels two weeks before Christmas and the night after the Astoria Fighting Fishermen had blown them out of the water. They'd won only a single game since that first one, and that had been only because half of their opponent's team had been battling the flu.

"At least Martin and Templeton are still hot," the assistant coach said as Matt passed to Dirk, who went in for a jump shot. He missed, but he managed to outmuscle his defender and get his own rebound.

"True. But even as good as those two kids are, two against six damn well isn't working."

"At least the town's still behind them."

"Again, that would be true." He'd been surprised that, if anything, attendance at the home games had increased. It was as if everyone was trying to pull their Dolphins up by sheer force in fan numbers. "But I wonder what's going to happen if we don't turn the program around."

"Other than Ken's head exploding, everything will be copacetic," Don said. "Hell, they didn't win before you came here. No one except Ken and his boosters ever seriously expected you to turn things around. And definitely not in the first year."

That was probably true. But, dammit, Dillon was not accustomed to failure. Even when he reminded himself that he'd been hired to be a teacher first, a coach second, the fact that his team was not only not on the road to state, but in danger of becoming the worst high school team in Oregon, stung.

"Failure," he said grimly, as he watched Johnny Tiernan-St. James throw up a brick of a free throw, "is not an option."

"Failure," Matt said to the team, who'd gathered together in an empty banquet room of the Crab Shack, "is not an option."

He still thought Dirk was a tool. And from the way the guy ignored him off the court, except when he was flaunting his rebound romance with Taylor, he figured the feeling was mutual. But there was one thing they agreed on. That somehow, some way, they were going to play at least one state tournament game on that glossy wooden floor in OSU's legendary Gill Coliseum.

"We might be able to outrun our opponents," Dirk said, "but shooting, rebounds, and steals are in single digits."

"And our free throws suck," Matt said. "Hell, we gave the game away to the Seagulls last week." He and Dirk had broken their own Dolphins scoring records against Seaside. But even that wasn't enough to pull out a win.

"There's a reason they're called *free* throws, ladies," Dirk said derisively.

"Did you call us here to ream us out?" Brendan Cooper complained.

"And if so," Jim Ryan, the team's power forward said, "I think the rest of the guys would join me in asking who died and made you coach?"

"Let's remember we're a team," Matt said, holding up both his hands. It had been his idea to hold this meeting, he'd been the one to go to Jake and ask if they could borrow this room away from the school, and he was damn well not going to let the dickhead screw it up.

"We're being outplayed, pure and simple. And watching the game films after practice, it's obvious that we're not going to be able to turn things around with our shooting fast enough to get a berth at state. So we're going to concentrate on free throws."

"You have to be fouled to get those," Johnny pointed out.

"And then you have to make them," Dirk said, "which you're not."

"He's not the only one," Matt said quickly, in defense of his friend. "But this is something we can fix. Dick—uh, Dirk—is right. There's a reason they're called free throws. So, starting today, every single person on this team is going to shoot two hundred shots. Every day. If you don't have a basket at your house—"

"Why the hell don't you?" Dirk demanded.

"Could you just let me finish?" Matt complained. They might be cocaptains, but the guy was still a douche. "If you don't have a basket, there are always the hoops at Evergreen Park. Or you can come over to my place. Or Dirk's."

"Or mine," Johnny volunteered.

"Great. Thanks. So two hundred shots every day. Even if it's raining fish and frogs. Because no way is any Dolphin player going to miss a free shot. But Johnny's right. We still have to get the foul calls to give us a chance to shoot. So we're holding Saturday practice at the fire station every week on how to position ourselves so the other guys will foul us."

Now that Aimee was no longer driving him to school, on the days when a storm didn't force him to take the stupid yellow bus, Matt rode his bike past the fire station. One day, when he'd seen the firefighters playing hoops in a side yard, this idea had sparked. He'd stopped and asked Flynn Farraday if they could borrow the court. Not only had the fire captain readily agreed, but better yet, having played high school hoops for the Shelter Bay Dolphins and for the Midshipmen at the Naval Academy, Captain Farraday agreed to give the team pointers.

"Is the coach going to be there?"

"No. We don't want to risk him getting in trouble for calling extra practices outside of the school week. So this is voluntary."

"What happens if I decide I don't want to show up?" Brendan asked.

"Then I track you down, rip your fucking head off, and piss down your neck," Dirk shot back. "Any more questions?"

Unsurprisingly, there were none.

51

Two days after having managed to pull off one home-made meal without poisoning her son or Dillon, Claire decided to try another recipe. The braised chicken legs with tomatoes, onions, and garlic was one of the most popular items on Lavender Hill Farm's menu, but Maddy had assured her that she was up for the challenge.

She'd just set the dish to a slow simmer on the stove when the doorbell rang.

She opened it to find Dillon standing in the yellow circle created by the front-porch light. And he was hold-ing a huge . . . tree?

"What in the world?"

"I brought your tree," he said as both dogs raced by her and began jumping and dancing around him in glee-ful welcome.

"In the first place, Marty Reynolds told me he'd de-liver it tomorrow afternoon." She'd bought the tree at a lot set up in the market's parking lot but hadn't wanted to even think about tying it to the top of her Lexus for the trip home. "And in the second place, that's not my tree."

"It's not your *original* tree," he corrected easily. "Yours was really, really short."

She folded her arms. "I bought a tabletop one because my house is really, really small."

"This'll be better. A friend has a Christmas tree farm up by Rainbow Lake. He's the guy who donated the town tree. He'd been pruning this one all year for himself, but since he's a Dolphins fan, he gave it up for the phenom and his mom."

"Tell me that you didn't play that stupid phenom card!"

"Sweetheart, you gotta play the cards you have. So are you going to let me in?"

Unlike the small, tidy tabletop tree she'd bought, the towering blue spruce filled the room.

"Don't you do anything halfway?" she asked as he adjusted the stand.

"That'd be boring." He stood back, tilted his head, and eyed the tree. "What do you think?"

"That it looks like the tree that ate Shelter Bay." Not only was it huge; he'd cut three feet off the bottom and the tip was nearly touching her ceiling.

"You don't like it?"

Because he looked honestly concerned, she shook her head in defeat. "It's beautiful." *But so large.*

"Maybe I did overdo it."

"No." She went over and wrapped her arms around his neck. "I love it. And I love that you brought me a tree when you're not getting one for yourself." He'd told her that because of the basketball schedule, he wouldn't be able to go back to Texas for Christmas with his mother, sisters, and new stepfather his mother had surprised everyone by marrying while he'd been in Afghanistan.

"Maybe you'll let me share yours," he suggested, drawing her closer and brushing his lips against hers.

The door burst open and Matt came barreling in, bringing with him a gust of wind and a winter chill.

"Whoa!" He came to an abrupt stop as he eyed the tree. "That is so freaking dope!"

"The kid's got good taste," Dillon said as he stepped a bit away. But he still kept his arm around Claire's waist.

"We can put all Gram's ornaments on it," Matt said, looking nearly as happy as he had the Christmas he'd come downstairs and found that shiny red ten-speed bicycle beneath the tree.

Her mother had collected ornaments, all of which had very personal stories behind them, over her lifetime. Some were expensive, others not. But to Claire, the most valuable of all were the ones she had bought for Matt each year to someday share with his own children on his own family's tree.

She should have thought of that. After what he'd said on Thanksgiving, about missing his grandmother, this was no time to be practical. It didn't matter that her house was so much smaller than the one she'd left behind; she should have bought a larger tree. One that, for their first Christmas in their new home, would hold all those ornaments and help keep alive the memory of the woman who'd been like a second mother to her son.

But once again Dillon seemed to have a knack for fitting perfectly into their lives. As Matt raced to retrieve the carton of ornaments she was temporarily storing in her bedroom closet, she realized that perhaps because he'd lost his father at such a tender age, he understood, more than she ever could, exactly what her son was feeling.

And it was at that moment, although she certainly hadn't planned it, and wasn't even sure she *wanted* it, Claire realized she'd fallen in love with this man who'd brought her son and her the most perfect Christmas tree she'd ever seen.

52

The first twinge came as Kara was getting ready to go to lunch. Assuring herself that she couldn't possibly be in labor, she decided to ignore it. This was her last day at work until after Trey's brother or sister was born, and since Maude Dutton, her day dispatcher/receptionist/secretary, had already thrown her a baby-leave party yesterday, she was determined to take time today for a girls' lunch with friends.

It wasn't as if there was that much crime this time of year. Once the tourists left, Shelter Bay pretty much went into hibernation until spring.

"It's raining," Maude pointed out.

"It's winter on the Oregon coast," Kara said. "It's always raining."

"Yeah, but they say this storm's gonna be a duck strangler." When Maude shook her head, Kara waited for the seventysomething's Marge Simpson beehive, which had been dyed a flaming Lucille Ball red, to tip over. It never had. But that hadn't stopped Kara from watching. And waiting.

"The cruiser does great in the rain," Kara pointed

out. Weighing in at two tons, her black-and-white Crown Vic was like a tank. "And I don't melt."

"You're pregnant."

"Why don't you tell me something I don't know?"

Kara struggled into her yellow county sheriff's rain slicker. The way her stomach had ballooned the past month, if she ate dessert, she might have trouble zipping it up again after lunch. It was Sax's fault, she decided as Maude helped her into the jacket. If he wasn't such a great cook and if she hadn't become addicted to hot sauce and spices this pregnancy, she wouldn't soon be rivaling the town's whales.

"Your father wasn't such a smart-mouth," said the dispatcher Kara had inherited from her sheriff father.

"That's because he was perfect." Ask anyone in Shelter Bay and they'd tell you that Ben Blanchard had been the best lawman since Wyatt Earp. Despite having worked as a patrol officer in Oceanside, it had taken Kara a while to win over the citizens she'd sworn to protect and serve.

Maude snorted at that. "That's what everyone liked to think," she said. "But your dad, he had his faults. Which didn't stop him from being a good sheriff. Just the way yours don't stop you from being good at your job."

The elderly woman didn't toss out compliments all that often.

"Thank you."

Maude, who was as round as a marionberry, shrugged padded shoulders clad in a stoplight red sweater with an ice-skating penguin on the front. When Kara had first returned to town, the dispatcher had seemed to own only elastic-waist jeans and bowling shirts. Apparently Dottie and Doris had convinced her to expand her wardrobe, because ever since St. Patrick's Day, you could tell what holiday was approaching by Maude's sweaters.

"Just telling it like I see it," the dispatcher said. "You may have been a little green when you started, but you've definitely grown into your daddy's boots."

For some stupid reason, that caused Kara to well up. *Hormones.*

Another twinge. Which escalated into a sharp, genuine pain.

"What's the matter?" The woman might wear trifocals, but she never missed anything.

"Nothing," Kara lied.

Those still-sharp eyes narrowed. "You sure you're all right?"

"I'm fine." She pulled down her hat from the hook on the wall. "Really."

"You went as white as bleached driftwood."

"It's nothing. The baby just kicked. I swear, if he's a boy, he's going to be a field-goal kicker."

"Or maybe a Rockette if it's a girl," commented Ashley Melson, whom Kara had moved from night duty to assistant day dispatcher. "Kenny and I saw them when they were playing in Portland. They're amazing kickers."

"Who undoubtedly all battered their mothers while in the womb," Kara said. Another twinge made her blink.

"You're in labor," Maude predicted. Having five children and a dozen grandchildren, over the last few months she'd been a self-proclaimed expert on pregnancy.

"I've been having these for the past few days," Kara said. "Sax insisted on taking me to the ER last night and they sent me home. The doctor on duty told me it was only false labor."

"Braxton Hicks contractions." The tower stayed straight atop her head as she nodded knowingly. "And the operative word there is *home*, which is where you should be."

"Sitting in front of the fire, knitting booties."

"Smart-mouth," Maude repeated. "You know, you don't always have to be Superwoman."

"I'm fine," Kara insisted. "Really."

Escaping any further argument, she walked out to the cruiser, which was parked in the small lot next to the office, just as her deputy, Marcus Jones, was returning from patrol.

"Storm's coming," he said.

"So I hear. You might want to get some barricades ready in case we have flooding." It was difficult thinking of her small crew of three deputies handling things by themselves.

"Sure thing, Sheriff. I was thinking maybe you might want to think about having Sax come drive you home. Or I could. Given that you're pregnant."

Apparently being the father of a young son himself made Marcus yet another expert on birthing babies.

"I appreciate your concern, Marcus. But pregnancy didn't take away my ability to drive." When he looked inclined to argue, she said, "And better get out the flares. Even if there's not flooding, if the rain gets too hard, or trees start coming down, we could have some fender benders."

She climbed into the cruiser and headed out of the lot before he could offer yet more unneeded male advice.

53

Claire had been pleased when Matt had asked to go on the ski club's annual trip two days after Christmas, because it was one more sign he was beginning to fit in. But it also was the first Christmas vacation they'd spend apart since he was born.

"It's only four days," she told the two dogs as she packed a small bag to take to Dillon's rental house on the bay. The past two nights he'd stayed at her cottage, but when he'd told her he had a surprise planned, she'd agreed to come into town.

She'd also decided to leave Jessie and Toby with Charity, just for this last night alone with Dillon.

"You like Peanut and Shadow," she reminded the dogs, who'd had a play date with Charity and Gabe's two dogs just last week when she'd taken Matt over to Johnny's. "And Angel and Johnny will play with you, too. It'll be like summer camp." She looked out the window, where the wind, blowing in from the sea, was causing the gigantic trees towering over the cottage to sway.

"Okay," she amended, "maybe winter camp."

*   *   *

Dillon's furnishings were somewhere between minimalist and college dorm. "I never bought much stuff," he explained as he took her coat and hung it on a rack by the front door, "because I was always getting transferred. So it was easier just to get new stuff wherever I'd land when I wasn't deployed. And since I've gotten here, I've been too busy to go shopping. Well, except for the TV."

Which, like the tree he'd shown up with, was enormous.

"Apparently it's true," she murmured. "With some guys, size does matter."

"Ha-ha. I prefer to think of it as an occupational necessity. When I'm stealing plays from the NBA teams, it helps to be able to see them."

The flat-screen took up half the wall. "I imagine you could see them from outer space."

He laughed, which he did easily and often, she'd learned during their time together. While the Oregon coast might be living up to its reputation for winter rain, Dillon had brought sunshine not just into her life, but into her son's as well.

"I did go shopping this morning, though. Why don't you sit down and I'll show you what I picked up?"

He left the room, went into the kitchen, and returned with an oversized wicker basket.

"What's that?"

"I thought we'd have a beach picnic."

"In case you hadn't noticed, Dillon, there's a storm blowing in. It's getting close to freezing and it's so foggy I could hardly see to drive here."

"I should've picked you up."

He'd offered. Even pressed, just a bit. But needing to hold on to her independence, she'd turned him down.

"Well, you're here now," he said. "And you're right—it

could get rough out there, which is why we're having the picnic in front of the fireplace."

Kneeling on the floor, he lifted the lid, allowing mouthwatering aromas to fill the room as he took out a red-and-white-checked quilt. "Chef Maddy told that me that setting the proper mood is important for the ultimate culinary experience," he explained as he spread it out on the pine-plank floor in front of the stone fireplace, where a fire was already crackling merrily. Matching napkins and a pair of stemless wineglasses followed.

"She came up with the quilt and dishes, but I thought of these myself," he said as he pulled out some clay pots filled with cheery yellow and purple flowers that brightened the darkening day.

"These are northern dune tansy," he said, pointing at the yellow ones. "And the purple ones are beach peas. Sofia De Luca has them both growing in her greenhouse for people who want to plant native wildflower gardens. She says the peas are actually edible."

"They're lovely. And perfect for a beach picnic."

"Gotta have atmosphere," he said, flashing her that grin she suspected would still thrill her when she was an old woman.

Not that they'd necessarily still be together by then. People fell out of love all the time. It was, after all, far more normal than the type of relationship she'd witnessed among the Douchetts at Thanksgiving.

Even as she tried to remain pragmatic about their affair, as Dillon proceeded to set the flower pots around the quilt, immeasurably moved by the gesture, and the trouble he'd gone to, just for her, Claire slid yet deeper into love.

54

The pains had vanished.

Kara didn't have a single twinge all the way to Lavender Hill Farm's restaurant. They were, as she'd tried to convince Sax last night, and told Maude, merely false labor. Hadn't she had them nearly her entire third trimester when she'd been pregnant with Trey? She'd simply made a mistake eating that spicy hot Cajun omelet for breakfast.

"This isn't your first rodeo," she said as she pulled up in front of the white front porch. "You've done this before." And there'd been a time, not too long ago, before she'd returned to Shelter Bay and fallen in love with Sax, that she'd truly believed Trey was destined to be an only child.

"So, are you getting excited?" Maddy asked twenty minutes later, as she, Charity, and Sedona sat with Kara at a table looking toward where the sea was draped in a steely gray fog. Rain streamed down the tall windows.

"Of course. But honestly, I'm more impatient," Kara replied as she took a bite of her salad.

The roasted organic chicken and fingerling potatoes

had been tossed with a creamy organic Dijon mustard
and sage dressing and served on a bed of baby spinach
and apples. Although Sofia De Luca's gardens were winter dormant, Maddy's grandmother continued to grow
her herbs and vegetables in her greenhouse, and the
chicken, Kara knew, had come from Blue Heron Farm.

"I'm not only looking like an elephant these days; I'm
starting to feel like one. I'm afraid Trey will be in college
before I have this baby."

"You're still two weeks away from your due date,"
Sedona pointed out.

"I know." Kara stabbed a piece of perfectly seasoned
potato. "It'd be hard to forget, since I have this big red X
on the magnetic calendar on the front of the refrigerator."

"Phoebe's been feeling the same way," Maddy said.
"She didn't want Gram and me to send her home last
week, but it was making us nervous watching her in the
kitchen with all those boiling pots and pans and knives.
Not that she hasn't turned into a really good sous chef,
but we managed to convince her that it couldn't be good
for her baby for her to be on her feet for so many hours
a day."

"I wouldn't think so," Charity said. "And how clever
to put the mommy guilt on her so she'd listen to reason.
I understand how independence would be important to
her, after what she's been through, but it can be over-
done."

She turned back to Kara. "And getting back on topic,
you don't look like at all like an elephant. In fact, you
look lovely."

"That's exactly what best friends are supposed to
say."

As the only woman at the table who'd had a child,

Kara wasn't going to fault them for not understanding how it seemed as if it'd been a lifetime since she'd shown Sax that pink plus sign on the home pregnancy kit.

Damn. Another pain, stronger than any she'd experienced thus far, wrenched her back and sent her abdomen into spasms.

"Yikes," Maddy said. "Did that feel anything like it looked?"

"I think maybe worse." Kara breathed easier as the pain abated. "But it's only false labor."

Charity braced her elbows on the table, put her chin on her linked hands, and gave Kara a long, judicious look across the glossy wooden tabletop. "Just because the pains were diagnosed as Braxton Hicks yesterday doesn't mean you're not in labor today."

"It's still early," Kara said, belying her earlier complaint about her baby seemingly taking forever to be born.

"It's your second child. It wouldn't be surprising for it to be early. Especially if he or she takes after its mother."

"What does that mean?" Another pain hit. "And I don't want to belittle your career, which you're amazing at, and I know you're a real doctor. But your patients just happen to have four legs."

"I suspect she was talking about the fact that you can be a bit impatient at times," Sedona suggested carefully.

"And stubborn," Charity said.

"I prefer to think of it as tenacious."

This time the pain started slowly, like a gathering wave, then increased in intensity as it moved across her abdomen until it reached a crest. Then blessedly subsided.

"Okay. *That's* not false labor," Charity said.

"I think you're right." Kara had no sooner admitted that when she felt a trickling of moisture between her legs, then a gush. Mortified, she looked down at the spreading puddle of amniotic fluid flowing across the polished wood floor.

Sedona stood up. "Let's go."

"I'm so sorry," Kara told Maddy, who waved away her apology.

"Don't be silly. Let's get you into the ladies' room and get you a pad, because it looks as if we'll be having our dessert at the hospital."

55

They piled into Sedona's SUV, which had four-wheel drive. The rain had chilled considerably while they'd been indoors, turning to hail that danced on the roof and hood of the vehicle and crunched beneath the wide tires. Gusts of wind battered the side doors, at times causing the SUV to shake.

"Wow," Charity said after Kara had called Sax to give him the news and assure him she was fine and on the way to the hospital. "Lucas did a really good job of insulating that restaurant addition to your grandmother's farm," she told Maddy, "because I sure didn't realize the weather had turned so bad. You could hardly hear this wind."

"The windows are triple paned," Maddy said as a trash can with a whale painted on it blew across Harborview Drive in front of them as they drove past the seawall, where white-capped waves were battering against the stone. "This is one time I regret that."

"We'll make it," Sedona said with an easy self-assurance she wore like a second skin.

As Kara concentrated on the controlled breathing she'd

learned in birthing class, it crossed her mind that Sedona's seemingly innate calm may have come from having grown up on a commune, where, it stood to reason, people would tend to be more mellow. Which also undoubtedly explained her leaving the big-bucks city accounting firm to bake cupcakes and pies here in Shelter Bay.

The single traffic light in town was no longer working, which had Kara hoping the electricity wouldn't go out at the hospital. Surely they had a backup generator. And shouldn't she, as sheriff, already know this?

The lights were still on as Sedona pulled into the parking lot and drove right up to the door of the ER.

"Wait here," Maddy said, jumping out of the backseat. "I'll go get someone to help."

"I can walk by myself," Kara complained.

The last time she'd been here as a patient had been after she'd been attacked in her own home by the bad guy who'd killed her father. The bossy nurse who'd wheeled her out to Sax's Camaro after she'd been released had insisted it was hospital policy. Even for cops.

"Of course you can walk," Sedona said. "But why make the nurse's day any more difficult by bucking policy and not letting her do her job?

Kara shook her head. "One of these days," she said, "I'm going to see you in something less than Zen mode. Like the rest of us mortals."

Sedona merely laughed, got out of SUV in what now was a sleet storm, and had the passenger door opened while Kara was still struggling with the seat belt.

Since she'd already filled out her paperwork ahead of time, the check-in went fairly smoothly, and soon she was being pushed into an elevator to be taken up to the second-floor maternity rooms.

Where, as the elevator doors opened, she came face-to-face with Ethan Concannon.

"Don't tell me Phoebe's in labor," she said.

"I brought her in two hours ago," he said. "And a good thing, too, since the roads outside of town are turning to ice."

She watched him wince as he remembered that she and Sax lived in a cliff house, as far out of town as anyone could get.

"He'll make it here," he assured Kara.

"Of course he will," Sedona, Charity, and Maddy all said in unison.

Kara could only hope they were right.

56

Claire knew that the picnic Maddy Chaffee had packed for them was undoubtedly exquisite. But between the wine that had mellowed out nerves made edgy by concern about her son and her first northwest storm building outside, and the shared kisses which grew slower, longer, and deeper, the world faded away and there was only Dillon.

After taking the dishes and basket into the kitchen, he returned, and apparently no longer content with her lips alone, he pushed aside the cowl neckline of her sweater and pressed his open mouth against her throat, where her pulse thudded hot and fast.

As she reeled from the touch of his tongue against her skin, a storm began to swirl inside her.

"Dillon." Even the sound of this man's name tasted lush and lovely on her tongue. "I need . . ." *Everything.* "More."

"More," he agreed, drawing her down to the quilt and undressing her with the exquisite care of a man unwrapping a precious Christmas gift.

Dillon Slater made love as she imagined he'd play

basketball—with a practiced skill that made every movement seem inordinately graceful.

Her skin flowed like water beneath his stroking hands. Beneath his mouth her senses tangled, brilliant layers, one atop the other, just as she layered stripes of color onto molten glass.

Through her swirling senses she heard him murmur her name. Over and over, like a promise. Or a prayer.

As he gave, she opened. Heart, mind, and body.

And as the wind wailed and rattled the windows and an icy rain hammered on the roof, inside they held each other tight.

And together, heart against heart, warm bodies entangled, they loved.

57

Even as Sax was going insane on the inside, he managed, for Trey's sake, to remain outwardly calm as he retrieved Kara's suitcase from the bedroom.

"You're about to be a big brother," he told his adopted son. Since Trey's teachers had scheduled an in-service day, Sax had left Bon Temps to Cody, his manager, and stayed home.

"The weather looks awful bad," Trey said. "What if we have a tsunami?"

"It'd have to be a really big one to reach up here to this cliff," Sax said as he took their parkas down from the hooks in the mudroom.

"But it could go into the bay."

There'd been a time, when Sax had first met the boy, that he'd been obsessed with watching disasters on the Discovery Channel. The counselor the widowed Kara had taken him to had said that was a normal response to his having lost his father to violence.

As far as Sax knew, those fears hadn't returned since he and Kara had gotten together and formed their family.

"Not going to happen," he said. "This is just a typical

winter storm." Which was mostly true, though the weather radio was also predicting the possibility of an ice storm. Which Sax so didn't need.

They'd managed to make it about a hundred yards when a Douglas fir came crashing down in front of them.

When Trey yelled, understandably, Sax began second-guessing his decision to bring him to the hospital.

"No problem." He flashed his son his most reassuring grin. The same one he'd use to assure Afghans that he'd come to their country to be their friend, and hey, don't pay any attention to that huge gun he was carrying.

The wind practically blew the door off the Camaro as he climbed out to retrieve the chainsaw he'd stuck in the trunk in anticipation of this possibility.

With the wind ripping at him like knives, he managed to cut the tree, which fortunately wasn't one of the huge ones lining the road, into hunks, which he rolled out of the way.

"Okay," he said with false bravado as he continued on. "No problem."

"That was great, Dad," Trey said. But as Sax glanced over at him, he saw that his small face was pinched with worry.

Join the club, kid.

The rest of the drive from the cliff-side home to the bridge thankfully was uneventful.

"No sweat," Sax told Trey. "We've almost got this nailed."

Then he turned the last tight corner and came face-to-face with the Shelter Bay drawbridge, which was coated, from pillars to soaring top wires, with ice.

58

The birthing rooms had been designed to calm fears and ease anxiety. Each room had two chairs and a love seat, the walls were painted in soft sea glass colors, and murals of local Shelter Bay landscapes had been painted on the wall opposite each bed.

Phoebe's wall depicted the Shelter Bay lighthouse, while Kara's was of the bay in summer, where boats with brightly colored sails skimmed across pure blue water while a pod of pelicans flew overhead.

"He's going to make it," Maddy assured Kara.

"I don't know how," Kara said through clenched teeth as another contraction rolled over her.

The contractions had begun in earnest right after she'd arrived at the hospital. Concerned about cord prolapse, her doctor had immediately ordered her confined to bed.

She couldn't believe her timing. Oh, having her baby come two weeks early wasn't that surprising, and if that was the only change in plans, she would have been grateful because it saved her sitting around at home for two weeks waiting to go into labor.

But to have that ice storm blow in from the sea, right beneath the weather radar, was really bad luck. She'd been forced to have Trey alone while Jared had been deployed, and it wasn't fair that she'd be alone this time, too.

Sax was less than twenty minutes away as the crow flies. Unfortunately, he was not a crow. And, as the highway signs always warned, bridges ice up first.

Although her friends were a wonderful support team, and she loved them, they weren't her husband.

"He'll get here," said Charity, repeating what Maddy and Sedona kept assuring her. "He was a SEAL. There's nothing those guys can't do."

"Except fly," Kara said as another wave rolled over her.

59

"What are we going to do now?" Trey asked.

"Got it covered," Sax assured him. "I'm calling in the cavalry. Your uncle Cole has chains on his SUV. He'll come and get us."

Which was a great idea.

Until Cole called back in from the other side of the bridge a few minutes later.

"It's not happening, bro," his older brother said. "It's too steep and as icy as a skating rink. I couldn't get half-way up it without sliding back down."

"Fuck," Sax said, momentarily forgetting Trey in his frustration.

"Fuck," the eight-year-old repeated.

Sax dragged his hand down his face. "Don't tell your mom I said that in front of you."

"I won't. But sometimes it's the only word that works."

Sax couldn't argue with that.

"She's not going to have that baby without us being there," he said.

"You'll think of something, Dad."

His son's confidence was encouraging. Their freaking nightmare of a situation was not.

He could handle this. He was a SEAL. And SEALs never, ever quit.

The only easy day was yesterday.

Too bad this day had to be so fucking lousy.

He sat there, staring at the bridge, tapping his fingers on the steering wheel as the wailing wind battered the Camaro and the sound of trees falling echoed through the forest. And he vowed that as soon as Kara had their baby, he was driving to a dealership and getting a real family car. Maybe not a minivan. But definitely an SUV like the one Cole had traded his fire-engine red dually diesel pickup for when he'd married Kelli.

"I have an idea." He pulled out his cell phone. He didn't have many bars, but he hoped he had enough of a signal to call Bon Temps.

"Hey, Cody," he said when his manager picked up. "Am I glad you're still there. Listen, I need some help, man. Like yesterday."

60

"I'm worried," Claire said the morning after Dillon's picnic. Matt was due back this morning, just as the storm had stalled overhead, bringing rare snow and ice to the coast.

"They're not predicting the storm to be as bad inland," he assured her as she paced the floor.

"They didn't predict *this* one," she pointed out. "At least it wasn't supposed to be nearly as bad as it's turning out to be."

"He'll be okay." He came up behind her and smoothed his large palms over her shoulders, easing out the boulder-sized knots in her muscles. "The buses all have chains in case of emergencies, and those ski-charter bus drivers are used to driving in bad weather, because it's a little hard to ski on a mountain that doesn't have any snow."

"Maybe it's mother's intuition," she said, staring out the rain-streaked window, as if she could will the bus to pull up in front of the house. She reached up and took hold of his hand, squeezing so hard her nails bit into his skin. "But I'm feeling really, really bad about this, Dillon."

She'd no sooner said those words when her cell phone trilled.

When she viewed *Highway Patrol* on the caller ID, Claire's blood turned as icy as the streets outside the window.

61

"Someone call for a coach?" Sax asked as he entered the room with Trey by his side.

"You're late," Kara said. The uncensored love Sax saw shining in her eyes belied her stern tone.

"I know. We had some stuff to deal with."

"A tree fell down across the road and Dad cut it up with a chainsaw," Kara's son said, recounting what Sax had already told her during one of his many calls before he'd lost both landline and cell service. "But then we couldn't get across the bridge."

"We heard no one was," Maddy said.

"Even Uncle Cole couldn't," Trey said. He was jumping up and down, still pumped with excitement from the ride into town from the coast. "But then Dad got the coolest idea."

"Which would be?" Kara asked. "To beam yourselves here?"

"Nah. That's make-believe. We rode here in a tank!"

"A tank?" In contrast to her son's, which were as wide as saucers, Kara's eyes narrowed.

"Cody's in the National Guard," Sax explained. "I

knew they were off doing winter training exercises at Mount Hood last weekend, so when I still had a cell signal, I called and asked whether they still had the cleats for the Abrams. Turns out they did."

He flashed his bad-boy cocky grin so she wouldn't realize how frantic he'd been. Even Trey, who'd been with him, hadn't realized that every atom in his body had been screeching like a Patriot missile while he'd been trying to figure out a way to make it to the hospital in time.

"We SEALs thrive on adversity," he said, quoting part of the oath he'd taken after surviving Hell Week so many years ago. There were times it felt like another lifetime. Which, he thought, as a wave of appreciation and love for his adopted son and wife rolled over him, it actually was.

"I never had a single doubt," Sedona said. "Come on, Trey," she said, holding out her hand. "Let's go down and see what kind of treats they've got in the cafeteria."

"Whatever they have won't be as good as your cupcakes," he said.

She smiled and ruffled his hair. "What is? But since the roads are an ice rink out there, we'll just have to suffer with what we can scrounge up here."

"I'm feeling hungry, too," Maddy said.

"Me, too," Charity agreed. She looked up at Sax. "We're leaving her in your hands now. Take care of her."

"I fully intend to." His voice was husky with emotion.

"So." He sat down on the edge of the bed, took a hand in both of his, and looked straight into her eyes. "How are you doing? Really?"

"I'm fine. Really," she insisted. "Better than fine now that you're here. Did you really come in a tank?"

"Yeah." She tensed as a contraction swept over her.

"Slow and deep." Sax reminded her about her breathing as he began massaging her abdomen, which had hardened with the contraction. "It's a long story." His fingers stroked upward and outward toward her hip bones, which he hoped would soothe the pressure and ease the pain.

"I'm obviously not going anywhere for a while," she said through clenched teeth, "so tell."

Sax had been to the classes. Watched the damn films, which, although he'd never admit it, even to her, had made him come as close to passing out as he had during Navy SEAL BUD/S drown proofing, where he was required to do a series of exercises in the pool while his hands and feet were bound.

He'd even reread the book three times in the past two days, preparing for this as diligently as he had for Hell Week and every mission he'd been on.

But nothing had prepared him for the sight of the woman he loved more than life in such obvious pain.

Reminding himself that his mission was to ease Kara's discomfort, not add to it by having her worry about his own, he forced himself to remain calm as he filled her in on his and Trey's adventure, leaving out the panicky parts and the F-words.

"This is going to be a walk in the park," he promised.

"You're as big a liar as the nurse-practitioner who taught the damn class." The contraction passed. She lay back against the pillows.

Her face was glistening with fresh sweat, her hair limp. But she was, without a doubt, the most beautiful woman Sax had ever seen.

They made a great team, although she was doing all

the work, while he was left to time her contractions, massage her abdomen, stroke her arms and legs to keep her circulation going, wipe her face with cool cloths, coax her on her breathing, feed her chips of ice, help her stay calm (not easy when every nerve in his body was more on edge than it had ever been, even while fighting the Taliban in the Kush), and, most important, the instructor had said, cheer her on as her friends and Trey took turns visiting.

"You're doing great, *chère*," he said, breathing in rhythm with her quick pants as she grew closer to delivery.

She was drenched in sweat.

The blue scrub shirt they'd put Sax in was soaked as well. More sweat dripped off his forehead onto their linked hands. With all their attention directed toward the mirror that allowed them to watch the birth, neither noticed.

"It's got hair," Sax said, enthralled by the sight.

"Of course my child has hair," Kara said indignantly.

"I thought babies were all born bald. Like Uncle Fester."

"Dammit, don't make me laugh," Kara complained on a sputtered laugh.

But the laugh seemed to ease the pain that had her panting again.

"My baby's beautiful," she insisted as the baby slid from her womb.

"She's also a girl," Dr. Parrish announced.

"Oh, my God." Tears welled up in Kara's eyes. "A little girl."

"A daughter." The thought was stunning. His own eyes stinging, Sax wiped the tears from her wet face.

He'd never loved any woman as much as he loved this one. He'd thought he couldn't love her more.

Until today.

"I am," he said, as he lowered his lips to hers, "the freaking luckiest guy on the planet."

62

Dillon was right about the storm not being as bad as they drove away from the coast. The caller had informed Claire that the bus carrying the skiers home from the resort had hit a patch of black ice on the twisting, winding road over the coastal mountains and rolled over.

Desperate for details, all she could learn was that ambulances from several surrounding small towns were taking the children to a community hospital nearly sixty minutes away. At the moment, the caller from the highway patrol could give her no other details as to what condition Matt was in.

"He's going to be all right," Dillon assured her as he pulled into the hospital parking lot.

"Of course he is," she agreed fervently, even as her nerves were screaming. "He's got a game the day after tomorrow. And he's never missed a basketball game in his life."

Basketball. He'd never been on skis before. What if he had injuries that could keep him from ever achieving the next step in his dream?

"He'll make it," Dillon said firmly after she'd shared

that fear with him. "And on the offhand chance he did sustain some sort of basketball-ending injury, he's young, with his entire life ahead of him. We'll help him handle it, Claire." He took hold of her hand and squeezed. "Together."

The other parents began streaming into the hospital. All were frantic, adding to the chaos of the scene, overwhelming the small hospital staff.

Dillon immediately took charge, obtaining information, calming everyone down, and working with the doctors and nurses, two of whom turned out to be Army vets.

Watching him, she witnessed the deep core of inner strength and leadership qualities that had allowed him to lead a team of fellow soldiers on one of the most deadly and certainly nerve-racking missions in the military.

She also realized that his wealth of confidence, which she had on occasion mistakenly taken for chauvinism, was what must have kept him and his teammates alive in war zones, where he definitely wouldn't have been playing games.

"Mr. and Mrs. Templeton?" a nurse asked as he found them in the waiting room.

"This is Ms. Templeton," Dillon said, standing up. "I'm Dillon Slater, Matt's coach."

"Well, I'm sure he'd like to see you both. He's in examining cubicle four. I'll take you there."

"How is he?" Claire asked, her heart in her throat.

"He has some bruises and contusions but nothing that'll stop you from taking him home." He handed them a clipboard with the paperwork. "Just fill out these forms and give them to the clerk at the front desk."

He led them through what seemed to be a maze of hallways, then stopped at a curtain. "He's all yours. And, I'm sure, ready to go home."

Refusing to worry about whether she embarrassed him, Claire threw her arms around her son.

"I was so worried," she said, clinging to him as she'd once wanted to cling when he'd first begun growing up and moving beyond the safety of her home.

"I'm okay," he insisted. And then Matt did something she'd feared she'd never experience again.

He hugged her back.

63

Sax and Ethan stood side by side in front of the nursery window, looking at the two infants, one bundled in pink, the other in blue.

"You realize, of course, that our wives are already planning to marry these two off," Sax said.

"I suppose there could be worse things," Ethan said. "Your daughter's very beautiful."

"And your son's handsome," Sax said, returning the compliment.

They fell silent as they continued to study the babies.

"Who are we kidding?" Sax said. "If you tell Kara I said this, I'll call you a bald-faced liar, but I think they both kinda look like aliens."

"That's because of their pointed heads," commented Ethan, who'd been through this before. "From the birthing. That'll change."

"That's a relief," Sax said. "Although I'll love her whatever she grows up to look like, I was worried I might have to reprogram my head around having a Conehead for a daughter."

"After I lost Mia and Max," Ethan said quietly, "I

never thought I'd ever be given another opportunity to be a father." He sighed heavily. Not, Sax thought, with pain. But with pure, unadulterated happiness. "This is the greatest gift. Ever."

The nurse behind the glass brought Sax's daughter over to the window and held her up so Sax could see her more clearly.

As he looked into the wide blue eyes of his daughter, something in his heart opened, allowing a wealth of love like nothing he'd ever expected to feel for this red-faced, cone-headed infant that he and Kara had made together to rush in, filling the last of those few remaining painful places that too many years in too many war zones had left him with.

"Fucking A," he agreed.

64

"Can you find Aimee?" Matt asked as he finally let go of Claire. He looked frantic, which wasn't surprising, given what he'd been through. "They took her away on a different ambulance and no one's been willing to tell me a thing."

"Things are a little confusing right now," Dillon said. "But I'll see what I can find out while your mom fills out all that paperwork. Then we can spring you."

"I'm not leaving." The little boy who'd needed his mother was gone. In his place was a young man who stubbornly folded his arms over his chest. "Not until Aimee gets the hell out of here, too."

Wanting to get him back home, where he belonged, Claire couldn't believe what he was saying.

"There's nothing you can do for her, Matt," she began. "She's in good hands, her parents are both here, and—"

"I'm not leaving without her," he insisted on a flare of heat. Then apparently realizing that anger wasn't going to get him anywhere, he softened his tone. And his attitude.

"I was a total jerk, Mom. I hurt her. That's why I went on this damn trip when I didn't even want to learn to ski, to try to apologize, but she refused to even listen to me. If anything happens to her before I can make up for the shitty way I treated her, I'll never, ever be able to forgive myself. As long as I live."

Although the circumstances were not remotely the same, his heartfelt words had Claire thinking of another man, one who'd turned his back on responsibility without so much as a backward glance. Even at fifteen, her son was a better man than his birth father would ever be.

She exchanged a look with Dillon. *Help me out here.* There'd been a time when she wouldn't have been able to ask. Matt, it seemed, wasn't the only one who'd changed since coming to Shelter Bay.

"How about a compromise?" Dillon suggested. "We check you out—"

"No. Way."

"Let me finish," the former EOD tech said with the calm, can-do attitude Claire had been witnessing since she'd received the call. "Just because you're no longer a patient doesn't mean we can't hang around in the waiting room until we know for a fact she's okay. And hopefully it will let you say what you need to."

Matt processed that for a long time, as if looking for the trick.

"Okay," he said finally.

The news was not good. But it could have been worse. The scrubs-clad doctor who'd come out briefly to talk with them had informed them that Aimee had suffered broken ribs, a head injury, a possible broken back, and a spiral break on her left leg, all of which required surgery. Together, Dillon, Claire, and Matt waited with her parents. Claire watched Aimee's father calm his distraught wife, his quiet strength reminding her of how Dillon had calmed not just her, but all those frantic parents. Which, in turn, gave her a glimpse into the older man Dillon would someday become.

Although the public cafeteria was closed at night, Dillon located a vending machine, but the coffee tasted like battery acid and the sandwiches could have been made from sawdust.

Not that any of them had an appetite anyway.

The food went uneaten. The coffee was drunk only in lieu of something stronger.

The nursing shift changed. New nurses, their scrubs clean, their manners brisk and efficient, came on duty. The waiting room became more crowded as the storm created more and more accidents from the coast to the mountains.

And still Claire, Matt, Dillon, and the Piersons kept their vigil.

65

It was early in the morning when Dillon invited Matt to go with him to the chapel.

"I can pray here," Matt had insisted. "I don't want to miss anything."

"If there's any news, I'll come get you," Claire assured him.

The chapel was mostly empty. A few people were sitting in the front pews, and an elderly man was down on his knees, totally oblivious to the others around him. The smell of burning wax wafted from the bank of candles set in red votive holders.

Gesturing Matt into a pew in the back, Dillon joined him on the wooden seat. "I want you to know something," he began.

"Is this about my mom?"

His tone did not sound encouraging.

"Yeah. I want to marry her."

"Marry? Like in husband and wife and till death do you part and all that stuff?"

"Yeah. Exactly like that."

"Have you asked her?"

"Not yet. I wanted to talk with you first."

"Why?"

"I'm going to marry her whatever you say about it, because I figure if you're not with the program, I can eventually change your mind. But it'll be a lot easier on her if you're on our side."

"I'm on *her* side," Matt said. "So you really love her?"

"I really, really love her. And hey, you're not so bad yourself."

"What do I call you? Coach? Or Dad?"

His tone was teenage nonchalant, but Dillon would've had to have been deaf not to hear the need.

"My dad died when I was younger than you," he said. "I still miss him. So you can decide for yourself, but I'd be honored to be your dad."

Matt was silent for a long moment.

The elderly man pushed himself to his feet and shuffled back down the aisle between the pews. Dillon hoped that whatever prayers he'd been sending up would be answered.

"I guess that works for me," Matt finally decided.

"Great," Dillon said, keeping his own tone casual, when what he wanted to do was shout *hoorah* to the heavens.

Now all he had to do was convince Claire that they belonged together. Forever.

Piece of cake.

He hoped, sending up a prayer of his own, just in case, because even hotshot EOD guys needed backup sometimes.

66

Dillon and Matt had just returned to the waiting room when the doctor arrived, looking every bit as exhausted as Claire was feeling. But as bad as Claire felt, she couldn't imagine what Aimee's parents were going through.

"Aimee's going to be fine," the surgeon assured them as Major Pierson immediately stood up when she entered. "She's still in recovery, but when she comes out of the anesthetic, we'll be moving her to ICU, where we can keep a close eye on her."

"What about her injuries?" Mrs. Pierson asked, her voice strained. Her husband sat back down and took both her hands in his.

"We fused the broken vertebrae together."

"Will she be able to walk?" her father asked.

That question had Matt flinching.

"Yes, but she'll need physical therapy for a time. Especially for that leg, which we put a plate in and essentially screwed back together."

At that, Mrs. Pierson made a sound like a whimper.

"It's not as bad as it sounds," the doctor assured her. "The good thing was that her head injury, which we were originally the most worried about, turned out to be fairly minor and shouldn't leave any lasting effects, other than a possible loss of memory of the accident."

"Which wouldn't be so bad," Matt said.

The doctor smiled at him. "From what I heard, that's true." She turned back toward his parents. "One thing I learned early in my practice is that kids are resilient. And tough. You can't ever count them out.

"Since it's going to be a while until she's ready for company," she said, directing her words toward Matt again, "why don't you and your parents go out for something to eat while I take the Piersons up to recovery. There's a place about two blocks away that serves a breakfast buffet that's not all that bad. And definitely better than cafeteria food."

"I'll wait here," Matt insisted yet again.

"We'll bring you back something," Dillon said.

"Thanks." They were at the door when he called out, "Hey, Coach."

Dillon glanced back over his shoulder.

Matt's grin was the first Claire had seen since they'd arrived at the hospital as he flashed Dillon a two-thumbs-up sign.

"What was all that about?" she asked as they walked out of the hospital. The sun was coming up, splitting the now clear blue sky into dazzling shades of lavender, pink, and gold. In the distance, the snow on the mountaintops glittered like the sugar crystals Sedona would sprinkle on her buttercream cupcake icing.

"I'll tell you in a bit," Dillon said. "Once I get like a gallon of coffee that isn't going to rust out my stomach." He stretched, rubbed the back of his neck, and looked around. "God, it's a gorgeous day."

"A good one," she agreed.

"Hell," he surprised her by saying.

"What?" She stopped and looked up at him, wondering what could possibly be wrong now.

"There's something I've been meaning to say. About our situation."

"Okay."

"I had it all planned."

"Okay," she repeated.

"But I didn't want to say it in a parking lot. Or over fried eggs in a greasy spoon."

"I'd rather have mine scrambled," she said.

"You're playing me."

"Only because it's so easy," she agreed, her eyes laughing as she took his hand. "It's a beautiful day. My son is alive and well, his girlfriend is going to be well and hopefully will have pity on him and forgive him for whatever youthful male mistake he made."

"I have a feeling Taylor Bennington might have been involved in that."

"From having watched her at the crabfest, I suspect you're right. But Matt's a good kid, Aimee's a smart one, so I figure they'll work things out after she makes him grovel a bit."

"Probably a lot." From what Dillon had witnessed the day they'd set off the cannon on the beach, the kid had a lot of s'plaining to do.

"It'll be a character-building experience for him." Claire said. "Meanwhile, the sun is shining and the sky is blue, and if you've brought me out here to propose, I can't think of a more beautiful time or place to accept."

His heart hitched. "You do realize that you've stolen

my game plan." Because his hands had gotten suddenly sweaty, he shoved them into the front pockets of his jeans. "One I've been working on for the past week. Longer," he admitted.

"Sorry," she said, sounding anything but. Her bold, teasing smile was one he knew would still have the power to thrill him when they were old and gray and watching their grandchildren shoot off cannons on the beach.

"Here's the thing," she said. "I thought I was in love once—"

"You were all of eighteen." And although he was sorry she'd had her teenage heart broken, he couldn't deny that he was grateful to that guy who never realized what he'd walked away from.

"True." She'd told him the story, not holding back her fairy-tale dreams, which had only made him admire her more. "And while that admittedly left me gun-shy when it came to men for a while, I didn't not give my heart to anyone else because I was afraid of becoming emotionally involved. It was because I was unwilling to settle for any man I didn't want to spend the rest of my life with."

"Bad enough you stole my game. You just stole my line about waiting for the perfect person to spend my life with," he complained without heat.

"Proving that once again, we're on the same page," she said. "So, since I've never been one to play games, and I know you're as crazy in love with me as I am in love with you, what would you say to getting married? And living with me in my little house by the sea? Forever?"

It wasn't the way he'd planned it. He'd intended candlelight, a romantic dinner he'd already figured out with

Chef Maddy, a night right out of one of those romance novels his mother had always loved to read.

But sometimes, even on the most carefully thought-out mission, you had to ditch the plan and just go with the flow.

"What the hell," Dillon said. "Since you put it that way—"

He took his hands out of his pockets, bringing with them the small box he'd been carrying around for weeks. The one he'd planned to give her on Christmas, but just in case she decided that she couldn't be engaged to her son's coach during the season, he'd reluctantly decided to wait to propose until after the final game.

After some consultation with her new friends, he'd booked a three-day weekend at a private cabin at Rainbow Lake that included a wine tour, which the women assured him she'd enjoy.

When she drew in a sharp breath as he slipped the aquamarine ring the jewelry designer she'd mentioned being friends with in Cannon Beach had designed especially for her, Dillon realized that he hadn't been so predictable after all.

Claire might have guessed his game plan.

But she'd misread his winning move.

He shoots! He scores!

"Yes," he said, drawing her into his arms. "Absolutely I'll marry you, Claire Templeton. And live with you in your little house by the sea."

His mouth lowered to her smiling one. "And forever's a damn good start."

67

Eight weeks later

Unlike the championships held for every other high school sport in Oregon, basketball championships took place in nearly every geographical region of the state.

As he paced the sidelines of what could be the most important basketball game of his life, Dillon decided it was a good thing that the 4A division had been assigned the famed Gill Coliseum, because from the noise practically raising the roof, it seemed nearly all the 10,400 seats were filled with Shelter Bay fans.

Surprising everyone, most of all him, the Dolphins had played the last half of their season as if they'd been drinking rocket fuel. Oh, they still couldn't shoot as well as their opponents, something he'd have to work on next season, but their passing skills were right up there with the best in the league, and they'd developed what some players never learned—a sense of reading the floor, knowing where not just the opposing players, but also their teammates, were at all times.

They also drew more fouls than any team he'd ever

seen. A fact that had not escaped the fans of their opponents over the past weeks and had drawn criticism from other towns' newspaper sports columnists and even the occasional editorial.

But Dillon didn't care. Because they'd accomplished what he'd hoped for. They'd meshed as a team, playing as a unit. Each had the others' backs, and together they'd proven unstoppable.

The score had been seesawing back and forth all evening. With less than five seconds to go, they were tied with the Klamath Falls Pelicans. As the crowd roared and stomped their feet in the bleachers, drowning out the sound of sneakers squeaking on the polished wood, Dirk Martin drove down the court, managing to power past his defender, only to be double-teamed.

He passed to Matt, who, feinting left, suddenly went right, revealing that the lesson Dillon had taught him that first day had sunk in.

When he, too, found himself facing a wall of defenders, he switched hands and, on the run, passed the ball to Johnny.

Who dribbled right in front of a charging defender, who crashed into him just as he went up for the shot.

The ball bounced off the rim as Johnny landed on his butt on the floor.

The opposing coach was apoplectic. Dillon wasn't sure whether the guy was more furious with his own player, or the Dolphin's number six, Johnny Tiernan-St. James.

"He's going to stroke out if he doesn't chill," Dillon told Don as the coach began yelling at the ref who'd called the foul.

"He's not the only one," the assistant coach said as he

glanced up at the clock. There was one second left. "This makes me really glad baseball doesn't have a time clock."

"It was a smart move by the kids," Dillon decided. "They knew no one was going to risk blocking either Matt's or Dirk's shot. But everyone knows Johnny's the worst player on the team. The odds of him successfully making any shot, under all this pressure, are pretty slim."

"That was the first half of the season," Don said as Dillon called a time-out to give the Dolphins their last pep talk of the season. "The last few weeks, I sure as hell wouldn't bet against any one of them."

"I'm not going to do the rah-rah thing," Dillon said as the team gathered on the sidelines. He only raised his voice loud enough to be heard over the cacophony of the dueling pep bands and screaming fans. "You guys don't need me to motivate you, because you've done that yourselves. What I am going to say is that whatever happens, you've done everything I've asked. And more.

"The Dolphins are a team everyone, even our opponents, look up to. A team admired for our poise on the court and leadership off the court. Over this season, every one of you has set an example, not just for every student in Shelter Bay High School, but for the younger kids, who dream of someday wearing a blue-and-white Dolphins letterman jacket.

"I'm proud of you." He looked at each player, even the benchers, one by one. "Now go out there and bring that trophy home."

"Hoorah!" they shouted as one as they ran back onto the floor.

As Dillon looked up at Claire, she flashed him a bold grin and a V sign. He viewed not an iota of doubt on her exquisitely lovely face.

The players lined up on either side of the basket.
Johnny took a deep breath. Bounced the ball.
Once.
Twice.
A third time.
Then sent it airborne.
Although Dillon knew it was a trick of the mind, like
the way an adrenaline rush seemed to slow time down in
battle, the ball seemed to take forever as it arced toward
the basket.

It could have been his imagination, or perhaps any
crowd noise was being drowned out by the roaring of
blood in his ears. It was as if a hush had come over the
sold-out arena.

Just when he was certain his heart was going to jump
out of his chest, the pebbled brown ball reached its des-
tination.

Swish.
Nothing but net.

Read on for a special preview of the next book
in JoAnn Ross's Shelter Bay series,

Castaway Cove

Available everywhere books are sold in July

Afghanistan

Disney Drive, the main drag of Bagram Air Force Base, was about as far from the Magic Kingdom as a person could get.

A river of bumper-to-bumper vehicles was headed out of the base, packed together like salmon swimming upstream.

"I swear it'd be easier to just get out and walk," Staff Sergeant MacKenzie "Mac" Culhane remarked to the cameraman and the female Airman correspondent from American Forces Network who were traveling with him.

"Is it always this crowded?" asked the "backpack" journalist from the *Seattle Examiner*, who'd been waiting for Mac when he'd arrived at the radio station that morning.

Apparently someone above Mac's pay grade had decided that some positive warm and fuzzy stateside press was in order, which was why they were traveling to the village for a meet, greet, and schmooze photo op with the locals.

"Actually, you're seeing it on a good day," Mac said. "At least we're moving." Though nothing near the posted twenty-five-miles-per-hour speed limit.

"So, is there a story why this street's named after Walt Disney?"

Jeez. You'd think the guy would've at least done some homework on the flight from the States.

"It's not. It's named for an Army specialist who died here when some heavy equipment fell on him," the AFN reporter said. Although her voice remained neutrally polite, Mac could tell from the very faint edge to her tone that she was as irked by the guy's question as he was.

"You definitely don't want anything on this base named for you," Mac said. "Because that means that you're dead." Another example being the Pat Tillman Memorial USO.

Mac might be a deejay, assigned to play songs and impart news and information, but like all the others he worked with, he took the AFN motto—"Serving those who serve"—seriously. Which was why whenever he could, he'd go outside the wire and travel to some of the world's most dangerous war zones to entertain the troops and film footage that was shown not only on AFN television, but also sent home to family and loved ones.

After having been assigned to bases around the world, he was now on his third tour in Afghanistan, where, in addition to entertaining with music and banter, he also delivered the news of troop deaths. More during the surge, but lately the bad guys had stepped up their game again.

"Damned if you didn't jinx us by saying we were

moving," the cameraman complained as the river of vehicles on the lane leading out of the base came to an
abrupt halt.

In less than a minute, the driver of one of the white
pickups civilian contractors tended to drive leaned on
his horn.

Yeah. As if that was going to help.

In front of the pickup, unable to move due to the
stalled traffic in front of him, the driver of a commuter
bus ferrying soldiers and civilians around the sprawling
base stuck a single finger salute out the window. Intended, Mac guessed, for the pickup driver.

Not wanting to be left out of the fun, a utility four-
wheeler, looking like a combat golf cart behind Mac's
MRAP (Mine Resistant Ambush Protected vehicle) got
into the act, adding his horn to the cacophony, which
wasn't helped by the roar of jets streaking overhead.

Meanwhile, pedestrians were packed as tightly together as the vehicles. Military personnel, who automat-
ically snapped out salutes, jockeyed for some semblance
of personal space with civilians and Afghans. Some, trying to speed up the process, had taken to walking or jog-
ging in the street.

Finally, they got beyond the gate and headed out into
the country, where the roads were even more of a joke.
While Bagram was definitely not a country club base—
with rocket attacks coming so often that diving into bun-
kers became routine, not to mention the constant threat
of insurgent attacks, and more recently "green on blue"
violence—Mac often thought that you really took your
life in your hands by traveling on any of the narrow,
winding roads.

The base was in a valley surrounded on four sides by

the Hindu Kush, where sunshine had the snow on the mountains gleaming like diamonds. Cutting its way through the nearly impassable mountains at ten thousand feet was the Salang Pass. Last spring, as the snow began to melt, an avalanche on the pass had swept over an entire village clinging to the edge of the two-lane roadway, burying it in tons of snow, ice, and stone.

There'd been a time a thousand years ago when Bagram was a wealthy, bustling city on the Silk Road. These days it was a village dependent on farming, base employment, and fighting.

The drive past the fields with the mountains in the distance could have been pleasant were it not for the metal signs warning of land mines leftover from Soviet occupation hanging on wires along the road, and the constantly blowing sand that had the consistency of talcum powder. Even when you couldn't see it, you could feel it in your eyes, nose, and throat whenever you went outside.

The market was bustling. Children, some of the boys wearing blue Cub Scout uniforms supplied by one of the majors at the base, who'd set up the Scouting program for the local population, dodged the traffic as they ran through the streets. Giggling, remarkably carefree girls jumped rope and played hopscotch on courts drawn in the dirt.

Women in dark burkas were focused on their shopping, while local police, trained by Allied forces, patrolled past the food stands. As the translator gave the reporter the tour, Mac chatted in his less than fluent Dari with the shopkeepers and his fans, who treated him like a celebrity every time he came to town. At first he'd been surprised by that, but then he came to realize that while Freedom Radio might consider the troops their target audience, a good proportion of the civilians listened as well. And even if they couldn't understand all the banter, music proved universal.

As he bought some goat meat and yogurt from an elderly man whose eyes were nearly black in his dark, sun-weathered face, a brightly colored vehicle, locally referred to as a "jingle truck" because of the bells drivers put on the top of their cabs, pulled up to deliver a load of *kaddo bourani*, Afghan pumpkins.

Which had Mac telling the Seattle reporter how he and his crew were going to set up a catapult for Freedom Radio's Thanksgiving pumpkin-hurling competition. He was just thinking how much he freaking loved his job when the world exploded in a fireball that sent him flying through the air.

Mac didn't know how long he'd been unconscious. But when he heard the Airman calling his name over the ringing in his ears, he managed with difficulty to open his eyes, which were even grittier with sand than usual. He hoped that explained the fact that everything he tried to focus on was like looking through a fractured mirror.

"I'm okay."

If you didn't count the crushing headache, the nausea, the blood he could feel pouring down his face, and the fact that he felt as if his body were peppered with fiery birdshot.

He wasn't sure whether he had managed to get the words out of his mouth or whether he'd just thought them. And although he could sort of hear her shouting, either she'd begun talking a foreign language or his brain wasn't decoding what she was trying to ask him.

As disoriented as he was, one searing thought flashed

through Mac's mind: *Please, God, don't let my brain be permanently scrambled.*

"Okay," he repeated, flinching as he turned his head to try to look around.

His left eye seemed to have been flash-blinded, while his right was like looking through cracked glass, but that didn't keep him from seeing that the explosion had ripped through the heart of the market, clearing a wide swath. At the periphery, burned and bloody bodies were piled up like so much cordwood.

He heard the cries and moans, but was grateful that along with the obnoxious ringing in his ears, whatever had happened to his hearing made the voices sound distant, like when his grandfather Culhane had taught him to listen to the sound of the sea inside a conch shell.

A mob of distraught people was rushing toward the scene, trying to dislodge the bodies, desperately searching for the living.

The Airman and her cameraman had lifted him up and were running toward the MRAP vehicle.

He was wishing he could assure them that he was fine, that they should leave him and go help the civilian women and children, when his right eye caught sight of what appeared to be a small arm wearing Cub Scout blue stretching out from beneath a jumble of human pick-up sticks.

As he felt himself being carefully placed into the vehicle, a burning pain began washing over him in hot waves. Even as he fought against it, as the MRAP roared away with its horn blaring loud enough that even he could hear it, Mac surrendered to the darkness.

After having shrapnel painstakingly picked out of his arms and legs and treatment for second-degree burns by the medical crew at Bagram, he was airlifted to Landstuhl Regional Medical Center in Germany.

"So, here's the deal," the doctor, a captain from next-door Ramstein Air Base told him. "You were lucky."

The weird thing was that although every part of him hurt like one of the lower circles of hell, even through the haze of IV drugs they were pumping into him, Mac knew the doctor was right.

At least he was alive, unlike the Afghan translator he'd worked with for the past eight months, or the newspaper reporter, who'd had the bad luck of joining the growing ranks of journalists killed while covering the war.

"You've got lacerations on your chest and arms, shrapnel in your thighs, legs, and shoulders, but fortunately your helmet, body armor, groin flap, and fire-retardant uniform prevented serious injury to your body."

"What about my eyes?" Mac was hoping the reason he couldn't see a thing was only because they were wrapped in sterile gauze.

"It's too early to tell." He listened for optimism in the female doctor's tone, but heard only exhaustion. "But they're intact. Which, even with your ballistic goggles, which I heard were toast, is really amazing given how close you were to the blast."

"I should've seen it coming," Mac muttered. The thought had been continuously circling through his mind, along with blurred but still-horrific images he knew he'd never be able to unsee.

"Yeah, with your X-ray eyes and superhero powers," she said dryly. "I know it's difficult for you warriors to get it through your heads, but you are, when it comes right down to it, human beings. Like the rest of us."

"I'm not a warrior," Mac said. "I'm just the guy on the radio."

He'd always been aware that his job was a walk in the park compared to so many others with whom he'd served. The troops worked damn hard, some risking their lives every minute of every day. His job, as he viewed it, was to always be there for them. To provide a little bit of home and bring some semblance of normal to a life that was anything but.

"Yet you were blown up, which I doubt would've happened if you'd chosen to remain a civilian deejay working in Albuquerque or Topeka."

Despite the pain, Mac smiled at that. "And how boring would that be?"

"Just what I need—another adrenaline junkie." She sighed as she pulled back the sheet and began examining his wounds.

"Explosions can work in inexplicable ways," she said. "We never know what we're going to be looking at when we get the call for incoming. In the instant of detonation, shrapnel and heat rush out at supersonic speeds. Which means that they should have been picking pieces of you out of the dirt into the next century. But there's no order to explosions. Some areas are thick with shrapnel. You could have just as easily been cut in half by a door or the hood of the truck that suicide bomber set off. But you happened to be standing in a partial seam that was empty of any lethal debris."

Unlike his translator and the reporter. Mac figured that just as he'd always have images of the aftermath running through his head, survivor guilt would become a constant companion.

"The surgery eased the swelling in your brain," she continued. "We'll want to keep an eye on you a couple more days to make sure you're out of the woods, and then we'll be shipping you back to CONUS for continued treatment." CONUS was military speak for the continental United States. "Your liaison will be visiting as soon as I leave, but he wanted you to know that your father called. My suggestion, not that you asked, is unless you feel you need immediate family support, it makes more sense for him to meet up with you at Travis, where you're ultimately headed."

"I'm fine," Mac lied, as he had been since he'd found himself lying on the ground surrounded by chaos. "If I'm staying only a couple days, there's no point in having him fly all the way here only to turn right around again."

"That was my thinking."

Mac debated asking if his wife had called. But he figured the doctor, who'd drawn the sheet back up, would have mentioned it if Kayla had felt moved to contact the hospital.

Of course, maybe his father filling her in was enough. Maybe, unlike her husband, she was still speaking to her father-in-law.

Two days later, he left Germany, spending a night layover at Andrews Air Force Base in Maryland before continuing on to David Grand USAF Medical Center at Travis Air Force Base in California.

His father was waiting for him.

His wife was not.

Which, unfortunately, didn't come as that much of a surprise since she hadn't e-mailed or Skyped with him for the past three months, ever since he'd informed her that instead of getting out, as he'd admittedly promised, he'd reenlisted.

Three weeks later, two weeks after he'd begun climbing the walls, he was transferred to outpatient status.

Although the bandages had been removed, his vision was still blurry. The retina tear on his left eye had been repaired, but the prognosis wasn't good. The doctors assured him that with a cornea transplant his right eye should be as good as new.

His father had wanted to accompany Mac to Colorado Springs, Kayla's hometown, where she'd moved with their daughter, Emma, three months before.

Not knowing what type of reception he'd receive, and needing to concentrate on repairing his wounded marriage, Mac insisted on going alone.

From the stilted phone conversations they'd shared while he'd been at Travis, he wasn't surprised when Kayla didn't show up at the airport. After giving the address to the house he'd never seen to the cabdriver, he sat in the backseat, practicing what he was going to say to make things right again.

The neighborhood was a typical American suburban, with neatly trimmed front lawns and tidy houses on each side of a street lined with trees ablaze in fall color. Even through his still-blurred vision, the high blue Colorado sky and red, yellow, and bronze leaves on the trees seemed blindingly bright after Afghanistan's unrelenting brown.

Most of the houses on the street were flying the American flag, which was to be expected in a city that was home to the Air Force Academy. Mac couldn't help noticing that the flag flying from the front porch of the white rambler the cabdriver had pulled up in front of was not the stars and stripes, but boasted three fall-themed pumpkins.

He rang the bell and waited for what seemed an eternity.

"Hi." His wife's tone, when she finally opened the door, wasn't angry, as it had been the last time they'd spoken in person. Nor was it the least bit welcoming. What it was, he decided, was disinterested.

"Hi," he said back, standing there holding his duffel bag while she submitted him to a slow examination.

"You look good," she said. Since his mirror revealed that he was gaunt and gray, and had a bald spot where they'd shaved his head for surgery, he translated that to mean that he didn't look nearly as bad as she'd expected.

"So do you."

It was the truth. She looked much the same. But different. Her long, straight slide of chestnut hair had been cropped to a chin-length blazing mahogany that echoed the leaves on the tree in the small front yard, and the snug purple sweater and skinny jeans revealed that although she'd always claimed to hate exercise, she'd been working out. A lot.

Silence settled over them as they stood there, she inside the ranch-style house, he on the narrow front porch. The only sound came from the blower the elderly man across the street was using to attack a mountain of leaves.

He glanced past her. "Where's Emma?"

"At a neighbor's." The unfamiliar, glossy bright hair swung as she tilted her head toward the house next door. "It's obvious we need to talk without a child present."

Mac's internal siren, which had failed to ring when

the suicide bomber had driven his jingle truck into the marketplace, had begun to sound. But feeling the leaf guy's eyes on them, he wasn't going to stand out here in public and point out that the child Kayla was referring to was his child, too. Ever since waking up to find himself in the Bagram ER, he'd gotten through the pain, stress, and guilt by staying focused on getting back home and holding his daughter in his arms.

Although patience had admittedly never been his strong suit, Mac held his tongue and refrained from starting yet another argument as he walked into the small foyer.

Where the two flowered suitcases sitting by the front door suggested that whatever conversation he and his wife were about to have was probably not going to go his way.